SEE BEYOND WHAT YOUR EYES CAN SEE

Other books by this author:

Eyes Never Lie

AZUREE OWENS

SEE BEYOND WHAT YOUR EYES CAN SEE

TATE PUBLISHING
AND ENTERPRISES, LLC

See Beyond What Your Eyes Can See
Copyright © 2013 by Azuree Owens. All rights reserved.

No part of this publication may be reproduced, stored in a retrieval system or transmitted in any way by any means, electronic, mechanical, photocopy, recording or otherwise without the prior permission of the author except as provided by USA copyright law.

All scripture quotations, unless otherwise indicated, are taken from the *Holy Bible, New International Version*®, NIV®. Copyright ©1973, 1978, 1984 by Biblica, Inc.™ Used by permission of Zondervan. All rights reserved worldwide. www.zondervan.com

Scripture quotations marked (AMP) are taken from the *Amplified Bible*, Copyright © 1954, 1958, 1962, 1964, 1965, 1987 by The Lockman Foundation. Used by permission.

This novel is a work of fiction. Names, descriptions, entities, and incidents included in the story are products of the author's imagination. Any resemblance to actual persons, events, and entities is entirely coincidental.

The opinions expressed by the author are not necessarily those of Tate Publishing, LLC.

Published by Tate Publishing & Enterprises, LLC
127 E. Trade Center Terrace | Mustang, Oklahoma 73064 USA
1.888.361.9473 | www.tatepublishing.com

Tate Publishing is committed to excellence in the publishing industry. The company reflects the philosophy established by the founders, based on Psalm 68:11,
"The Lord gave the word and great was the company of those who published it."

Book design copyright © 2013 by Tate Publishing, LLC. All rights reserved.
Cover design by Samson Lim
Interior design by Mary Jean Archival

Published in the United States of America
ISBN: 978-1-62510-695-7
1. Fiction / Christian / General
2. Fiction / Contemporary Women
13.06.17

Dedication

The eye is the lamp of the body. If your eyes are good, your whole body will be full of light. But if your eyes are bad, your whole body will be full of darkness. If then the light within you is darkness, how great is that darkness!

Matthew 6:22–23 (NIV)

I would like to keep this dedication simple and thank my Lord and Savior, Jesus Christ, for bestowing upon me a gift that continues to make room for me.

To my beautiful daughter, Ariel, you are my inspiration, driving me to achieve my goals and to never give up. I love you, and I will continue to push myself beyond my limits.

This may appear uncanny to most; however, I would like to thank the people who walked out of my life either by their own volition or as God ordained. Their absence released me from my past and taught me to embrace my present and move forward, with grace, into my future. I've learned obedience is better than sacrifice. Often, we as humans would rather please people and appear blessed than obey God. Isolation and obedience exceed sacrifice. It's far better to obey God and live covered, protected, guided, and favored because it yields an immeasurable reward. Obedience to God's perfect will is necessary to expose destiny.

I pray this book blesses the lives of those persons who fill the sanctuaries of churches worldwide, but continue to wear a veil. I hope you are able to remove your veil and experience true deliverance.

Dream

I used to dream
A life lived without fears
Without worries
Without stress
It was real
It was me
I was it and we were free

Happiness cascaded across my heart with peace bombarding
My innermost being until I had no choice but rejoice
I embraced my captor and promoted
to my peers the joy of being
A true prisoner of Christ
This was hope
This is my life
This is my reality
I am
A prisoner, captive in the bondage of serenity, faith, and love

I used to dream
Thoughts frolicked and welcomed
Passersby with greetings of joyous salutations
As adolescent dreams matured
Into full-fledged adult aspirations

I used to dream
Escaping into my mind
A place of solitude
That permitted my imagination to roam free
Free from the shackles of my reality
Life, lived to the fullest without limitations
I basked in the doubtlessness of God
My Father
My Protector

Forever confident
I hid in and behind Him
Awaiting Him to smite those who dared to permeate or
Invade my dreams

He protected me
As any Father would
However, He wanted me to mature
Maturation, a necessity
All while remaining hidden in the
shadow of his gentle protection
I matured
I continue to mature

Never wanting to release my dreams
I waited…I continue to wait
For the dreams my Father has shown me
For the limitless visions of my reality
Directly reflecting
The abundance of joy and peace that reside
In my dreams

Dreams that I could never have imagined
Or made up even in
The longest hour of capitulation
Due to my limited imagination

Waiting, remaining in wait…
Understanding now that the maturation
My Father wants and wills
For me to attain
Is all part of a plan

Dialogue, acceptance, and diligence in my mission and purpose
We talked, we danced, and we loved
Before He sent me off into the woman called my mother

Now I remain
A dreamer
Patiently awaiting the appointed time
Where the dreams I dreamt in my youth
Are introduced to the visions ordained by my Father
Where we embrace and progress forward
To the place of manifestation

I used to dream
I had to mature
I can still hide
All while waiting patiently
For that appointed time
The ordained manifestation
All stemming from my assignment and purpose
A vision
My Father's vision
My dream

Contents

The Suicidal Setup 13
Job Made Real 19
The Dream Stronghold 38
Angels Watching Over Me: Hannah's Help 48
Soul Therapy Meets the Past.. 54
Distant Past Appears Too Close 69
The Brotherhood: The Struggles of Men............................... 77
Can Love Truly Be Just a Friend?... 102
Reality Check 112
Mother's Presence: Prayer, Power, and Petition 123
Is Someone Expecting?... 134
Downtown Reunion 146
Uprooting the Past to Rendezvous with Destiny 155
I Had to Go Through That: Recognizing the Prince
    from the Frogs 169
The Plain 183
Family Deliverance 188
The Sanctuary.. 214
The Truth Shall Set You Free... 234
Confessions of the Soul 246
The King Within 274

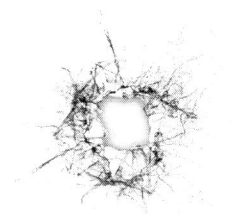

The Suicidal Setup

I eagerly expect and hope that I will in no way be ashamed, but will have sufficient courage so that now as always Christ will be exalted in my body, whether by life or by death. For to me, to live is Christ and to die is gain. If I am to go on living in the body, this will mean fruitful labor for me. Yet what shall I choose? I do not know! I am torn between the two: I desire to depart and be with Christ, which is better by far; but it is more necessary for you that I remain in the body. Convinced of this, I know that I will remain, and I will continue with all of you for your progress and joy in the faith, so that through my being with you again your joy in Christ Jesus will overflow on account of me.

Philippians 1:20–26 (NIV)

The school bell blared overhead as students bombarded the hallowed halls of this urban educational institution in supreme bliss of their last day for the academic year. Partially overjoyed of their newfound release from the scholastic shackles incarcerating their intellect, the students were more elated for liberation from the stifling Atlanta heat that suffocated their attention spans and ignited tempers faster than bullets. Sweat-stained clothing sat on skin like tattoos on fanning teen bodies, creating a cloud in the hallway as students pressed against one another in an effort to find the nearest exit. Though the temperature within the halls escalated within minutes to furnace-like temperatures, the students were mentally jubilant. Students basked in the knowledge that a return to the building would not occur for months, which gave cool to the sweltering compound. The seeming brightness of the day and the optimistic precept of freedom filled the air.

Though frenzy roused the atmosphere, one stood out amongst the crowd whose disposition was all but euphoric. Distanced from the crowd, one young lady stood contemplating her life's outlook. Unlike the towering basketball players hovering overhead at six-foot-three and above, she stood barely seeing over the locker at five-foot-six. Given a unique birth name, Evidence, that would prove to be the one word reflective of her life's journey, was unlike her peers. Going by her nickname Eve, she was framed with a physique like an Olympic gymnast. Her thick, jet-black hair was hostage to a ponytail with her hazel eyes hiding behind contemporary frames. She had a smile that would capture the attention of the sun. Her physical beauty was mind blowing, but her internal light fought to blaze. She walked slowly as she scoffed at her peer's excitement over their future plans. Eve bounced off heated bodies as she journeyed down the sweltering hallway; alone and submitting quickly to her melancholy thinking. With a dim attitude and irresistible rumination of suicide taking root in the garden of her mind, her attention was thwarted by her peer's mirth. The notion of detriment swam through her head like famished sharks in blood-filled waters seeking the source of their enticement. Before she could fully commit to her plan, she was jolted into reality by the one person privileged enough to be deemed friend. This friendship, established with church as a common denominator, ventured through the halls of her high school. Though they shared the same deistic belief, her heart remained sour at the thought of life.

Brooklyn, also known as Brooke, glided up to her friend as if she were a gaff-rigged sailboat floating in midair on the glory cloud with heaven's winds filling her sailcloth. With a smile that could make the angels tune up their harps and eyes that embodied eternal lamps, she was the epitome of optimism as she approached Eve. Brooke, unlike her half-naked peers who used the heat as their scapegoat, left room for the imagination rather than giving it all away at first glance. This vibrant young woman adorned with a peaceful presence reminded her dour friend of her promised participation in the youth retreat at their church. In her haste, she failed to inquire of her melancholy friend's demeanor, but mentioned of their gathering, "Hey, Eve, it's the last day of school, and I'm on cloud ten because nine isn't enough. You know I had to remind you about the retreat tonight. You are coming, right? You better! You better make sure you get on that van when it pulls up to your house! No excuses! I expect to see you there."

Before Brooke could get a valid response from her friend, she was pulled backward down the hall, quickly blending into the crowd. Pulling on the hand of a friend who decided to interject and abduct her body and attention, she paused briefly for some verbal or nonverbal clue of her friend's acknowledgement. Brooke yelled, "Well, say something, yes or no! It better be yes!"

Not wanting to disappoint and searching for some minuscule ounce of optimism, she replied before fully realizing her disgruntlement, "Yes, I'll be there, and it better be worth it!"

Turning around in utter anguish, she left school and proceeded home. She ignored everything in her view and escaped, yet lost in the darkened world of her despair. Eve found herself back at the start of her initial thought. Solitude had become her friend. Just when there appeared to be light at the end of her tunnel, she was confronted with a spiritual battlefield of her mind in full armor going up against a powerful enemy—thought of suicide.

Before her were options and avenues for quick fixes and torturous outlooks. To the left were pills, razors, and poisons. To the right was a rope, the roof of a building, and the lights of an eighteen-wheeler. They seemed to tower over her and draw in closer as she contemplated her life's escape route.

Vacillating over which suicidal road to take, she began to focus more on how dark and dismal the concept appeared. The battlefield, with the fiendish suicidal options, floated around, awaiting the selection process. Focusing to the left, her attention drew to the center where there appeared before her a cloud with light gleaming from within. The longer the cloud hovered, the larger it grew. Suddenly, the battleground didn't appear as detrimental as she conceived. All around her, she heard voices of encouragement as if angelic soldiers rallied with her in support of her victory rather than her demise. The more she focused on the voices, the smaller the enemy before her became. Ultimately, the angelic host silenced as her confidence and faith renewed. This spiritual warfare was no solitary victory, hence ending her concentration camp experience for any thought of suicide, at least for the time being. It would take more than this singular victory to overcome the torment that plagued her spirit. There would have to be strength so resilient and powerful to annihilate the devil's plans, and the only source powerful enough to prevail was God. That cloud was more than a visual emblem of power; it was evidence of the creator she desired most. If attending the retreat would invoke God's presence, then this was an open invitation where she would not be late.

∽o∾

Looking at her watch, Eve noticed she had enough time to go home, shower, dress, and head to the church. She picked up speed as she briskly walked toward the train station. Exhaling long and deeply, she pondered within, *is going to church really going to make a difference in how I feel?* Her entire body began to ache as her mental attitude generated a dismal forecast over her spirit. As fast as the darkness crept in, she rebuked it away even faster. Not knowing the entire Bible verbatim, but knowing enough to whip up strength to rebuke the demonic spirits wrestling for her soul, she journeyed home. Eve talked to herself in a faint whisper. She didn't want to bring too much attention to herself; there was no need to be considered as a psychotic candidate. Fortunately, she blended right in with the crowd awaiting the train.

Eve stood as she welcomed one last hope of optimism and pressed beyond her disbelief to acquire the mustard seed within. Smiling and looking up, she boarded the train and closed her eyes as the rhythm of the train nestled and eased her pain as a mother to a babe. For a brief moment, almost as if suspended in time, her time of solitude was replaced with serenity. However, the moment didn't last long because she'd reached her destination.

Leaving the safety of the train, she bolted down the street to her house, unlocked the door, and burst inside. Studying the time again she realized there was a small window for her to shower and change clothes. Making a beeline to the bathroom, she dropped her book bag and each garment along the way. Turning the shower into a sanctuary, she prayed silently with the grace cloud of expectation moving in. Time escaped her grasp, and she used enough water to bathe two small villages. Moving fast, but not fast enough, time raced away from her, but coming upon the final lap, she remained victorious. Walking to the door, she took one final look and quickly grabbed her keys, not realizing she would not return the same.

∽o∾

Staring at the church's emblem on the side of the bus caused her to pause for a moment. Reading the motto for Salvation Church, "New Life with Christ Begins with Salvation," aroused her intrigue as she boarded with expectancy of attaining a new life. After several pickups, they arrived at the majestic edifice. Eve observed the long street leading to the towering dwelling with floor-to-ceiling glass and nothing but a single chandelier and chrome cross illuminating the evening sky. The cross shined with a welcoming glow in the foyer. Her eyes were affixed to the church; she saw there was a purple carpet outlined in red with the church's emblem monogrammed. The church appeared fit for royalty but stood as a reminder that as a child of God, you are an heir and royalty is in your bloodline. Several of the youth huddled together as they whispered amongst themselves of the church's ambiance. Detainee to numerous vehicles creating traffic, she and her peers impatiently sat, anticipating their escape from their transportation.

Numerous vans and buses bombarded the church's parking lot. Teens flooded the sidewalk. She glared out the window in awe of the numerous peers who welcomed the evening's youth retreat. If polls and statistics were essential for demographic metrics, rubrics, and tabulations, Jesus' popularity and power demolished the competition. If you had a beating heart, you were invited and various hearts accepted their invitation.

Though suicide was the fiend housed to ascertain detriment in her life, replacing it would entail purpose and intent. Eve thought retrospectively about her life, circumstances, and solitude. Loneliness and pain with suicidal thoughts tugging at her mind created a veil of despair. The dim light within her soul desired to burn the veil and all associated with it, but that would require release and the risk of being exposed. After wearing a muzzle and shielding her torment for years, how could she possibly consider exposure? Was there another way to receive freedom? The moment this question appeared in her mind, three suicidal thoughts attempted to resurface from their rebuke. She shook her head as if dismissing the suicidal attack, but she was showered with more thoughts. This time, she wondered what others would think. Thoughts of her peer's opinions invaded her mind like a military squadron barraging enemy lines. Eve grew frustrated by the minute and found herself quietly erupting within. Sending off fumes of rage into the atmosphere, she searched for the nearest restroom, hoping to regain what little strength she had left. Splashing cold water on her face, she stared at her reflection and whispered to herself, "I refuse to leave the way I came. You hear me, Eve? We will not take this back home. Either it stays here or we die here. God, do you hear me? If you love me at all, this is my last plea; it's all I have left. Help me, please."

After considering her life's value to be least of those already dead, often referring to herself jokingly as Jane Doe, her introduction to a greater measure was the new catalyst in her life's saga. If suicide had a morsel of rationale, it would have come to the amicable resolve that its function was to catapult her into destiny, establishing God's glory. Suicide would take a backseat to a purposeful setup.

Job Made Real

After Job prayed for his friends, the Lord made him prosperous again and gave him twice as much as he had before.

Job 42:10 (NIV)

Driving away from Lenox Road and entering Georgia 400, the quickly diminishing silhouette of the Atlanta skyline was a mere reflection in the rearview of Bernie's luxury vehicle. Listening to her favorite gospel song and tapping her fingers on the steering wheel, Bernadette Josephson a.k.a. Bernie, the high-powered attorney, rolled down her window as she approached the tollbooth on Georgia 400. Extending her hand out the window and exchanging monetary salutations, Bernie noticed the woman's face. She instantly took a double take as their brief interaction created an immediate flashback and race for remembrance in Bernie's mind. She knew the young lady from somewhere, but putting her finger on their approximate previous encounter took a longer moment than she anticipated. Before she could reach Interstate 285, Bernie remembered where she met the young lady.

Tunneling back into the recesses of her mind, Bernie instantly saw herself in the room filled with her peers as they stood in mini-subgroups conversing amongst themselves. Her ex-boyfriend, at that time, embraced her elbow as he introduced the young lady and her companion to Bernie. Though the woman's name and details of their interaction were dismal, the woman's shirt was ingrained in Bernie's memory. Guised as a human billboard representing all atheists, the shirt read, *Death to God and God Believers*. Completely forgetting the details of their conversation, she only remembered reading the shirt, posing for a picture, and then embracing the young woman. Before she could dwell in the memories of her past, a driver honked his horn inherently at Bernie. Without delay, Bernie jolted the car back into her lane and clasped her chest. Waving her apologies for veering off into his lane, she began to silently pray. Tears streamed down her face and her prayer of thanks transitioned into a prayer of repentance. Drenched in tears, Bernie arrived at her destination. Taking a moment to gather her composure, she inhaled deeply as she massaged her moistened palms on the steering wheel and reached for her compact. Mentally encouraging herself to get it together, Bernie rubbed a fresh face of makeup on and took one final look at herself as she exited her vehicle. Bernie walked briskly with her head down as she meditated on her prayer time with God and entered the edifice.

∽∘∽

The youth retreat at Salvation Church caused youth to pour in from all over. Youth of all ages ran and gathered in their various age groups with their teachers preparing lessons. Bernie, the youth's most sought-after leader, journeyed to an overcrowded room full of anxious teenagers mentally, physically, and spiritually prepared to hear every word that fell from her lips. Though her approach with the youth was as radical as they came, she had the natural gift to bring this particular age group together. As a result, the youth ministry's numbers increased into the hundreds in less than a year. The immense growth within the ministry, and parents' exceeding joy having their children eagerly and regularly attend church, allowed Bernie the room to do what was necessary by any means.

Bernie journeyed to her room as she was greeted by one of her best friends, Hannah Winters. Walking with Bernie, the two continued to converse. To see Hannah, you immediately recognized how poised, distinguished, and professional a woman she was; however, what you could not identify was her quiet pain. She returned to God and the church after a tumultuous journey of fighting her fears and personal past. After being guised in the pews for several months, leading up to a year, she eventually stepped out of her shell and began her new journey of servitude within God's house. Somehow, helping others and being there for people was the therapeutic outlet in a safe environment she needed to get her through her darkest hours. Knowing the sincerity of heart Pastor and Lady Woods have for people were an added bonus.

Though Hannah was an active member in the church, working with the youth was clearly the gift anointed for Bernie. However, the youth retreat always captured Hannah's attention because it afforded her the opportunity to teach those interested in the world of the arts. Amber Dawson, one of the youth advisors, line sister, and close friend of Taylor's, stopped Bernie and Hannah. Taylor Woods, Pastor Woods' daughter, approached and joined in the conversation as they briefly discussed some topics they were teaching their classes.

For some reason, Bold Bernie was the go-to person whenever people had questions. Never hesitating to be of assistance, Bernie entertained her peer's inquisition, "Now you know I have to go see my children, but I will stop in my tracks for you ladies. How are you beautiful women doing today?"

Amber responded joyously as she explicated her point and position of change for both her Taylor's students: "Ridiculously excited for some reason. I sense something great is about to happen! Lately all of the kids have had so much frustration, hurt, and questions bottled up, so we're stepping out of the box on this one. You know Mother Jenkins can't stand stuff being out of order. She's always screaming about how God likes stuff in decency and in order, but we just want to take it to another level, while still getting the Word of God in their spirits. If anyone understands how we feel, you would."

Taylor followed up her friend's retort: "Bold Bernie, we know your time is valuable, but for tonight, we want to combine the groups? We wanted to focus on the scripture, '*We are overcome by the word of our testimony.*'"

Bernie, understanding her peers, responded, "Well, Mother Jenkins has her reasons for being structured. Structure is good, so just understand where she's coming from. The spirit is powerful! This is only confirmation of what the Holy Spirit spoke to me while I was in prayer this morning. Absolutely, ladies! Get your classes and I'll meet you in the Overflow Room."

Without responding to Bernie, the two bolted away to their classes to retrieve their students before Mother Jenkins showed up. Having a confrontation with Mother Jenkins wasn't on the list of things to do. There was a need to go beyond the established traditions, and being lured into formality by a biased leader compelled to keeping things "normal" was subject for dismissal. However, Mother Jenkins stood afar observing the congestion and behavior of all the bodies clamoring throughout the halls within the church. Addressing the youth, Mother Jenkins commented of the noise. Meanwhile, Taylor and Amber proceeded as planned to rustle up their students for a night of power and God's presence.

Socially acknowledging their peers, the youth clapped hands to unite on one accord about their Lord and Savior. More youth continued to trickle into the room. There was one teen far off in the corner that wasn't connected in any way to any of the other youth gathered in the room. Nestled down on the floor, this unnamed worshiper rocked unhurriedly on her knees, praying to God from her heart.

Tears poured from her face as she intimately sought God, "Heal her and speak to her pain. I don't know why I'm hurting for someone, but please, God, take the pain away and move like only you can. Help her, God, and give her a spirit of boldness to release the pain. Touch her and make her whole. I know you hear me and answer prayers, so I'm thanking you in advance. Be glorified in this place. Let her light shine so you are glorified and hearts surrender to you. Thank you, God! Thank you, God! Thank you, Jesus!"

This teenager rocked, pouring out her soul not for herself, but for some stranger whom she felt the Holy Spirit required her to stand in the gap as an intercessor. While her peers stood around in small groups whispering, some proclaimed with boldness that she's always a little different. This teenage intercessory prayer warrior, immersed in the secret place of God, gradually moved from the outer court to the inner court of God's own presence for some stranger. Her lips moved as though she was replicating the prayer of Hannah in 1 Samuel, but her tears flowed so heavily and plummeted to the banks of her shirt that it created visual evidence of her time spent in prayer.

Slowly ceasing from rocking, she began to smile through the tears. Her prayer of pain immediately transformed to tears and verbal expressions of joy as she realized she'd just had another encounter with God. With the noise of voices faint in the distance of her spirit and the clamoring of bodies and chairs being moved from their original positions, this teenage girl heard the voice of God speak, "Arise, I have heard your prayer. The glory of the Lord is evident in this place. She is already delivered, restored, and healed."

Thankful that God's presence manifested, she slowly arose from her personal sanctuary and paced the floor, still worshipping God. This worship was personal and didn't require music. This worship to God didn't invoke others to participate. This worship session was so intimate yet so profound that those with a connection began to worship God. The atmosphere went from a social climate to immediate worship. The youth who began to praise, pray, and worship God began making noise that poured into the halls.

Eve could hear the transition in sound from the restroom and quickly gathered her composure. Immediately, she left the bathroom and blended into the crowd trying to enter the room. As she approached the Overflow Room, she could hear the youth in worship. She immediately walked in, and before she could assess the environment, she began crying profusely. It was as if the spirit of release drew to her and all self-restraint diminished. Her tears swelled faster than ocean waves at high tide and crashed against the banks of her skin. God's spirit embraced her. Yelling and crying, she was finally free and uninhibited in praise, "I'm letting it all go, God! Tonight, God, right now, no more evil thoughts! Release me! I'm letting it all go! I'm letting go, I'm tired!"

Other youth began to distance themselves from conversation, closed their eyes, and lifted their voices in prayer to God. Though the worship initiated with silence, it transitioned, roaring into praise. Youth musicians began to utilize their gifts and operate in their anointing through instrumentation as they played harmoniously and melodiously ushering in the angelic host of the glory train. The music only enhanced the already evident worship that was taking place in the room. A teen worship leader with the voice of angels began to sing. Soon, other teens held hands and sang, lifting their voices as one to reach heaven's gates and bombard God's throne with thanksgiving in their hearts. Some jumped up and down, others waved their hands, and dancers from the liturgical dance ministry began to express themselves through dance. The sound of praise and worship to God escalated to concert decibels. The glory cloud enveloped the room and everyone worshipped. Tears and repentance filled the air, deliverance was in demand, and salvation was at an all-time high. The Holy Spirit was more intense and spread faster than a California wildfire in the middle of a dry field on a windy day. The more the people began to worship, the faster the Holy Spirit touched lives.

Bernie and Hannah finally entered in the room. Bernie immediately exclaimed, "Oh, the blood of Jesus! The blood of Jesus! The blood! The blood! The blood! I feel the presence of God in this place! Hallelujah!" Before Bernie could completely posture herself for teaching, Amber, Taylor, and a host of adult mentors and adolescents filled the room. Instructed by their proctors to move swiftly and quietly, the youth all scattered to find seats by relatives and friends alike. The atmosphere, set for worship, drew the additional youth into praise. This measurably large room turned into a sanctuary filled with bodies of maturing youth, hungry and thirsting for God's presence. Glancing around the room, Bernie paced the floor engulfed in the favor of God.

A fresh wind of anointing filled the room and circled everyone who entered into the glory cloud of the Lord. In a matter of minutes, the entire atmosphere shifted and the youth unilaterally made a joyful noise unto the Lord. After an hour and a half of continuous praise, singing, dancing, and the immense shout of a war cry, people slowly paced the floor as they continued their worship in silence. Although some continued sporadically shouting out a sound of praise, the order and norm of the gathering had taken a detour to God's divine and welcomed intervention. After several minutes of gathering her composure and smearing more makeup on her face, Bernie fanned off the notion of even trying to be pretty at this point. She was already exposed as a worshipper, and this exposure was worth the mess. Steadily pacing the floor and shifting gears into her radical mode, Bernie addressed her children.

"I'm convinced that God's presence is in here, and there's going to be a major transformation. I'm convinced that God is going to show himself mighty. Allow me to help you understand. See we often hope, which is what we're supposed to do. Most of us even believe, but when you're convinced of something, there's absolutely nothing anyone can say to alter your belief. That's where I am right now. You need to learn that there's a difference between believing and being convinced. You don't have to be convinced with me, I'm accustomed to standing out by myself."

Not wanting to preach, but finding herself swept away into God's perfect spirit, Bernie was in another place. She entered the inner court of God's own presence, and in this position, she was completely uninvolved. Her intent was to proceed as planned, but there was an apparent shift in the atmosphere, elevating evidence of a spiritual takeover. She knew there was something that was necessary to discuss, and she was going to initiate the night with a touchy subject. Unbeknownst to Bernie and all present, their level of understanding would soon be obliterated. Returning to her natural self, Bernie addressed the room with capitulation to the leading of the Holy Spirit.

Standing before this room filled with eager hearts prepared to receive the word of God, Bernie stood confident in boldness, prepared to relinquish all God deposited into her belly. Her presence alone commanded attention. Towering at five-foot-eleven-inches, with a muscular physique fit for a fitness magazine, and a powerful commanding voice with the bass of a man but the gentleness of all her feminine wiles, Bernie smiled, allowing her finely polished teeth to escape, and warmly welcomed all of her beloved children.

"I'm thankful to God and the Holy Spirit that is present in this place. For those who are our honored guests, you have officially been inducted into the family. For those unfamiliar with me, I am a servant first and foremost here at Salvation Church in the Youth Department, and my name is Bernadette, but everyone calls me Bernie. Some even go as far as saying Bold Bernie, but either way, I'll declare I'm a child of God.

"I know we're all swimming in the depths of glory, but we're also here to feed hungry souls. My intent is to discuss a non-churchy subject. So let me forewarn you, I have no problem submitting to the lead of God and his perfect will. So instead of me skating around the matter, I'll get straight to the point. Please listen with your heart and spirit. I love each of you and consider you all my wonderful children.

"I want to discuss something with you your parents don't want you to hear within the church. Honestly, the old folks say we should wait. Without further ado, our topic of discussion is sex! Just like that! Get comfortable because we're going into a place many run from in the church! Now let me say this for the record, sex really isn't everything. You think about the time you spend having the actual sex act with someone and you'll realize that life is more than just sex. However, when—"

One teen blurted out a comment before Bernie could complete her statement.

"Yeah, I hear what you're saying, but you're old, and we have more to deal with than you did back in your day."

"James, what does that mean—back in my day? I'm not that much older than you." Bernie surveyed her audience and decided to take yet another approach to her topic of discussion. "Okay, since you think I'm so much older, would you all like to have some real talk?"

In undisputed agreement, the youth said, "Yeah!"

The adult mentors sat anxiously waiting to hear Bernie's approach to this subject. Amber and Taylor clapped hands and whispered amongst each other, smiling over the subject at hand. Glancing over her comrade's shoulder, Amber alerted Taylor that Mother Jenkins walked in the room and took a seat along the wall. Taylor rolled her eyes, fanned off the notion of her interrupting, and whispered something to Amber. Bernie, recognizing Mother Jenkins's conspicuous and dour demeanor, ignored her and commenced to teach.

Before Bernie could proceed, an unfamiliar face interrupted her. Eve raised a question that ignited the conversation to levels beyond everyone's understanding. "Ms. Bernie, I'm sorry to interrupt, but I have a confession and a question. I come here sometimes, but I don't participate in many activities. I've seen you and heard your name before and some of the other teachers, but I may not be that familiar to you. To be honest, the only person that really knows I'm a member here is my friend, Brooke. She always harasses me about coming to the retreats and being involved, so here I am. She also told me the retreats you all have are like little therapy sessions for teens, and this is a safe haven for me to be around other young sold-out believers. If I can be honest and blunt, I'm tired of walking around parading the person everyone wants to see. I'm hurting, and I have to let it go. I can't take it anymore!"

Bernie couldn't believe the question, but she stood still and silently prayed for God to allow the Holy Spirit to take full control. Immediately, calm overcame her, and she knew instantly that her submission caused her to take a backseat to God's lead. Walking over to grab a chair and pulling it to the front of the room by some of her children, she motioned to the young lady that she had the floor. Before taking a seat, Bernie walked over to give her a hug. She greeted her warmly as though she'd known her for years, then took a seat and addressed the young lady.

"Honey, let me first say, welcome into the family. Now, I don't want to assume anything, so let me ask. Have you ever confessed Jesus Christ as your personal Lord and Savior? Before you even say a word about who you are, I want you to know that you are truly welcomed into the family. What you've done in the past, if you ask, can and will forever be forgiven."

"Yes, Ms. Bernie, I've confessed to Jesus, I've talked about Jesus to others, and I pray on the regular, but this brings me to my statement and question."

Bernie threw her hand up and shrugged her shoulders down as she said, "Okay, sorry for interrupting. You have the floor. Would you like to share your name with us?"

Eve thought for a moment, "Is it okay if I just start? I'm not sure just yet. It might not make much difference anyway, but I just have a few things to say and ask."

Bernie understood how confessions and teens could be. "Absolutely, whenever you're ready." Bernie walked over to her seat between her children and sat attentively as Eve postured herself in her seat. Unsure if she should sit or stand, the petite young woman opted to stand so she could be both seen and heard. Clearing her throat and standing with an air of confidence as though she towered like a runway model, the young woman began to address the room.

"Let me start out by saying that this is truly one of the hardest things I've ever done. I've been isolated in my mind so long–the darkness seems brighter than light. I almost didn't make it here tonight, literally. I know that everything happens for a reason, but there are some things that will never make sense to me–no matter how much I believe. You are looking at someone who has had an attitude with God. I've been at war in my heart and spirit so long, that I'm surprised I'm still standing. Just today, I thought of several different ways I could commit suicide!" Waving her hands as if they were white flags she continued, "Ewwwww, I know I'm in church talking about the one sin that could send you straight to Hell, but I'm being honest and this pain, heartache, and spiritual torture is unbearable. Maybe you all are stronger than me, but I'm exhausted."

Eve paused briefly while fighting to maintain her confident disposition. Slowly dropping her head, she battled her thoughts and emotions. One part of her wanted to run out of the crowded room, but the other part refused and wanted to finish what she'd started. Growing frustrated from another internal struggle, she breathed deeply, raised her head, and decided to press forward. For the first time all day people had taken notice of her–all because she had something to say. Since fear was chasing her down, she opted to stop running, look fear in the face, and denounce any stronghold over her mind. Emotionally strengthened, she left the mental battleground and proceeded.

"Well, I'll give you the short version. My life is true, and though harsh, it is real. Quite frankly, people my age would say, 'TMI' or, 'shut up and be quiet.' I'm so tired of hiding and to be honest it's emotionally and mentally draining. People who sit on the outside looking in have no clue what really rests behind the tormented walls of my life. Before you sit there prepared to judge me, I just ask that you check and make sure you're not living in a glass house. I know I'm a nameless face in the crowd. Some of you may even want me to stop talking right now and some could probably care less, but time and life are rapidly declining for me so I'm not easily embarrassed. Perhaps I'm the only one with the issue and I can tell I'm the only one willing to speak up about it, but I'm beyond being fake so people will love me or care about me. My issue you ask yourself—since it's taking me a long time to explain—well here it is."

Giving no place to fear, she exhaled deeply and took command of her testimony as though she was a highly trained and sought-after orator. With self-assurance emanating through her pores, she towered over her peers and mentors with unequivocal fortitude, causing royalty to submit to her incidence. Gazing into the eyes of her audience, she continued.

"Well, I'm not here to bore anyone, so here's the deal. I'm sixteen, I was beaten severely, literally almost to death, and brutally gang-raped by my uncle and three of his drunken friends when I was only twelve. Abandoned, I was left in the company of a family member all because no one cared. My 'I could-care-less-mother' would leave me with whoever was willing to keep an eye on me. Since nothing ever happened before, what was one more time? She left me there with him and his little drunk friends, so she could be with her man, who didn't like the fact that she had baggage. I'm only baggage because she was a loose cannon and had sex like preachers pass offering plates, so I can't tell you who my father is.

"Long story made very short, look at me! Take a good long look at what *sex* looks like. I have full-blown AIDS at sixteen. I had a baby that died, only because I was scared as hell and hid my pregnancy until I couldn't hide it anymore. I know this is church, sorry for the profanity, but I'm angry and hurt. What was I supposed to do? I didn't know anything about how to care for myself, let alone while pregnant. I was paranoid, and I swam in anxiety all day.

"My mother finally showed some emotion, but said she refused to be a grandmother. It didn't matter because my baby was premature and too weak to survive. She never made it out of the hospital. Where she should have been frantic and apologetic for leaving me, she opted to be angry for having her world interrupted by me. There was no '*I'm so sorry for leaving you.*' All I came home to was '*I don't want to be a grandmother*!' If that didn't suffice, by the time I was thirteen she kicked me out, told me to never come back because I wasn't welcomed by her man, and I was making her look bad.

"After roaming the streets, agonizing over where to go, I was infuriated and hysterical over the reality of being hated and rejected by my own mother. I was orphaned, literally! Ms. Lorna, a woman in my neighborhood, took me in. My mother hated me so much that my case worker tried to talk her into *not* signing over her parental rights! My mother auctioned me off like a slave to Ms. Lorna without putting up a fight. I never felt such pain in my life! I never knew the human heart had the ability to be so desolate. We eventually moved away to give me some stability. I thank God for Ms. Lorna because she taught me about God and it really settled *some* of my anger and hate, but my questions are quite simple. What did I do so wrong that God would have me rejected by my own mother? Why would God allow a man take my life away before I started living? Sex was the furthest thing in my mind.

"I thought I would come here tonight and leave strengthened, but you all want to talk about the same thing that was used to punish me and now wants to take my life away. I don't even know what I did to make God so angry that something like this happened. I'm sorry for throwing everything off, but this subject gets very personal with me. You know, sometimes I would actually pray that God would help me and take me away to a better place.

Maybe I'm the only one! I know no one in here has ever wished to die or had suicidal thoughts, but that is just how intent I've been on giving up.

"Maybe you all are holier than I am, but I'm admitting it right here and now. Thoughts of suicide and death–in my mind–come as natural as breathing.

"Even though I know suicide is against God, what do you do when you're hurting? What do you do when pain is so familiar that laughter is a foreigner in your own pool of emotions? Why should I want to continue living when death accepted an open invitation into my life unannounced? In my mind, suicide has been more of a friend than life itself.

"For some reason, I keep trying my hand at life. I can't leap into the act of suicide just yet. I must admit, I went as far as trying little things to see if I could go through with it. Just when I'm ready to take the full plunge, I can't commit to it. Instead, I'm slapped right back to my reality. I have AIDS, so what's the point of rushing death? I don't look like I have AIDS, do I? Is there a specific look or face for AIDS? Is there an age restriction? Obviously AIDS isn't gender biased? Do I fit your presumed profile for how AIDS should look and act? I don't look sick. I go to school just like you? Guess what, AIDS is everywhere. Wake up people! This is reality! This is my reality! This isn't a commercial. This isn't a magazine AD with a model getting paid to look despondent. This isn't some enticing picture posted on some social network for giggles, likes, comments, and a potential meet-and-greet. This is real. I am real! *Sex* is not something to be taken lightly! Life shouldn't be taken for granted! Look at me! This is *sex*! I am a voice screaming out and the spokesperson for *sex*!

"Better yet, I'm more than that. I know you may have questions and opinions swirling around in your minds. I can feel the judgment, and I can see your thoughts on your faces. So to answer your question, this is what AIDS looks like. I'm sixteen and I'm dying from AIDS at the hands of rape by a family member and his friends! I don't even know why I came here tonight. I was really convinced I was supposed to be here."

With tears plummeting from her face, she searched the faces of her peers and the adults within the room so they could take an introspective thought to their irresponsible actions of having casual sex. Though her circumstance was not contingent upon her own doing, she was the result of the flagrant negligence of her adult attackers. Bridging the gap between the hidden truth behind sex and the reality of the rampant viral disease nestled within her body; Eve chuckled nervously and proceeded with her confession.

"Ha, be careful what you ask for, right? I love God! I need God! Doesn't he know that? I hope he is listening and loves me enough to see this is my plea and my submission before him. I didn't ask for this. I was a kid. I wanted a childhood. I wanted a real family, but instead I got death. So, Ms. Bernie, what do you say to someone who knows the darker side of *sex*?"

The room fell silent with the pressure of solitary confinement consuming each person's mind. Tears rolled down faces like salted rivers crashing against banks of clothing. Some nestled their peers in their arms, only imagining the pain she must have felt. Others considered the reality of AIDS and the conviction of their careless actions impregnated them with fear. Even with a surfeit of emotions encapsulating the room, some considered their own problems obsolete. Bernie sat in silence; meditating intently in solitary prayer for the wisdom and discernment for her flesh and carnal spirit to take a backseat to God's voice completely. Bernie, not speaking for herself, submitted unto the Holy Spirit of God as she responded in the prophetic.

"Your suffering was not in vain, and there's greater purpose to your testimony than you know. This is a divine encounter beyond all of our levels of understanding. You are the man born blind with the disciples inquiring to Jesus who sinned, the man or his parents. You are the Obadiah connecting two different worlds: the prophetic and that destined by the prophesy. You are the slave girl who linked Naaman to the Prophet Elisha. You, my beautiful child, have purpose greater than you know. It's God's perfect will for you to be here."

Bernie noticed the tears streaming from the faces in the room and continued, "I can't help but think of the lepers who sat outside the gates contemplating their fate. They were thrust in a position to either hold their position and not speak a word to the king, which would bring death upon themselves, or if they should share the information and bless the lives of others, hence bringing life for themselves as well as others. If they remained where they were, they would surely die, but it was not until they changed their position that they not only received life, but a plethora of blessings. Though I cannot nor would I dare lie to you about why these events had to occur in your life, I will tell you because of those events and the power in your testimony, you are healed.

"God told me to tell you to see beyond what your eyes can see. You're not going to die, but you will live and be made whole. Your health shall be restored, and you will live a long life in this land. Your generations shall be blessed. The curse over your life has been broken. This is the first time you've ever spoken boldly, but your life and this fellowship amongst believers was not by chance. Though your journey to get to this place caused you immense pain, your living shall not be in vain. Every prayer you've ever prayed was received in heaven.

"Even when the devil asked for your life, God rebuked him because you shall be used to bring God glory. The doctors have spoken their sentence, but there is a name above every name, Jesus, son of the living God. God is *I am that I am.* He is Jehovah Shamah, Jehovah Niecy, Jehovah Sikenueh, he is Jehovah Jierah, and God is your source. God's word to you is 'never be deceived for my love for you extends beyond your understanding and my glory shall rise upon you.'"

~o~

There wasn't a dry face in the place. Even Mother Jenkins was elated that she'd witnessed the praise, the worship, and the testimony given by Eve who'd transitioned her outlook of service from traditionalism to contemporary. Mother Jenkins flashed back to the days of her youth when God's power was evident in the church and testimony services concatenated with prayer produced deliverance. The stark difference between her experience as a youth and the experiences of the present day was simple, the ceiling of time entrapment. Mother Jenkins, like many elders in the traditional church, placed blinders on the all-seeing, all-knowing God. Shackled to the God of yesterday, somehow, she, like her counterparts, neglected to realize God is always moving and time never waits. Synonymous to Mother Jenkins's pious perception, some elders were awaiting God to show up the way he did twenty years prior. However, had they received God and a better understanding, they would recognize he appears in greater form.

~o~

In this instance, God appeared before his sheep in the form of a young unfamiliar face with a medically diagnosed deadly disease. However, like the lepers of Jesus' time, of the ten who were afflicted, only one returned to the priest. Eve opted to return to God and the spirit of God was with her. She was the one who acknowledged her source. As a result, she awakened the spiritual eyes of the old and the young, the traditionalist and the radical contemporary. Her testimony alone bridged an established gap without argument. Rather, it was formulated on truth, matured in spirit, and released in love. Eve was the missing link to reconnect lives engulfed in sin and bring them to humbled repentance. Her peers meditated on truth.

Some teens created an altar in the room, falling to their knees and shouting out to God for forgiveness and in prayer for Eve.

Some paced the floor, praying for this young woman. Others laid prostrate in the presence of God, while some remained astounded, lost in a trance of reality. Slowly, the teens began holding hands and created a circle around Eve, praying to God from their hearts. Teens began sharing their testimonies about various experiences with sex.

Sex had many faces. There was no barrier between the gender, the ages, or the races. Sex was hidden behind the fortified walls of beating hearts, but the power of God exposed the sin. There was a breaking, and the silence of sex shattered to the floor at the altar before God. Adults, encouraging teens not to rush, began to cry and share their personal stories and experiences that brought them into the sex-stained sin. Meanwhile, both male and female teens shared their testimonies about being molested and raped. Eve transitioned from an unfamiliar face in the crowd to mentoring her peers. Finally, she wasn't alone. Rather, she was strength for the brokenhearted.

There was an inevitable unveiling. Faces of the youth were tattooed in tears after being masked behind the shrouds of their privatized pain. Makeup ran down faces being washed away into cloth as truth was exposed. Those who always appeared put-together were broken and abused. Stories and testimonies filled the air as layers of hidden pain were placed out in the open for all to hear. Some cried out and confessed their curiosity of homosexuality because of their forced sexual encounters.

One preteen male, dressed in a bold graphic tee inscribed *I Was Born This Way*, confessed to being molested and raped by a family member. Ignoring the underlying issue that resonated within the private realm of his memory, he opted to engage in a homosexual lifestyle because he thought it was the norm. Though he cried out and told his family and the relative was exposed for his actions, they refused to identify that there was a problem. His rape went unnoticed and he went untreated. The testimonies grew in number, and the absolute shock of what these teens had experienced in their young lives was astounding. They poured pain from their hearts and joined in unity for healing.

∽o∾

Taylor left the room to get her father, Pastor Woods. Not wanting to take anything away from the prophetic utterance established through Bernie, he walked into the set atmosphere and submitted himself to the glory of God. Healing and deliverance consumed young lives. His prayer only solidified that God had already been glorified. Teens rallied together and exalted God together in prayer. Each prayer catapulted straight to God's heart as the youth pulled on his presence. This room of young people stood unified in sincere worship before the presence of God. This was not your average youth retreat. God's presence was known and apparent. People from other rooms bombarded the doors as the atmosphere was engrossed with worship.

Every preconceived agenda was immediately discarded as young lives were forever changed. The initiator of this transformation would become the example of God's miracle-working power.

∽o∾

Hannah, trembling from her emotional outcry, walked over to Eve and held her in her arms. Tears consumed Hannah's being so immensely that she knew divine connection brought her to the retreat. Though many teens shared their testimonies, Hannah remained silent of the pain of her past. Hannah never uttered the pain she endured, but she whispered in Eve's ear, "I can relate more than you know. I was a teenager just like you. Thank you for being courageous and taking authority over your fear. You're stronger than most adults–even me. Thank you."

The Dream Stronghold

> *But if out in the country a man happens to meet a girl pledged to be married and rapes her, only the man who has done this shall die. Do nothing to the girl; she has committed no sin deserving death. This case is like that of someone who attacks and murders his neighbor.*
>
> *Deuteronomy 22:25–26* (NIV)

After leaving the youth retreat, Hannah returned home dazed. She couldn't stop thinking about Eve's testimony and the sea of testimonies shared by many of the teens. She reflected on her own torment that she sheltered within the dungeon of her memory. Peeling off the thin layer of clothing and showering to wash away the burden of reflection, Hannah prepared to end the event of the emotional evening.

As much as she didn't want to reflect upon her past, she removed several drawings and portraits from the closet. Incredibly gifted as an artist, Hannah received a full four-year scholarship and traveled the world with her art displayed in international galleries. Unfortunately, her darkest collection would remain riddled with pain for observation by the artist alone. Each drawing reminded her of that night. From black-and-white sketches to the portraits painting a full scene, she lined them up as they retold the events of her torment. Frustrated from memories, Hannah opted to relax the best way she knew. After a nightcap to help ease her into a relaxed state, Hannah prayed on bended knee and attempted to lie down for a full night's rest. Unfortunately, Hannah wrestled within her thoughts. She fought to keep her eyelids open as she lay in the dark with her eyes affixed to the ceiling. She envisioned that dreadful night she tried so hard to forget. She could see everything clearly as though it happened just yesterday. Before she could dismiss the memory, she saw herself seventeen all over again.

∽o∾

Walking away from a small crowd of friends, Hannah paraded the residential street with a partial skip in her step. She smiled and twirled around, waving good-bye to her friends one more time as the small group parted ways. Retracing the steps of her adventurous day, she tuned out all sounds and tunneled back to specific conversations.

Of all the conversations she had for the day, the one with Thomas stood out. She recalled how he brushed her wind-blown hair out of her face as they sat gazing in one another's eyes on the courtyard bench.

"Hannah, listen, you know I've been watching you for a long time. I know all of you sit around and talk about me and some of the guys, but I like you. Not because of the reasons you think I should, but because you're different. To me, you stand out in a crowd, like there's a spotlight shining on you and no one else is around. Hannah, what I'm saying is I want to know if you'll be my girl. I mean, my lady? My mother told me something about a difference in a girl, a woman, and a lady. I don't remember everything, but I do know I want you to be my lady. Hey! You would already have a nickname, just from me to you. So what do you say?" Hannah tried to pretend she didn't understand.

"Nickname, what nickname?"

"Lady, not in a rude way, but something personal between us."

"Well, before I say yes or no, I did want to say this. Don't expect anything extra from me because I'm not for that. The same way you want to do things with your life, I want to do things with mine."

The untouched virtuous young lady who marveled in her self-preservation knew the value of chastity. This valuable treasure was the key element in attaining the interest of the most popular guy in high school. Hannah refused to rush the process for selecting a recipient of her chastity. Unlike several of her female counterparts, Hannah deemed virginity to be more valuable than millions of dollars. It was the one thing she could control and select who would be privileged enough to partake her personal prized possession. Witnessing her peers succumb to teen pregnancy and the staggering hold parenthood had at an early age, she maintained a mind-set of patience versus eagerness. Family members were there to assist some of the young parents, but more were left in the cold rushing wind of expedited parenthood. Though many attempted to smile amid their decision, others were emotionally grieved within the shackle of new innocent life that halted their teenage years.

Hannah gazed into Thomas's eyes, searching for the truth through his words. Though she was elated to be chosen, he too would have to be chosen, and the ball was in her court. Thomas, not wanting to mess up the golden moment, said, "Whoa! I promise I don't expect anything from you. If I wanted anything extra, trust me, there's an entire school of girls who will give themselves freely. Why do you think I'm sitting here with you and not them? I told you, you're different, and I like different people because I'm a different man." Hannah smirked and threw her hand on her hip.

"Man! Thomas, why do you call yourself a man?"

"I was raised to see further into the distance. So many people see into the now. I like to see into the future. And since we are talking about seeing into the future, I don't see myself going to prom without you, but you would have to be my lady in order for me to be there with you. I take it your answer is no because you never answered my question."

Hannah laughed as she thought of his definition of the future. Thomas's long-term vision, with Hannah, only saw up to prom, while her vision saw beyond her collegiate years. He didn't envision a relationship with her beyond high school. Thinking that far into the future did seem a bit much, and besides, there was no guarantee she would stay with him after high school and throughout college, so being his high school sweetheart was welcomed with great joy.

"Thomas, you should already know my answer is yes, but for the sake of formality, my answer is yes."

Receiving an answer from Hannah almost made Thomas more nervous, but he didn't want to come across as excited. Maintaining his cavalier composure, he proceeded with sealing the deal of their relationship.

"Okay, sometimes formality is good. This way neither of us walks around assuming anything. Hey, just for the sake of making it known, how about we always remain good friends? I mean, I want you to be my lady, but I want us to be good friends also. Don't get caught up in the titles, but just be great friends. You think you're up for that?"

Hannah knew instantly that she not only wanted to be his girlfriend, but she was more elated that he had common sense to want to be good friends. Hannah knew the best relationships were rooted in great friendships. Hannah smiled and said, "Finally! A man that has a brain! Sure, I know I can handle that."

Thomas wanted to run down the street screaming with excitement that he finally had the one beautiful girl in the school that engulfed both physical beauty and internal beauty. Rather than embarrass himself before his newfound love, he opted to maintain his calm demeanor. Clapping his hands together and smiling, he extended his arm toward Hannah. Exhaling a sigh of relief coupled with enthusiasm, he responded, "Well, my lady, I know we should probably hang out longer since we're now official, but I have to make a run before I go in the house. I know you all will be out here longer, so I'll call you the moment I step foot in the door."

"Okay, I'll talk to you then."

Before parting ways, he gently brushed her cheek with a kiss and popped up from the bench where they were sitting. Saying good-byes to their friends, he jumped in his mother's car and drove off. Hannah's friends sat in utter amazement; she walked over to tell her friends about her new union.

Of all the girls in the city to ask, he asked Hannah to be his number one. All the girls wanted Thomas. He was six-foot-four, senior in high school, with a full academic scholarship for the fall, athletic, and borderline genius, which only made him sexier than the other athletes. Thomas had a vision of where he was going and what he wanted to do. He didn't just want to be a famous athlete with a few endorsements. He wanted to own a team. Only the best and the brightest sign checks. This visionary young man was what all the young girls wanted but who was solely Hannah's. There was something about him asking her to be exclusively his girlfriend that poured a smile on her face that made this day, time, and year seem more noticeable than any other. Her success as an artist, not because of him, but because of her own achievements, combined with his vision were a few of the thoughts that pranced around her mind. With only two short blocks left and a turn around the corner, Hannah would be home ready to receive her first phone call as the girlfriend of the most popular guy in town.

∽0∾

The darkness of the sky nestled the earth with the stars used as nightlights paving the way. Everything seemed still and serene. The gentle breeze caused the treetops to dance as the moon shined spotlight upon her. The beat of her steps and the clapping of leaves applauded her new transition as she walked by. The buds from new flowers rustled on the ground, creating a soothing melody and sense of calm in the atmosphere. With the occasional sound of a car in the faint distance and the song of a grasshopper in the yards as she passed by, she felt this was the safest place on earth. Suddenly, safety took a backseat as she jolted backward. In an instant, a hand covered her mouth. This world of serenity was snatched up in the blink of an eye.

Hauled off into the back of a van, Hannah found herself in a position of intense fight. Within seconds, her eyes were affixed to the rustic décor of the interior of the van. The walls were padded as if the owner took time to prepare for this moment. There was a soft carpet beneath her back as she snatched fibers from the vehicle's floor, attempting to flee from her invader's clutches. There were no distinctive signs within the van, with the exception of current newspaper articles plastered as additional insulation and a bobble head hula dancer dangling upside down. Her eyes ran around the van in search of a window to kick or something she could use to impale her attacker. To no avail, all she had were broken nails, bleeding from her nail beds, with carpet burns pressed into her skin. With the few nails remaining, she attempted to carve her name into his skin. Using every tactic possible, as seen in movies, she tried vigorously to free herself from her forced position. Releasing distorted cries for help, her fight grew more concentrated. The heavy breathing and grunting of her fight echoed in the air as some stranger tussled with her, attempting to silence her from screaming. Hannah was in for the battle of her life, and she gave it everything she had. With the piercing shocks of pain that penetrated her nervous system like the screeching brakes of a runaway train, she was temporarily paralyzed from the intense fear of not knowing what was to come. With thoughts racing through her mind, her world suddenly moved in extreme slow motion completely contrary to her thoughts. The more fight she put up only appeared to react as though she never budged. After minutes of a struggle, she was finally pinned in his masculine grasp. The heat in the van soared to volcanic temperatures as her heart pulsated rapidly almost causing her to gasp for air. Beads of sweat poured from both their bodies. He used one hand to secure silence from her lips. In a low, almost indistinct voice, the invader finally spoke, "I've been watching you for quite some time, so I was already prepared for a fight. I like that about you. I appreciate and love your willingness to never give in." He taunted Hannah. Wanting her to make him earn submission was the fuel used to drive his mentally thwarted sex drive. Licking the side of her face slowly as he tasted her skin, he leaned in closer to her ear and yelled, "Come on! Don't make it easy for me!"

He loosened his grip for Hannah to fight back. Hannah seized the opportunity and continued to squirm in his arms, but suddenly stopped when she realized that her fear and fight enticed him. She felt his arousal and sunk deep into the recesses of her mind, doing the only thing she could think and know to do. She prayed silently, asking for some kind of help. Irritated that she was motionless, her reaction not giving him his momentary pleasure, he leaned in closer to Hannah, breathing his suffocating breath in her face. Despite the darkness of the rustic van, she was able to see clearly the eyes of the man who decided to assault her. The hazel brown eyes of this predator seared deeply into Hannah, almost molesting her vision in search of her inner soul. Momentarily, he stared deeply into her eyes searching for any sign of fear. She was emotionally removed from his presence, disabling him to see her fear. Unable to contain her tears, a single stream of tears fell from her eyes. Hannah stared blankly into this man's eyes as she fought to turn her head to look away from him. Realizing she still had fight in her, he forced her to make this impersonal experience as intimate as possible. As he extended his manhood into her, she screamed repeatedly. From the outside, her screams appeared muffled.

Whisked away in his moment of passion and her boundless moments of agony, he groaned in pleasure as Hannah's screams faded into the night. He reached the height of his release, but Hannah withdrew into her own darkened hole. This visionary had her life stolen forever for one man's moment of selfish pleasure. Hannah now found herself in a hole of despair and desolation. Not wanting to stick around for any recourse, the man of every woman's nightmare began to speak again.

"I had the chance to kill you, but I didn't, so you should be thankful that I had a change of heart. Here's what you're going to do. You're going to go home. You're not going to call the police because I will be watching. If I see a cop, the moment you step foot out of your house, you're mine. Better yet, I'll get you in your home and your mother, who is beautiful by the way. Not as beautiful as you, but she'll do. That mouthy sister of yours and your father will be easiest. No cops! Understand?"

Ignoring the very words he spoke, Hannah remained lost in a sea of thoughts. Pain chased fear as her tears rounded their seventieth lap in a five hundred mile race. Hannah was slow to move, but never wanted to set her eyes upon the face of this man who permanently scarred her emotionally, physically, and mentally. For years, this street, this block, this neighborhood was considered the place of safety. Instantly, it became the concentration camp of her life.

If raping her wasn't enough, the man was pleased when he perceived his threats propelled her into shock. Unbeknownst to him, not one word penetrated her senses. Attempting to throw Hannah back into reality, he repeatedly hit her in the face and clasped her jaw in his hands, forcing her to stare once again into his mischievous eyes. As he hovered over her, smiling and laughing, she burned the image of his face in her mind. If he really watched her, like he said, he would've known a majority of the artwork in the Arts Department at her school was drawn by her. She engraved the image of the man who robbed her of purity in her psyche.

After several minutes of torment, which seemed to equate to days, Hannah was emotionless. He left Hannah lying on the floor of the van. To ensure her position remained unmoved, he tied her wrists to the base of the driver's seat as he peeled away from the scene of this heinous crime. Driving in circles to throw her sense of direction off, he ultimately came to a screeching halt. Bolting away from his seat in absolute haste, he loosed Hannah's wrists and leaned in for one more look. Torturing her vision, he clutched her face with one hand and opened the back door with the other. Pushing Hannah out in the street, she fell to the pavement weakened from the attack. For the first time, she inhaled the crisp air as steam arose from her body. The heat from her body coupled with the night air left Hannah in a cloud of anguish. Slamming the door behind her, he returned to the driver's seat and sped off into the dark of the night.

Riddled with pain, Hannah pressed for the morsel of strength left to arise from the pavement. Scarred from her fight and her fall, she looked around. Realizing she'd been released farther away from her destination but within range for her to reach her home, she stood, as bodily fluids and blood ran from her body and gathered at her feet. Standing in the road, dazed over what just happened, she aimlessly walked in the middle of the street. In the dark of night, she looked like a drifter wandering the street with nowhere to go.

※

Even in her sleep, tears rolled down her eyes. She felt pain in her body as though she endured the torment once again. Opening her eyes in the darkened room, she sobbed. After crying into the night with no comfort, she embraced herself and attempted to lull herself to sleep.

Wishing she could've done this in the van, Hannah's breathing became forceful. The more she drove into her attacker's face, the more she shook within her bed.

Crying within, she fought to yell, but silently suffocated her cries as the pressure swelled. If she were only able to kick, scream, or harm him the way he tormented her soul, it would've been better; instead, she found herself fighting a dream.

She fought this dream for over ten years, yet there had been no resolve. Hannah continuously returned to the same state of panic and dysfunction as though her tormentor was hovering over her all over again. This dream, this nightmare, this torment has been the stronghold, the thief, and the burden resting on her shoulders. Embarrassed to share her private pain, she did what became familiar: attempt to scream and wrestle with the demonic force of her past.

Hannah no longer maintained a record of the countless fights she had with her attacker in her dreams. The numbers grew into the hundreds as she never revealed her innermost pain with anyone. She was a prisoner of war, still tied up in the back of the rustic van. There were times she would still smell his searing breath or the scent of the van. She could still feel the moisture of the air on her skin and loathed over the assault. Unfortunately, Hannah would remain bound to her dream of emotional and mental agony until she resolved within for liberation.

How could she heal when the memory of pain was ever present? There were times when she had a sense of wholeness, but she would revert back to her familiar torment. How could she rejoice in life when innocence produced pain? She pondered within if she truly earned liberation. She'd marveled in discontent so long, that the concept of peace appeared obsolete. Depression and despair decimated her heart, striving to convince her to believe she deserved what occurred. A continuum of self-punishment was her inner battle. This war lasted longer than any other obstacle in her life erecting to mountainous heights. Her rape was the one mountain she was unable to move. Why was it so hard to release her captor? How is it he was able to release her physically, but she remained emotionally? Hannah argued within repetitively and grew frustrated when an answer lacked the validity she desired. Emancipation from the memories, restoration of self-worth, confidence to love without a hint of fear with the purest heart, strength to let go, and the ultimate objective to forgive—were the things Hannah wanted to attain, yet failed in one area or another. Being made whole and completely unashamed would be the hope she cleaved to as each day provided new grace to drive her to this goal. Though the path of success had more detours than she'd prefer, she'd find herself unwavering in attaining restoration and confidence, but the greatest of all forgiveness and love of self and others without fear.

Angels Watching Over Me: Hannah's Help

> *Do not forget to entertain strangers, for by doing do some have unwittingly entertained angels.*
>
> Hebrews 13:2 (NKJV)

Pastor Woods and his wife, Yolanda, prepared to leave Salvation Church after completing Bible study for the evening and encouraging parishioners. Pastor Woods tried earnestly to persuade Yolanda to expedite their departure. Before they could make it to the door, one of Pastor Woods's eldest deacons flagged them down for a few minutes of their time. Pastor Woods exhaled, knowing a few minutes meant a minimum of an hour. After the three conversed over ministerial outreach initiatives, Pastor Woods, tired from the evening, motioned for Yolanda to get in the car while he finished the conversation with Deacon Giles. Pastor Woods laughed and joked with Deacon Giles until he realized the older gentleman was in no rush to leave. After ten more minutes of saying goodnight, Pastor Woods was finally free of the shackles of dialogue with Deacon Giles. Jumping behind the steering wheel, he exhaled a sigh of relief and drove away from the church.

Hannah remained lost in the darkened memory of her rape. Though her mind focused on her experience and the fear that help her captive, she had no clue of the hidden blessing that was headed her way. Though unable to stop the crime from happening, Pastor Woods and his wife would play an intricate role in Hannah's life. With Pastor Woods and Yolanda detained across town, Hannah wandered aimlessly down the street dazed after her brutal attack. Her rapist fled away and continued almost running head on into their car. Yolanda, seeing the van, screamed to her husband at the top of her lungs, "Oh dear Jesus! Honey! Blow your horn! Jesus, stop that crazy driver! Cover us, Lord!"

With the excessive blowing of the horn, the rapist swerved missing a head-on collision with their car within inches. Pastor Woods, astonished by his near-death experience, yelled out to God, "Lord, keep that man from hurting or killing someone. Lord, thank you for your covering and protection from dangers seen and unseen. Lord, it has brand-new meaning to me now. Thank you, Jesus!"

Turning the steering wheel with immense pressure caused the invader to careen in the road. Swerving in the street, he focused his attention on his recent victory of raping Hannah. Not paying attention to what was before him, he focused on the side mirror, cursing the driver of the car he just missed. With the Interstate 75 just two blocks away, he revved the van as he accelerated to sixty miles per hour, gloating in his success. Distracted, his eyes remained affixed to the side mirror as he used his right hand to reach for a cigarette. Unable to find the cigarette he desired most, he banged repeatedly on the dashboard before he turned to look straight. No sooner than he could maneuver control of the van and avoid the jug handle, he swerved and plowed into the guardrail and plummeted over into a deep embankment. The van went through a series of rollovers, leaving a trail of fluid and gas. The sound of crushed metal and breaking glass could be heard from a mile away. Without a seatbelt, his body bounced around uncontrollably until he was eventually pinned—a prisoner in his own vehicle. The van finally stopped after it crashed into a tree upside down. His foot, wedged beneath the collapsed dashboard, pressed against the gas pedal, revving the engine. Vehicular fluids and gas began creating a puddle in the dried grass and leaves overhead. Electrical components sparkled like firecrackers in the dark of the night. The scent of the gas became stronger as the rapist sat dazed. Fear and pain penetrated his body. Confused and disoriented, he feverishly looked around trying to gain understanding. He tried continuously to move his arms, head, and legs, but there was no movement, not even a flinch.

Distracted by the pain, he felt his heart throbbing as the steering wheel pressed deeply into his chest. Gasping for air and grunting heavily in disbelief, he wanted to scream, but he quickly exhausted himself in a continued attempt for oxygen and his freedom. His legs were crushed and pinned beneath the dashboard. A piece of metal projected through the windshield and pierced his right shoulder, holding him hostage to his seat. The flips from the van severely cracked several vertebrae. Though he initially felt his situation, he would soon learn how quickly things changed in the blink of an eye. Pain crept away as its dominant nemesis took its place—numbness. Agonizing pain was a hero in contrast to the villain that sought to take over his body. Numbness raced through his body chasing suffering away and cleaved to his central nervous system. Proving dominance over pain, paralysis had taken complete control. The rapist who once dominated over innocence was now victim to the power of paralysis. The only part of his body he was able to move were his eyes as blood streamed into them.

Jolted back into reality, he thought to move his hands to wipe the trickling blood, but was unable to help himself. He tried profusely to move his body, but to no avail. After minutes of mental anguish and the unwelcomed truth that his body was no longer responsive, panic and frustration swelled within him. Anger brewed, but still there was no physical response. He looked around and there was nothing but darkness and the occasional electrical spark. Sounds of cars and trucks barreling by made his world within the van seem stranded in time and space. Life as he knew it was moving rapidly, yet there he was, captive as a result of his own doing. The only thing left to do was yell out for someone to help him.

Tears swelled in the ducts of his eyes, but his pride choked him–refusing to submit. Under duress, he abused himself mentally.

The oppressor had become the immobilized seeking liberation. However, as fate would have it, he remained a prisoner of his own mind, body, and van. There was nothing he would fathom or imagine that could reverse the paralysis from his broken body. With nothing but his eyesight left intact, tears flowed like a rushing river washing away the blood on his face. Option less and unable to withstand the pain, his only resolve was to cry for help.

His outcry, though faintly heard, resounded in his ears as echoes in a cave. He belted out screams of agony from within the battered vehicle. The same sound he heard moments prior from Hannah were now the sound of his own voice. He gasped for air between screams, but pain shot through his body like bolts of lightning crashing to the earth. His heavy panting grew faint as he began drowning in his own blood. The minutes turned into hours. A small crowd gathered at the top of the guardrail. Onlookers pointed at the vehicle's odd position and other called highway patrol and emergency responders to the scene. The once bustling highway was shut down and traffic detoured.

It took several hours for rescuers to recover the tortured van. What was originally the scene of an accident became the scene of death. Once crews fully retrieved the vehicle, they found the rapist dead–choked in a pool of his own blood. He died at his own hand, tortured, and alone; never to harm another person.

Meanwhile, death ceased its latest victim in a van, but angels recued a young woman across town. With no regard of the oncoming headlights and excessive horn blowing, Hannah remained isolated in her mind as she continued to walk in the middle of the street. The couple in the car continued to discuss the speeding van, but immediately shifted their conversation when they saw a young lady in the street. Pastor Woods, irritated by their encounter but thankful for the best, inquired to his wife.

"Why would this young lady be out wandering in the middle of the street?"

"Woods, honey, something must be terribly wrong."

Pastor Woods slowed the car down in the near distance and came to a stop as he continued to address his wife sarcastically.

"Yolanda, you think? This girl looks familiar, but I'm not sure if I know her or not. These young people are all starting to look the same. I think we should stop and ask her if she needs help. But let's wait a second."

"There's no time to wait. There's a stranger in need, and obviously, God sent us here to meet the need. There was a reason why we didn't leave that church on time. For once, Deacon Giles's running off at the mouth paid off. Had we left earlier, we would've never been here to help. Get out the car and go help her."

"Now, Yolanda, just wait a second!"

"Woods, if you don't get out this car and help that girl I'm getting out!"

"Hold on a second! I understand but—"

"No! You wait."

Yolanda jumped out of the car and walked over to Hannah. The closer she came to Hannah only confirmed her husband's previous assumption. She recognized Hannah from their church. Hannah, still lost in her own mind, was removed from answering any of the questions Yolanda threw at her like an out-of-control pitcher. Yolanda immediately wrapped her arms around Hannah and gently guided her to the car.

Pastor Woods put the car in park and got out. Looking at his wife, he shook his head and stood with his hands on his hips. Yolanda yelled, "Come quickly!" as she noticed the bruising on Hannah's face and body. She wrapped her arms around Hannah to shield her from the cool air. As Pastor Woods ran to approach them, Hannah jumped back and began shaking uncontrollably in Yolanda's arms. Yolanda yelled out to Pastor Woods for him to stop coming near them.

"Honey, stay right there! Better yet, get the phone and call the police! Have them send an ambulance immediately. It shouldn't take that long for them to get here."

As Pastor Woods listened to his wife, Yolanda continued to try to talk to Hannah and get through to her. After a few questions, she ceased from further inquiry. Instead, she nestled Hannah in her arms. Receptive to the nurturing arms, Hannah finally released the anguish she suppressed from her night of torture. As the emergency vehicles approached, Hannah cleaved tighter to Yolanda. Yolanda, a registered nurse, was fully knowledgeable of the protocol and procedures for dealing with special victims, so she accompanied Hannah in the ambulance as Pastor Woods followed behind to the hospital. Since Yolanda was the only person Hannah would talk to, she was able to retrieve personal information from Hannah to contact her family. Arriving at the hospital, Yolanda remained in the room, patiently waiting for Hannah to give more detail of what occurred.

Hannah gestured to Yolanda for something to write. Scrambling around the room for paper, Yolanda gave Hannah some paper and a pen. The artistic genius surfaced in Hannah as she tattooed all her frustrations onto the paper. Recreating the scene, Hannah grew more frustrated by the second. Before her parents and the police could arrive bombarding her with ten thousand questions, Hannah already drew the entire scene of the van, the invader's body in the background, and the almost caricature blowup of the invader's face. Stabbing the picture in the eyes, Yolanda tried to grab Hannah's hands as she scratched the paper fiercely as if digging into her tormentor's face.

Soul Therapy Meets the Past

Reflect on what I am saying, for the Lord will give you insight into all this.

*2 Timothy 2:7 (*NIV*)*

The haunting of Hannah's dream was the concrete continuously pouring on her present happiness. Wanting nothing more than to escape the concentration camp of her mind, Hannah inhaled deeply as she prepared to exert all the pain that suffocated her serenity chamber. Before she could yell out a scream, her alarm clock went off. Startled into a state of shock, she attempted to regain consciousness. By the time she reached over to shut off the alarm clock, the phone rang. Snatching the phone in an intense moment of fury, with the proverbial bellowing of her friend Patricia Wilmington, she heard, "Hannah, Hannah, Hannah!"

"Patricia! Why are you yelling in my ear so early in the morning?"

"Early, it's almost ten o'clock, and if I'm not mistaken, today is Friday and you were supposed to meet me at the spa. Hello!"

"Oh my goodness!"

"Yeah, oh my goodness is right! Are you coming or what? You know how I feel about my time. I could've gone in to work, but I carved out this day just for you."

Spending time with her friends was the furthest thing on her mind, but it was the on-time remedy necessary to get her day and life in perspective. Hannah reassured Patricia, "I know, Pat, I know. Listen, give me a few minutes. I'll meet you there. I need to be relaxed anyway. I'll see you in a few minutes. I'm on my way."

If anyone watched time closer than Father Time, it was Patricia. As the senior vice president of finance for one of the largest financial firms in United States based in Atlanta, Patricia was acclimated to people adhering to her demands. When Patricia called a meeting, any person showing up *on time* was asked to leave. This tardiness, though considered by many as on time, immediately placed the latecomer on the reduction in force list faster than premium stock rising. Patricia was notorious for quoting her life's mantra, "To be early is to be on time. To be on time is to be late. To be late is unacceptable." She said this so often that her staff arrived early at every function. Though Patricia's staff was trained on her punctuality expectations, she couldn't get her closest friends to honor her demand. She loved her friends dearly; however, it didn't negate her frustration.

Patricia retorted while exhaling discontent, "Okay, well hurry up! I hope you plan to bathe before meeting me in a few minutes. You sound like your breath stinks. Hurry up, so we aren't stuck with Man-Hands Maggie. I want Cedric to rub on me. So hurry your butt up! Bye!"

Hanging up the phone, she wiped her face and gathered her thoughts. Momentarily staring out the window, she thought about her dream. The young woman's testimony from the retreat only reminded her of the pain and torment she endured in her own teenage years. She thought she suppressed her feelings, but the retreat experience called her to see that there may be a need for her within a ministry at the church. Her reality shifted; she tried to gain perspective on her day. Nothing could get her into the frame of mind like encouraging herself with the word.

"I am blessed. I am highly favored. I am strong! Yes! I am strong. *No weapon formed against me shall prosper. If any man be in Christ, he is a new creature. No good thing will he withhold from those that love him.* God loves me, and I'm his child. I am victorious! Devil, you thought you had me, but I got away! It's going to be a great day! Nothing will steal my joy. All right, God, this is the day the Lord created, I'm already rejoicing, so let's go!"

She leaped in the shower and darted out as if she were back in college with ten minutes to get to an 8:00 class. After minutes of preparation, Hannah looked herself over in the mirror before she grabbed her keys and headed for the door. By the time she locked the door and headed down her front steps, the mailman was walking up to her. The two exchanged greetings and he inquired for her to sign for an envelope. Hannah signed for the certified letter and tossed the mail in her front seat.

Sitting at the light, Hannah glanced over at the letter. She observed the sender and immediately opened her mail. After years of continuous doctor appointments and hoping that time would literally heal all her wounds, she found herself in the reality of her nightmare—yet again. The continuums of daunting nightmares were troublesome when she slept, but now—awake—the attack threw another bone in her skeletal closet. Hannah gasped for air as tears gathered in her eyes. Dazed and distressed, her eyes couldn't leave the words on the page. Anticipating exoneration from her horrific past, she read her medically diagnosed fate and detriment of her future.

Frustrated motorists raged for Hannah's attention. Horns blew as Hannah unconsciously sat through the green light which turned red again. Ignoring the activity, Hannah belted out in anguish, brutally attacking her steering wheel with no outlet other than screams and tears. Pedestrians and motorists with a clear view gaped at her tantrum. No one dared lay hand upon their horn or inquire of her rage. Infuriated at the news, she bolted through the light just as it turned green nearly hitting a car.

Hannah tried to bury the letter at the bottom of her bag as she rummaged through her purse. Feeling for her antidepressants, she wanted an immediate escape from her harsh reality. Her emotional instability sought refuge, and pills were the calm after the storm. Without using a water chaser, Hannah popped two pills and wiped her face, fighting to regroup before meeting Patricia. Vacillating between positive encouragements and anger were a familiar routine that Hannah knew how to suppress. Anything to guise the inner turmoil was welcomed and going to the spa was the perfect distraction.

∽o∾

Patricia stood in the foyer as if she were royalty awaiting servants to tend to her needs. Towering over the staff, her stiletto heels echoed against the Spanish marble floors as she poised herself for attention. The sun beamed across her caramel skin as she removed her glasses to see what disappointment was attempting to capture her attention. Her lean muscular frame grabbed the attention of some gentlemen who sat patiently waiting for their spouses. Others sitting with their wives were caught looking, but were thrust back into reality when they were slapped. Looking all of the employees over as if they were unacceptable, she smiled gently whenever Cedric, Josh, or Danny walked by. She bit the end of her sunglasses as she monitored their masculine presence, then placed them back on her face. Walking over to the concierge, she emphatically stated her expectations and demands for the royal treatment. Pulling her designer frames to the tip of her nose as though disgusted, she said, "You must be new here. I'm Patricia Wilmington, and I have an appointment. There should also be an appointment for Hannah Winters and Bernadette Josephson." Trained and well prepared for the most uncouth person, the young lady smiled and greeted Patricia despite her unwelcoming presence.

"Hello. Yes, I am. My name is Heather, how can I help you?"

"Well, let's see, I just told you my purpose for being here, but apparently, you didn't get the memo, so you can start by finding Hailey for me. She knows everything I expect, and I don't need to converse with you regarding details. That'll be all!" Heather maintained her smile as she said, "Sure. Not a problem."

Walking away, Heather looked back at Patricia and scoffed. Passing by Maggie, in route for Hailey, she informed Maggie that her client arrived. Unbeknownst to Patricia, Hannah was walking up behind her.

"You know what, Pat, God don't like ugly! You better stop running around here as if you own something and treat people right. Someone is going to cuss you out one of these days."

Patricia didn't particularly care for reprimand. Convinced her way of taking action proved successful, Patricia saw no need for change. Turning her mouth and staring into Hannah's hazel brown eyes with her powerfully convicting tone, she replied, "Humph, they know better than that. Where did you come from? Rolling up in here all late! You act like my time isn't precious! You know my mantra!"

Hannah laughed at her friend, "I know all about your mantra. I actually prefer to be early myself. I might not be a corporate executive, but I pride myself on punctuality whenever I see my clients. Speaking of which, don't you want to buy another property?"

Patricia smirked, "If you weren't my friend and realtor, I'm pretty sure we wouldn't be having this conversation. I'll buy the property when you arrive early for our next lunch date. How about that?" The two laughed as they walked.

If Heather could only see that there was indeed someone close enough to Patricia to stand up to her bold personality, she would've been pleased to know the cavalry had arrived. Hannah reaffirmed her position with, "Pat, shut up! Don't forget I know you, and I know who you think you are." Patricia shrunk back into friendship mode rather than dictator mode and laughed.

"You're lucky I love you like I love myself because no one else can talk to me like that! Watch what you say around here. I don't want anyone thinking they can talk to me like that!"

The two smiled as Hannah spoke up Maggie.

"Come on, Pat. Keep it up! You're going to end up with Man-Hands Maggie!"

"Hannah, don't play with me, girl! You know how I am about speaking stuff up. I will scream if I see Man-Hands Maggie! I could understand if she was good, but she's rougher than a man. Ouch, see now, I'm more uptight just thinking about it."

"Pat, I'm almost convinced you were born uptight!"

Patricia and Hannah walked off laughing out loud as Hailey walked up to meet them and escort them to the spa area. Following closely behind Hailey, Hannah exhaled deeply as she shared with her good friend the shackled reoccurrence that captivated her dreams transforming them into nightmares.

"Pat, on a serious note, it happened again."

"Hello! Hannah, I need a little more than that. For all I know, you could've farted again. What are you talking about?"

"My dream, I mean my nightmare about my past. It's starting back up. I'm right back to my youth with all my pain swelling up in me. Every time I'm about to scream, I wake up, or something wakes me up."

Patricia showed little to no sympathy for Hannah's plight. She considered her emotional discomfort as important; however, since Hannah took no authoritative steps in changing her position as a victim, particularly after being advised by Patricia, she perceived her pain and distress was a result of preferred posture. Patricia looked at Hannah and chastised her as if she were a child.

"I told your hardheaded butt last time to go see a shrink. Get your money's worth and find out what the root problem is. Bury it, talk about it, whatever. Just move on. You can't let the past from years ago hold on to you. Trust me, honey; whatever is in my past is just that, my past."

"Well, that's easy for you to say. I can't just let go of my past like that. I live with my past in my present."

"Hannah, please! It is just that easy for me to say as it is for you to do. You live with your past in your present not by force, but by choice. No one from your past is tracking you down with a billboard sign in your front yard, shouting, '*Please remember me*!'

You're the one running around like whatever it is will kill you if anyone ever finds out. For goodness sake! All you tell me is that you had another dream. However, you've never said what the dream is about. I never bothered asking because I figured if you wanted me to know, you would've told by now me. If you let the devil ride, don't get angry when he takes the keys and drive!"

Hannah was astounded at her friend's truth on confronting issues. Though she was well aware, she was taken aback that she was the recipient of her bitter reality. The devil had been driving for years because she voluntarily cowered and permitted him access over her life. With all the blessings and abundant grace provided by God, she opted to focus on the past and the power of the devil rather than optimizing on the promise of Christ.

Before Hannah could seriously respond to Patricia's surprisingly wise remarks, her phone rang. Patricia exhaled, closed her eyes, and responded, "Good! Now I can finally relax. You have me up in here preaching and helping you out, and I need to focus on Cedric rubbing me into a state of ultimate peace." Hannah couldn't help but send Patricia into overload before she diverted her attention to the phone.

"Hold on a second. Well, before you think about that ultimate peace, open your eyes. Hello, Maggie!" Hannah exploded in laughter as Man-Hands Maggie walked in the room and headed straight for Patricia. Completely distracted, Hannah ignored Elias on the phone yelling because Patricia was causing a scene and demanding Hailey's presence.

Bernie arrived late after leaving a deposition for a client in her office. Her sun-glazed skin massaged in the deep love of God's own light glowed beneath her canary and azure dress. Her bangles, coupled with the base of her walk, created a melody as they highlighted the echo from her stilettos. Finally approaching the doorway, Bernie heard Patricia's voice loud and clear as she looked in and laughed within.

Bernie stood in the threshold and shook her head, partially embarrassed and partially amused at Patricia's behavior. Bernie knew how Patricia felt about Maggie and could not help but laugh as Patricia went into full theatrics. Walking in the room, she sat on the table and said, "I stopped for a second, wondering where you were. Then, I heard mouth-all-mighty over here and knew exactly where to find you. What is going on in here? Hey, hey, hey, Drama Queen! Shut that noise up! You're in here making us look bad like we're straight from the projects." Bernie redirected her attention to Maggie and apologized for Patricia's behavior. Looking at Maggie, she said, "Um, please excuse my friend here. She's a pill short today. Can you give us a minute and ask Hailey to come in, please?"

Maggie smiled and walked out of the room to give the ladies time to converse. Patricia waited until Maggie was completely gone before she charged straight for Hannah, directing all her frustration toward her for speaking Maggie up. Hannah laughed with tears streaming from her eyes as she rolled over in laughter. Bernie began laughing even harder as Patricia's fury arose. This financially well-established woman who gave a persona of being upper echelon proved that she was still in training. Every ounce of urban finesse rolled right out of Patricia as though the designer clothes, makeup, and money were as invisible as the air she breathed. Hailey entered the room and paused while Patricia scolded Hannah, "See, it's your fault! I told you not to speak up Man-Hands, and what did you do, you spoke her right up to me. Now, I'm tense! I need some relaxation. See, teasing me you forgot to help yourself. Hannah you should get Maggie instead of Liza just for taunting me. I hope she's off today, so you'd be stuck with Maggie!" Patricia redirected her attention to Hailey, "Honey, please get Cedric or Josh! I'll take any male over Man-Hands Maggie. My fearful friend would like Liza." Hannah had been completely distracted by Patricia that she neglected to make her preference known to Heather and Hailey. Contrary to her counterparts, she was uncomfortable with a male masseuse, so she nodded in agreement.

Hailey gaped as she tried to maintain her composure. Hearing the nickname come from Patricia threw her off guard. She responded, "Sure, I'll see who is available and ensure your requests are satisfied. I'll send them right in."

Bernie lay back on the vacant table and began to relax. Hannah, still laughing, finally returned to her phone as Patricia and Bernie talked about Maggie.

"Hello."

Elias sighed as he replied, "I was wondering if you forgot I was on the phone. I see you and your friends are having a good time over there. I was trying to see if we were still on for dinner, or if I would be off the hook since you're having a women's day?"

"What makes you think you would be off the hook? You're talking as if you're being held hostage or something." Hannah crossed her arms and listened attentively as her fiancé, Elias Christenson, attempted to explain.

"Come on, Hannah, that's the furthest thing from my mind. Some of the brothers were talking about getting together tonight to prepare before we take over two hundred of these young men into the mountains. Pastor Woods wants to address the concerns of the youth from the retreat a few weeks ago. He believes this is all in perfect alignment with the vision God gave him for the youth of the church. After what happened in Bernie's class, he's been focused on the youth. He's spearheading the young men, and I think he talked to Bernie about her leading the young women. Did she talk to you about it yet?" Elias cleared his throat and waited for a response to his inquisition. Hannah, elated to hear of the great response, replied, "Wow, that sounds fantastic, Elias. She actually just walked in when you called, so I'm sure she'll tell us all about it."

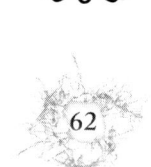

Hannah couldn't contain herself. Elias professed he would never let a woman know his next move, but he always found himself letting Hannah know what was going on. Hannah was the first woman, other than Taylor, he'd ever considered sharing the details of his day and life, let alone marrying her. He looked forward to marrying Hannah, just as much as she looked forward to marrying him. Hannah was the only woman he'd asked God about and received an answer. Though Elias was acquainted with Hannah, after meeting her at a conference, he patiently observed her behavior and actions for two years. He needed assurance and clarity from God that she was indeed the virtuous woman of his prayers. Not wanting to expedite any process or go ahead of God to miss the anointed, appointed time, he waited those years until God finally gave him the answer to his prayer in a dream. He saw everything plainly in his dream; it was as if déjà vu occurred. All he could do was thank God.

"Well, so you know, I'm not canceling out on you. I know you would nag me for hours later."

"Eli, little do you know. I'm perfectly fine, but you do know I'm going to remind you later that you have to consult with me first on everything."

Picking up on her sarcasm, Elias began stuttering, "Ha-Han-Hannah, do you see how women are? This is what I mean when I tell the brothers that women go to the extreme."

"Let me gloat and rub it in. I thought we'd have to be married for twenty years before I'd have you reporting for duty."

"You know what, woman? I'm hanging up this phone."

The two laughed uncontrollably as they shared a private moment of understanding. Before Hannah could proceed to indulge in further sarcasm, Elias's laughter simmered as he recognized Pastor Woods standing in the doorway of his office. Holding up his finger to acknowledge Pastor Woods' presence, he quickly changed gears and told Hannah, "Honey, Pastor is here and I have to go, so are we good?"

"Absolutely, Eli, love you. Tell Pastor I said hello. I'll talk to you later."

"Love you, Hannah. I'll call you later tonight. Oh, and remind me to tell you about these dreams I keep having about you getting pregnant. Now, run and tell that to your friends! You're going to have a whole tribe of my children running around that spa with you. Do you still want to gloat? Ha, got to go! Talk to you later."

"Okay, you know I'll remind you about that! Love you, later."

The two agreed early in their relationship never to say bye, so they agreed to always say, "Later."

Hannah's thoughts were ready to take off from the gateway, but before the bugle horn could blow, she was drawn to her thespian friend's voice. Hanging up with Elias, she spun around and returned to her comically and dramatically stricken friends. By this time, Bernie was enthralled in laughter that couldn't be contained with tears filling her eyes at the overdramatized Patricia. Though Patricia endorsed the replica of being five star, every now and again, the two and a half stars would shine through. This was definitely one of those moments.

Hailey returned to the room and stood listening to Patricia's bantering about Maggie. Barry, the extreme eye candy masseuse, proceeded to walk by on the way to another room. Hailey attempted to contain herself; however, she internally collapsed under the ceiling of hysterical comedy as Patricia continued to bellow over having Man-Hands Maggie be her masseuse. Hannah shook her head and waved for Hailey to come in closer as she walked over to establish some order in the room. Talking loud enough for her friends to hear, Hannah apologized to Hailey, "Excuse me, Hailey, you know Pat is over the top. I'm not sure if you were aware we were coming in today, but I know if you were or if she saw you first, we could have avoided this entire scene. You know how Pat feels about Maggie, but is it possible if we could have the gentlemen service us today versus a female masseuse? You know the masculine touch can sooth the cares of the world away. This way the sooner they come in, the faster we'll be able to move forward in our spa treatments for the day."

Before Hailey could respond to Hannah's request, Patricia chimed in with her voice echoing as if she were speaking into a cave. Patricia sat up to address Hailey, "I'm glad you jumped in and asked because apparently, this heifer didn't hear me the first time! Whatever happened to *the customer is always right*? Didn't I tell the new girl I wanted a man when I arrived? She's over here trying to be funny, sending Mr. Man up in here. Hannah, Bernie, y'all better help her get her mind right before I have to take it up a notch. As a matter of fact, why am I even wasting my time? Where is the owner? I don't even want the manager. Take me straight to the top. That's how I get things done!"

Hannah jumped up and walked over to Hailey, laughing and talking indistinctly as she apologized again for her friend's abusive and ignorant behavior. Bernie pulled Patricia back down to the massage table as Hannah walked out the door with Hailey.

Patricia, convinced she had to add one more comment in, yelled out to the two, "Hannah, you better make sure the finest man in the building walks through that door when you get back! I'm not playing!" as they exited the room. Hannah ignored Patricia's comments and joked with Hailey about Patricia and Maggie as they continued walking.

Bernie, embarrassed by her friend's inappropriate behavior, began chastising Patricia for her actions in their private argument. Meanwhile, Hannah and Hailey returned to the reception area as Hailey scrolled through the system, checking for any form of masculine availability. Hannah apologized immeasurably to Hailey for Patricia's over-the-top performance. Hailey was always excited whenever Patricia came to the spa because there was never a dull moment. Finally, she had an opportunity to laugh from the first ounce of a comedic action received for the day. Clients were generally stiff and extremely short with the staff, so any excuse to laugh was welcomed. Hailey dismissed the encounter in its entirety and called for Liza, Cedric, and another gentleman to meet Hannah. Shaking hands with the gentlemen and hugging Liza, Hannah exhaled a sigh of relief and walked away, explaining what they were about to walk into. The four laughed and entered the room.

Patricia ignored Bernie's persistence to keep her prostrate and stood perfectly erect as she examined her options while observing their names monogrammed on their shirts. Patricia yelled out to Bernie, "See, every now and then, you have to let people know you mean business. That's what gets results. Hannah, you did a good job, but next time, don't have these people in here wasting my valuable time. I should charge you two by the hour for my pain and suffering. Now come over here, Cedric, and make me feel brand-new!"

In a complete state of shock over Patricia's comments, Hannah and Bernie scoffed and disregarded Patricia's comments. Lying on the table in utter pleasure with sensuous sounds filling the air, Bernie began to elaborate on upcoming events at the church. Before she could go into detail, Patricia's phone rang. Expelling a loud and frustrated sigh, Patricia looked to see the number on her phone, completely cutting Bernie off.

"I am so sorry, Bernie. I'm finally starting to relax, and this phone is ringing. I don't even recognize this number. I'm not answering that. Sorry, Bernie, go ahead."

Bernie responded emphatically, "Well, you've already cut me off. They'll probably just call back anyway, so answer the phone!" Patricia, refusing to submit to Bernie's demand, emoted her position, "Now you know I don't answer numbers I don't recognize." Not taking one step back, Bernie opted for a resolution and yelled, "Well, hand me the phone!"

"Here, take it, and tell whoever it is if they aren't making me more money, I don't want to talk. I'm relaxing with Cedric, the body motivator. Girl, my muscles are thanking him in tongues, like those sanctified people talk in church. I don't have time to be bothered."

Bernie snatched the phone and laughed as she put the phone to her face. Bernie answered Patricia's phone with every ounce of cynicism, laughed, and greeted the unknown caller, "Hello, this is Patricia's answering service. If you're not making her more money, she doesn't want to be bothered. May I take a message?"

The giggling in the background threw the unfamiliar person answering the phone off guard. The caller responded with curiosity, "Huh? Is Patricia available?"

"I'm sorry, but if this isn't a business matter that involves compensatory benefits, Patricia is unavailable. May I ask if this is business related?"

"Did I call her office? I thought this was her cell phone. Is this a joke? Is Patricia available?" The caller became more aggressive and demanded, "Who is this?"

Bernie immediately assessed the frustration of the caller and responded, "I'm sorry, can I have your name please?"

Growing irritated by the reception on the phone, the caller inquired of the intent of the person answering the phone. Before Bernie could respond, Patricia yelled from the background for Bernie to hang up. Instantly, the caller retorted, "Excuse me, but I would like to speak to Patricia. I know this is her phone. I just heard her voice. Who are you? Did she tell you not to answer the phone when I called? Is that why you're playing games? Who is this, and where is Patricia?"

Bernie cuffed her hand over the phone and whispered to Patricia to take her phone. Patricia, irritated and reduced to entertaining someone else versus enjoying the masculine touch of Cedric, reached to receive the phone. Exerting her frustration, Patricia clamored, "Bernie, hand me the phone. This better be worth it. I finally have a man making me feel right and now this. Who is this? I don't recognize your number, so I must not know you!"

Astounded by the derisive greeting from Patricia, the caller gently responded to the now familiar voice.

"Hello, Pattycake." In a sensual, but subtle tone, the caller arrested Patricia's attention. "How are you? Are you surprised to hear from me? You do recognize my voice, don't you? Or was the nickname the icing on the cake?"

Frozen in time and space like a prehistoric fossil, Patricia lay still and silent with her face pressed in the small opening of the table with the phone against her ear. Captivated by the voice, Patricia, for the first time all day, was betwixt with silence.

Her sudden physical response to the caller's voice sent red flags to Bernie and Hannah. Instructed by their masseuses to change positions as they continued working diligently, Hannah and Bernie whispered amongst themselves. Hannah pounded Bernie with questions of whom the person could possibly be that created a drastic shift in their friend's demeanor. Scurrying for answers, the dynamic duo began hitting Patricia in an attempt to thrust her back into reality. Unable to gain Patricia's attention, they continued to inquire amongst each other. The only response Patricia gave was, "What do you want? I have to go."

Completely isolated in thought, Patricia reflected on the last time she'd heard that nickname, and it was not a pleasurable experience.

Distant Past Appears Too Close

Do not take revenge, my friends, but leave room for God's wrath, for it is written: "It is mine to avenge; I will repay," says the Lord.

Romans 12:19 (NIV)

Senior year at Grandeur University was the highlight of every twenty something's educational career. Patricia was ecstatic and celebrating her matriculation with honors in international business and moving into her MBA program. However, before the commensurate ceremony with parental guidance, there was the party. This twenty-one-year-old knew the ins and outs of the party scene like a New York cabby knew the cross streets. The atmosphere was set and the music blared indistinctly from the four corners of the earth, or so it seemed. College students from near and far piled into cars to partake in heavy consumptions of alcoholic beverages of all types. When there was a Student Government Association (SGA) party, there was entertainment for every culture, gender, and personality. Spring break was the angelic counterpart compared to the parties around campus prior to graduation. As the hours passed and the consumption of alcohol transformed the most disciplined of personalities into their alter ego, the SGA party, comprised of every organization from Greeks to dorms, was the party of the decade.

Patricia and her female entourage of sexy bandits were fashionably timely to their third evening event. The dimly lit fraternity house turned into a club-like atmosphere when one of the best mix-tape DJs appeared on the scene.

The frat house had bodies pressed upon each other with minimal room for breathing let alone dancing. The collegiate cared less. The liquor kept coming, and the music grew louder. Finding some small space and opportunity, small huddles of girls cleaved to one another like they were making a XXX version of *Collegiate: Extreme Naughty*, while sex-driven guys preyed upon the weak and those with intolerable alcohol levels. If there was a time for seizing the girl you'd had your eye on but would never give you the time of day, grasping her in her drunken state at this party was the prime outlet. Drunk guys seized the moment with their overly drunken female counterparts and whisked them away to the nearest available location for the sexual enticement. Among those was Braxton and his good-looking drunk friends. Braxton was the definition of sex appeal with his masculine physique in prime condition. Poised for attention, he stood completely erect among the crowd and his peers. His green eyes peered through the crowd as he cracked a smile revealing his natural dental perfection. Though the room was immersed with beautiful women, one caught his attention. When he noticed Patricia, he immediately flashed to their first conversation when she completely embarrassed him in front of his teammates and left him standing there alone. Noticing the cup in her hand, he prided himself on getting the last laugh. Approaching this bold and audacious young lady, he had no clue that her cup was full of ginger ale that she brought. Patricia, unlike many of her female counterparts, preferred not to drink since she'd witnessed the darkness of liquor by the experiences of others. Besides, she was the one in the group to keep everyone else in line.

Braxton noticed how the light enveloped her. Her smile was brighter than the moon shining on this clear night, yet it was warm enough to melt the hardest heart. He licked his lips as he observed how she stood with the light cascading across the long wavy locks of her hair. Pointing his hands at Patricia, he announced, "Ladies, ladies, ladies, I would ask you how you're doing, but you'll only say fine, and that's already obvious."

Patricia showed no acceptance of his rehearsed compliment and canceled his flight before he could book it. She replied, "Oh please! Try running Grandpa's line on some idiot who's desperate for attention. Go change your diapers and let a real man walk up to me. You're in the way! Go somewhere, anywhere other than standing right here, please!" Braxton was aware that Patricia would put up a fight, but he was ignorant to the level of potency she possessed. Braxton ignored Patricia's rude comment and asked, "Why are you trying to play hard to get? You know I'm the man around here. My reputation speaks for itself, so if anyone needs to recognize a man, it's you, unless you're so accustomed to being familiar with women that you wouldn't recognize a man if he pressed into you right now."

Patricia looked at her friends. She turned to Braxton with her eyes burning with fury as if she were watching his cremation and responded, "Are you serious? Braxton, honestly, are you serious about saying your reputation? Apparently, you haven't heard the latest news. The word around town is that you are the worst thirty seconds a woman could encounter. Not only are you a waste of time, but your hardware is smaller than a Vienna sausage. If that couldn't get any worse, the added word to your reputation is that your breath smells like raw sewage. Better yet, I want to know if the Grim Reaper is your dentist because your breath smells like death. One of your little friends should check your pulse to make sure you're still alive.

"As a matter of fact, here's what I want you to do. Go to the nearest, and I do mean the nearest, mortuary and ask them if they have any embalming mints or formaldehyde binaca that you can ingest to hoard off the smell of death spewing from your lips. We all don't have to suffer, you walking corpse. I'm surprised rigor mortis hasn't set in. So as much as I would like to make you feel important, I'm trying not to embarrass your dead-smelling ass any further."

Braxton's anger grew inside of him faster than a torpedo racing out of the tube of a submarine. His friends were temporarily sober hearing Patricia's comments and stood attentive to hear his response. Others who were close enough to hear chuckled and pointed while repeating what they heard, acting as validation for the rumors they'd heard. The scariest part of embarrassing someone who proclaims to be the best is not knowing the silence of their action. Silence is often mistaken for weakness; however, it is also the fuel used to invoke revenge.

Braxton rubbed his face and laughed, trying to dismiss the words he'd heard. Before he could retort, he stared deeply into Patricia's eyes and raised his hand. Before he could rub her face, Patricia chimed in, "I wish you would put those feminine hands on me. I'll have you tattooed to a jail cell with a four-hundred-pound lover man calling you Sweetness while tossing your salad and rubbing the back of your neck with your face buried in the pillow faster than you can blink and scream for help. Go ahead! You feeling froggy? Leap and see what happens. Come on, Vienna, let's see what you're man enough to do. When the men in the state pen find out about your little manhood problem and the need for tweezers, they'll flip you over and give you a new nickname like PB. Oh, you know what PB is right? It's Pillow Biter! That's because all you'll have time to do is bend over and bite pillows grunting in pain. That's going to be your name once you put those nasty hands on me."

Braxton's spirit changed faster than seconds on a clock. He looked at Patricia as though he'd already committed the crime of his thoughts. Patricia, not fazed by his newfound disposition, retorted, "Don't look at me like that! I'm not afraid or intimidated by you. Hell, for that matter, your friend can get it faster than you. He has more of a reputation than you do! You know what, Braxton, I'll take you up on that. Better yet, come on."

Raising her voice and drawing attention to the situation, Patricia made sure everyone in the immediate vicinity knew that Braxton's manhood was the highlight of the conversation.

"Hey, everybody, Braxton wants to prove he's a real man, and he's tired of lying to himself and everyone else, so he's going to show us how it's really hanging. Isn't that right, Braxton? What's the matter? You afraid everyone will see, and the rumors will be proven true?"

Patricia knew how to invoke the wrath of a man in a matter of seconds. When it came to confrontation, she was first in line for the task. Backing down from an argument or a fight was the furthest thing from her mind. Unfortunately, she lacked the ability to know the difference between appropriate timing versus inappropriate timing. What she didn't realize was Braxton's insecurity always drove him to the brink of violence. His temper was shorter than a new blade of grass and more hazardous than a biochemical spill. While she assumed she gained the upper hand in the situation, she neglected to realize the demonic force that consumed Braxton.

"Yeah, Patricia, you've already told everyone here you're ready to go all in with me, so by all means, let's go. Better yet, you're not that fine, now that I look at you. Come on, fellas."

Braxton and his renegade armament of pals pushed past the crowd of mockers and escaped to the cool of the air. Braxton's retreat from Patricia caused the crowd to disseminate and fade back into the concentration of the party. Though several of the partygoers centered their attention on the music, there was one in the crowd whose eyes remained affixed to Patricia.

Bobbi observed every move Patricia made. After minutes of watching, Bobbi recessed into the crowd, paving a small path to the doorway for some air. Patricia and her friends disregarded the encounter in its entirety and moved on beyond the conversation with Braxton. With the music wailing in the background, Patricia was unable to hear her phone ringing. Enjoying her last party before going overseas, Patricia made every effort to enjoy this evening with her friends. Before she could get completely settled into the nightlife, a freshman, unable to handle the consumption of mixed alcoholic beverages, spilled her drink on Patricia and threw up on the floor right in front of Patricia and her friends. Pushing the young lady out of her way, she stormed out to go change her liquor-stained clothing.

∽o∽

Drunken bodies clothed the streets like sidewalks in suburban neighborhoods. The outpour of laughter and the faint sound of vomiting were among the evening highlights. The moonlit sky painted a mysterious picture, causing the trees to play phantoms to the buildings in the night.

A beautiful and vibrant young woman entered this inebriated scene. Astounded by the scenery of her peers, she combed through the crowds in search of Patricia. Continuously making an attempt to contact her cell, to no avail, this young woman approached small clusters of students inquiring of her whereabouts.

Braxton stood afar pacing the parking lot in a cloud of anger escalating to tornado winds within seconds. Having some of his friends return back to the party, he was left with the devious duo who never left his side. Flashing back to the insults he'd received from Patricia were the catalyst used to drive his rage. The devious duo didn't aid in calming this ravenous beast; rather, they added insult to injury with their proclamations of some of the rumors they too heard. With Braxton's rage gaining speed like a turbine jet engine, he noticed Patricia's beauty as she walked toward them in an attempt to get to the dorm in the midnight light. Consuming more and more liquor, the trio concocted a diabolical plan of revenge.

Clouds swelled in the sky covering the moon's illumination. Before she could comment to this group of men, she was whisked away like a leaf captured by the wind. In the blink of an eye, the triple threat invaded her personal space while her screams were lost in the faded sounds of music blaring in the near distance. The intoxicated souls wandering aimlessly ignored the sounds as they screamed out like a crowd cheering at a sold out NFL game.

In an effort to silence her, she was punched and beaten like an unwanted doll. Blood ran from her face like tears of a newborn child. Innocence of life and personal value diminished into the dark of the night. Each man took his turn as she was helpless and unassisted. Her body grew weak as every morsel of strength within her vanished into the night like the oxygen she cleaved to for air. If assaulting her wasn't enough, Braxton decided to gain control and lean in to take a closer look at his victim. With his vision partially blurred and his heavily intoxicated breath, he shook his head as his vision doubled. Abrasively rubbing her face, he paused and condemned his victim.

"There's no way you'll ever embarrass me again. This time, I'll make sure of it. Let's put her in her car."

The young men whisked her away and carried her motionless body to the car. Following their poorly concocted plan to make it appear as a brutal car crash, the trio decided to scar their victim, leaving permanent marks. Using broken glass from a nearby bottle, they carved into her skin. With blood coloring his skin, he motioned and yelled for one of his trio to hand him a stone, rock, or brick, and a bottle. Jamming the gas pedal with a liquor bottle and stone, they poured alcohol inside the vehicle and all over her body. While taking the final sips, Braxton started the engine and whispered into her ear.

"We'll see who gets the last laugh, Patricia."

The trio watched as the car peeled off and crashed into some trees where it remained wedged with the engine revving. Laughing in amusement while massaging their manhood as a sign of success, the demonic trinity piled into a car and sped off into the night.

Running to the scene, the crowd of drunken bodies clamored to sober up. However, immersed in their intoxication, they sought humor in this tumultuous situation rather than wisdom in notifying the authorities. Among those in the crowd was Bobbi who was the only sober individual on site. Plugging one ear and pressing the other into the receiver, Bobbi notified the campus police, demanded an ambulance, and ran over to aid the young helpless victim. Climbing into the trees and pressing past broken glass, Bobbi was able to pull the body out of the car. The amount of blood made it hard to clearly see the victim's face, but in a moment of absolute shock, Bobbi instantly knew who it was wept and whispered, "Pattycake? I love you so much. I'll get whoever did this to you. I'll never stop until they pay for this. I love you, Pattycake. Why didn't you listen to me?"

The wailing sound of sirens nearing the campus ignited a widespread bellow of bodies to sober up. Cups were emptied into bushes and grass, illegal paraphernalia was dumped into sewers, intoxicated drivers staggered from behind the wheel and stood in the warm breeze fighting for sobriety as the campus police, local authorities, and an ambulatory crew entered the campus. Bobbi held the mutilated, motionless life using a shirt as a bandage while screaming their location. The medical crew dove in immediately while authorities began taming the crowd. The two were whisked away in the back of the ambulance while the crowd murmured over what happened. The police only pressed pause on the party, but eventually left to answer another call. It didn't take long for the music to return to high decibels, and the ambulance that ignited panic was a quick and distant memory in a matter of minutes.

The Brotherhood: The Struggles of Men

My brothers, if anyone among you wanders from the truth and someone brings him back, let him know that whoever brings back a sinner from his wandering will save his soul from death and will cover a multitude of sins.

James 5:19–20 (NIV)

Jackson Wilmington walked with a smooth glide as though walking on air. His long bowlegs hid beneath the Italian silk slacks of his navy pinstriped suit. His expensive designer shoes made music as they tapped against the Spanish marble floors in his office building. At six-foot-three and physically prepared to win a triathlon, Jackson waved his hand above his head at the on-duty guard for the last time of the day. He looked up and pointed to the sky while silently thanking God for his success and accomplishments. This daily ritual had a more profound effect today since God favored him with the ability to gain additional wealth. A powerful and successful marketing company owner, he stood in front of his business in the glow of closing a multi-million dollar deal. Walking to his luxury vehicle, he peeled away the layers of professionalism and relaxed behind the wheel as he began commuting to his upscale apartment.

After months of long days and nights, preparation, and prayer, his patience and labor met its reward. With success before him, wealth chasing him, and love absent, Jackson found himself at a crossroad of achievement. Elated for his overwhelming blessings from God, he also shared a certain level of sadness. According to what others could see, Jackson had arrived. Jackson's successful place in life was the conceit of every proud parent. What was supposed to be joy on the mountain after surviving the tumultuous valley experience, Jackson struggled with greater thoughts on his mind. Exhaling and rubbing his head in discontent, he exited his vehicle, set the alarm, and slowly walked to the elevator. Immediately, the doors opened, and he pressed the button to the top floor. The elevator chimed, and the doors parted as he slowly crept out and walked a few feet to his door. With no sign of enthusiasm or excitement over his success, he pressed the key into the locked door. This day was the celebratory achievement and milestone in his professional career. Statistically, he would go home and share the great news with his wife and children. However, contrary to politically correct perceptions, Jackson opened the door to his lavish loft and found himself alone. Exerting a sigh of discontent, he threw the keys down and walked over to the refrigerator. Searching through the refrigerator and grunting in disgust, he noticed the highlight of his meal would be the choice of takeout menus or microwavable dinners; he slammed the door shut. Before he could wallow in self-pity, Jordan, his always jubilant best friend, managed to show up on the scene.

Jordan Brensen, Jackson's best friend since high school, always managed to be the light in Jackson's darkness. There was something about old adages and clichés. When the two stood together, everyone thought they were brothers. Although not brothers born of the same womb, this divine brotherhood destined them both for greatness. In the case of this dynamic duo, birds of a feather literally do flock together. Jordan towered as a six-foot-four reflection of God's handiwork. He stood as eye candy to a blind woman. His smile gleamed through his perfectly chiseled lips with dark brown almond-shaped eyes that saturated a person's vision in a trance when conversing with him. This dominant personality coupled with a masculine physique similar to an NBA player at the top of his game, injury free, was matured and ready to live life. Jordan, like his high school counterpart, was handsome, successful, and worth having around. Although extremely serious, particularly work related, he was the life of the party. His perception of life was always positive. Even in the darkest, loneliest years of his life, his attitude and positive spirit convinced him without doubt that he would look back and laugh. Jordan absolutely held on to this belief and laughed himself out of any pit that tried to make a bed for him. Jordan never succumbed to the pits and traps set for him, and he refused to witness his best friend Jackson submit willingly. Jordan knew everything about Jackson, including the main things that always bothered him the most.

Before Jackson could completely break down for the evening, his doorbell rang followed by a melodious drumbeat of knocking on the door. Jackson scoffed while looking at the clock knowing that only one person made their presence known like this. Opening the door without even asking, Jordan burst in.

"What's up, my multi-millionaire comrade? You know I know the entire deal, man… all I have to say is I'm more worthy, but since it happened to you first, congratulations!" Jordan imitated a servant bowing before his master as he congratulated his friend on his major success. Jackson immediately responded by extending his hand for their signature handshake. "Thanks, man! You know I'm almost afraid to ask how you found out, but whatever. What are you doing here?"

Jordan was prepared to go into his dissertation, but decided to take the more comical route.

"See, you're asking the wrong question, brother! If I was someone out to get you, they could put you on a clock. Switch up the routine. Listen, I can tell you need to get out, so we are going out on the town. We're going to celebrate and enjoy the fruits of your labor. Call up some women and have them meet us. Oh wait…," Jordan kidded, "you don't have any friends, let alone female friends! Yo, when are you going to come out of this trance of no women? If I didn't know you personally, I would have to ask a few questions, but then, that would make me suspect, so I'm not even going there. Because 'Big Jo' was the only brother you know that applied to an all girls college, so that's not even an option. Seriously, look here, call your sister and have her meet us with some of her friends. Now she has some fine friends. Whew, they almost make me want to go to church and actually be serious about being there."

Though Jordan would attend services at church, his presence on the pew came with a contingency plan and purpose. Jackson tried to redirect his comical friend's thought process.

"What? Man, *no*! I'm not calling her! You should go to church because you want to have a relationship with God. Come on, Jo!"

Jordan grabbed his chest and stood as if receiving an award. "Oh, I have a relationship with God. As a matter of fact, did I ever tell you how my relationship started?" Jordan came down off his imaginary platform and laughed as he prepared to explicate truth to his ignorant friend.

Jackson leaped over to the couch and sat with one leg hanging over the arm. Removing his tie and throwing his jacket over the back of the sofa, he sat prepared to be amused by his exuberant comrade. Jackson not only needed the laughter and entertainment, but it was the highlight of his day of success. It wasn't the picturesque life with the wife and kids he wanted, but a great friend with nonstop jokes and stories to bust a gut would suffice. Smiling, he said, "Probably, but tell me anyway."

∽o∾

Jordan, prepared for his theatrical debut, was soaring with elation ready to explain his divine process on the foundation of his God and church relationship. Taking a seat on the chaise across from Jackson, Jordan laughed thinking about his true story of finding God.

"Jack, I remember it like it was yesterday! You know my mother always went to church and my dad would go so he wouldn't have to hear her mouth. At first, it would seem like he was trying be late on purpose, but eventually, I noticed that he would be ready before my mother and would rush her. Man, we went to a Pentecostal church, and they were guaranteed to start shouting and dancing. Well, every Sunday, all the kids would go to children's church, but for some reason, we didn't go this particular Sunday. So I had to sit with my parents. My mother wanted to be in the preacher's face, but my dad wanted to sit on the end around the middle. I guess he thought if he got too close, Jesus would get him or something. I don't know. All I know is everything would be service as usual until that organist hit some chords. It was okay, but then the music broke and they went jumping and dancing. There was this lady named Sister James," Jordan paused and rubbed his face as he reminisced. "Now that I think about it, she was fine. It's almost like having a crush on your teacher. You don't want to, but you look at her and you wish you were older. I'm telling you, brother, if you saw her, you would've said the same thing. She was fine. I almost think that's why my pops kept going back. Hold up, seriously, now that you have me thinking about it, all the fine women went to our church! Jack, Sister James broke out in a shout, and all of a sudden, those breasts started flying, and when she hit the floor and I saw that thong, brother, I was done! My father and I looked at each other, and he started waving his hands and yelling, 'Praise the Lord! Don't hold it in, Sister! Hallelujah, let the Lord use you. Praise him! Let that sister shout and release!' Man, I was damaged goods after that. My mother couldn't get me back in children's church. That was when I truly started paying attention in church. It was to the point I would beg God to let them start shouting. Without fail, the sanctuary would light up, and the women would completely loosen up. Jack, I'm telling you, jiggling breasts and the sound and sight of thighs and butts clapping sparked my relationship with God and church. Every time I think about it, I want to say, 'Thank you, Lord!' Man, just thinking about it makes me want to go to church right now! I'm telling you, Jack, it's better than the strip club!"

Jackson jolted from his seat as if five government agencies rammed his front door. Just when Jackson thought he'd heard every story of Jordan's life, there was always the element of surprise with Jordan. This flash from the past was the icing on the cake.

"*What*! Oh my god! You can't possibly be serious. Jordan, you know there's a spot just waiting for you…man…that is not the…man…I don't even know what to say to you right now!"

The two sat and laughed uncontrollably as Jackson replayed the image in his mind. Jordan was ready to share more, but Jackson laughed so hard that tears began rolling down his cheeks. He'd completely lost sight of all his bottled-up frustration. Jordan was the perfect release to forget any problem or worry. He tried to drink some soda between breaths, but envisioning Jordan in church and knowing how his father is, the soda started coming out of his nose. Grabbing for some tissue, partially choking and laughing, Jordan chimed in, "Yo, man, you okay? Don't fall out on my watch. All I'm saying is I have no problem with going to church. That's where you go to get the honeys."

"Take it from me…that is not why you go to church. Listen, you've been my best friend for years, you haven't learned anything from me yet?"

"Oh heck yeah, man! You've taught me how to run from women, chase your dreams, and run from your purpose! Run from more women while making your dreams manifest. Did I mention being single and miserable? I wasn't sure if I threw that in?"

Jackson swatted away at Jordan like he was an irritating fly. Sneering at Jordan, he maintained his position on the subject, "Whatever, man, I'm not miserable, and I don't run from women. You have the nerve to talk. You're the most meticulous man I know when it comes to women. So don't talk about me."

Jordan, unconvinced of his partner's stance, proceeded to enlighten his unaware associate. Taking the position as the subject matter expert, Jordan yelled, "Jackson, Jackson, Jackson!

No! See my situation is different. At least, I'll have a relationship. It's not my fault the woman turns out to be psychotic. If she's not a psycho, she's too needy, or she comes with too much emotional baggage. Oh, and let's not forget the sister with a mini tribe with multiple DNA tests running through the village. Nothing against the kids, but clearly, there is some insecurity there if you couldn't get it right past man number 3.

"Now you want me to play Daddy to all these kids and none of them look like me. Some brothers are up for the challenge, and I have nothing against them. I applaud them. However, I would like to have the mental imagination that I'm the *only* train pulling into the station. I don't want any reminders that another train ran in that tunnel. Even if she had heavy traffic, let me just imagine when I see her, there was no one there before me.

"So when the sister has three, four, and five kids with three, four, and five men, I can't think past the process of conception. Every time I look at those kids, my stomach starts to turn from the thought of what she might have done with those men. Nah, I'm good. I'll know the right one, I mean the *one*, when I meet her, but I haven't met her yet. Now you on the other hand, you my good friend, you won't even get the number, let alone the relationship. What's the deal with that?"

Jackson laughed as Jordan paced the floor as though he were an Ivy League professor speaking before an audience of hungry men famished for a relationship. Unbeknownst to Jordan, Jackson was very much heartbroken. His heart sank and his light within flickered as if fighting for oxygen as he thought about his last experience with love.

∞

In a daze, Jackson reflected upon the memory of love. Staring blankly into the room, it was as if all the memories became a reality. He saw the day he walked out the cleaners in a rush to meet a client for a late lunch. Effortlessly walking without paying attention to his direction, he bolted right into her, nearly knocking her to the ground. Jolted into focus, he locked eyes with her and saw himself walking down the aisle. Though her natural beauty sent him in a temporary trance, her eyes told the story her lips would never utter. He almost wanted to console her in his arms to ensure she would forever remain safe in his presence, but he didn't want to come scare her away. He opted to gently reach out to her. Partially surprised of her abrupt encounter, Alexandria smiled at Jackson, received his hand as she gathered her composure. When she smiled, Jackson knew he wanted to see that look on her face again.

Adjusting her clothes, she excused herself and prepared to walk away. Jackson recognized when opportunity met destiny, and he refused to let her slip away into the crowd. He apologized for nearly knocking her over, and after minutes of adorning her with apologies, he pleaded for her forgiveness and requested she accompany him to dinner. Alexandria gladly accepted his dinner request, the two exchanged numbers, and this coincidental encounter would lead to a two-year love affair turned engagement.

Unfortunately, before they could prepare for their future, Alexandria's life would take a sudden turn that neither of them prepared for. After experiencing extreme stomach and lower abdominal pain and heavy menstrual bleeding for several weeks on end, Jackson urged Alexandria to visit her gynecologist for an examination. Assured it was best, Alexandria and Jackson went for a physical. After several tests, the doctor discovered malignant cells that were multiplying and spreading so rapidly that having surgery would prove more detrimental than beneficial. He would never forget the look on her face when the doctor informed her that she had stage 4 ovarian cancer.

He watched himself in the office consoling her for the devastating news they'd received. He began to massage his face as if wiping away the thoughts, but he delved deeper into the past pain of his love's transition.

Like lightning flashing in the darkened sky, so were the memories that illuminated his mind. He saw her undergo chemo and dialysis in an attempt to reverse the diagnosis and spare what life remained. He remembered the photo they took with her completely bald head and jubilant smile imprinting her signature peaceful essence in the lens. He recalled sitting in the room, observing how she encouraged other chemo and radiation patients and sang hymns and worshipped softly while connected to the machines. Patients and the staff looked forward to her coming because despite her sickness, she approached death with life.

Unfortunately, he also considered the plans they wanted to make for their dream wedding. Not wanting to risk something detrimental happening to her if they left to get married, he devised the next best plan. Jackson wanted to surprise Alex by marrying her without delay. Jackson called and spoke with Pastor Woods explaining his plan. Pastor Woods consulted Jackson and agreed to come to the dialysis center without hesitation. Prepared to surprise Alex, Jackson changed his normal routine and sent Alex to the dialysis center unaccompanied. Instead, he detoured to the jewelry store and purchased her ring. Excited that he would finally marry Alexandria despite her sickness and the threat of death, Jackson headed to the dialysis center. While in route, he called to ensure Pastor Woods had arrived and prayed with her prior to his arrival. Rushing with excitement, Jackson arrived at the dialysis center. Pastor Woods stood by Alexandria and held her hand as Jackson walked in, hugged, and thanked Pastor Woods, and kissed Alex on her forehead. He could feel her smile beneath his lips. All he could do was look at her and smile. Seeing the smile on her face brought tears to his eyes. Unable to ignore there was something a little different about her disposition, Jackson inquired if she was okay. Never wanting to cause alarm, she merely smiled and nodded. Her body grew weary from the treatments and she was physically exhausted from the fight. She didn't want to alert Jackson that she was fighting within to retain strength, but Jackson noticed how Alex's eyes appeared weaker. Her blinks grew longer and longer as if she was preparing to go to sleep. Though bright, they seemed to grow dim. Despite her physical feeling, she took solace in the comforting touch of love's hand. Jackson massaged her face and embraced her. Receiving the gentle touch of love, Jackson pulled out the ring and cried as he knelt on one knee and proposed to Alex. Jackson, filled with emotion, confessed to Alex Pastor Woods's presence at the dialysis center. Alexandria laughed and gladly accepted Jackson's hand in marriage. The staff and patients with enough strength clapped and rejoiced for Jackson proved that he would love Alexandria in sickness and in health. There wasn't a dry eye in the building, and Alexandria was overwhelmed with joy. She reached a heightened level of peace, and with the peace in her heart, she kissed Jackson and whispered in his ear, "I love you so much." Before they could proceed and bask in the joy of the moment, something went terribly wrong. Alexandria inhaled deeply and exhaled in slow long breaths. In a final exhale, she smiled, and the sound to follow would forever remain engrained in Jackson's ear: the machine flatlined and Alexandria stopped breathing while in dialysis before she would become Jackson's wife. Everything thereafter became a blur. He remembered screaming out her name, yelling at the staff, and weeping uncontrollably. To no avail, the noise from machines, the clamoring from personnel moving chairs and other objects to get to her funneled out. Everything moved in extremely slow motion around him as he lost a grip on love. This reflective moment made Jackson feel as if he was right back in the thick of the day, and he became emotional. In an attempt to escape the tormenting grip of Alexandria's death, he rubbed his face repeatedly. Not wanting to give notice to his current state, he attempted to speak, but remained choked in his words. After a few minutes, he tried to regain the jubilant disposition he presented to Jordan, but the dark cloud of despair still hovered over him.

Saddened by the thought of his one true love, Alexandria, he retorted, "Listen, Alex was special and it's been a long time." Jackson cleared his throat as he modified his emotions. Regrouping to regain his original state, he looked at Jordan and continued, "Look, I made a vow to God after Alexandria, and I'm keeping it. After she died from cancer, I wasn't right. I don't think I can handle someone I love suffer like that ever again. I'm still trying to get right. She suffered so badly. Everything happened in the blink of an eye. She found out she was sick, and then she died. There wasn't even time to get adjusted to the news. I don't know, but I told God I don't want to meet anyone, date anyone, or love a woman if she isn't the wife God placed on the earth just for me. Even if it meant being alone. *No* women until the *one* comes."

Jackson thought about his perception of love and marriage.

"Unlike many men, I have a high level of respect for God and marriage. I believe if more people concentrated on the intended purpose behind marriage, the divorce rate would decrease tremendously and the family would be restored to God's intended purpose."

Jordan inquired, "Okay, Jack, you have my undivided attention since this is a conversation I don't think we've ever entertained. So reveal the great mystery. What is God's intended purpose?"

"Jordan, it's quite simple. In my opinion and personal belief, I believe God intended marriage to bring glory to himself. That is the great revelation, my friend. Marriage, if truly ordained by God, will be blessed and will bring glory to God."

Jordan sat up and looked at Jackson quizzically as though he made no sense whatsoever. He waved his hands in the air as if requesting a time-out. Not completely understanding the direction Jackson was headed, he replied, "What are you talking about? First of all, Jack, how is a marriage going to bring glory to God? Brother, you're losing me faster than a doctor in hospital with a dying patient. I'm trying to stay with you, brother. I'm almost afraid to ask you to explain this, but if you don't, I might be messed up forever. A brother won't ever make it down the aisle." Jordan fanned for Jackson to continue so he could attain a greater level of understanding on the subject. Jordan proceeded, "Come, Jack, reel me in, brother. How exactly is glory going to come to God?"

Jackson had no problem making his perception clear. "Jordan, God will be glorified because the marriage will return to him. Hold on and let me explain and don't interrupt. A relationship developing into a marriage initially starts out as a trinity."

Jordan's eyes grew larger as he assumed Jackson was referencing a ménage à trois. He wanted to interrupt so badly, but Jackson had already required him to hear him out.

Jackson refused to entertain Jordan's demeanor and he continued, "A couple in a relationship are two individuals who come together. You have a man and a woman. Once they are joined, the two become one. They are one because the husband submits himself to God, so those two within the trinity are bonded. The wife submits herself to her husband because he is the head, under God. Basically, by her submitting to her husband, she's merely returning back to God who is the original groom anyway. Don't look lost. The Bible says it clearly in Ephesians 5: 22, 'Wives, submit to your own husbands, as to the Lord.' Now before you fly off the deep end, please understand that submit is a choice–it's an action. So the wife's act of submission is a choice. The husband also has a requirement that comes with an even greater responsibility. When you read further, verse 25 states, 'Husbands, love your wives, just as Christ also loved the church and gave Himself for her.' That is unconditional, uncontaminated love. Christ gave His life for the church and Christ/God is faithful until the end. This is the ultimate commitment. I firmly believe a husband must be as committed to his wife and family as Christ is to the church. God, who was once evident within the two, is unified unto himself. The Bible says, '*Greater is he that is in you, than he that is in the world.*' If God is in you and you marry someone with God in them, hence being equally yoked, then between the two, God is one, or like I said, the two becoming one. When the husband and wife see each other, they are both seeing God because he is in them and they are one. Now with everyone unified in submission to God, the one, in essence, marries God. When the one—the couple—comes to God, God is marrying himself, hence bringing glory to himself."

Jordan smiled as he thought about Jackson's explanation. Nodding his head in agreement, he continued, "Man, if I didn't know you, I would've thought you might have been a preacher. Is there something you're hiding from your brother? You need to talk to God for real. You know I'm under serious heavenly construction, but that's interesting. I've never really thought about it that way, and I've never heard your perspective on marriage. I'm a long-term work in progress, so I'm not sure how quickly I'll completely convert. I'm almost scared to say submit, but a brother is definitely listening. I'm convinced you're the only man I know who can keep my attention when it comes to serious God conversations. I'm not sure if I should be embarrassed by that or not, but it'll give my angelic foreman another area of concentration. Wow, Jack! I might have to use that, with the Jordan twist of course."

"Jo, by all means, brother you can have that, it's real though. I take marriage seriously. If God ordains it, he'll bless every aspect of it, spiritually, emotionally, financially, mentally, and physically. That's why I have no problem staying focused. When I see some of these women, I don't see a morsel of God in them. Plus, I'm convinced God will let me know. Then you have the realistic aspects of it too. Some of these women are a trip. Man, once you reach a certain place of success, you know how it is, they want what you have, not you. I told one female that I worked in the mailroom and she dropped me like bad stock. Then I told another one that I was wealthy, and I brought her to my old house in the suburbs, and next thing I know, she had me meeting her entire family. They were trying to tell me that God told them I was the one for her. How's God going to tell complete strangers that some woman is my wife, and he completely bypasses me? No! I said I'd wait and that's what I'm doing. It doesn't make me gay, and it doesn't make me bisexual. It's called restraint. It's called discipline. It's called patience. It's called being a man of valor. I don't care what you or anyone else thinks. Man, they even talk about me at work. I'm the boss, but they spread rumors about me because I don't want any of the ladies in the office. At church, they talk because I don't want any of the women there. Darned if you do, and darned if you don't. I don't care if I come in here and eat microwave dinners until they come out with some new way to take a pill and eat. I'm waiting. I'd rather wait for the right one than to be trapped in a dead-end relationship or, even worse, lead some woman on in a relationship that I know isn't going anywhere beyond the bedroom."

Jackson's mood shifted drastically. He talked to Jordan with optimism in his decisions. Jordan was receptive because he had news to share with Jackson. Secretly, he wanted to transition to the place of family himself.

Jordan interjected, "Now, I did meet this beautiful woman that makes me want to invest in a diamond, but we've only been dating a few weeks. I look forward to seeing her because I actually enjoy her company. I will say women are like leaves on green trees in a forest. They're dancing everywhere in the wind, and it's getting my attention. I must say, I love the view, but I know all of that viewing will grow old until the right leaf lands before me. I think it just did, but a brother has to be sure. You know, since I'm all about investments, I have to research what I'm investing into. Leaves, forest, brother, you have me going soft in here, man. It must be your house, Jack. I don't know, Jackson. Eventually, I want to get to that ultimate settle-down place. I know it's in me, but until then, I'm pitching a tent in the forest. I believe nature's calling me."

Jordan laughed uncontrollably as he envisioned women's faces on leaves. He laughed while trying to get focused in his thoughts. There was only one problem, his thoughts shifted into high gear, and the comedy poured through Jordan like a waterfall crashing into a new river.

"Jackson, I respect you on so many levels, but I still want the honeys. Nothing against you waiting, but you're telling this to a grown man who enjoys going to church to see thongs, so until I get where you are, I hear you. I support you. I love you like my biological brother. Hell, I'm closer to you than I am to my real brother, but pray for you, man. Now are you going to call Patricia and tell her to roll in with some fine friends or what?" Jackson laughed at his friend and said, "What? You're ready to what? Why do you want Pat to bring some friends if you're ready to pick a leaf? You're going to have to tell me about this chosen leaf, I mean woman, brother. What's this I hear?" Jordan calmly received his friend's queries and countered from the boardroom of his heart. "I need more time to review the data, and I'll let you know more upon further review."

Before he could change the subject, Jackson's phone rang. Walking over to answer the phone, Jordan chimed in while clapping his hands and laughing aloud.

"Yeah, man. See, I spoke her up. That's Patricia calling, saying she's on her way. Make sure she brings Bernie. No wait…Bernie is in deep with Jesus. Wait, ask her who's available and bring her."

Jackson looked and laughed saying, "Jordan, please, this isn't my sister. Man, this is Eli."

"Eli, what's going on, brother?"

Elias and Jackson became mutual friends through the brotherhood ministry at the church. Jackson's firm was a sponsor for an event to bring awareness for men's health and wealth that Elias was chairing. After seeing his diligence and efforts to bring massive awareness to the community, their friendship grew. Jackson made sure the event was well marketed causing an immense turnout, bringing more men into the ministry and greater awareness to the community. Since the event and a host of other ministerial duties, they established a good, lasting friendship. Whenever Elias needed Jackson, he would always support him in ministry. Jackson too learned more about being a man of God, and he witnessed the true essence of Christianity through the life of Elias. This genuine man was sincere in his love for God and serving God's people. It was Elias's character, which served as evidence, causing Jackson to continue assisting when Elias called.

Elias responded to his spiritual brother's greeting, "Jackson, my brother, what's going on? What are you getting into these days?"

"Eli, I'm living and enjoying life. All the while trying to get Jordan to understand the real reason for coming to church."

Jordan laughed in the background while he rummaged through Jackson's refrigerator. Elias responded in amusement, "What is he talking about now. I know he has some crazy story behind why he comes to church."

"Brother, if you only knew. I'll have to let him hit you with that story. Man, I almost choked to death when I heard it myself. I'm telling you, Jordan knows how to keep the jokes coming."

"You're right about that. On a serious note, there's a reason for me calling. You know Pastor Woods request that the men get together to help some of these young brothers. So you know I had to call you."

"Eli, I'm glad you called me. Of course, I'll participate. What do you have in mind?"

Elias, ready with his selling pitch to recruit volunteers, explained, "All the ministers are going to have a group and men from the brotherhood pair up and help these young men in every aspect and walk of life, just men being men. We're hitting all the topics, questions, and curiosities of these men and embedding the truth through the Word in them."

Welcoming any opportunity to help was up Jackson's alley, but it always came with some reservation, partially because it required extended hours. Elias wanted to seal the deal, but couldn't help to point out what he'd recognized about Jackson.

"Jackson, seeing how you interact with these kids is amazing. When I heard you ministering to some of the brothers at the health and wealth initiative, I could see it all over you. Some men call themselves, others run from their calling, and a small remnant are lined up and being prepared by God to be raised up at an appointed time. Now, I'm the last person to tell someone they are called to preach and teach the gospel. That's between you and God. I've seen men and women crash and burn carrying themselves before God's people. I will admit there's a unique anointing and spirit about you. I'm praying that God opens your heart and that you're receptive to whatever he tells you regarding your calling and purpose. It's definitely there, but like I said, that's between you and God."

Jackson quickly sank into the recesses of his mind while Elias continued to talk. Even though Elias was a great friend and a true man of God, when he began to talk about God, he'd take over a conversation as if he was one of the disciples on the Mount of Transfiguration with Jesus himself. Elias continued to talk while Jackson reflected upon a conversation he had with his mother.

Being the matriarch of their family, his mother, Esther, was a woman endowed with wisdom. She raised her children with the fear and admonition of the Lord and took no shame in making sure they all knew Jesus as their personal Savior. She told Jackson early on that he was special and God had a special divine connection and purpose in his life. Jackson often found this hard to believe since his father, Silas, would speak contrary to what his mother spoke of God.

Silas, a retired colonel for the US Marine Corps with gruesome experiences and life tribulations, often argued with his wife concerning God, church, and faith. He was a modern-day Saul before meeting Jesus on the Damascus road. He often shunned and ostracized people for their religious beliefs and, without intent, spiritually abused his own wife and children. He had a response for every situation and questioned if God were as real and powerful as Esther portrayed, then why the continuous calamity in the world. Regardless of the treatment and spiritual abuse of his father, his mother never cowered when it came to her prophetic utterance to her children about God.

Jackson tunneled back to one of the last arguments his parents had before his father had the massive heart attack that changed his father's life, attitude, and conversation about God, about church, and about faith.

Though every detail of their argument wasn't clear, Jackson distinctly recalled his mother defending herself and God against his father's slanderous statements and boldly prophesied his future to him, "Silas, hear me now and hear me well, the Bible declares that 'every knee shall bow and every tongue shall confess that Jesus Christ is Lord.' So help me, you will submit to God and serve him with your whole heart, even if God sits you down himself. Keep it up, and you'll have a heart attack as a warning! Don't let your heart stop before you surrender. You will mistreat me no longer! You better seek God for forgiveness. If God shuts you up or closes a door, there isn't a man on earth that can help you. I've prayed, fasted, and believed, now I'll witness the power of God at work in you and through you."

Silas, for the first time, was speechless and didn't have a strategic response to his wife's statements. It was as if the lion's jaws were sealed shut by the hand of God himself. Silas merely looked at Esther as if he'd seen God's face. Not sure of what to say, Silas haphazardly uttered his own life's transition, "I'm healthy as a man in the prime of his youth! If I have a heart attack, I'll serve

God with everything in me. Better yet, I'll even get baptized. No, wait, I'll even start preaching, that's when I'll know that your God is real. If he makes a preacher out of me, there has to be a god! If I live and your Jesus does any of this, then maybe I'll surrender! Highly unlikely, I'm the colonel and surrendering isn't an option! But if I don't, and I assure you I won't, I never want to have this or any conversation relative to this again! End of story!"

Esther walked over to her husband fully assured and smiled between her words before she left the room, "Well, Mr. Preacher, watch God, the true general, work, Colonel. You're already outranked!" Silas remained in the room in the presence of Jackson, speechless. The look on his face spoke intimidation, but he remained silent. For the first time in their marriage, it was as if he never spoke a word to his wife. This wasn't her, but in actuality, it was her with a power so evident within her that even he couldn't retort. There was something in Esther's tone and stature that left Silas at war within. Unwilling to submit to Esther's words, Silas devised a plan to deceive Esther that he assumed was fool-proof—be the "preacher" his wife declared he would be.

Jackson endured his teen and early adult years watching his father play preacher. The earlier years of his childhood were joyous and memorable, but once Jackson became a teenager, his father called himself into the ministry. Elias had the right idea that many men call themselves, and Jackson's father was one of those examples. No one really knows what ignited his father's willingness to go from not being interested in going to church or reading the Bible to waking up early one Saturday morning and announcing he was going to be a preacher. He never heard his father say, "God called me," "God spoke to me," or "God" anything. His father literally sat the family down and said he was going into ministry. As his family, they had to support him. Though Jackson's mother knew it wasn't God calling him, she prayed adamantly and finally received an answer from God about the purpose and intent of her husband's newfound revelation. Once she received confirmation from God that his perfect will and plan would be revealed in time, she settled within herself to see God's plan unfold. Many people didn't understand Jackson's mother and her support of her husband. She really didn't warrant any reason to explicate to anyone because she trusted God enough to know that his plan would outlive a man any day. If a man was issued a role to play in God's plan, then there was no escaping until the plan and purpose was manifested. This was the case with Jackson's father. As a result, Jackson wasn't in a rush to follow the dreams God spoke to him through and the obvious revelation from the Holy Spirit at work in his life.

Just when Jackson thought he'd achieved his greatest level of success, his calling always managed to chase him down. He would try to veer his thoughts in a different direction, but the invisible spirit of God always drove his mind to envision him submitting unto God and yielding to his perfect will. He always saw the fork in the road with the sunny, elucidated cloud in the right and his tangible attained wealth on his left. The only difference was the light, though emitting upon his tangible wealth, always compared dim to the illumination that cast over the acquired wealth he'd received. There was nothing there to call his own. Though it appeared everything was there, it was quite barren.

Shaking his head to erase the visual, Jackson was thrust back into his reality. Elias was still bantering on the telephone about God. Jordan sat quietly as he channel surfed and snickered at various commercials. For some reason, every channel he turned to showed women dancing, shaking, or walking around half-naked to promote a product. Jackson, not knowing a thing Elias was talking about, abruptly cut him off.

"Eli, man, listen, I don't mean to cut you off, brother, but you know you can keep going and not let a brother get a word in edgewise. What's up, man? You need something or you want me to do something?"

Eli, understanding and realizing he'd completely taken over the conversation, took no offense. He was well aware of his talkative character trait because many people addressed to him before. The only person that never complained was Hannah, and that was merely because she had tendency to do the same thing. The two were literally meant for each other on a number of scales.

Elias, understanding Jackson was always busy, replied, "Sorry, man, you know I go in, and once I get started, it's like a waterfall. I will say I have purpose for calling other than preaching to you. Pastor Woods is preparing for the brothers to take the young men on this retreat. I wanted to know if you'd participate as one of the mentors. Since Jordan is there, see if he'd like to be a part as well. We need as many brothers as possible that can talk real with these young men and answer their questions in a safe and secured environment. I know you've participated in other things with us, so what do you think?"

Jackson didn't waste any time in responding, "Absolutely, Eli, Jordan and I will go all in for these young men. When do we need to be there? Will there be a briefing to outline the goals and objectives?"

When Jordan heard Jackson speak on his behalf, he was immediately snatched from the television to the telephone conversation.

"Jack, what are y'all talking about, and what are you volunteering me to do? If the women aren't going to be in the building, don't count me in."

Jackson fanned Jordan away in the background, but the more he fanned, the louder Jordan became. "Let me talk to Eli! What's going on over there that I need to know about? Give me the phone, Jack. Eli, what's going on over there? What are y'all getting me caught up in, man?"

Jackson sneered and ignored Jordan's outburst, while Eli responded to both inquiries.

"Jack, we're going to meet at the church in about an hour or so. Sorry it's short notice, I was going through so many calls, and time caught up with me, but if y'all can make it, that'll be cool, if not, then I'll let you know when we're meeting up to give you more details."

"Well, we're not doing anything now, so we'll meet you over at the church."

Jordan chimed in again, but this time, he refused to be ignored, so he snatched the phone from Jackson.

"Eli, what is Jack volunteering me to do? You already know if fine women are not going to be present, I can't guarantee my presence in the building. Tell me the sisters are coming out in droves!"

Eli laughed, knowing how adamant Jordan was when it came to women and answered, "Jordan, you will be in the company of all men. From every corner of the building, there will be men there swarming like NFL players in a huddle with thousands of fans in the stands. Not a skirt in sight. At least there better not be a skirt in the building, on a man in particular."

Jordan didn't try to keep any couth or composure about himself or his perception of preferring the presence of women.

"What! Eli, as much as I would like to be there and assist in whatever you have planned, me plus a group of men don't sound right to me."

"Hold on, Jordan, it's the brotherhood ministry at the church, and we're volunteering to help get these young men going in the right direction. Jackson said you'd be cool to volunteer as a mentor."

"Oh well, I can do that for a couple hours. Yeah, man, I got some stories to tell that'll have them on the floor dying laughing."

"Well, it won't be for a couple of hours. It'll be for the weekend."

Jordan tried to wrap his mind around being trapped in an enclosed place with men for an extended period of time. It was evident he'd never experienced a men's retreat, but for him to be a highly educated professional, he was rather ignorant when it came to matters of servitude. More disgusted as he thought about the time he'd have to spend with the men, he shouted, "What! Forty-eight hours of nonstop men! Y'all are going to have a cook or something to ease my mind. That's a long time to be with men. This isn't going to turn into some group therapy where some dude is going to be crying on my shoulder, is it? Look, I'll be there and I'll help out, but the first dude that cries on my shoulder or wants a comfort hug…I'm out! All you will see is my back, and I might leave y'all with a few words to remember me by. It'll turn into a healing and deliverance retreat then, I'm telling you right now, that's how it's going down. Now if none of those things occur, then we're straight, and both you and Jack owe me at least two hookups with some of the finest women in the city, better yet the state, because I know Hannah has some fine friends. All the good-looking ones hang out together."

Eli took a sip of water to quench his thirst from talking, but was overwhelmed with a surge of laughter. He literally couldn't control himself and eventually ended up spitting out the water he was sipping. He didn't even know how to react to Jordan. Jordan was always running off at the mouth, saying something that made perfect sense to him, but at times may not have been necessary for the public to know. However, since their friendship was established, Eli understood how Jordan was when it came to the opposite sex.

"Jordan, I want you to come because you bring laughter and realism about manhood to the table: doubts, fears, failures, success, and so much more. You're the man these young brothers need to know, so I need you in the place. How about this, I'll make sure you meet a nice young lady, if it's the last thing I do. I have a question though: do you want to be married? What's the sense of me introducing you, if your intent isn't to marry?"

"Absolutely, I don't want to end up like Jack over here. Everything you could possibly want and nothing to show for it. I want to be married. My parents are still married, but, man, so far, God hasn't pointed the one out to me, so until then, I'm on the hunt. Brother, I must say, I like this jungle landscape. I have a lot to offer the right one, but until we meet and God gives the green light, I'm like a fat man at a buffet on an empty stomach. I'm going in!"

Jackson couldn't contain himself. Listening to Jordan and Eli, he was amused when he heard Jordan. Unbeknownst to them, Jordan was more prepared and ready to head down that aisle than either of them. Eli knew exactly who he'd introduce Jordan to.

"Okay, Jordan, here's what I'll do. Since you've decided to spend forty-eight hours of your life with about five hundred men, I'll have a cookout at my house and invite a few folks over. I'll get Hannah to invite some women, and I'll be sure the person I have in mind comes. Does that sound like a plan? This way you'll have options."

"Eli, see you're messing up already. You were supposed to invite me to church, man. That's where the ladies are."

"No, man, you're supposed to be there for God, not women. Why do you want to come to church to meet women? That's why I said we'll have something at my house. Let God handle the rest."

"Eli, one day I'll tell you exactly why I go to church, but we'll have to talk about that later. Let me just say this for the record, and since you're a man of the cloth, I know you'll understand what I mean when I say this. Me going to church is like Saul, when Samuel anointed him king. Chasing some ass, he got a huge blessing—that's all I'm saying. Now after that soaks in, hold me to telling you that full story, but, brother, I don't think you can handle the pressure. When you're ready, I'll call you. As far as it goes for this retreat, you can count me in, man. I'll see you at the church. Here's Jack." Jordan handed the phone to Jackson.

Jackson busted out in laughter and couldn't contain himself. The image and reflecting on the story Jordan just shared overwhelmed him before he could calm down. Gathering his composure, he informed Eli.

"Brother, let me tell you, when Jordan gives you the uncut version, you're going to need some equipment to lay hands on him. He needs help. We'll see you at the meeting."

"Okay, I'll keep that in mind. Talk to you later, Jack."

Hanging up with Eli, Jackson prepared to jokingly chastise Jordan like a parent enraged over having to commit to something unwillingly.

"Man, he better have this cookout and she better be the finest thing there, and I don't mean cute outfit fine, I'm talking about full package beauty. If she's remotely ugly, I'm going to pay you back in the worst way for volunteering me like this. Now because you're my best friend, I'll cut you some slack. However, if I see a gold tooth, nappy weave, and tracks combo, spandex, a pinky toe hanging out the side of the shoe, one row of naps, toes hanging over the shoe holding up the sidewalk, or enough fat to start a brand-new diet craze, I'm going to let you and Eli have it." Jackson dismissed the loquacious banter of his friend, and the two looked at each other a laughed hysterically.

Jackson didn't anticipate his day ending in such a manner, but it was much better than sitting on the sofa in his echelon loft alone. This laughter with a great friend was the element necessary to aide him and distract his focus from the things lacking in his life; however, there was a small part of Jackson that wanted to reflect on the memories of his father. Synonymous to Elias's comment of his calling, Jackson tried to bury his thoughts toward what God called him to do. Before Jackson could delve into the deep waters of his thoughts, Jordan was there to rescue him from the childhood reality he'd hidden in the recesses of his mind. After hearing his overly comedic friend, the thoughts washed away in the current, but a tidal wave would eventually resurrect his past.

Can Love Truly Be Just a Friend?

Where has your lover gone, most beautiful of women? Which way did your lover turn, that we may look for him with you? **2** *My lover has gone down to his garden, to the beds of spices, to browse in the gardens and to gather lilies. I am my lover's and my lover is mine…*

Song of Solomon 6:1–3 (NIV)

Elias continued working to finish the list of calls in his office when the always vibrant Taylor Woods walked in. To any human being with eyes, Taylor was an absolute beauty.

It didn't seem like seven years elapsed when Elias first came to join the ministry, the two immediately cleaved to one another. Elias was waiting in the lounge of the pastor's office for their meeting when Taylor came to pick up paperwork from her father. Elias missed his mouth and spilled grape soda on the front of his perfectly pressed white shirt as he gazed upon Taylor for the first time. Elias jumped and exerted a sigh of discontent, which immediately caught Taylor's attention. After chuckling at his misfortune, Taylor walked over to help Elias. Once the two connected eyes, their friendship would only grow.

Taylor looked at Elias and immediately knew he was a fresh fish in deep water. She couldn't help but burn the image of his features into her mind, purple-stained shirt and all. She looked in his eyes and saw this man's love. Shaking her head to erase the thought, she walked over to this muscular handsome man, dressed in a clean suit presented like business, and found herself say, "Someone would probably call me rude for saying this, but I've never been known to care much about the opinions of others, so I'll just come out with it. When did you grow a hole in your mouth? You're about to meet the pastor with a huge purple stain on the front of your shirt. Hello, Mr. Clumsy, it's a pleasure to meet you."

Elias couldn't help but notice the beautiful woman in front of him. He tried not to focus on the physical and he was insulted, but her beauty was partially blinding. Before he could subject his thoughts to the desires of the flesh, the cold soda trickled down his shirt making the stain larger as he arose to greet his rude acquaintance. Elias looked at Taylor, attempting to not give away his attention and replied, "That would be considered rude particularly since you don't know me. Hello, Ms. Rudy, how are you?"

Taylor clasped her chest, put her hand on her hip, and gasped, "I know you didn't call me Ms. Rudy. Where did that come from?" Taylor didn't know she'd finally met her match. Not submitting to her response, he said, "If I'm Mr. Clumsy, then you're rude, Ms. Rudy." This one comment transitioned two strangers and matured into two friends laughing about spilled soda. Taylor guided Elias to the restroom while she went to the closet in the hall of her father's office and found a spare shirt that looked like it might fit. Shaking the shirt and laughing, she knocked on the door and handed him the shirt through the crack. After sharing that embarrassing moment, the two laughed, and their friendship journey began.

For years, Elias and Taylor had a friendship that remained private. It was evident they loved each other deeply. Their always playful gestures and open displays of affection raised eyebrows whenever they were around one another. The two never quieted the whispers and found no fault in their actions. To the public, there was always talk about their relationship, and to the unknowing, it was understood the two were a couple. Elias spent countless hours in counseling with her father regarding his calling. For some reason, Pastor Woods welcomed him likened to the relationship Elisha had with the Elijah. The closer Elias was with Pastor Woods, the closer he grew to Taylor.

Pastor Woods wanted to give Elias an opportunity to serve within the ministry. He acknowledged that his responsibility as pastor was to groom and build the house with servants. He took Ephesians 4 to another level and would welcome any servant who was willing to labor for the kingdom. There was enough work to be done, so the moment Elias spoke of his calling and continued diligently to serve Pastor Woods provided an outlet for Elias to build the kingdom. As a result, Pastor Woods put him over the singles ministry. This catapulted the relationship between him and Taylor beyond their own understanding.

Elias recognized the church grew tremendously with young professionals, so he opted to have a retreat at a vacation resort in the Florida Keys. Not anticipating an immense turnout, Elias was astounded at the overwhelming response from those wanting to participate. What should've been roughly seventy-five people turned into over two hundred and seventy-five people. The four-day ministerial weekend was compact with singing, preaching, dancing, and laughter. While some were delivered by the preachers, others opted to be delivered in other areas. Among those present was Taylor who had helped Elias promote and organize the event.

Saturday was the last night, and the atmosphere had been set in worship. Once the people dispersed to enjoy their last evening in the Keys, the natural atmosphere was just as powerful as the spiritual. Elias was ending his phone call with Pastor Woods after giving him a briefing of the retreat's success. Although others briefed Pastor Woods, because it was Elias's ministry, he also updated Pastor Woods for the real highlights. Pleased the events occurred with great success, Elias lifted his head and exhaled a sigh of relief.

Coming back from his personal trance of relaxation, he looked around the room to see the cleaning crew clamoring briskly to set up for the next event. Elias took a glance across the room, only to see Taylor sitting on the veranda watching the waves crash into the sanded earth. She managed to capture a moment of serenity to herself after pulling off a triumphant affair. Smiling within, he noticed his right-hand woman taking in the moment she deserved; he walked over to see her. After taking a few steps, he stopped in his tracks as he noticed how the sunset arrayed her beauty. With her head turned into the light, she had a hue that made her glow. This one moment of Taylor's raw beauty caused Elias to become hostage to the light that permeated her presence.

"Eli, this is your friend. She's like a best friend to you. Don't think about it. Man, she is beautiful. Nope…focus, Elias, this is Taylor. Little Ms. Rudy, she's your Taylor. Aw, man, I can't believe this…okay. Get it together. Just walk over there and be yourself."

∽∘∾

Elias began walking over to Taylor when he noticed she extended her hand to welcome his presence. Turning her head slightly in his direction, she smiled and silently greeted her friend. Shifting her body in the oversized chair, Taylor pulled Elias's hand and guided him to sit beside her. They sat suspended in time, basking in the breeze that caressed their skin with the sun massaging their bodies as they nestled in the chair. This moment of floating time spoke volumes though neither of them uttered a word. If love had a moment where neither beat nor lyrics could capture in their melodious clutches, this moment was the sound of love and friendship. Elias smiled and laughed within as he parted Taylor's hair, brushing it to the side and sealed their love with a gentle kiss on her temple. Resting his head upon hers, they were carried away into the arms of love's own melody. Without hesitation, the sounds of chattering personnel and the clamor of furniture disappeared into the distance as a new sound arose and imprisoned these two beating hearts.

The heat of the sun began to recede, and the crashing waves found calm as Elias glanced at his watch. Taking a double take, he inhaled as he noticed the moment had quickly elapsed into an hour. Not wanting the moment to end, he gathered his thoughts for his next move. Wrestling within himself, he thought to keep their relationship on the course it had taken, but her solace in his masculine arms was a feeling he welcomed. Instead of treating her like she was just another woman he knew, he wanted to make sure she was well aware that she was an exception to the rule. Rubbing her face gently he whispered in her ear, "My Rudy, come on, let's go. These people are almost done, and they're going to kick us out. It's getting late. Let me walk you to your room, or can you make it alone like a big girl?"

Taylor laughed at Elias's comment. Though she was partially upset this moment would be lost in time and space, she knew it was only temporal. With an exasperated sigh, she said, "Man, now that is how you relax after some serious work. Eli, once again, the dynamic trio, you, God, and me, have created a hit. This retreat was definitely a home run for the kingdom."

The two smiled at each other and did their secret handshake. Continuing to hold Taylor's hand, Elias pulled Taylor from the chair as she slowly obliged his gesture. She inquired, "Do we have to move? They are still doing the arrangements. I'm tired… the heels have had their fair share for the day, the week, and the month. Why did my room have to be so far away? Jesus, I asked for the upgrade, but the feet are seriously having a battle, and I'm not winning right now. Lord, this would be a great time to give me some wings. Not saying I want to see you in glory, but these feet of mine are talking in tongues. Eli, don't pull me too fast. Be gentle."

Taylor, clueless, had no understanding of just how gentle Elias wanted to be, but he shook himself trying to remain focused.

"Tay, you know I'll always be gentle with you, but I thought you might be able to handle a little pressure."

Instantaneously, Taylor was thrust into the flesh and her thoughts raced through her mind, "Eli, what are you talking about?"

Elias didn't know exactly how to respond to her question. He knew exactly what he was referencing, but her tone threw him off. Was she saying it with sarcasm or was there a hint of flirtation in that voice? With his emotions thwarted, he laughed and fought to see Little Ms. Rudy. Only this time, Taylor stretched, clearly exposing her entire captivating frame. The vision of this fully matured young woman reminded Elias that Little Ms. Rudy was Taylor Woods, mature and elegantly sexy. All attempts at focusing on Little Ms. Rudy sank like a torpedoed submarine, with no survivors. Massaging his manicured goatee, Elias allowed his perfectly mastered smile to pierce through his succulent lips. Looking off and pulling Taylor close to him with a quick jolt, he embraced her. Elias whispered in her ear, "Taylor Woods, you are one of the strongest women I know. I know you are not about to allow some heels to outdo you. Trust me, you can handle the pressure. Now if you like, I can carry you, but I've never known you to be the damsel in distress type."

Unbeknownst to Elias, Taylor's thoughts of Elias elevating her in the air in those caramel masculine arms took her mind into overdrive. All she could see were things that would involve serious repentance, fasting, praying, and more repentance. When she thought about the anointing oil, her thoughts flashed to using the oil for much more sinful purposes. Her heart skipped seven beats trying to escape from the desires of her flesh, but just in case, she exhaled to get a second wind for one more lap. Taylor didn't want Elias to know the thoughts that swam through her mind, but she never successfully managed the poker face. Had it not been for her caramel-tanned skin, Elias would've seen nothing but red. Trying to keep her always sarcastic personality, Taylor welcomed the flirtatious challenge, "Every damsel has her day, so are you going to whisk me away or what? It's a long walk from here to my room. There's no telling who'll see you carrying me and what they'll think. So the question is can you handle the pressure when it's thrust back to you?"

Elias knew it was best to leave the question unanswered, but he couldn't help himself.

"How about we find out and answer questions later."

Before Taylor could muster up a response, she was repositioned into Elias's arms, and he carried her all the way to her room without as much as a grunt of weakness. Taylor immediately felt weightless. Not quite sure how to respond, Taylor threw on the dramatic role and pretended to faint as though she were a damsel being rescued. After a brief moment of a farce faint, she planned the perfect response to Elias's act of chivalry. Taylor decided it was best to role-play this act of heroism. Batting her eyelashes and in the drawl of a southern belle, Taylor replied, "Oh, Eli, how will I ever repay you? You've managed to save me from the treacherous fiends attached to my ankles. What would I ever do without you in my life? Oh, Eli, you're my hero." She looked deeply into Elias's eyes, smiled, and massaged his masculine arms as she awaited a response.

Elias couldn't do anything but laugh. He almost dropped Taylor in the hallway once they came around the corner from laughing so hard. The two laughed until Taylor started to stutter through her words. Before she could gather her composure, Elias arrived at her room.

"My-my-my-my hero Eli has sa-sa-sa-sa-saved me once again. I guess this is where I'm supposed to kiss you and bid you ado. How can I ever repay you?"

Taylor's movement shifted her weight around. Weakening from laughter, Elias said, "Can you start by getting down and opening the door?" Taylor was pressed into her sarcastic mode. With her lips pursed, she said, "Well, since you put it like that, how about no. No, Eli, I actually, kind of like it up here. I'll have to make you start carrying me more often."

Elias laughed as he finagled the door open while holding Taylor in the air. They had successfully made it to the room without any witnesses. The delay in the hallway was witnessed by a man who came to the retreat. Neither knew the man personally, but they both recognized him. Smiling and exchanging a long distance salutation, Taylor looked at Elias and laughed. Elias pushed in the door, and the two burst out in laughter as he tossed her on the bed.

With Taylor lying on the bed, Elias helped take her shoes off as he contemplated massaging her feet. Not sure what to say, he kept the banter light, "Tay, you know I'd hook you up with a foot massage, but, man, you've been walking on those fiends all day. Go wash them or something. These hands are delicate, and I can't let just anything touch them. Besides, you have stinky feet."

Gasping and tossing a pillow at his head while pulling a wrestling move on him, Taylor jumped on Elias. "How about I take it up a notch and take a shower, but before I do…smell this."

Taylor pinned Elias down and pushed her toes as far into his face as she could, but the more she laughed, the weaker she became. Elias enjoyed their playful gesture and laughed even harder than she did. However, the more they remained pinned together, the more he was reminded that this was Taylor and not Little Ms. Rudy. As much as he wanted to focus on Little Ms. Rudy, his hands rubbed up against Taylor's body. Between his physical senses and his mental sensitivity, the mood changed and scorched his once mildly cool thoughts and pressured the carnal thoughts with volcanic temperatures. Taylor, sensing the shift in the atmosphere, jumped up and ran to the bathroom before she could melt in the moment. Yelling from the bathroom, she inquired, "Are you going to wait here for me, or are you going to your room to take a shower? I'll be clean, and you'll be funky. You can take one here like you do at the house, but you won't have any tighty-whities."

There was a huge difference between being in a lavish hotel, in an extravagant room, with a ridiculously gorgeous woman, and being in her father's house. At Dad's house, pressing your way into the woman you've secretly loved is not an option; however, in this hotel room, hundreds of miles away from Daddy and his all-seeing eye, the sky is limitless. Speaking before thinking through his response, Elias answered, "You're just going to have to move over in there and make room for me. This way, I'll make sure all those parts…"

Carnality seized and bombarded his spiritual walls. He reserved the remaining words with expectant hope that he was ignored. With the silence in the air as deafening as an abandoned cave, Elias nervously paced around the room abusing himself for his comment. Meanwhile, Taylor soothed her body beneath the massaging showerheads and meditated quietly on his words. Before she could escape into the realm of fantasy, Elias snatched the room key and yelled, "I'll be right back!" In an instant, Taylor was disappointed that he decided not to fulfill the acts of his comment. Encouraging herself that it was the best thing for the two of them, she made every moment in that intensely hot shower count. In order to bring her flesh under subjection, it was going to take heat, prayer, and quietness to set her straight. The heat from the bathroom created a huge fog in the air. By the time she surfaced from the sauna, she screamed in shock to see Elias was back in the room. She never heard him reenter the room. Completely paralyzed in her essence, Elias's mouth dropped. The last ounce of strength used in controlling his flesh whisked away in the breeze along with the exhale released as he gasped. Though his intent was to return and do what they'd always done at the house, relax and crack jokes, he was mesmerized into the carnality of his fantasy. Taylor observed Elias's frozen state as he observed her wet satin skin. Without a morsel of covering, Taylor mustered every ounce of sarcasm and added a hint of flirtation to Elias, "Now that you're full, is it possible for you to at least turn around or hand me something to cover up?"

Elias closed his mouth, looked around the room, scrambling to find something to use as a towel, and snatched the entire comforter off the bed. He wrapped it around Taylor while massaging her warm silky skin. His fingers pulsated against her body tenderizing her muscles. As she turned around, he neglected to let her go and closed his eyes, briefly inhaling the fragrance from her clean skin. This was the second time Taylor welcomed the sensuous masculine incarcerating grasp of her cherished friend's love. Only this time, she wanted him to release all he kept bound. Elias and Taylor stared deeply into each other's eyes with silence roaring in their ears. Their hearts pulsated rapidly resounding as one beat generating a melodious sound. Silence echoing between them as Taylor was enveloped in the hands and arms of a man she sincerely loved, Elias no longer wrestling within. Time escaped them as Elias single-handedly lifted Taylor from the ground and journeyed to the bed on the other side of the room. Peeling away her layered shield, he sensuously and seductively danced into her love.

Reality Check

Therefore God gave them over in the sinful desires of their hearts to sexual impurity for the degrading of their bodies with one another. They exchanged the truth of God for a lie, and worshiped and served created things rather than the Creator— who is forever praised. Amen. Because of this, God gave them over to shameful lusts. Even their women exchanged natural relations for unnatural ones. In the same way the men also abandoned natural relations with women and were inflamed with lust for one another. Men committed indecent acts with other men, and received in themselves the due penalty for their perversion. Furthermore, since they did not think it worthwhile to retain the knowledge of God, he gave them over to a depraved mind, to do what ought not to be done.

*Romans 1:24–27 (*NIV*)*

Patricia was never one for returning home, but at her mother's request and the need for a relaxing place to hide, Pat found herself running away back to Manalapan, New Jersey. Walking through Newark International Airport with her designer luggage in tow, she graced the marble floors of the airport with the air of royalty. People gazed upon her presence as though she was an Academy Award–winning actress. Basking in the glow of attention, Patricia found the limo driver and immediately demanded his servitude exceed her expectations.

Exhaling from the rear of the limo, she silently mourned being in the city she vowed never to return. Looking out the window at the bustling metropolis near the airport, she was reminded why she preferred southern living with a city feel. As the driver entered the Garden State Parkway and headed toward Patricia's childhood residence, she was betwixt with emotions. Nearing the township of Manalapan, she was surprised at some of the changes in the city. There was such an immense change in the environment from when she was raised. Rather than looking aged and traditional, the city had a new burst of life that caused her to peer out the tinted glass as a tourist on a New York City tour bus.

The driver pulled in front of her mother's house and proceeded to retrieve her items, as Patricia stood on the curb and admired the upkeep of her childhood residence. The eastern sun rained light on the four thousand-square-foot red brick house with picturesque floor-to-ceiling windows. On the western side of the house was a bay window serving as a canvas with the perfect picture of the baby grand piano in the music room. The magnolia tree in full bloom scented the air perfectly. The tiered walkway, draped in fresh flowers from her mother's own touch, looked like a perfectly organized bouquet. Though Patricia never focused on the house, growing up, she marveled at how it resembled that of a model home in a popular magazine.

Tipping the driver generously, Patricia proceeded up the walkway and unlocked her mother's home using the old hidden key. Before stepping through the door, she whispered a prayer beneath her breath, "Please don't let this house be a horrible instant replay from the sixties and seventies. Pat, you know if this house isn't modernized, you're staying at the hotel whether she gets upset or not." Exhaling a sigh of release, Patricia was elated as she looked around and noticed her mother's modern contemporary transformation evident throughout the house. The old chair had been replaced by a plush charcoal tufted loveseat. The contemporary color palate of charcoal, cranberry, and black with varying minor accent colors were approved by Patricia's critical eye. Talking aloud and complimenting her mother's design style, she marveled over the modern appeal engrossed throughout the house.

"Okay, Ma," she said to the empty room, "I see you've been listening to me and watching a few episodes from the home channel. Now I can finally relax."

Walking to the family room, Patricia was surprised to find that room was suspended in time, unchanged like the rest of the house. Though biased in her preference to the modern amenities, Patricia recognized there was something about the memories of laughter and joy that echoed through the room. This was the only room in the house that displayed pictures from her youth. Slowly picking up pictures and holding them as her mind reflected on the day and time of each event, she held the photos until she felt peace. Patricia sat on the couch, and before she realized it, she was sound asleep.

After a few hours of much needed rest, Patricia was awakened by the sound of laughter coming from the other room. Looking at her watch and stretching, Patricia walked in to the echoes of laughter. Leaning against the doorpost, Patricia watched Gabrielle and Kendall flirtatiously fondle each other in the presence of Payton. Payton didn't regard the adult presence nor did she notice Patricia leaning against the doorpost. Rather, her focus remained concentrated on the preschool cartoons airing on the television. As a new episode came on, she began to sing the introductory song and twirl around in front of the television. Snacking on her favorite lemon cookies and quieting as the show began, Payton looked to dismiss the actions of the two adults; unfortunately, Patricia's opted to focus directly on the adult activity. Patricia's anger immediately went from zero to a hundred. Her presence and voice startled Gabrielle, Payton, and Kendall, and they all screamed simultaneously. Of the three, Kendall was in a state of utter dismay. Kendall's jaw hit the floor. Just when Kendall assumed the relationship with Gabrielle seemed predictable, this element of spontaneity was unsuspecting and almost heart-wrenching.

Every ounce of religion and Christianity flew out the door once Patricia went into full gear. Patricia looked at Gabrielle with a death stare to let her know her repulsion. Patricia, not vexed by Kendall's alarm, sneered and immediately moved to enact her antipathy, "How about you do us all a favor and get the hell over it. You're sitting in here on my mother's furniture, looking like an idiot with your mouth hanging open. Brielle, you look just as dumb, but you're the epitome of dumber. Why the hell are you up in here playing husband and wife in front of my daughter? What the hell is your problem?"

Before Gabrielle could welcome her sister's presence, she took immediate offense to Patricia's inquisitions. Gabrielle leaped off the couch and walked over to Patricia. Kendall remained seated with hands clasped to mouth as if frozen in ice. Raising her voice, Gabrielle yelled, "What! How are you going to come in here and begin to scold me in front of Kendall and Payton? You haven't come around after all this time, and now you want to play hero mother to the rescue! Who do you think you are?"

Kendall remained in shock. Patricia's rage swelled within as she retaliated to her sister's rash inquisitions.

"I know I'm the one that needs to slap some damn common sense into you—playing house in front of my daughter. How long has this hot mess been going on? You can't be responsible after all these years. Do I have to do everything?"

She paused in her words and addressed Payton, "Payton, do me a favor." She immediately smiled with lemon cookie crumbs spilling from her mouth. Patricia thought of where she could send Payton so she wouldn't witness what was about to happen.

"I know Mrs. Stone is still next door because she and Grandma are always together. See if she's home and go over there for a little while. If she isn't there, just go in the backyard and play for a while, I'll come get you when I'm done."

Patricia rubbed her hands across the top of Payton's head and leaned in to kiss her forehead. After kissing her daughter, she knelt down to look Payton in the eyes. With a smirk on her face, she completed her thought, "Mommy has to choke your Aunt Brielle in a few minutes. You look fabulous, honey. I'm proud of your aunt for keeping up my standards with you at least, but I'm so sorry you had to witness this. We'll talk more later. You know I love you, right?"

Leaning in to give Payton a hug and another kiss, she looked at her smiled and apologized again, "I'm so sorry you had to see all this, but I promise we'll talk more. I pinky promise." Payton chuckled and hugged her mother on the hip as she nodded in acceptance. Squeezing Payton, Patricia turned her daughter toward the door and she skipped out the door. By the time Payton made it off the front porch, the yelling from within the house went up to concert decibels.

"I can't believe you, Brielle! You're lucky I'm trying to get right with God, but I'm about to backslide on a magnanimous level that'll have God himself shaking his head, asking, 'Why, my child?' by the time I finish with you in here."

Patricia spoke to Gabrielle and assumed they were teenagers again when Gabrielle would cower before her sister's authority. However, Gabrielle was grown and able to stand on her own two feet. Ready for battle, Gabrielle shifted her weight to one side, put on the coat of confidence, and spoke boldly to her sister.

"Patricia, you don't have a right to stand there and judge me! If anyone needs to be judged, it's you! You neglected your own child because she didn't fit into your life plans, and you want to judge me. You don't even know me. So don't come in here looking down on me!"

Arrayed in confidence, Gabrielle slowly approached her sister as though each word and step were the hammer and nail to pierce Patricia to the wall. She waited years to face her sister with this level of supremacy, but the opportunity never arose. This wasn't the time to delay any further. Though Gabrielle, fully garmented in assurance, faced the verbal attack head on, her words were to no avail. Patricia's ferocity was fueled by pure wrath. She couldn't see beyond what her eyes saw. To Patricia, her eyes didn't lie, and Gabrielle's actions combined with seeing Payton as a witness caused her adrenaline to heighten. Patricia only focused on Gabrielle's steps, but she immediately paced the floor like a ravenous lioness on the hunt. Gabrielle paused in her steps and braced herself for impact, but remembered that she was fully capable to stand against her sister and any other force that attempted to come her way.

Patricia overruled what should've been recognition for Gabrielle's newfound behavior without consideration. Patricia took no notice of her sister's newly developed attitude and proceeded full steam ahead.

"Gabrielle, please! I should punch you in the mouth! Who are you talking to? You can't seem to get anything right! Don't try to tell me about my parental abilities. My child knows exactly what is going on with me, and our relationship is better than you know. God had enough common damn sense to create animals to follow the correct order of things with the opposite sex. One male and one female, and you can't even figure that out, Brielle! Not only have you chosen to mimic porno scenes in front of my kid with a woman, but you also chose one that looks like a damn man." Patricia looked beyond Gabrielle and redirected her attention on Kendall.

Exasperating a sigh of discontent, she threw her hands up and clapped them, creating a sound of thunder in the room, "To be honest, I don't care what lifestyle you've chosen or the decision you made. My problem is you're sitting here promoting it, in a pornographic manner, in front of my five-year-old! Then you have the nerve to have a partner that looks just like a damn man! What's the point? To top it all off, you want to preach to me about being responsible! Are you kidding me?"

If there was an anger meter in the room to gauge whose fury soared to dangerous levels, Gabrielle would've caused the meter to break. Gabrielle thought about slapping Patricia, but she didn't think it would be enough. She paced the floor looking for something to grab and throw at Patricia, but instead, she attempted to coerce herself into being the bigger person and dismiss her sister's ignorance toward her lifestyle. Unfortunately, the seven seconds that tried to warrant calm were overshadowed by the three seconds it took for Gabrielle to pick up the empty vase from the table. Turning the vase upright and walking over to Patricia, she retorted with an even more immense level of anger as she proceeded to scream at her sister, "You ever disrespect me again, I'll shove this vase down your throat! I've been more responsible than you! You haven't been responsible in five years. Ma has been raising your child because your stuck-up, wannabe ass been living the high life, trying to escape real responsibility. Now you show up and want to disrespect me!"

"Gabrielle, first of all, we both know you ain't hitting nobody, so put that expensive ass vase down! Secondly, don't try that irresponsible mess with me. Payton knows exactly who I am, and we spend more than enough time together. I'm here to get her, and she knows it, but now that I know she's been mentally and emotionally abused by witnessing your lesbian lifestyle, I have to take her to a more morally sound environment. Thanks to you, now I have to invest money into shrinks so she won't grow up confused and mentally distorted."

Kendall, an activist in the gay and lesbian community, took extreme offense on Patricia's bold comments. No longer bound by her initial shock, Kendall refused to remain silent. Stimulated by anger and her newfound position, atop the verbal abuse, Kendall immediately chimed into the argument.

"How dare you stand there and be as ignorant as you are. I perceived you to be intelligent, but now I see your ignorance is shining and making you extremely unattractive. Do you know we have rights?" Kendall took a bold and courageous step to interject into an argument Patricia invoked. Her comment and inquisition was the lighter fluid Patricia needed to send the flames dancing in the air.

"Who the hell invited you into this conversation? I was talking to my sister. When I asked a question, you stared at me like you saw a damn ghost, so shut the hell up. You need to learn how to speak when spoken to. When I asked you a question, you didn't answer, so shut up!"

Kendall realized just how different Gabrielle and Patricia were. She'd never received a morsel of dialogue like this from Gabrielle. Patricia spoke with authority and showed no sign of intimidation, in stark contrast to Gabrielle whose passive-aggressive behavior was more Kendall's speed. If there was an alter ego or multiple personality that Gabrielle could ever have, it was evident within Patricia. For the first time within their relationship, seeing Gabrielle stand with boldness against Patricia was the audible alert that Gabrielle had just as much temper in her as Patricia.

Patricia realized she was insulted by Kendall and immediately sought to devour Kendall with the might of Samson, "Wait, what the hell did you just say to me? Ignorant… rights…do you know I have a right to shoot your ass for talking to me in my mother's house? Do you know I have a right to sue you for flagrantly displaying your personal lifestyle in front of a juvenile? Actually, it was downright pornographic in nature. I'm feeling like calling the police to come arrest you for child abuse—you and my ignorant sister."

The entire weight of the argument shifted from Gabrielle and Patricia to Patricia and Kendall. Kendall showed no signs of intimidation or fear even though Patricia always intimidated people with her presence. Kendall made sure Patricia knew she was not subservient to her slanderous verbiage.

"Look here, don't threaten me! Do you know who I am? I'll have you exposed on a level so deep, you wouldn't be able to discern whether you're innocent or guilty for a heinous hate crime."

Unfortunately for Kendall, Patricia didn't take kindly to threats and often looked forward to confrontation. Patricia was in the right environment to follow through on her threat. She knew her father kept the house with enough handguns to arm a small village.

"I don't give a damn if you're the lesbian mistress to half of the United States female population! How about I help you out by committing the crime, this way there will be no confusion. Wait right here! I tried not to let Pashequah out, but you asked for it!"

Patricia turned around and bolted to the rear of her mother's house, talking to herself and trying to keep her alter ego asleep. Kendall didn't stand a chance if Patricia's other side controlled her behavior. Unbeknownst to Kendall, Gabrielle's father had taught all of his children how to use firearms. He even went as far as teaching them how to disassemble bombs. As a retired U.S. Marine with over thirty years of active duty in covert missions and defense weapons tactics, he assured his family's safety in light of his absence. Kendall was in imminent danger and had no clue Patricia's threat was more than likely going to become a harsh reality in a matter of minutes.

Fearless and immersed in rage, Patricia mumbled beneath her breath as she loaded her father's S&W 500 .50-cal magnum. Patricia almost forgot how heavy the gun was unloaded and how the weight changed once loaded. Determined to get her point across, Patricia yelled to let Kendall know she was coming for her. Locked and loaded with five in the barrel and Kendall in her sights, Patricia headed to the living room.

Meanwhile, Gabrielle and Kendall stood arguing over Patricia's comments. Gabrielle defended her sister and tried to get Kendall to understand the level of danger she faced if Patricia found her father's weapons, "Ken, I'm telling you. I love you and I love my sister, but you really don't understand. This is not a good time for you to jump into our argument. Let me handle this."

"Let you handle this!" Kendall bellowed in fury. "You haven't said a word. Gabrielle, how can you stand here and let her disrespect me, disrespect us, disrespect our love, and disrespect our lives? How can you permit her to say whatever she chooses? I thought you loved me. Now you're standing here defending her?"

"Ken, listen, we can talk about this later, but let me handle Patricia. Trust me, if you knew what I know, you'd let me handle this!"

Kendall dismissed Gabrielle's previous statement and continued to yell at Gabrielle with her arms swinging in the air. By the time Patricia reached the doorway and looked up, all she saw was Kendall's arms swinging, Gabrielle's hands covering her face, and distorted words escaping Kendall's lips. The words leaving Kendall's mouth never touched Patricia's ears. She had tunnel vision, and that was far more dangerous than anything else, particularly with a loaded handgun. Patricia shifted gears faster than a NASCAR driver fresh out of pit row beating the pace car. Although Patricia's pistons were revving at an all-time high, Kendall was soaring in rage like a runaway meteor with nothing to crash into. Kendall paced the floor, bantering about her despondency.

"I'm so disgusted with you right now, Brielle! You're such a backstabbing liar! You've left me alone to fend for myself against your psychotic sister! Who the hell are you? You didn't even tell me you had an identical damn twin. I'm freaking out over here that I'm seeing two of you! Then the other half is a gay-basher, while I'm in love with her lesbian sister. I'm standing here trying to figure out how the hell this all happened. You told me Payton was your child, and I accepted her even though I didn't prefer a woman with a kid. Now I find out she's not yours, and there's someone walking the earth that looks just like you! What is going on? You've been lying to me, and now you want me to let you handle this! You haven't handled anything that I can see!"

Before Gabrielle could respond, Patricia leaned against the doorway with the magnum pressed against her crossed arms, fully visible for Kendall and Gabrielle to see. Lowering her voice and shifting all her weight to one leg, Patricia spoke clearly, so her words were not ignored.

"Kendall, you may not know who Gabrielle is, but in seven seconds, you're going to know who I am, and you'll definitely know who my heavy friend is right here. See I'm not that, threaten you, talk garbage all day, and have no plan a, b, or c type of woman. I'm the do it first, ask for forgiveness later type. Now I'm not sure if you just hit my sister. Perhaps if you have, then you've probably done me a favor, but you have five seconds to get your stuff and head out that door before the county coroner shows up. Trust me, I am a perfect shot."

Kendall's eyes were immediately affixed to the ridiculously large gun in Patricia's hands. For the first time during this argument, both Kendall and Gabrielle were a bit fearful. Gabrielle knew her sister's capabilities, and Kendall was shocked that she went through with her threat. Pressing beyond the fear pulsating within her spirit, Gabrielle opted to turn her fear, anxiety, and suppressed emotions into power and courage. "Patricia, you have the gall to stand here in our parents house and threaten us with Daddy's gun! Aren't you the same hypocrite that goes to church every week? Now you're standing here holding my father's handgun, threatening to use it! This is why I don't respect you! This is why I don't respect half the people in church. You parade around like you're better than everyone else, but you and I are more alike than you know."

"Gabrielle, be quiet! Don't give me the rehearsed speech! Do I look like I care about all that? What does that have to do with you and He-She over here playing house in front of Payton?"

The argument continued to elevate between the three, but there would be a shift unbeknownst to the three adults. Esther, Gabrielle and Patricia's mother, would soon shift the entire atmosphere in her home.

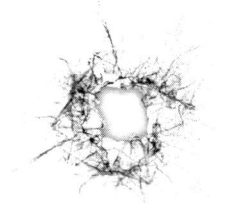

Mother's Presence: Prayer, Power, and Petition

For this people's heart has become calloused; they hardly hear with their ears, and they have closed their eyes. Otherwise they might see with their eyes, hear with their ears, understand with their hearts and turn, and I would heal them.

Matthew 13:15 (NIV)

Turning into the driveway, Esther—Jackson, Gabrielle, and Patricia's mother—listened to the sounds of shouting from within her house. Esther exhaled an infuriated sigh of displeasure. She was more despondent as she realized they were even louder outside the car than inside. Instantly she knew, Patricia's presence had to be the cause for such uproar. Esther paused, partially elated for her daughter's return and partially angered that her appearance alone could invoke such discord within her house. Esther sought solace in God. Refusing to be drawn into the confusion, bitterness, and rage within her house, she opted to be arrayed in peace, if only for a moment.

∽∽

Engrossed in her own troubles, she lifted her head and whispered a prayer to God with the belief that he already answered the prayer. Her sole responsibility was to call on him, but he'd already assessed the request of her prayer.

> God, you have said in your word that in this life there will be trials and tribulations, but be of good cheer, for you have already overcome. God, I haven't seen Patricia in several months, but she's home. I don't know why these two can't get along. They grew up perfectly fine, then

something happened, and I have no clue what created this division in my family. I need peace and deliverance from the past, Jesus. Not just for me, but for my entire family. All of my children need deliverance from the past, from the pain, from the shame, and from the disappointments. Lord, your freedom dwells within us. I know you hear me, and I believe you've already answered my prayer. Father, thank you for bringing Tricia back to me, but please, Lord, mend both of my daughter's broken hearts. You are the potter and they are the clay. In order for deliverance and healing to take place, I know they both had to be broken, but let this be a time of healing, restoration, and release. I rebuke any confusing spirit, any demonic spirit, and any spirit that is not bringing glory to you. I rebuke the spirit of division in my family. In the name of Jesus, amen.

∽o∾

Esther, filled with contentment, was propelled back to reality when the papers from her hand fell by her feet. Reaching to pick up the papers, she was drenched in the veracity of her own discouraging news. She paused and stood alone, reading the results of her cancer screening. If having a positive test result of malignant cells in both breasts wasn't damaging enough, coming home to screams and discontent wasn't healthier. Fortunately, Esther never allotted room in her life for negativity. Assured in her spirit by God's own power to heal her body, she nestled the paperwork in her purse and looked toward heaven–praying silently within. Smiling with poise and resting in reassurance, Esther proceeded to head in the house. Before she reached the porch, Payton bolted toward her running an Olympic dash and winning the gold medal. Overjoyed to see the one person who knew no different, peace and joy, she welcomed her granddaughter with open arms.

Though elated to see Payton, Esther was startled and inquired of her granddaughter, "Hey there, Pretty Pay, where are you coming from?" Payton always honored her grandmother and loved her more than life itself. Responding with the joy of any excited five-year-old, she bounced and pointed toward Mrs. Stone's house. When Esther looked up, she saw her good friend and neighbor waving to ensure Payton's safe arrival. Esther smiled and waved at Mrs. Stone. Mrs. Stone yelled out, "Hey, Es, I'll call you later, my phone is ringing." Esther replied with a smile, "Okay, we'll talk then. Thanks for watching Payton. Talk to you later." Mrs. Stone waved and turned to close the door and retrieved the phone. Payton and Esther smiled at one another. Esther realized she was blessed when she saw the smile on Payton's face. Payton, full of excitement, wanted to tell her grandmother about her mother.

Jumping up and down, Payton exclaimed, "Grandma, guess who's here?" Esther, already fully knowledgeable, pretended unaware and responded, "Oh my goodness, who's here?"

Payton stood laughing, "My mommy is here," pausing briefly she pointed to the house, "but her and Aunt Brielle are yelling at each other. My mommy wasn't being very nice. My teacher said you shouldn't yell at your friends, but my mommy and Aunt Brielle were yelling pretty loud. So my mommy told me to go see Mrs. Stone."

Esther smiled at Payton's report. There was something about a child's version of an adult situation. Thinking about Payton's comparison of her mother and aunt with her teacher's instruction caused her to chuckle within. Responding with a smile, she continued, "Your teacher is right, but the same applies to sisters, and your mommy and aunt are sisters, and they should know better."

~~~

With the power and presence of love existing outside, malice and bitterness took residence inside. They delved deeper into their feud only this time, Gabrielle completely opened a new closet of skeletons. Gabrielle decided to throw a more personal javelin at Patricia, "See, Tricia, this is exactly why I stopped going to church. This is why Ma keeps preaching and praying. It's people like you

I despise most! You talk one way when you're in church, then you turn around and treat your family and people a completely different way when you're not in church. You have no regard for life and how to treat people. People who have sacrificed life and limb for your selfish ass, and you turn around and quickly judge! You're supposed to be my sister! You're supposed to be the person I turn to when I need help! You're supposed to be there for others! Even if you don't care about me, you could at least care enough about Payton to be responsible over her life. But if it's not all about Patricia, and if it doesn't fit into your delusional state of grandeur, then it's to hell with everything and everyone."

Patricia was amazed to the witness of power Gabrielle's retort. Growing up, Gabrielle would cower behind Patricia, but today was undeniably a day of deliverance. Patricia stepped back and leaned in closer as she stared at Gabrielle. In an attempt to calm the savage beast looming within, she smiled, chuckled, and said, "Oh, I see you're finally coming out of that little shell you've been cleaving to all these years. So your Mrs. Man over there really did turn you out! I'm almost proud of you, but it still doesn't change anything. You're standing there ridiculing me, but I never said I was perfect. Did I ever say I go to church because I'm better than you or anyone else?"

Patricia's emotional and mental instability began to prevail as her agitation swelled within. "I go so I don't have to walk around shooting people like I'm about to up in here."

Kendall paced the floor. Her movement distracted Patricia. Wanting to maintain control, she redirected her focus to Kendall, "Look here, I see you pacing back and forth. I know you may not have a clear understanding, but allow me to make a suggestion. Stand still before I help you! I don't even know why you're still here anyway!"

Gabrielle finally chimed in to lure Patricia away from Kendall. Taking her defense, she shouted, "Leave Kendall out of this, Tricia! You're still doing it, and you don't even see what you're doing! Either you see, or you just don't care!"

Patricia squinted her eyes tightly, making her face as serious as the sight of death. Using all of her intimidation tactics, she gawked at Gabrielle and waved the gun around in her hand and raised her voice, "Oh please, Gabrielle! You're judging me!" Patricia managed to return to a state of emotional and mental stability, but her temperament was still in the red. "I'm working hard on getting better. Is that what you want to hear? I go to church because I want to be better! Does that make you more comfortable? Why do you think I'm here to get Payton? You think I don't know what I've been doing?"

Patricia paced the floor trying to physically walk herself into a calmer state, "I do my best to suppress my angrier side. She's the reason why I go to church. My alter ego isn't as sane as I am, so church keeps her away from the public. I'm in prayer to have her removed, but it's situations like this that wake her up."

Grunting in frustration, Patricia continued, "Ugh! I can't believe you have me in here talking like this! You should be grateful that God propped me up in that church because if I act out what's really on my mind, both of y'all would've been dead right now."

∽o∾

Patricia was never that parishioner that attended church weekly, but recent events caused her to begin attending more regularly. Having good friends like Hannah, Bernie, and Taylor always talk about God seemed to help. Even though they weren't really great at quelling her aggressive personality once ignited, they were great at piercing her soul and ministering to her heart with their lives and their actions. Seeing God at work through them played an intricate role in bringing Patricia closer and closer. Being saved in her adult years was not like her adolescent years when she, Gabrielle, and Jackson, their brother, were considered saved because they repeated a sinner's repentance after the preacher and made their mother happy. This version of salvation was by force because their mother made them join the church, as most parents with children. However, they initially had no personal intimacy with getting to know God. Though they would pray as a family, mainly with their mother, they developed a relationship with God vicariously through Esther. As children, they modeled what they saw. As they grew older and more life trials occurred, there would come a time when the personal relationship with God would be put to the test. Of the three, Patricia was thrust into the tribulation experience prior to her siblings. Patricia immediately began to experience various trials that she'd never experienced prior to. This extreme argument with her twin and her jilted relationship with her daughter immediately soared to the top of the charts.

One thing Gabrielle was right about, if Patricia backslid, there would truly be some smoke and at least one body resting on her mother's floor. Gabrielle knew Patricia's temperament, so she quickly shifted her tone and gears so she could be both heard and received. Once Patricia was agitated and her vision became tunneled, everything in her path would be utterly destroyed until she satisfied her quest with absolute victory. Though this provided great wealth and success for her in the business world, when it came to matters of the heart and family, this proved detrimental.

Kendall's pacing and commenting beneath her breath snatched Patricia's attention away from Gabrielle as she began to ignite the torch of fury all over again toward Kendall. Gabrielle recognizing her sister's temperament attempted to dilute their qualm. Before Gabrielle could address Kendall, Patricia interjected, "Ken, since Gabrielle refers to you with a male identifier, you need to know I don't like to repeat myself. Clearly, you haven't seen this gun so let me help you get a better view." Patricia repositioned her body so the sunlight gleamed off the freshly cleaned magnum almost blinding Kendall, while forcing Kendall to relocate in the room. Waving the gun, making it more visible for all to see like a fanatic psychopath, Patricia continued, "I'll assume that you didn't understand me the first time so I'll say it again, for the hard of hearing and downright dumb. Stop moving and pacing the floor! Now you've turned Brielle out, but I'm not my sister and you don't know me. I strongly suggest you listen and stop ignoring me when I tell you to do something! Better yet, how about you leave! Get out!"

Kendall, realizing the instability in Patricia's disposition, came to the understanding that she should've listened to Gabrielle. Gathering her belongings, she addressed both Gabrielle and Patricia.

"You know what? I don't have to take this abuse from you! You're not worth my time. This entire family is dysfunctional and delusional. You all need help! Gabrielle, it's over! I don't need this! If you come with her, as a family pack, I don't need you in my life!"

Gabrielle, growing more and more discontent with the yelling and arguing, threw her hands in the air and shouted at the top of her lungs, "That's enough! Both of you just shut up! I can't take it anymore! I'm tired, I can't take it anymore! Kendall, if that's what you want, then leave! Patricia, you have no clue, do you! You have no clue! You'll learn, then you'll regret everything!"

Esther and Payton decided to come in the house as they laughed through their personal love moment. Kendall almost knocked Payton over as she excused herself and stormed out of the house. Meanwhile, Gabrielle darted past her mother brushing against her and headed for the bathroom. Patricia, proud of her work, commented to her mother.

"See, Ma, this is why you need me to come around here. I'll set some order up in here. I got them devil's running. Whew, now what's for dinner, I'm buying!"

Esther, being as calm and harmonious as she always carried herself, laughed at her own daughter's ignorance. With her hand on her hip, she slowly replied, "So you think that you're coming into my house and establishing some sort of order? That would imply that my house wasn't in order and that I allowed the devil to rest in my house. You don't know the word because it says, 'As for me and my house we will serve the Lord.'" Walking in closer to Patricia, she proclaimed, "You waltz in here and create mayhem and havoc, and deceive yourself into thinking you're bringing about order. Patricia, there are some things you need to learn. Have a seat and let me explain a few things to you so there's no confusion but clarity."

Whenever Esther was present, you instantly knew that she was not alone. People would always comment that there was something special or different about Esther. Others would demonstrate their discomfort when in her presence. Those who were spiritually connected cleaved to this wise woman of God as they acknowledged the different presence about her was none other than the Holy Spirit. The spirit within her was so potent and powerful when she prophesied or prayed there was change. This is why she remained at peace when given the diagnosis of breast cancer. With the doctor's diagnosis but God's final answer established in their private covenant, combined with discord in her house, Esther clearly ascertained to Patricia what true order entailed.

⁂

Meanwhile, Gabrielle cried uncontrollably in the bathroom. Gabrielle emoted to God as she removed the scarf from around her neck as she examined her scars. The scars stood as symbols of life and of God's promise to keep her alive. Unbeknownst to Patricia, the scars Gabrielle bore were a result of being Patricia's sister. Patricia knew nothing about the scars nor the story that supported the devastating event causing Gabrielle to remain mutilated until her years on earth would end. Gabrielle wept as she prayed aloud.

"God, my sister has no clue what I've gone through for her. How can she stand there and judge me? She doesn't even know anything about Kendall. God, you were there. You know we weren't doing anything. She always goes over the top and personifies things so it will make everyone else look horrible. I would never abuse Payton. I love her too much to abuse her. I admit this lifestyle isn't exactly the way you would have us to live, especially if we live by the Bible's standards, and I've felt guilty, but, God, you know why I'm this way.

"How can I trust a man, when it was a man that tried to take my life? How can I trust a man, when it was a man that robbed me of my purity? How can I trust a man, when it was a man that ripped my womb, and now, I can't have children! The one gift that comes precious to a woman, the one gift I'd treasure, you robbed me of that too. Now Patricia is here to take the only child I'll ever be able to have! You refuse to let me enjoy life. You take everything away from me. Tell me, how can I trust anyone! Now, I can't even trust women, not Kendall, not Patricia, not even myself.

"Why me, God? What did I do so wrong that I deserve this? All I did was go to my sister's school to visit her. All I did was be born a twin. Why didn't you warn me? Why did you let this happen? Why did those guys do this to me? The entire time they kept calling me, "Patricia, Patricia, Patricia." I'm not Patricia, God, I'm Gabrielle, but you let this happen to me because she's my sister. Why did you even let me be born only to take what little life I had? Look at me! Look at what they did to me! What did I ever do so wrong that you couldn't make this go away? Why didn't you just let me die? Now, I'm tormented and agonized. I don't even talk to you anymore because of this, because of these scars, because of this pain, because you hated me enough to let me suffer because I was born Patricia's sister. You're supposed to be this big all-knowing God my mother's has been teaching us about all these years, but you allowed this to happen to me. I thought you were a loving god! You don't love me! You hate me! Now this, I can't take it anymore! Why me? Why?"

The tears crashed upon Gabrielle's flesh, rolling down her face and beneath her chin as they rested on her scarred throat. Tears nestled in the bosom of Gabrielle's suffering of being her sister's twin. This had been the first time Gabrielle prayed to God in years. She believed God allowed her to suffer for being Patricia's twin, so she targeted her anger toward God for years. She never told people exactly what happened. Somehow, she managed to remain evasive when someone inquired about her throat. Gabrielle only confided in one person. Even then, she vowed never to speak to her confidante if she ever told Patricia or her father. Her mother, her only living bearer of her secret truth, knew of her grief, yet she too was distressed.

∽o∾

Esther raised all of her children in the nurture and admonition of the Lord, but the teenage years transitioned them all. Unfortunately for Gabrielle, had she only taken a moment of her time to embrace her mother's prayer before leaving to visit Patricia, she would've been covered. Esther tried to get Gabrielle to slow her pace and listen as she prayed. However, Gabrielle, caught in her ignorance, verbally expressed that she didn't need God to be with her, she was grown and mature enough to handle herself. Though Esther redirected her daughter's professed insolence, she prayed for her safekeeping as any mother would. This created a battle that Esther tarried with for years. The instant she was aware of her daughters assault, she questioned her prayer life and relationship with God. It was the first time in her years that she had to go seek wise counsel with an increased amount of iron. Knowing iron sharpens iron, in order for her to attain vigor and encouragement, she humbled herself to God in what she knew to have great effect: in prayer.

∽o∾

Esther reflected on her emotional state that was the kidnapper of her solace. Esther felt culpability for letting Gabrielle go visit Patricia. Gabrielle begged her for weeks to go to her sister's campus until Esther finally submitted to her daughter's request.

Knowing she'd financed Gabrielle's trip brought penitence upon her that she wrestled with for deliverance. Just when Esther would think she was completely delivered from the hurt and pain of her daughter's silent misery, Gabrielle would come to visit and the war would ignite as though it had never been won. Though Esther knew the word and her personal relationship with God taught her enough to know not to condemn herself, she would manage to trust in this until she would see the scarred body of her daughter. That hurt, that experience, that personal struggle within is what Esther cleaved to while simultaneously creating a stronghold after Jesus bestowed deliverance. Seeing the tangible on Gabrielle only reminded her of the sorrow she felt. Ringing her hands in grief, Esther tried not to reflect on the past and think negatively.

❦

Meanwhile, Gabrielle didn't wait long enough to hear a response from God. She'd shut God out of her life so long she almost forgot what it was like to truly hear his voice. Restless from crying, the destruction of her relationship, and parental involvement, she cleaned up her face and left the bathroom. Leaving no time for further discussion, she waved good-bye to her mother and bolted straight out the door. Before Esther could yell out to Gabrielle for her to talk and explain what went on, Gabrielle was in her car and pulling out the driveway. Esther turned and looked at Patricia with a chastising look that intimidated Patricia in a matter of seconds. Patricia hadn't seen that look since her childhood, but immediately knew not to speak. Esther slowly rose from her seat and walked away to her room. Payton ran in the room, confused if she should follow her grandmother or spend time with her mother. Patricia opened her arms, making the decision for Payton. Running and leaping into her mother's arms, Patricia and Payton sat in the stillness of the large house and caught up on lost time.

Is Someone Expecting?

If we confess our sins, he is faithful and just to forgive us our sins and to cleanse us from all unrighteousness.

1 John 1:9 (NIV)

Pastor Woods held a meeting with all of the men and volunteers who participated in helping the young men of the church during their retreat and the subsequent events that followed over several months. After months of ministerial efforts going toward to the empowerment of all men in the church and community, it was time to relax, rejoice in God's glory, and laugh in peace of their servitude efforts. To their surprise, he planned several activities for the men, and they all enjoyed a wonderful lunch with, for the first time in their church's history, all of the women from every ministry serving and assisting, thanking them for building the kingdom of God.

Laughter and endless tales filled the air as voices echoed throughout the Fellowship Hall with men, women, and children uniting for a great cause and purpose. It was evident that change occurred, deliverance took place, and lives, once imbedded in pain, were under submission to revitalization. Among the participants of this pastoral gesture were Jackson and Jordan. Fortunately for Jordan, he would encounter his request of being in a sea of women. As the women continued pouring in, Jordan grinned from ear to ear like a kid in a candy store convinced and emotionally charged to trying one of everything. Jackson noticed Jordan's silence, which was very seldom, and glanced to observe his friend's countenance. Chuckling within, he tapped his best friend on the arm and calmly but jokingly spoke.

"Look, man, this is the church, this is not a social networking scene. These are God-fearing, pure, praying, submissive, loving, confident, and holy women. They're not here so they can be attacked by a hungry, lonely, wealthy, single man like yourself. Keep it together, brother. Go easy, this is the church. Hallelujah!"

Jordan made sure Jackson had a lucid understanding of his position. Verifying his physique and attire were in order, while massaging his manicured goatee, Jordan tilted his head toward Jackson and replied with every ounce of cynicism he could muster up.

"Brother, the best freaks hide behind all those titles. Why do you think the women in the church have just as many, if not more, children than the strippers in the strip clubs? That's exactly what I'm talking about, Jackson. Give me the submissive ones first, better yet, let me get the pure ones. You know the pure ones are the freaks, teacher. All that pinned up frustration looking for an outlet. That reminds me. Jack, I forgot to tell you about the woman I want to marry. I thought she was going to get me off the playing field for real. We were going out, laughing, and having fun. Now we've been seeing each other for quite some time. It started out very slow. I had to ensure she wouldn't surprise me with the 'I'm married, but separated' or the 'I have children, but they don't live with me'. I got the FICO score, the police record information, medical history, we went to take HIV tests together, and I even got the college transcripts, Jackson! I've never taken an HIV/AIDS test with a woman, but she was the only one to ask. No one else ever asked or demanded it. A brother is in for real. From there, it slowly progressed to us seeing each other a little more often. It kept growing, that's why I told you I might be ready one day to settle down. You know a brother always wants a freak, but with her, she's different. I want to know her, I want a lady, a queen, a classy, sophisticated, intelligent woman that can complement me as I would her. Can you believe this? I have to get my manhood back."

Jordan shook his head in disbelief over his confession of believing in love again and admired his own proclamation of wanting to settle down. Knowing Jackson was the only person who would understand or relate, he knew his outlook would be received. Jordan looked and Jackson and smiled as he mentally gathered his composure to complete his love update. Clearing his throat, he continued, "After a few weeks, we finally crossed over to the inner dimension one night, then she hit me with the whammy. She had me ready to add her to my will! Jack, I was shocked when she left in the morning. Man, I woke up and felt dirty. She left a note, man. She did one of my moves on me with the note and the *'I'll call you.'* I never heard from her since. That was a couple of weeks ago. I was ready to let her in, and she took off on me. Man, I need her to be the first in line at the confessional booth. Jack, I can't even fake it. I thought I might marry her, but she jilted me in my own crib. I love it!"

∽o∾

Jackson grabbed his chest in supreme consternation at the words flowing from Jordan's lips. It was as if Jordan had been lost in the *zone,* and there was a surrogate in his place.

"Wait a minute. You have to slow it down. Watch it or you'll end up falling in love with her for real."

Jordan shook his head and hands as he attempted to reassure Jackson of his decision.

Jordan stretched his hands out to Jackson, pointing out his friend's disbelief. Realizing talking about love exposed his vulnerability, he leaned back in the chair to rethink his perception of love and women.

"See how you treat your best friend. Jackson, please, let me get my head back into the game. I don't want these women to think I've lost my touch. Honestly, I hope she surfaces. Until then, since you're afraid of women, I'll help you out by sending the ones I don't want over here.

Jordan laughed and leaned over as he exerted a sigh of relief. He quickly shifted gears and headed to the next crowd of beautiful welcoming prey. No one could throw on the charm like Jordan. He was always the life of the party. His personality always made the most pessimistic person see optimism by then end of their conversation. He demanded the attention of the female gender and welcomed the first recipient. Within minutes, he had a small crowd up in laughter with women leaning in and whispering privately amongst themselves over his marital status.

Jordan was not the only person perusing genders. This immense hall housed various subsections and groups that often quarantined people unintentionally. It was as if watching the migration of animals on a science channel to see how the people instantaneously formulated their own groups and circles. The matured married men were grouped together, keeping their sights on their wives, while conversing amongst themselves of how they were back in the day. Keeping the conversation mature with underlying tones of suggestion made this group of men isolated from the others as their coded language was kept within the confines of their age range.

On the other side of the room was a cluster of young singles. Jordan, in full swing, was the life of the luncheon, while his loner friend, Jackson, dug in his pocket to retrieve the vibrating phone. Walking over to a somewhat quiet place in the room, Jordan smiled as he joyously greeted his mother.

"Hey there, pretty lady. How are you?"

Esther loved her son dearly and welcomed his loving voice.

"Hello, my son! You know I love hearing your voice. How are things in the bustling metropolis where you are? What's all the noise in the background?"

"I'm at the church, and we're having a luncheon where all the women are serving the men. I've been mentoring some of the young men to help them with some issues they face. How are things with you and Dad?"

"Well, all is well here, but I would like to see you. Do you have any time to come home to the small town-big city where you were raised to visit a little lady? I need you to come home if you can."

Worry filled Jackson's heart and sent panic straight to his nervous system. His mother never inquired of him coming home nor requested for him to come home expeditiously. "Is everything okay there? What's going on? Are you okay? Is it Dad again? Talk to me! You never ask me to come home." Esther heard the fright in her son's voice and reassured him calmly, "Son, don't worry, I would like to have all my children home. I've already spoken to the wonder twins, not sure how that'll turn out, but I would like you all to be here as soon as possible. We only wait until the holidays or other quick weekend trips in order for you all to come home. I would just like to spend some time with my children. I don't want to alarm you, but if you have time, I would like for you to come visit. I know you have your own life down there in Atlanta, but if you can squeeze time in your schedule at some point to make it to New Jersey, I'd appreciate it."

"Ma, you know all you have to do is give the word, and since you've already given the word, I'll be home as soon as possible. I'll call you once I get my flight arrangements made. I love you, are you sure you don't want to talk to me over the phone?"

"Son, take your time. There's nothing to worry about. Plus, you need to talk to Pat, so all of you can be here at the same time. When your schedule allows, just come on home to visit your mother, we'll talk plenty then. Are you sure I'm not imposing on your life?"

"I only have one mother, and she never asks me to come home. At your request, I'll be there as fast as I can. I'll see you soon. Love you!"

"Thank you, my son. I love you too."

Hanging up the phone, Jackson wanted to delve into the recesses of his mind over his mother's request, but he was immediately distracted by a beautiful woman walking clear in his path. Thinking about Jordan's comment to send him the rejects, he decided to laugh and ignore the woman's presence. However, he couldn't help notice the essence of her beauty. She wasn't built like a model nor was she exposing every aspect of her flesh; she was elegant, astoundingly beautiful, and walked with her head held high. Not in an air of arrogance, rather, she exuded confidence.

In awe, he stared at this woman as he noticed there was something different about her. She wasn't mingled into the pack of worshippers. She stood out amongst the crowd like a single dove in a bed crows. She was different. For the first time in months, his spirit quickened within as he clearly heard the voice of God speak, "Receive her. She is the one I have chosen for you. I shall bless you and give you exceeding favor."

There were no bells, no whistles, and no angels playing harps, there was only a peace where he knew his time and season of wait was over. As she neared, his heart pulsated, and for the first time since his teenage years, Jackson was nervous. His palms began to moisten and his throat almost sealed shut. Jackson wanted to prepare for an emotional war, but the peace was so calming that he opted to surrender to the spirit of God. Hailing the white flag in his spirit, Jackson found comfort and all acts of anxiety disappeared as though they never arrived. Before he could muster up the strength to speak, she smiled and addressed him.

"Oh, excuse me please. I need to get these plates from behind you."

Reaching behind Jackson, her long-layered hair draped across her shoulder and her perfume penetrated his nostrils creating a burst of fresh sweetness his senses desired. Grabbing the plates and some other utensils, she smiled, pardoned herself, and turned around. Before she walked away, she looked Jackson square in the eyes and said, "Hope you enjoy the fellowship. Let me know if you need anything." Jackson stood there feeling foolish as he found himself paralyzed in a trance of perplexity. He'd waited to hear God speak after not dating, seeing, kissing, hugging, holding, loving, rubbing, or embracing a woman since he committed himself to God and waiting. Finally, he hears from God, and she addresses him casually as if ignoring him and gives her undivided attention to some plates with a general extension of kindness. Jackson shook his head with his forehead wrinkled and began to speak without thinking.

"Well, as a matter of fact, yes. I do need something. Let me ask you a question."

Turning around toward Jackson and shifting all of her weight to one side, she relaxed the plates and utensils in her arm as if tending a baby. She stood there, smiling within, elated that he wanted to talk, but anticipating his inquisitions with relevance to food. She braced herself for impact, but in her sassiness replied, "Yes? I didn't think you would really ask, but I suppose that's my fault for asking. So how can I help you?"

"Well, you can start by giving me these plates. Someone else will pick them up. Then you can let me know your name."

She tilted her head slightly, looking as if she'd heard it all before. With a slight smirk and curiosity to see how this episode of life would play out, she responded, "Okay, since there's no need for me to let you know we're in church, and since I am serving, sure, why not. My name is Amber. What is your name?" Jackson wanted to jump out of his skin and yell about the revelation he just received from God's divine express. He looked off at Jordan and thought about how he just ridiculed him for falling in love and having a one-night stand; now, he's here trying to converse with his future wife. Life has a funny way of showing you just how much you're not in charge of fate.

Returning to reality, he smiled at the attractive woman standing patiently before him, "Hello, Amber, I'm Jackson, pleasure to meet you. I couldn't help but notice how you walked over here. I thought you were paying attention to me and coming over to see about me, but I have to admit I was a little thrown off when all you came for were the plates."

Amber rolled her eyes and snickered as she realized he was making small talk to lead to a dinner request. Ready to walk away at the first sign of unnecessary dialogue, she paused to hear his response. Still not wanting to assume, she commented on his motives.

"Okay, I see you're like the guy over there trying to run game on all the single fish in the sea."

Jackson knew she was referring to Jordan, but pushed to persuade her he was not operating with a hidden agenda. It was evident Jackson wasn't involved in the dating arena for quite some time. He was like a widowed man getting back into the dating game after being happily married to one woman for over thirty years with no goal in seeking other interest. He couldn't believe it, yet he still stumbled over getting his point across.

"Wait, no, that's not it, okay, that didn't come out right. I was thinking, but wait. Okay, let's start again Amber. What I wanted to say was I noticed how you walked over, and I couldn't help but think that maybe you wanted to talk a little instead of rushing and serving everyone."

"Well, to be honest, the point of me being here is to serve, so if you would like to talk, I guess I have a minute. Okay, you have my attention."

Jackson was relieved at her welcoming demeanor. It helped to take some of the pressure off. Finally returning to his normal cavalier personality, he continued, "To be honest, that's not what I want. So let me just cut to the chase. I believe you're different. There's something about your presence that's intriguing to me. I would like to learn who Amber is and what's in your heart. I think that's why I'm having the teenage, pimple skin, messing up the words thing going on. I don't want to come across as just another brother running game, but I would like to know if you have time to talk outside of church. The only way I can get to know you is to spend time with you. Perhaps I can run into you for lunch or just happen to bump into you at a restaurant for dinner. I don't want you to think I came to church to meet a woman. Even though, I guess that's what I'm doing. Oh, I can't believe this. What's going on with me?"

Laughing within, Amber thought of his nervousness and sincerity of his approach. She gently smiled and responded to Jackson's request.

"I must admit, you are a little different yourself. I mean, you seem to come across a bit sincere. I'm not sure though. You are friends with the deep-sea diver over there, so let me think for a moment." Amber paused briefly. Jackson was ready to interrupt to reassure her again that he was not like Jordan, but before he could interject, she continued, "Well, how about this, we can just happen to run into each other at The Plain tonight. It's poetry and jazz night and I'm reading. Maybe I'll see you in the crowd, and perhaps we can sit and talk. That's only if you just happen to be in the vicinity. If not, then eventually, I'll see you around, if that's God's perfect will. Sound good?"

"I knew you were different. I knew there was something about you. Now I've gone to The Plain before and I've never seen you there, so you know I would enjoy seeing you read tonight. I'll make sure I just happen to be in the crowd. Thanks for letting me know where you will happen to be. I'll see you there. It was nice to meet you, Amber."

"Likewise, Jackson."

Amber began to walk away with a schoolgirl smile on her face as she nodded in salutation to Jordan as he approached Jackson. In the interim, Jackson couldn't believe what just happened. This was definitely a left fielder for him, but he welcomed this new encounter with optimism and expectation. Just when he wanted to remember his thoughts about his mother, Jordan returned gleaming from ear-to-ear.

"My man, Jackson, you know I saw you talking to thickness over there. Now I remember Alexandria was a little thick, but, man, I have to give it you Jack, she's gorgeous. I overlooked her, but, brother, the women are all over me. Listen, I've been invited, I mean, we've been invited to a dinner party at honey's loft. Apparently, she's having a party for one of her artist friends. I'm going, you down?"

"Jordan, I'm going to let you give me the details on this one after it's all over. I'm meeting Amber, not thickness, at The Plain."

"That's my man, finally getting back out there. Man, I should've taken you up to the mountains a long time ago. You're like Moses with the Ten Commandments. You came back with a whole new set of rules. That's my man. I'll call you later. Just in case I need a rescue mission to save me from the women. Who knows, maybe I'll find my future wife. Whoa, I almost got carried away. Later, man."

"Don't hurt 'em, Jordan." Both Jordan and Jackson parted ways. In the meantime, mingled in the crowd, Elias looked around, hoping to see either Taylor or Hannah, but to his surprise, neither was present. Walking past Amber, Elias inquired of Hannah's whereabouts. Amber shrugged her shoulders and mentioned not seeing her since they were preparing the food. Walking off, he dug in his pockets in search of phone to call his lovely fiancée. Finally reaching Hannah on the phone, Elias smiled as he talked to the woman he was preparing to marry.

"Hannah, honey, how are you? How's your day going?"

"Everything is fine with me. How about you?"

"I'm here at the church for the luncheon, I thought you were coming?"

"I was there, but I left because my mother called. I'm waiting for her to get to my house now. Sorry I left early and I'm not there to support you, but my mom needs help today."

"I understand completely, listen, I still want to talk to you about these dreams I've been having for months now."

Wanting to hear what brought such great excitement to Eli, Hannah waited patiently for him to tell of his dream.

"Hannah, God has been letting me see it plain as day. I told you before I've been having dreams about us. Actually, I told you about you having a tribe of my children. I know you brushed it off like I was joking, but, Hannah, I'm serious. I saw us in a park with little ducks swimming on the pond. They were all coming toward us, and when I turned and looked at you, there was a baby in your arms that looked just like you. Then when I looked down, I was holding a baby that looked just like the one you were holding. It was a sunny day and people were walking by us congratulating us and telling us how beautiful the children were. Then, an old woman walked up and told you to tell me all about it, and then, it would come. You dismissed her and we kept walking. Then the ducks went and got back in the water and I woke up. I'm not rushing us to have children because we have to wait to do it the right way, but, honey, I saw us with our family. God is going to bless us, I know it. I've been thinking about this ever since I had the dream. So how are you? I never even asked, I just went straight in. Oh, wait, I did ask, but I can ask again. I'm just excited and I'm telling you, Hannah, this is a sign. I'm not sure about the old lady, but I saw the kids. Twins, Hannah, twins. I hope you're ready."

Elias went on and on, but Hannah sank into her mind, completely ignoring Elias's bantering. His excitement carried away the conversation, so he didn't notice Hannah's silence. Thinking about the pain and of her own nightmares, she was motionless. How could she tell the man who prayed for her and she loved the truth about her barrenness? If he ever found out, he wouldn't want to be with her any longer. Here he is having dreams about children and a family, while her medical diagnosis and re-enacted nightmares proved otherwise. A single tear crawled down her cheek as she loathed over Elias's revelatory experience. Completely removed from their conversation, Hannah abruptly cut Elias off and hung up the phone without the normal prolonged salutation. Before she hung up, she wanted to know if his love would be an undying agape love.

"Elias, would you love me even if we didn't have children? Would you love me if there were more flaws with me than you see? Better yet, how can you have a dream and know that it's what God wants? You want us to get married, and I'm ready to get married today, but can and will you love me regardless of your dream? Hold that thought, that's my mother on the other end, she must be outside. Let me call you back."

Before he could respond, their call was dropped. Elias was standing there gazing at the phone. Dismissing the abruptness of her tone, he optimistically considered her excitement in telling her mother and proceeded to go about conversing amongst the parishioners.

Downtown Reunion

But when completeness comes, what is in part disappears. When I was a child, I talked like a child, I thought like a child, I reasoned like a child. When I became a man, I put the ways of childhood behind me. For now we see only a reflection as in a mirror; then we shall see face to face. Now I know in part; then I shall know fully, even as I am fully known. And now these three remain: faith, hope and love. But the greatest of these is love.

1 Corinthians 13:10–13 (NIV)

For the vision is yet for an appointed time and it hastens to the end [fulfillment]; it will not deceive or disappoint. Though it tarry, wait [earnestly] for it, because it will surely come; it will not be behindhand on its appointed day.

Habakkuk 2:3 (AMP)

With the day turning to night, Jordan was on the east side of town in an art gallery surrounded by young twenty- to thirty-something socialites. The loft was pouring with people of all walks of life from aspiring models, producers, artist, professors, professionals, and authors. The music was perfect, and the champagne was crisp. Enjoying the atmosphere and laughing with people he'd met at various functions, Jordan couldn't help but notice the young woman at the top of the staircase. She stood there more gorgeous than he'd pictured her last. Grabbing an extra drink, he walked over through the crowd to meet her once she touched the last step.

Laughing with her friends, she turned her face forward to see a champagne glass with bubbles rising in her face. Lowering the glass, she couldn't help but notice the debonair man masking his handsome features with chilled champagne. Smiling at one another, the two grabbed hands and exchanged a kiss on the cheek. Excusing herself from her friends, she walked over to a corner of the loft by the window with a view of the Atlanta skyline and sat on the elegant chaise. Jordan postured himself above her and held her hand. Finally having her near, he wanted to make every second last longer than the first.

"I must admit, you look extravagant sitting there. May you indulge me in a personal greeting? I would like to embrace you in my arms again."

She arose, slowly taking in the moment, and embraced Jordan. Once their bodies parted, they gazed into their souls.

"I haven't seen you in a while. How are things going?"

Jordan was shocked that she was so nonchalant about their last acquaintance, but proceeded to follow along before taking the lead.

"I was going to ask you the same thing. I never heard from you. I have to admit, that was a bold move, leaving the way you did."

"I only left that way because it dawned on me how it was the wrong way to go about getting to know you better. I wanted, I mean, want to get to know you, but I jumped in feet first not thinking. I was embarrassed, so I figured I'd do it to you before you did it to me."

"See, I guess that is a misconception women have about men. You classify us as if we're all the same. I assure you I wouldn't have thought nor do I think any less of you. I was just telling my friend about you today. So I'm glad that you're here."

She looked at Jordan quizzically, trying to figure out exactly how much he told his friend. Wondering within, she looked concerned as to what aspect of her personality did he share with his friend. Pushing past this immature thought, she pressed her way forward knowing there was a greater issue pursuing her.

"Well, you say that now, but I'm not sure if you'll say that later."

"Why would you say something like that? I thought we were getting along fine. We saw each other all the time for the most part. Then you jumped ship like I was sinking. I must admit, I was starting to enjoy being around you."

She turned her head and looked down in a state of embarrassment, knowing her confession would more than likely change his temperament.

"Like I said, Jordan, you say that now, but you won't say that when I tell you what I have to say."

Jordan's tone changed. He slowly transitioned from the in-love man to the successful professional acclimated to bearing news of varying aspects. He reached for her hand.

"I'm a grown man, I can take anything."

She turned to look at Jordan and was reminded of what captivated her attention, but prepared for the worst. Releasing a somber sigh, she said, "I'm pregnant, Jordan. Now, do you still want to get to know me better?"

Jordan was relieved. He was mentally prepared for more devastating news. This was much easier to assess than hearing her give a terminal illness report or serving him notice that she's moving out of the country. He visually pictured her eight months and smiled at his vision.

"Let me get this straight, Taylor Woods. I don't want you to ever be confused. I want to get to know you better. You're grown and I'm grown, so that immature teenage fear needs to be called out. Do you anticipate on keeping the child? I know we talked about our views over several conversations, but talking about it and experiencing it are two different things. Why didn't you call me?"

This conversation was overdue, but necessary to proceed in getting to the next level. Taylor fought to put aside her fears and spoke to the man who fathered the child growing in her womb.

"Jordan, being honest, I was afraid. I didn't want you to think I was a stray bullet flying aimlessly, hitting every man in sight. I've never been the sleeping-around type. Then when I found out, I just clammed up. On top of that, you know I have to deal with my family, and I'm not even ready for that challenge. I'm still trying to figure out how to break it to them without breaking their hearts. Besides, it's not like I've known for months, I just found out last week. And I refuse to make a selfish decision when I know I needed to talk to you about it."

Jordan massaged her hand and gently guided her face to look him in the eyes so she wouldn't miss a word he wanted to share. Jordan took the serious road since this conversation was the epitome of a serious situation.

"Well, I enjoyed being with you and around you. Honestly, this isn't exactly the way I hoped we'd get to know each other better. I want to embrace you as a woman, not you as a sexual partner. I'm not a teenager fearful of the onus that is before us. I want you to know that you are in the company of a mature man. Now, I'm not a preacher and I'm definitely not a saint, but since we've jumped into sin, I know enough about God that if we repent he'll forgive us. I hope that God will bless our friendship, our relationship, and our child. As a man with both his parents married, I respect marriage and the covenant between a husband and a wife, but I refuse to subject you and myself to a lifetime commitment for the sake of appeasing others and for appearances. I know how women get with the married thing, and I'm not saying let's go to Vegas, but we have had numerous conversations about marriage and longevity. Now what's going on in your mind?"

Taylor wanted to scream and leap in his arms. Everything they'd discussed and the positive take on life manifested in this moment. All her preconceived notions of his absence and parental negligence disseminated and were replaced with matured masculine acceptance.

"At this point, I need, I want…okay, no. Take a deep breath, Tay," Taylor exhaled deeply to start over in response to Jordan.

"If God approves then, I want to move forward in my life. Hopefully, that movement will have you journeying with me. I know what the shock value effect of finding out I'm pregnant can do to a man. As a woman, I know how I felt when I found out, so as a man and after our last encounter, I can imagine what might be swirling around in your thoughts. So talk to me. Not just about the pregnancy, I mean talk to me."

Jordan was pleased to see their conversation to develop. He was also glad she wanted to hear and listen to his perspective, but he was prepared to tell her the truth, whether she was emotionally prepared or not. He looked off into the lights and turned his head back to Taylor and proceeded.

"You want to know. I'll tell you. Taylor, I was shocked when you left, but since you're here now, I can't focus on the past. You telling me you're pregnant is something that goes along with the territory of adult irresponsibility. Not just on your part, but on my part. As a man, I am responsible professionally and I've grown successful as a result, but taming the flesh is not like investments. There's nothing emotionally attached to work, but with you, I was starting to finally see some light at the end of my tunnel, then you jumped ship on me like I was the *Titanic*. So part of me is wondering if you'd do it again. Honestly, I wanted and still desire having a loving relationship with you. Having a child is the added bonus. Being honest, I would've wanted to date you a little longer and probably get to see you in the morning with funky breath and raccoon eyes, but now, that may be a little different. Since we've already taken the lustful step, how about we revamp this and reconsider a few things. I personally want to get to know the real you, not the churchy Daddy's little girl, always dressed to kill, keeping up appearances for people, and of course your mother's angel version. I want to know the real Taylor Woods, the good, the bad, and the ugly. I want to see that angel your parents see. Well, I think we passed the angelic portion anyway because you are definitely a skilled woman. See, I'm having flashbacks and my flesh is rising. Pray for me."

Jordan took a deep breath as he tried to remain focused on the matter at hand, but thinking of their intimate time together threw his body chemistry and testosterone level into overdrive.

Driving back down to his present reality, Jordan exhaled, "Whew, okay, sorry I'm focused. I want to get a chance to know and fall in love with Taylor Woods. I want to be your friend, your man, your lover, and one day your husband. Now, I've been around the neighborhood, so I know when a woman doesn't want to be bothered. Trust me I'm not fit or putting my heart out there, but we did start this process so that's my position. Now we just have to grow and continue to learn from here. Girl, let me tell you, I told my man I was going to buy a confessional booth and put it at my front door. That's where we need to go right now."

Taylor laughed nervously, but with joy that he didn't want to reject her. She wanted the relationship, but guarded her heart and braced for the impact of his rejection so it wouldn't hurt as badly. During their time apart, she'd rehearsed in her mind numerous times how she would respond if the conversation went in the opposite direction.

"Jordan, I'm not saying this because I'm pregnant. We talked about taking our relationship elevating to a higher level before that night, but I do want you to know I want to be with you. I was starting to love you, like you, and I told my mom about you. I have to ease her in before my father because that's a monster I'm just not ready for. I love my dad, but under the new circumstances, I'm glad I'd already told my mom about you so it's not as bad. If I know her, she told him, but that's for another day. I want to get to know you. I want to get to know you in your action figure underwear and I want to hug you when you feel like you're all alone. I want to be there as your new best friend, if you'll have me."

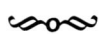

Taylor sat, trying to submit her tears and emotions to her command. Winning the battle over her emotions would take more than a mental antidote for a hormonal pregnant woman. Speaking with maturation and confidence since she too played a significant role in the life growing within her womb, she welcomed his stance on relationship.

Momentarily, she stared off in the distance at the lights of the city to seek peace and silently pray to God for repentance and guidance. Returning from her private altar, she was pleased when Jordan said, "I can tell you're in deep thought about this, so how about we go somewhere, pray, repent, pray, repent some more, and ask God what he wants so we don't mess this up. I might not be a deacon, on the usher board, or a minister, but I have been in church and my mother has preached and rubbed enough oil on my head growing up to last me a lifetime. What I know about God is that's he's loving and forgiving. So we just need to talk with him together. My mother has always been adamant about going to God for major life-altering decisions, so I believe that's what we need to do. Besides, I've learned that the favor and blessings of God are more powerful and sustaining than my hands."

It was as if he was in her private prayer closet. The answer she sought was right before her. With a sense of calm caressing her soul, Taylor replied, "That is why I was starting to love you, Jordan. Now I'm sure that's why. Promise me one thing: let's keep God at the forefront from now on. No more jumping ahead of him. I have a good feeling God's going to lead us in the right direction."

Jordan was overjoyed with Taylor's response and smiled both internally and externally. He reassured her of his position and their new position together.

"I'm a grown man and you're a grown, mature woman, so if this is how we'll grow together, then let's raise our child. Now listen, don't go doing anymore disappearing acts or tricks on me. I need and will be there for every doctor's appointment, kick, turn, and craving. Heck, I'm craving pralines and cream with some warm apple pie and caramel right now. Our son is going to be handsome just like me. Wait a second, let me have a one-on-one with God real quick." Jordan went into Tony Award–winning comedic role within seconds. Between his hands and voice inflections, he fought not to laugh at his own thoughts as he prayed aloud, "Uh,

God, this is Jo, I mean Jordan. Listen I need you to be on my side on this one. You know I had a few run-ins with some fathers in my day. Oh, and I would like to apologize in advance for some of the problems and heartache I may have caused over the years. I hope this makes us good 'cause little girls are…whew… little girls make a man angry. You just want to hurt him because you know what he's thinking. God, seriously between me and Taylor come on, God, you know I'm going toned some military hardware to keep those boys away from my house. I know you're God, so if you decide to bless us with a baby girl, please give me a piece. I mean peace, just in case these boys come knocking on my door. Oh, and keep me out of jail. Amen, hallelujah, glory! It's a boy! In Jesus's name, son of God! Amen!"

Taylor laughed uncontrollably as she envisioned Jordan trying to pull a gun out on some boy for wanting to take their daughter out. Coming out of her laughter, she replied, "You know we can't have any of that."

Jordan looked at Taylor and laughed, "Tay, please, you know I was a piece of work, so I have to make sure God doesn't try to play me for some of the foolishness I did. Girl, I'll have to tell you about this girl's father who pulled out his gun on me. Man, I went Olympic gold that night! Whew! Now that we're going to move forward, don't try that running off thing. I told you I have running-on lock. Girl, I felt naked when you left. Straight role reversal. Seriously, I would never tell you this, but this is me and you, so I'm just going to keep it real. Taylor, you had me feeling like a prostitute taking money out of offering plates, thinking it was payday. Now you see how that doesn't make sense? Neither was the way I felt when you left, so no more of that. I'm putting my foot down. Might be the last time, but I'll always be able to say I did."

The two laughed as Jordan always found a way to make a joke out of a serious situation. Exhaling a sigh of relief between laughs, she looked at Jordan and realized he was as sincere as she'd believed.

"You know what, Jordan, how about we go some place quiet and private and pick up where we left off. Actually, not where we left off, more like, a few days before we left off. If my memory serves me right, you were challenging me to a game of pool. I remember you talking garbage like you could beat me. So instead of us having confessionals, how about we go to your place and get that pool game in so I can shut you down."

Jordan smiled from ear-to-ear as he looked at Taylor and marveled over her beauty. This time, it wasn't the physical beauty, it was that inner glow that made him glad he'd met her when he did. Leaving the loft, Jordan and Taylor journeyed across town and into their future. They opted to ignore the repercussions of their actions, even if for the night, as they agreed to face life's new challenges together. Little did Taylor know Jordan had plans to ensure she'd never leave his side again. He was prepared to add her to his will, along with his child, not out of obligation as the child's father, but out of love as a husband. The decision, however, would be up to Taylor to accept his hand.

Uprooting the Past to Rendezvous with Destiny

The tongue has the power of life and death, and those who love it will eat its fruit. He who finds a wife finds what is good and receives favor from the Lord.

*Proverbs 18: 21–23 (*NIV*)*

Elated to finally have an evening out where the anticipation of meeting someone worthy of company was at hand, both Jackson and Amber were preparing for their date with one goal in mind: have a good time. The emotional baggage they both carried would be put to the test in this one encounter. They both experienced the emotional instability of previous relationships and personal insecurities, yet they found themselves betwixt with decisions. On one hand, destiny gleamed with such illumination that the angelic host hailed this momentous occasion. On the other hand, they had to discern if they were to move forward without doubt and fear from their past or cleave to the familiar pain of previous lovers and miss their God-ordained opportunity.

Jackson showered and groomed himself while wrestling to focus on his evening rather than meditate on Alex. However, he would seldom pause in reflection of her and abruptly thrust himself back into his present state and continue in preparation to meet Amber.

※

While putting on her makeup, she paused momentarily as she looked herself over. She rubbed her hands across her face gently as if appraising her own feminine beauty. Running her fingers through her hair, she moved her head from side to side in a moment of decision making for the perfect style. Pausing, she observed the overall view of her essence. This moment of defining caused her to clearly see dualities. From the side, she was curvaceous and adorned with a figure that numerous women pay surgeons thousands to enhance, yet this side profile also portioned her pain. She saw herself on her side, lying in bed anguished and frustrated. The countless days and lonely nights she stared out her bedroom window with her tears absorbed into her pillow were seeds sown into a hope that one day she'd reap joy. Returning to see her frontal view, she saw a confident woman who knew beyond a shadow of doubt that she wasn't crazy for remaining faithful to God and eventually, like Rachel and Hannah, God would remember her. Exhaling deeply, she continued to prepare for her evening.

∽o∾

Though Amber exuded and noticed her confidence, she too had a past that rendered her great pain and left her riddled with bouts of depression. This coveted woman attained a deeply rooted relationship with God that was put to the test more often than not. Frequently frustrated from the observances of other's relationships, she would find herself warring against despair. However, her faith in God and determination to surpass the pain of her previous experiences ignited a life within. Although sparked with intrigue to overcome, she couldn't help but reflect on the dream she had a few nights prior.

> Surrounded by darkness, she saw herself in her own house. She looked herself over quizzically as she noticed the broom in her hands. She paused, partially choking on the agitated dust floating in the air. Putting her broom to the side, she walked over to her door and left her house, open. She looked around as if in an unfamiliar place; she noticed a bench. Flummoxed over her surroundings, she sat, still and quiet, watching couples and singles roam aimlessly engulfed in their own world of happiness with

Sin caressing their lusts. Amber witnessed others prosper in life and love. She felt anger brewing within as she warranted Sin to sit beside her. If people were able to actively participate in living freely without guilt, then she deserved that same happiness. Almost taken over by the temporal emotion of the moment, she'd almost forgotten her vow to God. Silently weeping, she cupped her head in her hands. Taking up solace in being abandoned and left alone on the outskirts of darkness, she sat weeping while watching others live freely before her. Though Sin lingered in this darkness, it left a temporary opening. Without an invitation, Depression found an opportunity in her soul where Sin left off.

Depression was no stranger and a known visitor to her spirit. She immediately arose from her position in an attempt to escape from Depression. She began walking with haste and eventually running away from Depression. Unfortunately, Depression chased her just as fast, if not faster than Blessings. Though Blessings could easily overpower Depression, her mental and emotional inability to rebuke Depression caused it to appear greater and stronger than Blessings; hence, impeding Blessings' victory in her life. The precious gift of Blessings would forever chase her. Proving strength and ability, Blessings would catapult delicate gifts ahead of her that she may stumble upon them and receive. Unfortunately, Blessings would go unopened as she passed some by while others were caught and carried away by the twins, Doubt and Fear.

The villainous offspring twins of Depression were present to coax her into believing she would never attain Blessings. The evil twins managed to surface whenever Depression was temporarily suppressed. Fortunately, as she continued, there in the distance with a small glimmer of light before her in the midst of the cesspool of darkness, she saw Hope. Taking a second wind, she fled at top speed, yelling out to Hope. Though she felt herself yelling, her screams went unheard, and Hope, too, began running from her. Unwilling to give up, she still managed to chase Hope. As she sought out Hope, Blessings gained strength and chased after her. Every time she appeared to have Hope in her grasp, Hope would continually escape her like a fleeting gust of Wind. This was truly the challenge of her faith. Exhausted from her marathon, she stopped and stood. Panting in desperation to catch her breath, she noticed her present state. The Wind hurled around her violently. Waving her arms in an attempt to quail its disturbance, she found herself fighting against an unknown force. In that moment, she realized she was encircled in the brewing of a vicious storm with the complete inability to grasp it, the Wind.

Wind hurled around her harshly with an arctic chill that cut against her skin with ever-brazing touch. She tried covering every exposed portion of her body as she jilted, jumped, and ducked in different directions, attempting to escape the jagged forces of Wind. Suffocating from the calamity and power of Wind, she began falling to the ground. Fighting to get back to her feet, she escaped and sought shelter. Carried in the powerful arms of Wind, love and relationships, hope and chastity, vows and time, obedience and carnality whirled around her, creating a brutal storm. They whipped around taunting her for she deemed them to be chasing in the Wind. Unable to control it, hold it, see it, direct it, coordinate it, contain it, manipulate it, or convince it, the Wind, like Depression, had no face and no visual direction, only its touch. She knew it was there by the evidence of her battered body and mutilated emotions. Prolonged time didn't help alleviate this forbidden unsolicited feeling. As time progressed, her uninvited guest, Depression, along with the twins Doubt and Fear, would begin to affix themselves to her in a rogue triple-threat attempt to discredit Righteousness. Highlighting what she could see with her carnal eyes and hovering a darkened veil over the light of God's promise, with blurred vision from tear-filled eyes, she battled within as God made her walk down the path of Righteousness. The path was narrow and more tumultuous than her former encounters. This path required that she be held accountable. Sin only lingered, Doubt and Fear robbed her of precious gifts, Depression taunted and hovered, Blessings chased after her, Hope ran and escaped her grasp, Wind violently whirled and beat against her, yet Righteousness was the only one to come and speak to her.

In a soft, still voice, Righteousness said, "Know who you are and who is in you. You have Authority." The voice of Righteousness spoke to her as if asserting all she knew to be true was evident from within the core of her being. Since the voice was so faint, the moment she questioned what she'd heard, Doubt and Fear quickened in her spirit, feeding strength to her nemesis, Depression. With a new door fully opened and the dust unsettled, Depression relentlessly continued to tether the darkened veil before her eyes, generating a dense fog of chaos. Unable to see the path and have a clear sense of direction, she froze in her steps. Unmoving and unclear which way to go, she wept aloud for help. She wiped her eyes profusely in an attempt to attain clarity, but again, Righteousness spoke, and this time, she recognized the voice. Oddly enough, the other tormenting spirits, particularly Depression, never spoke. It was merely there to create a distraction; unfortunately, it had been extremely successful. Although Depression's track record was immense, Righteousness would overpower the fiend in this battle. Batting her eyes but failing to preserve the outpouring of her emotions, she heard the voice of Righteousness speak, "You must sweep the house clean. Use the Authority God has given you. Resist the enemy and he will flee, but you must overpower the adversary with Faith and Trust. Properly replace that which leaves with the power twins Faith and Trust and you will experience God. Serve and surrender, then the one God has shall come, but you must fill the house with the Authority and Righteousness of God." Not waiting for feedback from Amber, Righteousness vanished. She immediately obeyed the call of Righteousness, and suddenly, she could see without delay. She looked herself over and looked about as she wrestled to cleave to the voice of Righteousness. Assuming the archenemies of her soul would leave because of her newfound revelation, she was shocked to see them remain, desperately awaiting the moment she would open the door for their return.

To the external eye, she was put together, but the internal battlefield of her emotions created a mountainous region of turmoil that often hindered her ability to perceive God and receive the promises of God. Likened to the prodigal son, in a moment of coming to herself, she prayed and repented to God with all humility. Drenched in the tears of her emotional pain, she prayed for the strength to move forward with confidence in the only one who never left, abandoned, or emotionally scarred her, God. She asked for a heart to forgive with absolute sincerity for every person from her past she cleaved to as an excuse to harbor resentment and anger. Amber prayed for a sign so obvious that she'd know without hesitation, doubt, or fear it had to be the hand of God answering her silent but humble prayer. Amidst her prayer, she still arose betwixt with grief.

Somewhat sullen from the recollection of her dream, she pressed forward while encouraging herself internally. Determined to live victoriously she ousted depression and began to hum worship melodies that served as an angelic choir elevating her spirit by the minute. Giving no second thought to depression, peace had taken up residence and hope was finally within her reach. In her spirit, she cleaved to both hope and peace as she left her home prepared to face destiny with her soul affixed to destiny. Like Amber, Jackson rallied to journey forward respectively, though there were some strongholds that were up for battle. Only this time, destiny would ultimately set these captives free with Midtown Atlanta being their conjoined destination of independence and victory.

Midtown Atlanta was the place to be if you wanted an evening of sophistication and relaxation. The city offered hidden treasure troves and gems strategically placed to entice every aspect of personal preference. Restaurants' sweet signature scents lured famished people into their doors. Clubs were draped with people awaiting entrance to dance the night away. Couples and small groups of friends gathered throughout the streets gallivanting to their various destinations. The occasional luxury condo resident merely strolled down the street while taking in their residential and high-priced environment. Jackson drove and smiled with anticipation of seeing Amber and patiently looked forward to being an active participant in moving forward in life and love. Driving toward The Plain, he noticed the crowd and searched for a place to park. Jackson pulled his luxury vehicle into the parking lot and walked to the entrance. The sight of couples holding hands while walking, with women gazing intently into the eyes of their companion, heightened his sense of being in good company.

The atmosphere at The Plain was eclectic and vibrant with youthful life and passionate lovers for the arts taking up residence. The moderately large venue was filled to capacity with bodies spilling over into the courtyard. Other onlookers eagerly sought a glimpse of the action in passing. The warm weather encapsulated the evening. The weather was perfect, and the women were dressed in their finest garments. The men paraded confidently with an air of sophistication that caused heads to turn. The melodious sounds filled the air as lips touched wineglasses while voices echoed lyrics to their preferred artist masterpiece. Professional socialites were sprinkled in the crowd along with notable artists adorning the streets of Atlanta for an evening out. If you were a lover of live instrumentation, great food, and superlative ambiance, The Plain was your destination location.

With his expectations high, Jackson entered and immediately enjoyed a melodious evening of jazz, hip-hop, rhythm and blues, and smooth poetry. Jackson stood momentarily and observed his surroundings. There was something quite sensuously aesthetic to the soul with live instrumentation. Various scents from candles created a keen sense of ambiance as Jackson sought and located the prime location to nestle himself with absolute anticipation of seeing Amber. Taking in the rhythmic environment, Jackson felt like a fish out of water. He'd almost forgotten how much he enjoyed mellow evenings out. He hadn't realized how much he'd sheltered himself from society after Alexandria died of cancer. Her death spawned his longing for patience in loving someone. Who knew it would take years for his heart and soul to heal. Happenstance caused the opportunity to present itself, and Jackson looked forward to the journey.

Jackson smiled as Amber took the stage. He sat in the dimly lit corner close to the stage with nothing but candlelight glimmering across his face. Jackson's eyes remained affixed to Amber as her soulful, melodious voice mesmerized the entire club with her poetry in song. Her sultry singing whisked Jackson away into an entranced vision.

Hearing her voice destroyed the fear that wrestled for first place in his spirit. His heart submitted to the groaning within as he envisioned himself soaring to levels beyond his understanding. He looked above as the heavens opened with angels singing, playing, and rejoicing for his time had finally come. In an instant, he saw Alexandria standing with a warm smile on her face as she waved good-bye, pointing for him to look to his future. Turning his head, standing before him with an illuminating light surrounding her was Amber. After waiting patiently, he finally saw the woman he knew would be his wife. Before he'd realized it, he opened his mouth and said faintly, "She's going to be my wife." This one statement after the confirmation to his revelatory experience was entrusted to Jackson, in a vision, in a poetry club after waiting patiently to hear the voice of God. Returning from his trance, Jackson smiled as bright as the sun in the candlelit corner. A single tear swelled in his ducts as he momentarily reflected on seeing Alexandria's face and realizing that he'd received closure on his long-awaited journey.

Jackson thought he was only coming to hear Amber read, but he was astounded when she opened her mouth and sang like an angel from God's personal choir. The melody was as calm as the Caribbean Sea. Bodies swayed rhythmically to the bass cello, muted trumpet, drums, and Fender Rhode quartet that made musical notes take flight and land gently upon eardrums. She stood gracefully with an air of confidence that made the eyes of everyone in The Plain either bow their head in a trance from the music at the sound of her voice or move in closer to their significant other. Either way, the mood was set for lovers and the lyrical poetic prose only enhanced the atmosphere. His heart swelled and peace blanketed his spirit as he closed his eyes and escaped into the soul of her voice. In a low, hypnotic, seductively sensual sound, Amber arrested Jackson and her audience's attention with merely the title of her piece, "Love-In-You."

> No longer limited
> Myopic in view
> I explore…
> Conjuring up belief
> To gain and attain
> That which is intangible,
> Yet has no limitations
> On what it can perceive or receive…
> Your heart—
> There I find, Love-In-You
>
> Nights filled with despair, but my
> Nightmares vanished at your touch

Now, I live and love the dream
A dream that is now my life
And my reality of Love-In-You

You drive me to believe again
Past pain and heartbreak are no longer perceived
I gracefully float on clouds of favor and harmony
Elevating to new heights never imagined
I let you in, limitless and without boundaries
You have caused my fainting heart to believe in Love-In-You

I think you're beautiful
Both internally and externally; simply beautiful
Should we never speak again
Never exchange melodious greetings of salutations
In the warmth of summer breezes
Engulfed in the aromatic fragrance of lavender, magnolia, and juniper trees
Always believe
I perceived
Love-In-You

I want to receive your love
I want to believe in our love
No longer bound enslaved, living in concentration camps
I would be free
Emancipated to creatively enjoy and explore
Love-In-You

Growth-In-Us
Creates trust
Springing forth
Rejuvenating life in my deserted place
I rest in the peace of our hearts
Resounding and beating as one
When I thought love
I vacillated in black and white
When I believed in love
I dreamed in color

When I trusted love
I learned to release without fear or intimidation
And you blessed me with my greatest gift
Love-In-You

Leaning back out of the candlelight, Jackson finally felt tranquility. As she exited the stage, he arose to acknowledge her. With the small crowd of well-wishers greeting her, she smiled to see the friendly face from church that happened upon her location.

"Let me just say you were phenomenal. I am completely taken aback. I would have never known you were such a beautiful poetess and singer. Your voice is soothing. I'm really blown away. I'm sure you're acclimated to receiving accolades for such an astounding gift."

Amber smiled so hard that her eyes almost appeared shut. Amidst a deep blush, she paused as she intently gazed into Jackson's face. Though she observed how handsome he was, she actually had an opportunity to see him in another light. Not wanting to appear dazed, she replied, "Well, let's just say, in order to get to know me, you would have to see beyond what your eyes can see." Jackson, intrigued by such a statement, leaned in to learn more.

"That is rather interesting, what do you mean by that? It's somewhat obvious, but I'm curious to see your perspective."

Amber thought to herself how he deflected the conversation to open the floor for her to speak, but being cautious of saying too much, she opted to keep her response minimal and afford him the opportunity to open up.

"It's obvious that we met at church, but I like to think people solely identify with a persona rather than a person. I can't speak for everyone, but in all honesty, you met me at church, perhaps you envisioned a Holy Roller completely flawless, lacking imperfection. I implore you to take the limits off and see my heart versus a persona."

Fascinated with her statement, Jackson responded, "Persona. People wear veils cascading their true being that will inevitably be revealed at an appointed time. Character in a person is just as pertinent as morale. Some actually demonstrate who they are, holistically. Would it be safe to say I am sitting with your persona, or am I sitting with your person? I am interested in getting to know you as a whole."

Amber smiled and wanted to leap out her skin and shout. After relinquishing her motivation for entertaining every man that approached her or appeared to have an aspect of dignity, she was finally in a position to engage in dialogue with a man. Curious and intrigued by his response, she wanted to know the level of Jackson's intent. The initial conversation was the foundation she used to assess if she'd create an excuse to leave or slam him with a barrage of inquisitions.

Embracing the newness the opportunity afforded but also cautious of moving forward, Amber inhaled deeply. She hadn't postured herself to meet anyone, neither was she incessantly hounding Cupid for love. Her past relationships and the dark cloud of resentment that hovered over her like space were the driving force to keep her focused on career, family, and her personal relationship with God. Her prayer, though simple, embodied a biblical principle she believed God honored, forgiveness and love. The hardest prayer she had to pray was for peace to forgive the men of her past. She also had to learn to accept love, which is and has always been the greatest commandment.

Jackson pondered if his response created tension in their conversation as Amber sat quietly. Regrouping, he countered his own statement to bring Amber back into the conversation and clearly identify his purpose.

"I don't want to be presumptuous, and I don't believe in leaping off skyscrapers, but I recognize that someone has to take a step of faith. I want you to know my intent is sincere. I'm not in a rush or race to the bedroom. Playing mind games isn't my preferred method of attaining companionship. I sincerely think you are an astoundingly beautiful woman, and I know a great thing or woman when I meet one. As a professional, I aim high. I organize and establish relationships that often take time to develop. As a result, I've learned that patience in establishing relationships with my clients has proven quite beneficial. I apply that same approach to my personal life. I'm patient enough to know when to wait, when to pursue, and when to sow or invest wisely into what I know and believe will produce abundantly. I hope I'm not offending you. I almost think this is a bit much, but the bottom line is simple for me. I can't speak for every man out there. However, for me, Jackson, my sole intent is to get to know you, establish a friendship, and humbly follow God's lead and vision for his perfect will to be done. My vision is clear, and I must stay in alignment with God's vision so the promised blessings arise as a result of obedience. Okay, I've said more than enough, and I'm sounding a little churchy, which isn't really my thing. At least, now you know where I'm coming from so you don't misinterpret me as just another brother about frivolous mind games or trying to meet you at church and test you as a Christian. I'm sure there are plenty of people out there for that battle, but it's not my purpose. So now that I've scared you into a state of shock, by all means, let me know your thoughts."

Amber could've slapped him with excitement and leaped into his arms. She almost wanted to scream out, "Finally, God, a man with a heart! I do! I will marry you!" However, he never asked for her hand in marriage, but she saw herself in a couture Amsale gown, standing before God, him, and the preacher. Shifting in her seat, smiling from ear-to-ear, she thought briefly. This man is before her, affirming and clarifying what she'd desired and needed. For a brief moment, she wanted to poke him to make sure he was real, but the music in the background reassured her that she was awake and the man sitting across from her with the flickering candlelight highlighting his masculine features was no hallucination. Her silent prayers and tears guised as seeds in heaven's garden were growing into matured trees bearing great fruit. The sign from God couldn't get any more obvious than this. Amber knew instantly this was the moment God prepared her for.

Without hesitation but a confirming smile to assure him she was pleased, she said, "In the event I never let you know because we get lost in the conversation and time elapse, let me use this moment to thank you for being forthright and honest. I have a greater level of respect for you for exposing yourself. I know men seldom opt to walk in the nakedness of honesty, but I appreciate you and honor you as a man for doing so. Also, thank you for letting me know that you are a man of vision. Without a vision, the people perish, so your submission to God and his vision is worth more than a nation of diamonds and gold. Well, since I know where you're coming from, will you accept this simple response if I said I'm willing to journey forward and stand by your side as we both walk forward and follow God's lead, taking it one day at a time?"

Jackson wanted to take Amber by the hand and physically walk her into her future with him by her side. Instead, he smiled and graciously accepted, "Amber, that sounds like an offer I'm more than willing to accept." Amber and Jackson continued to talk and laugh softly. The music stirred the crowd, and Jackson reached for Amber to dance with him. Accepting this prince's hand, they moved to the dance floor. Lost in the music and melting away the past in her future's embrace, Amber was finally free from the amphibious reptiles of her past.

I Had to Go Through That: Recognizing the Prince from the Frogs

After dealing with so many frogs, toads, bullfrogs, snakes, burrows, and just about every other amphibian, reptile, and mammal, she was equipped and prepared to move forward in her life. Like the clicks of a camera's shutter, so were the reflections of past relational experiences that led her to The Plain. Tunneling in her mind like the speed of light yet slow enough for her to capture, she envisioned her past.

It was as though each man stood before her in a lineup, waiting to be identified as the key suspect. She saw Marc, the promising athlete, with a professional basketball career before him snatched away as a result of his poor decisions, not on the court, but off the court. She recalled the conversation turned argument they had resulting in a devastating reality check of his perception. Amber advised Marc not to go to the park and play basketball with his friends. Marc responded by informing her that his friends were his family and she only wanted him because he was about to sign an NBA contract.

Before turning away, he told her it was over and he never wanted to see her again. With tears streaming from her eyes and pain piercing her heart, he made matters worse by embarrassing her in front of his friends. Though he once regarded her as perfect, she was now deduced to being fat and negative too. Marc even considered her the very least of those worthy of his time. Crushed, she pleaded as he scoffed and never looked back. Neglecting the one person who sincerely cared about him and his well-being, Marc made a decision to walk away from love and follow his friends. Unfortunate for Marc, these same friends' actions would deflate his dreams. After an altercation with a group of guys, shots were fired. Frantic and running from the scene, Marc was pierced in the back by a stray bullet. He was paralyzed from the waist down while his friends walked away unscathed. The fleeting NBA promise and abandonment by his friends left this rising star alone. Crushed beyond belief, he became depressed and addicted to pain medication. With malice in his heart, he cursed Amber for not staying by his side, though he himself chose to walk away. Any way to place blame for his decisions was the road he opted to take. He was bound to a wheelchair; within which he planted the root of scorn.

Next was William, the cheating, sexual manipulator, who too had potential, but never met the mark. He never wanted to overachieve. He seldom applied himself except at things that were of grave interest to him. He was always the victim and blamed everyone for his failures. Taking no accountability for himself, he failed to realize his success factors. He may not have been the best according to societal ratings, but he excelled in women, sex, and financial manipulation. William didn't have a pot to piss in or a window to throw it out, but he knew how to move in with a woman in record time. He identified his strength as a lover and a woman's weakness for being pleased. Appealing to her lustful desires, he lured himself in, and before she could blink, she was fronting the cost to have a warm body in the bed.

Amber, like her predecessor's, became his Chief Financial Officer (CFO). She released her budget to appease him, fronted the cost for everything, invested in pleasing her flesh, but yielded no profit on her investment. Growing frustrated, she prayed and asked God for a sign and a way out of the money pit relationship. Promising God she'd move on and never return if he'd show her a sign. Abruptly, a series of illnesses and deaths occurred in his family, causing him to be gone out of state for several weeks. Unfortunate for his relatives, but fortunate for Amber, her prayer had been answered. Time without him opened her blind eyes.

Using the time apart to sweep her house clean, she learned there were layers of deceit versus dust under her roof. She found receipts for gifts she never received purchased from high-end stores, hotel bills, and baby clothes. Perplexed and distraught, she fell onto her chaise lounge, searching for answers to the obvious. Asking herself questions aloud, she inquired, "Who's Ms. No Name and how long have I financed her lavish lifestyle? I can't believe this man is playing Robin Hood with my money! When did he become a father? Who is she? Are there multiple women? Who is this man?" Exerting a sigh of discontent and smacking herself, she questioned her own ignorance, "How could I not see thousands of dollars gone? How long has *this* been going on? Dag, how could he hide stuff in *my* house? What else is in here?" Enraged, she leapt off the chaise, curious to find more evidence for his permanent departure. Pausing for a moment of celebration, she screamed, "Thank you, Jesus, for opening my eyes!"

As CFO, she financed her lover's affair and never realized what was happening. Unbeknownst to Amber, *she* was playing mistress. For months she poorly assumed she was his sole lover. Though Amber's time away from William was her blessing, the financial shock, mental and emotional anguish derived from humiliation was her curse. But she wasn't alone. Victims of a cheaters lies, neither knew of the other.

William's actions created turbulence with Ms. No Name. His absence and Amber's revelatory enlightenment severed his ability to maintain a monetarily meaningful relationship. She was no longer interested in him. His masculine charisma was not enough to retain her attention. The manipulator was being manipulated by Ms. No Name. Disgusted by his bone-dry funding, their relationship ended faster than it began.

Amber confronted William about the money and the child. He tried every trick in his book, but to no avail. She laid the evidence before him and he turned pale instantly. On trial for his deceptive ways, he refused to concede and pled not guilty on all charges. Frustrated by his negligence, he grew egotistical. In his arrogance he made statements that tattooed to her heart, "I'm proud of you. You won't make the same mistake twice. But rest assured, what *you* won't do, another woman *will*. No one likes to be alone, and some women are more than willing to pay for my time and loving." His arrogance filled the atmosphere and exposed his true character. Convinced it was God, she walked away and never looked back.

After realizing she'd submitted her body, time, heart, and wallet to a man, she vowed to wait faithfully until God sent the one he'd ordained just for her. In a heartfelt prayer, she cried unto God and vowed to save herself until God sent the one who would be her husband. In a faint whisper, she heard God speak, "*Be still and know that I am God. The husband I have chosen shall come. Trust and believe.*" It was a promise that she would hold on to for dear life. She then realized it wasn't her job to find a man and make him her husband. The days of chasing men were over. She recognized she'd reversed the roles and wanted God's order to take control in her life. She knew the Bible said, "He that seeks a wife finds a good thing, and attains favor from the Lord," and she'd considered herself to be a good thing. Unsure of how long she would have to wait, she believed God could do a much better job than she had done for herself.

After nine months of celibacy and waiting, had her time come? Unfortunately, just when she thought it couldn't get any worse, then there was Jake, the six-figure architectural engineer, who considered himself to be the catch of the century. Convinced he was placed on earth to be every woman's dream, his conceit and selfish ways created division before unity was conceptualized. He demanded to be identified as Daddy and wanted constant recognition for his physical attributes. A bored three-year-old with no toys had a longer attention span than Jake. Within a month's time, he began speaking to her as though she were subordinate and unworthy of his time.

Of their many conversations, one echoed in her memory like the reverberating gong of the Liberty Bell. Not wanting to rush a physical connection, she asked him if he'd consider waiting and getting know her. Without hesitation, he proclaimed, "I'm not the type of man to wait. Baby, you have to realize my options are limitless. Why are you acting like a scared teenager? We're adults, so you know how to act like an adult woman. What's the problem?"

Continuing with a hurl of insults for not giving it up and acting like a teenager, he typified this by saying, "The way I see it, you're not an asset, you're a liability. You're costing me valuable time, seeking more of *my* valuable time and for what–friendship? You want friendship, okay, but let's be mature about *this* type of friendship. I don't see where I benefit from your request." Scoffing, he continued, "You don't even make six-figures. You're not financially or intimately on my level. I expect my woman to give me what I need when I need it." Of all the insults, these penetrated her core. In less than one month's time and in one conversation, this man caused her to take an introspective look at her life, and it looked bleak. Though she was confident, for the first time, she'd considered herself unworthy.

The months progressed, transitioning into two years without any prospects. Not one man was willing to see Amber for the woman God ordained and created her to be. Apparently giving your body, heart, and soul were essential and provided no recourse of action for others. Surely, she was foolish for waiting on a magical moment to occur. Feeling foolish about celibacy, she began to choke emotionally. Sitting back and witnessing others prosper in life and love, she'd almost forgotten her vow to God and taken up solace in being abandoned and left alone. Presuming an external defect, she took time to invest in her health and well-being. For ease of mind she attempted to eliminate the possibilities. She began going to doctors, getting blood work, checkups, and dental work to ensure she was medically clear of diseases, flaws, and blemishes. Still, there were no prospective companions. In denial of the obvious, she over analyzed her isolation. Charting and mapping characteristics of each man over her two year journey, she identified the source of her problem. The root cause analysis determined the hindrance was her unwillingness to engage in physical intimacy.

When the time arose and a potential companion surfaced for a date or series of dates, their desires and interest were solely encompassed by sex and temporary fixes. Dates would come and go the moment she mentioned no physical intimacy until marriage. There was Lawrence, the dentist; Daniel, the small-business owner; Jonathan, the journalist; Cedric, the firefighter; and Bradley, the investment banker. Each one bolted for the nearest exit at the mention of no sex until marriage. Amber began feeling that she'd been abandoned, rejected, and ousted by man and God. There were times she would have encouraging moments of strength, but there was a cloud of loneliness hovering over her as if she was destined for darkness and solitude. Feeling marked like the plague, she redirected her focus on healthier living and pouring her life into serving at the church. Alienated in isolation, she shut down emotionally. Batting her eyes, she noticed one more person, her elderly neighbor, and remembered their conversation.

※

At a moment of breaking, she was ready to quit completely, turn away from her vow to God, and revert back to what was familiar—bitterness. On a normal day, checking her mailbox, her elderly neighbor approached her randomly and began talking. Shocked by this impromptu interaction, Amber realized this woman barely gave her nonverbal acknowledgement, let alone her entire life story. For some reason, on this particular day, this woman was open for communication. For a moment, Amber attempted to leave the woman's presence, but the woman's tender hands reached out and held on to Amber as if she were destined to remain. The woman shared how God's timing is perfect and never rushed. She spoke of how vows to God are not to be taken lightly as it was written in the Bible. She warned of remembering what God spoke to her and to not lose sight.

"Young lady, I don't really know you, but I notice everything and I wanted to tell you that you're special. I see that you are always alone, but it won't last much longer. I don't know if you're harboring past pain, but whatever is impeding your progress, get to the root of your heartache and dig it up.

What was, what is, and what shall be are three things that do not operate in the same time and space. Nor shall they be treated as such. Your past grazed the plains of your life's journey by teaching you lessons while molding your thought processes and patterns. You are destined for greatness, yet you hold yourself in contempt of past obstacles and genuine commitment. However, consider greatness is on the horizon and there is no condemnation for your life and sins of your past.

You're riddled with anguish and scarred from situations that were created to protect you. So you tarnish your present with residual garnishing of familiar pain. Why? So you may dominate or have control over fear or pain? Control over what exactly, darkened and distant memories suffocating the very breath from your innermost being? You're overly consumed and neglecting to live in the moment of sustained grace, favor, and truth. Had you been neglected you would've died in that desolate valley of your life, but God didn't allow you to remain there. It was for a season. As with life, that season—as you know it—has passed. You embrace who you were, fear growth in who you've become, doubt who you shall be, and ignore the vital signs of repetitive behavior. Dear, don't dwell in what ceased to exist since what was can no longer *be*. You've learned a thing or two, now live without regret.

The glimmer of hope must remain! Renew oil to your lamp and see the glory of God move powerfully in your life. You have loved and you have cried, yet God has sustained you in both. Your latter days shall be greater than your former days. Believe in the plans of God. You shall receive the favor of God, so believe and trust God's timing. Then you'll experience change."

The elderly woman paused and sighed deeply. Amber was in awe and became emotional. She dropped her head nodding in agreement. This humble gesture let her neighbor know her words had not fallen on deaf ears, so she continued, "You're in this place by God's own design and order. Get your house in order! God will place the blessings in your path. You have to forgive, let go, and move forward. If you've experienced disappointments in the past, don't consider that to be the final outcome of your future. Who are you harboring in your heart that you refuse to forgive? Find out who it is. I bet the answer isn't what you've assumed all this time. When you figure it out, confront the person with a mind expectant of a favorable outcome, release it, and move forward without fear. This time of loneliness was to get your attention. It's to help identify some things in your life so you don't carry that burdened baggage into your promise. Sweetheart, don't be upset by it. Embrace the time and place God has temporarily placed before you. If people would understand and embrace the values ordained by God, the world would be better off. Let me just say this, I'm seventy-seven years old. I've seen and experienced so much over these years. You can take what I say for what it's worth or disregard it all together. Sweetheart, you are a beautiful young lady, you carry yourself very well, and I can tell by your spirit you are truly close to God's own heart. Be a great, faithful wife to God, and he'll bless you with an astounding earthly husband. Sometimes, God just wants your undivided attention. You know, God's jealous like that. He's also close to the brokenhearted, so trust him despite what you can see.

This temporary place you're in is just that, temporary. Sometimes you'll never know God is all you need until God is all you have. Keep moving forward and trust that your steps have already been ordered. The *one* God placed on this earth just for you will see you when you least expect it. When he comes, remember to go through the open door and don't judge that man based on the men of your past.

Have you ever heard of Hannah in the Bible? I love her. You should read about her, she'll surprise you. When you do, remember this one thing—special orders take time. When your order is up, God will bless it and favor it because of your willingness to stand, trust, and obey. I'm even willing to believe that he'll surpass anything you've ever thought or dreamt. Just keep the faith. It's not over. Others may appear to go before you, but you'll surpass them with something greater, an honored vow and favor from God. When God blesses, he likes to show off. Take it from an old woman who knows. Nice talking with you, Dear." Parting ways, Amber captured this conversation in her heart. This was the added strength she needed to move forward.

※

Resonating on the obvious God-ordained conversation with her neighbor, Amber decided it was time to remove excess baggage. In order to move forward with her life, she had to ensure her spiritual and emotional house was in order. The first order of business was to identify the source of the filth that leased out vital space in her heart, spirit, and mind. It was time to serve the invaders overdue eviction notices. Rather than merely kicking out unwanted residents with the possibility of return, she opted to tear down the building blocks of resentment, malice, and rejection and replace them with a garden of clarity, forgiveness, hope, love, and peace. From her mental perspective, this was going to be a wonderful new oasis. Amber knew that creating a beautiful mental landscape required getting interactive. She wrestled to replace fear and doubt with positive thoughts and grand expectations while speaking confident positive expectancy into her future. She thought about how her future would be hindered if she didn't take a stance on relinquishing her past.

It's one thing to think and speak, but taking a step of action changes the outcome of the challenge, and at this juncture in her life, Amber was up for the challenge. Realizing she had nothing to lose and everything to gain, Amber took that ever so apprehensive step that comes across the path of life and began to journey forward. The employees of her mind worked busily as they funneled through rows and rows of archived files, searching the key component of her unresolved hurt and anguish. One stood out among the rest charging from the rear to the forefront with the pertinent news of having found the originating culprit. Blowing the dust from the resource, she reviewed the memory that stood out like an infrared light beaming on the all black target of her darkened spirit—her father.

After not speaking to him for years, she mustered up the nerve and pressed beyond her pride to pay him a visit. She argued within if she should warn him of her coming, but her thoughts of not being received outweighed her motion. Rather, the open road would allow her time to see something different and think. The four-hour drive to her father's Charleston, South Carolina, home would allow her all the time she needed to wrestle through her mountain of questions while encouraging the peace she so desperately sought.

She mentally prepared a speech in her mind. Practicing her questions and potential responses, she delved deeper in thought. Focused on what to say, she envisioned her conversation. Confident in her position she asked, "How could you consider me your daughter when you walked out of my life? Do you know that I've endured several failed relationships? Each one was a direct result of our failed relationship. For one reason or another, each man possessed some characteristic or trait that reminded me of you, yet in their own right drove a wedge in the relationship." She shook her head in disbelief, growing frustrated with her own thoughts. Arguing within, she pondered on placing blame or releasing pain and moving forward. The internal battle created an external outpour of sweat.

Though the time of year identified the season as spring, it was evident this season would take a backseat to the bombarding heat of the summer. The blistering heat of the spring to summer seasonal transition caused sweat to pour off her body though she was in the air-conditioned car. Perhaps the temperature of her mind, which was as high as the thermostat, reading 92° Fahrenheit, added to the additional pressure. After driving through the city, she'd finally arrived, without prior notice, to her father's house. She drove slowly as she observed the fully bricked welcoming-arms stairway surrounded by Spanish moss trees with a gardened pathway of juniper trees. The Spanish moss branches frolicked and swayed gracefully in the fresh breeze. The whirling wind of pollen and budding flowers were inviting as the clear blue sky confirmed no indication of calamity in the atmosphere. Rather, it warranted calm and tranquility as she journeyed to the porch. The four white wicker rocking chairs rested, awaiting someone to take comfort in their arms. After a few deep breaths, she rang the doorbell and was partially astounded at the immediate response.

Looking in the eyes of her paternal reflection, she smiled as she saw herself. He stood there poised with the definition of confidence as he looked at this young, beautiful, and vibrant woman. Returning a smile at the warm and inviting face of this beautiful woman, he peered into her eyes with excitement at seeing the fruit of his seed stand before him. However, his smile turned into sadness as he recalled the last time he saw her face. A wrinkle creased his forehead. Utterly amazed, he stood envisioning the little girl he once twirled in the air with her arms extended laughing joyously, as the man she loved carried her into the wind as if she were weightless. There she stood before him—a woman. His emotions were evident in his face. He stood before the little girl he loved dearly and was ashamed to have never known her as she matured into womanhood. This created a mountain of emotions that melted into a river of tears. Before they could exchange greetings, he willingly released his pride that burdened him for years and beseeched her for forgiveness. This was the moment in life where the rehearsed conversations and overwhelming urge to retain anger over the past vanished into thin air without the possibility of reincarnation. It was as if he anticipated the day where he could release the tsunami of apologies on her. Fortunately for him, time, space, and opportunity literally knocked on his door.

Their relationship had always been unstable even though he was always there financially. Despite his instability and continuous revolving-door relationship with her, she remained in love with the first man she'd ever known to love. They talked of how he was the first to take her on a date to a fine dining restaurant. They discussed how he modeled the behavior of a respectable gentleman. She even reminded him of the day he taught her the waltz in preparation for her wedding day father/ daughter dance. She saw the glimmer in his eyes as his mind returned to that day. He remembered the look on her face as he gazed upon his daughter as she followed his lead.

They talked for hours amid their tears of reflection.

Feeling unresolved and compelled to attain an answer to the one question that haunted her greater than the plague, she inquired, "I know we've talked and ran down memory lane. I'm thankful that we could have this conversation. But I must admit, our relationship placed an immense damper on my personal life with men. I felt so rejected and abandoned by you that I successfully managed to pick every man that would eventually reject me. Of all the men, why you? Why would you reject me?"

Her father almost feared responding, but knew it was her sole intent for coming. Exhaling, he crossed he legs and massaged his hands, "Amber, I left because I had an issue with gambling. You never knew how much pain and torment I put your mother through because she always remained strong despite my addiction. However, like any person with an addiction, I was in over my head and began to spiral out of control faster than I could recover.

I managed to get myself and our marriage into a hole that was immeasurable. I had people following me and making extreme threats to get their money back. It was the day when a bookie told me that he'd kidnap you and sell you to the highest bidder that I knew I had to leave to protect you and your mother. It was a cowardly way to assess the situation, but I didn't know any other viable way to keep you safe while I recovered financially. I thank God, even though some may say I shouldn't include God as my help for getting me out of trouble with my gambling addiction, but I honestly don't know who else to thank. I messed up and it almost cost your life. I couldn't let that happen. In my mind, I wasn't rejecting you; in my mind and heart I was protecting you, from afar. Even after I recovered financially, I was still afraid that someone would retaliate and come after you or your mother, so I convinced myself that it would be best if I stayed away. It's no excuse, but it's the truth. I never meant to reject you or leave you feeling rejected or abandoned. You've always been my most valuable treasure, and it would have killed me to see someone harm you as a result of my foolish addiction. I wish I could've been there all those years, but I would have been more harmful than helpful in your life had I stayed. I know I've asked you repeatedly to forgive me, but I want you to know that I love you and I plead with you to forgive this old man for being a young fool. Can you please forgive me, Amber?"

Tears streamed down her face as she saw the sincerity in his eyes. His soul spoke to her, and she was able to capture truth at the essence of his core. Finally, the truth behind her pain escaped from the mouth of her greatest embedded root. Sniffling and inhaling in an attempt to gain her composure, she replied, "Every nightmare and every bad relationship, I assumed was a reflection of me. I thought that I was being rejected as a form of punishment, but as I think honestly upon some of the men I've encountered, I can see how God was protecting me along the way. Yes, I noticed it before, but it's even clearer now. Coming here today was therapeutic for me. I needed this. You know I never talk much, I think more than anything, but after hearing the truth and knowing within my heart that I have no reason to harbor any form of resentment toward you, I want you to know that I forgive you, and I'm grateful that you're still alive to tell me the truth, ask me for forgiveness, and I am able to relinquish all resentment without the desire of holding on to anything that once was. I love you. You're my dad, I just needed to know and now I can move on and embrace a healthy relationship. The dark cloud that hovered over my heart is no longer present. I am free and I believe it." Her father didn't want to say anything beyond the obvious, for God had answered his prayers. However, he was compelled to thank God. He prayed silently for Amber, "God, thank you for a heart that forgives. I pray she'll never have to walk a mile in my shoes because her own steps will be divinely blessed, ordered, and favored causing her to soar above the pits I stumbled upon. I pray she can surpass any challenge she will ever face. Bless the man that would call her wife. Let him see, know, and value her life. Thank you for everything, God." Getting up from his chair, he reached for his daughter and embraced her while whispering in her ear, "I love you so much. Always have and I always will. Maybe one day, if you let me, I'll be able to have that dance with you." Amber looked up into her father's eyes and said, "There's no time like the present." With a smile on his face and a rhythm in his heart, he asked, "Amber, my beautiful daughter, may I have this dance?"

"Yes, you certainly may," Amber stated with a hint of shyness, but overjoyed that she had the opportunity to dance with her father again. While following his lead, they danced in the spring breeze under God's own light with nature creating a melody that carried them away in time. Exchanging questions with truth and conversing the day away, they both resolved to forfeit what was familiar to them—separation—and embrace the new season of restoration. With that final thought in mind, she glowed radiantly and smiled with the intent to enjoy moving forward into her future.

The Plain

The light and mood in The Plain was calming and soothing. This was the perfect place and moment to establish independence from her past. Swaying effortlessly to the rhythmic sensuousness of the melody, Jackson grabbed her hand and twirled her around. This temporary gesture was as if God was turning her focus and bringing her back to the center so she could look her future in the eyes. Amber was nurtured in the arms of a man that wanted to release her from her past. Smiling and enjoying her time with Jackson only reminded her of how frustrated she once felt. She remembered how aggravated she was and considered herself to be worthless as a result of the men who mishandled her. She reflected on the countless times she watched her friends enjoy dates that turned into long-term relationships, engagements, and even marriages without the consideration of virginity or celibacy until marriage. Enjoying the moment of her present, yet reminiscing on her tribulation, she was finally able to attain closure while trusting God for his timing on the dance floor in an intimate setting. They returned to their table for drinks and more conversation. For a brief moment, Amber wrestled within if she should open up about her celibacy. On one hand, if she spoke to soon, then he'd flee in the darkness of the night. On the other hand, if she held on and their friendship developed into something more, it would be devastating for her to relinquish her feelings. A decision had to be made, and without fear, Amber asked God, "Is my season of waiting over? Is Jackson the one? Lord, if this sign is true and if he's the final chapter, then he'll stay, right? Should I tell him now or wait until later? If I wait and develop feelings, then I'll be right back at square one. Oh, God, can you tell me yes or no, make it just that simple, and I'll tell him now. Please answer this prayer a little quicker than you've answered some of my other prayers. Amen." It was as if God had been waiting to hear from her. Amidst the noise of the venue, a peace came over Amber and an answer in the form of a faint whisper arose, "Yes." Partially shocked at the immediacy of her prayer, she accepted God's decision and posed a few questions.

Transitioning back to her current state, she exhaled and addressed Jackson, "Quite frankly, I respect you as a man, both as a man who has identified God as his head and as a man of vision. I can tell that you are set apart from the wolf pack, and I like that about you. In the event I neglect to thank you for such a wonderful evening, please allow me to thank you in advance. We've laughed and danced and I can honestly say I've enjoyed your company. I gather you're a sincere man, so if you are as sincere as you proclaim and have presented to me as of late, then there are some things that I think we should discuss. You may deem this rather inappropriate, but if I may be selfish for a moment, for my own safety I would feel much better if it is addressed earlier rather than later. This way, we will both have the opportunity to make a sound decision with absolutely no remorse. Since you've opened the door candidly with expressing yourself, I'll follow your lead. I have no problem following a man's lead, based on the situation. Men need to realize women would submit and follow their lead, as wives, if they would surrender to God and follow God's lead and vision. Without a vision, the people perish, hence the reason why marriages don't last, in my opinion. I threw that in there even though it was off the subject, but I felt the need to say that. So I have a few questions if you're prepared to answer them."

Jackson wasn't sure what impact to brace himself for, so he didn't run a list of possible questions. He reminded himself of what he'd heard from God and responded, "I see you aren't shy. I respect a woman who is poised and operates with humility and boldness. Please always talk to me. Tell me what's on your heart and mind. Don't be shy. I can handle anything you throw my way."

"Are you sure? I hope you know that was a rhetorical question. Well, we certainly will find out. Since you say you can handle it, then here it is. I prefer *not* to engage in physical intimacy or sex until marriage. I believe that it should be an intimate moment shared with the man God has ordained to be my husband. Would you, if this were to transition beyond tonight and develop from a friendship into a relationship, be willing to wait until marriage?"

Jackson exhaled and smiled while partially in shock of her question. Though some men would have been turned off immediately, Jackson was more than pleased that he'd met a woman with standards. Even though he left the dating scene after Alexandria, he recalled how women were entirely too easily available. Unlike many men, he was disgusted with women's societal preconceived assumption that the prerequisite for keeping a man and his attention was to submit their bodies within hours or days of meeting. Having women in his life that he sincerely loved and knowing the standard he held himself to, he expected any woman he'd considered to advance in life with to maintain a level of superlative self-worth. This question allowed him to see Amber's value and self-image of herself, and he loved the beauty that emanated from within. Jackson was completely convinced that God confirmed what he'd heard with her question. He smiled and responded, "Amber, I want to get to know you. I respect a woman with standards and I'm willing to grow with you, get to know you, and wait for you. I'm a confident man, and if I may confess, I've been celibate myself, so I'm willing if you're willing."

Amber was overjoyed. She extended her hand as if preparing to shake his hand as a nonverbal contractual agreement. Jackson laughed, pulled her hand from around the table, raised her up, and embraced her. This subtle gesture joined two people who were in wait, but met their destiny in one place. The two talked and laughed the night away as if they'd known each other all their lives. If this was the reward for being patient, Jackson silently thanked God for trusting him to receive his blessing.

This one evening transitioned from weeks into months. With the change of the seasons, so was the growth of their friendship and relationship. It was evident their meeting was divinely ordered by God. The invisible wind carrying their love into the heavenly realm was pure and natural. The time shared between Jackson and Amber was sincere and not rushed. Amber was the first woman Jackson prayed for and with since leaving his mother's house. Not even Alexandria had a committed relationship with God like Amber. Jackson slowly became more and more involved at church, dedicating his time to the various ministries. He even began listening to Elias while paying more attention to the details of his conversation rather than daydreaming while Elias clamored on and on about God and life. Simultaneously, Jackson continued to have dreams and visions of his calling that he privatized. Convinced he was on the right path, but fearful of deceiving himself, he continued to crawl rather than run. Enjoying their personal and spiritual relationship, Jackson and Amber continued to discuss God's word and began to model their lives according to God's road map, the Bible.

When they weren't in church, Jackson would look at Amber in awe, noticing how her natural beauty was reflective of true virtuosity. He would sit and take in her perfume and embrace her for no reason, other than letting her know he enjoyed having her near. There were days when he would look at Amber and sit in wonderment at just how different she was. He loved being in her company and discussing every aspect of life from politics to saving the animals. Their relationship ignited with true friendship. To Jackson, this was what he'd known real love to be. Not wanting to veer off course and head down the road of desire and temptation, Jackson made no effort to advance their relationship in any direction that would yield God's anger.

Amber embraced a love that wanted to be in love with her for who she was. Amber, too, waited patiently for a meaningful bond. She was finally involved with a man whose sole purpose was not rooted in harvesting fleshly desires. Finally, a man that didn't just want sex, want to feed her flesh, or want to lead her into sin and damnation. This wasn't the love that had a hidden agenda or self-seeking. This was that love she'd waited for and expected after all the false, lustful relationships that left her emotionless and void. She too decided to commit her life and ways to God and vowed to wait for the man God ordained and placed on this earth solely for her. She finally learned her love lesson: a temporary fix can lead to a permanent problem, but a patient promise leads to prosperity. Love truly must be patient. Amber knew if God's hand was orchestrating the love, then she'd have nothing more to do than wait and receive with great expectations.

If Jackson or Amber were ever asked did they expect to find true love, they'd probably respond with a cliché explaining what the inquirer wanted to hear. However, God ordained this patient, growing love. As a result, their relationship matured and elevated with increasing revelations that this was meant to be. Jackson knew Amber was the one and his wait had finally been over. Spiritually, financially, and emotionally prepared to journey into his future, he mentally planned the day when he would propose to Amber.

Family Deliverance

He who conceals his sins does not prosper, but whoever confesses and renounces them finds mercy. Blessed is the man who always fears the Lord, *but he who hardens his heart falls into trouble.*

Proverbs 28:13–14 (NIV)

Then Peter came to Jesus and asked, "Lord, how many times shall I forgive my brother when he sins against me? Up to seven times?" Jesus answered, "I tell you, not seven times, but seventy-seven times." Therefore, the kingdom of heaven is like a king who wanted to settle accounts with his servants.

Matthew 18:21–23 (NIV)

When an evil spirit comes out of a man, it goes through arid places seeking rest and does not find it. Then is says, 'I will return to the house I left.' When it arrives, it finds the house unoccupied, swept clean, and put in order. Then it goes and takes with it seven other spirits more wicked than itself, and they go in and live there. And the final condition of that man is worse than the first.

Matthew 12: 43–45 (NIV)

Jackson cleared his schedule in alignment with his siblings and his mother's request was granted. He walked down the tarmac at Newark International Airport with a seemingly calm but rushed pace, knowing if his mother called and said it was important and she needed him to come home, it must truly be urgent. Hailing a cab and giving the driver instructions on the fastest route to get to Manalapan, Jackson refused to entertain the negative thoughts that knocked at the threshold of his mind. The cabdriver glanced in the rearview as he noticed Jackson whispering to himself.

Since the ride would take several minutes, even with the fastest route, the cabdriver spoke to Jackson anyway.

"Young man, listen, I see you're in a bit of a rush, but it's a little obvious something's troubling you. I don't know if you're a God-fearing man, but I'm telling you, your life is about to change for the better. God is amazing. Take it from me. I may not look like much, and there isn't enough time for me to tell you my story. Now, since you have no place to go and we're on a highway, so you can't jump out of the car, let me just say this, after all the hell I've gone through with fighting God and trying to do it all on my own, I've learned that God's will cannot be overthrown. He has a way of getting our attention. He got my attention, and I haven't looked back. Take it from this old man: God is going to do something so great in and through you that you will have no other choice, but to surrender. Once you do, you'll never look back. Don't you just love God?"

The cabdriver didn't mind asking rather thought-provoking questions, particularly since he was in a car driving with his passenger unable to exit the vehicle. This older gentleman deemed the cab ride the perfect place to ask the perfect questions. Albeit, Jackson was thrown off since this cabdriver proved he wouldn't submit to silence. Trying not to appear disturbed by his driver's inquisitions, he replied, "Excuse me, sir, I know cabdrivers are talkative and tend to create conversation with people, but do you always talk to your passengers about God?"

The cabdriver smiled as if he'd just won the lottery. The joy of the Lord and the blessing of surviving life was the fuel used to drive this man's worship. Without hesitation, he exclaimed, "I sure do! I may not have a mega-church, a church, a congregation, or any of the things associated with what you would think a preacher or man of God should have in order to reach God's people, but this little cab, this car you're in right now, is my pulpit, my sanctuary, and the place where God positioned me to reach any person that needs a ride to learn of him. So many people overlook their calling in life because they think they need members and bylaws in order to fulfill God's plan for their lives. Not I, this old man has been around the block, and I know that it doesn't take all of that. At least it doesn't for me. Now some are called to reach the masses, but this disciple for Christ is just an old man in a cab driving down the highway telling one person at a time that Jesus lives and is able to do exceedingly and abundantly above all you could ask or think. Generally, the people who hop in my cab all need a word from God for one reason or another. Some I may see again and they'll remind me of something I said. To be quite honest, half the time, I don't remember because it's not me they're talking to anyway, but I don't need recognition to believe that God uses me to touch people's lives. Like I said, I may not look like much to you, but to God, I'm larger than life. Trust me, young man."

Jackson rubbed his face and stared out the window. He looked quizzically in an attempt to attain some form of understanding in how he was positioned to sit in a cab with the one cab-driving preacher on earth. It would be just his luck to get the one cabdriver that wouldn't stop talking about God. Unable to derive a cumulative answer, he comforted the driver, "Well, Sir, it sounds like you know what you're called to do. That's great." Jackson leaned back in the seat, anticipating this would be the end of their conversation. For a brief moment, he chuckled beneath his breath as he looked at the cabdriver and instantly thought about Elias. Just when he thought Elias was the only man on earth that would go on and on to no end about God, he was sitting in the back of a cab with Elias's competition. He tried not to look at the driver or appear interested, but the cabdriver looked at his comment as an open door for dialogue. The cabdriver was truly a blessing, and Jackson was on the border of missing it because it wasn't wrapped in the familiar or assuming packaging. It was evident God was working things out for Jackson's good while doing a new thing in his life. The professional success and wisdom Jackson attained in the business world created an ignorant man in the realm of understanding God's strategic plan. Unfortunately for Jackson, he was only expecting great revelation to come from greater people. God would use this opportunity to validate how he could use the foolish things to confound the wise. Not easily intimidated and convinced he had to fulfill his mission and purpose, the cabdriver persisted.

"Young man, it sounds like you're hiding from what you're called to do. One thing about God, you can run, but you can't hide. God has a way of presenting it before you when you're unable to hide. Then you'll see and know it was no one but God. Look at the Bible, people tried hiding from God, but he always knew where they were. Even gave them the benefit of the doubt and asked them, like he didn't already know. Ha, God is truly a wonder." As much as Jackson tried to ignore the cabdriver, he was drawn in to respond, "Since you know so much, let me ask you a question, if you call yourself rather than God calling you, isn't it worse than running?" Jackson asked, thinking he would get a clear-cut answer to his undying thirst for clarity. This time, Jackson's eyes were focused on the rearview mirror as he sat anticipating a profound response. The cabdriver was the right person on the job to answer his question.

"Absolutely, the Bible speaks of false prophets and God's judgment will be upon them, but when God truly calls you and God makes your calling evident, there will be no doubt. When God calls you, at the right time, he positions you before man, if that's where you belong. If God positions you, then he'll keep you, but if you call or position yourself, you'll suffocate trying to keep yourself positioned. Just read up on David. Even though he was chosen and anointed, he still had to work in his father's fields tending the sheep, he worked for Saul, he fought Goliath, and served under Saul until the appointed time. Don't wait for man to validate when you should move if you're called, or wait for man to call you in front of the masses. If you do, you'll never fulfill your purpose because you'll deceive yourself of the proper timing. God knows when the time is right. Sometimes, God even uses situations, people, and enemies to drive us into our destiny, even when we think the time isn't right. Have you ever heard someone share their testimony of how God wanted them to help someone or minister to someone at a time when they were struggling or hurting themselves? This is what I'm referring to, young man. If you wait for what you consider the right time, you'll miss the timing of God all together. Follow God's lead, then he'll do just that, lead you in the path that you should go. I don't know why people think they can lead God, this is why Jesus told the disciples to follow him. Son, that's your answer, follow God's lead. Well, as I said, God's plans will not be overthrown. Young man, you'll see and know firsthand, trust this little old man. That certainly was quick. We're here. I guess that was a faster route. I'll have to keep that in mind."

Jackson paused as he ingested the words of wisdom from an old cabdriver that insisted on being a vessel used by God, "Well, thanks for the advice, but I'm not sure if all of that was for me, but I appreciate your opinion and your wisdom."

The cabdriver turned around in his seat and looked into Jackson's spirit, saying, "Young man, I'm always on assignment and I know that word was for you. Do an old man a favor. When you get a little time, do some reading. Go to Hebrews 13:2, and pray on it. I have a big feeling your life is about to change for the better. Oh! Congratulations on the new wife." Jackson sat flummoxed as he gaped at the old man's face, knowing this was something he'd kept very personal. The driver now seized Jackson's attention.

"Sir, what are you talking about? I never told you anything about a wife. You're giving me scriptures, advice, and prophesying. What kind of cabdriver are you? Please don't answer that, it was a rhetorical question." Jackson shook his head, but was in awe at the old man's comments. His thoughts scrambled through his mind, but the revelation of this man's knowledge was precise. Jackson exited the cab, retrieved his bag, and nervously reached in his pocket to hand the cabdriver a fifty-dollar bill. Leaning into the cab, he handed his God-driven driver his fare and said, "Thanks, here you go. Have a nice day." The cabdriver received his fare with a generous tip and bellowed, "Remember, young man, Hebrews 13:2."

Stepping away from the cab and standing on the sidewalk in front of his parents' house, Jackson watched the cab as it drove off into the sun. Before he turned around, he looked up to heaven and said, "God what are you up to? God, first, you had Elias preaching to me about my calling, then Amber comes into my life and you tell me she's the one for me, and now preaching cabdrivers?" Jackson shook his head is wonderment, but he proceeded with observing his present location.

Jackson was right back to his college days of returning home to Manalapan on breaks. The house looked better than he remembered, but he didn't realize just how much he missed home. Before he could bask in the moment, the door flew open and his mother stood there with a smile brighter than the noonday sun, waiting to embrace her son. Jackson rushed without delay at top speed to envelop the woman he'd loved all his life, as though she needed a friendly reminder. Twirling his mother around in the doorway and she squealing like a teenage girl, the two laughed and Esther continually touched him as though she needed to convince herself his presence was not a figment of her imagination. Rushing him into the house, she whisked him away to the kitchen to prepare something for him to eat. This was something Esther had always provided for Jackson because every time he would arrive home, the first thing he would ask was what time were they eating. This time, Esther was prepared for her son's arrival. Sitting down to the island in the kitchen, Jackson smiled in awe at the glow of his mother's excitement. Though she was aging, she was truly aging gracefully. She looked extremely elegant to him for a woman in her sixties. Flirting with his mother, he commented on her beauty.

"Dad is a lucky man, but if I didn't know him or you, I might have to ask you out on a date. You are looking flawless and you still have it like I remember. Ma, do you remember my crazy roommate who kept trying to flirt with you when you came to my school? Then, when his father came in the room and saw you, he tried even harder to ask you out? Man, all my friends would say, 'Your mother is fine.' Even Jordan, with his crazy self, always asked you to drop him the secret formula so he could patent it and get wealthy. You are truly the epitome of exquisiteness, and I'm not just saying that because you're my mother."

Esther stood there, gleaming over her son's compliments and excited he viewed her in such a positive light. Esther enjoyed conversing with Jackson and quickly began probing into his personal life. Looking over her glasses, she handed him a plate with all his favorite culinary treats as she inquired, "So when can I expect to have you make this fine young lady a grandmother again. I love Payton, but I'd like to have a house full of noise again. It gets quiet around here and with your father involved at the church, it's even quieter."

Before he could get a full scoop of food in his mouth, Jackson paused in his tracks to process his mother's request. Jackson looked at his mother with a smirk and laughed as he mustered up the right response to her maternal yearning for a noisy house.

"I've met a young lady whom I've grown quite fond of. Her name is Amber and she is almost as gorgeous as you. I have to honestly say this is the first time in years I've heard God speak so clearly about a woman in my life since Alex. I want you to meet her and tell me what you think."

Esther twirled around the kitchen like a child with Christmas morning glee. Clapping her hands, she raised her arms and began calling on the Lord with thanksgiving, "Thank you, Jesus! Son, I was a little worried. You know after Alexandria passed,

I wasn't sure if you were going to bounce back. You took her death extremely hard and you went so long without having a relationship. So when can I meet her? How soon do you want us to come to Atlanta and visit? Don't worry; I'll make all the arrangements. We are coming to Atlanta."

Jackson couldn't get a word in edgewise. Esther walked around the granite island and continued her bombardment of questions as she processed Jackson's new relationship. Inquisitively, she continued, "Better yet, why didn't she fly here with you? Did you get her a plane ticket? Did you invite her to come? I hope she doesn't think you were being rude. I want to meet her. Get on that phone, get on the Internet, and get her a ticket! I want to meet her today. Make it tomorrow. Just hurry up and get her here. I need to probe her and see what my potential grandchildren are going to look like. I want to see her now! Is she cute? Is she almost as gorgeous as me? What does she do? How old is she? Can she have children? Is she saved, sanctified, and filled with the Holy Ghost? Wait a minute, did you say God spoke to you? What did he say? Was it about her? Jackson, say something! Better yet, what's her number so I can call her and ask myself? You aren't answering any of my questions."

Jackson laughed so hard he began coughing, choking, and crying all at the same time. Esther laughed along with him, but she was serious in her inquisitions. Jackson was her only son, and keeping the family name going was on him. Trying to regain his sanity, Jackson repeatedly cleared his throat, trying to collect his composure. In the interim, Esther looked over his shoulder as his sister entered the room. Screaming at the top of her lungs, Gabrielle ran and jumped on Jackson's back before he could completely turn around. Gabrielle greeted Jackson with a hug and extra punches for not coming around as often.

"Jackie, where have you been? What has taken you so long to get here? Who is she and what does she look like. You're not swimming in back waters, are you?"

Esther, shocked by Gabrielle's question, chimed in to cut her off.

"Brielle, please, your brother is getting married and I'll be a grandmother again. Jack, give me her number, son."

Jackson began choking all over again by his mother's comment. Taken aback, he was shocked at how his comment regarding Amber skyrocketed from having a new friend to going down the aisle with children on the way. Gabrielle and Esther began talking and planning out the description of the young lady who was obviously keeping Jackson's undivided attention. If he managed to stay away from home as long as he did, there had to be a woman involved. Finally clearing his throat, Jackson waved his arms almost in distress and banged on the granite countertop for the two to stop. Laughing only prolonged their lack of silence, but eventually, Jackson was successful.

"Wait a minute, wait a minute, can I please interject. Brielle, I'm not swimming in back waters nor have I ever swam in back waters and *no one* is swimming anywhere near my waters, so you don't have to worry about that. Now let me clear the air so there's no confusion, I am dating a young lady. Her name is Amber, she is gorgeous and I'm falling, okay, I've fallen for her, this is true. She just happens to remind me a lot of Mom. I can honestly say she is just as beautiful both spiritually and naturally. Mom, I wasn't looking for a replica of you, but she's the only one God spoke to me about who just happens to have some of the fine attributes and qualities that remind me of you. For example, both of you are voluptuous, thick, curvy women with beautiful skin and a radiant smile that belongs on billboards across every major interstate in the United States. Look at you, when I see you, I see a bombshell. For you to be in your sixties, you are phenomenally beautiful. When I see her, I envision her growing into a beautiful woman and me coming home to her just like Dad comes home to you." Gabrielle's eyes gaped as she stared at her brother. The sound of him talking about another woman and seeing himself in the future with a woman was unheard of, not even Alexandria received such compliments.

Patricia's timing was impeccable. She walked in the house just as Jackson was preparing to continue his speech. Jackson noticed Gabrielle's excited demeanor and looked at his mother's eyes swelling with tears of love and continued.

"Mom, don't you start crying, I love you. Now we're having a great moment, please don't start crying." Esther fought back the tears of joy, but one escaped her eyes as she made haste to retrieve it. Turning his head, Jackson tried again to address his mother and his sister.

"Before you two finish planning my wedding and naming my unborn children, at least let me make sure she agrees. Gee whiz, you two went in so quickly. Did you plan this? Man, I'm glad Tricia isn't here to chime in because it'll never end."

Patricia chimed in instantly to quail any doubt of her presence. With her aggressive voice, she expelled her knowledge, "See how much you know, I already know all about her. Hello, Jackson, we both live in Atlanta. We just happen to live on opposite sides of the city, so you can't spy on me, even though so many people know us and we end up at several of the same events and venues. Ma, you know I know all about Amber. Let me set the record straight up in here, she doesn't look like you. Don't get me wrong, she an attractive woman, I mean she's very pretty, a little thick, but definitely not you. Now, I will give you credit, Jack, she's definitely a candidate to enter this family, but come on now, comparing her to the queen?"

Patricia turned toward her mother and addressed the latter portion of her statement directly to Esther. "Let's be very clear here, I like her, but you're my mother and she's not you. Besides, Jackson, it's about time because you know people ask me all the time about my fine brother. I have no problem with screening all the undesirables, trust me! Not just anyone can get in this family. We don't have time for letting some ghetto lab rat try to come up in the mix, not in this family. We have standards, right, Ma?"

Patricia immediately changed the mood in the room with her judgmental comments and overpowering statements. Always looking for support from her mother, she resolved to address her rather than Gabrielle. Esther rolled her eyes and peered over her glasses as she responded to her daughter's comments.

"Patricia, that is unnecessary and uncalled for. We have a standard, and that is to love our neighbor as we love ourselves. If this is the woman God has chosen for Jackson, then God's plan and his perfect will is what I want for him and for you. Let go of that judgmental attitude. It's not very attractive. If anyone is ghetto, having a nasty attitude like that is what's ghetto. Don't come in here depressing everyone because you're having issues."

Gabrielle could have leaped out of her skin when her mother spoke up about her sister's malicious attitude. She waved her arms pointing at Patricia as she chimed in on cue, "Ma, I'm so glad you finally said something to Patricia about her spiteful attitude. Thank you, Jesus, finally someone else recognizes that malevolent, hypercritical, mind-set of hers."

Patricia's nostrils flared as the anger within her began brewing and rising faster than good stock. This was round two and Patricia brought the fight to the ring. Before the cling of the first bell, she had her fist up ready to throw the first jab.

"Gabrielle, who are you talking to? Don't get me started about being spiteful after I caught you and Mr. Man making out in front of my daughter. If you want to talk about nasty and ghetto, let's talk about that! And for the record, I don't have any issues."

Jackson began choking all over again and laughing at his sister's refusal of her intervention. The distress over hearing about his little Brielle was a mouthful, but suddenly, he was right back to his college years hearing Gabrielle and Patricia go at it. They were fine up until college, and Jackson never knew what ignited this internal family war between them, but whatever it was, it was enough to cause them to stay away from home for prolonged amounts of time. When the two were in the same house around the holidays, it was like forcing lava to remain in an erupted volcano.

Esther, mentally, spiritually, and emotionally equipped for battle and casting out demonic spirits, was prepared for this moment. Before Patricia could go for the rib cage, Esther stepped in as the ref with an announcement.

"Pat, hush, leave Brielle alone. Before you two get the fists flying in here, let me throw this in, then I want to move on immediately afterward because I don't need questions or worrying. I have you all here and your father is late, so let me clear the air why you are all here. I found out I have breast cancer. Pat and Brielle, I want both of you to go with me to get mammograms and, Jackson, get you a screening from top to bottom. I think your father wants you to go with him to get your prostate checked. He won't go unless you go with him, and I need him to go so we're both not sickly, so those are your instruction. I know you're a grown man and you can make you're your own decisions, but in this case, I'm still mother and I trump your decision. You will go a get a full examination with your father. We will live and not submit our bodies to sickness and disease. An ounce of prevention is worth a pound of cure. Now, since I know my children and I know your thoughts are racing through your minds, I'll reiterate what I said. Don't worry about me. I've already started my healing process, and since God promised me long life and great health, I just wanted to let you know what the doctor's said, but I believe Jesus' report over the doctor's. As of my last visit, heaven is winning the battle. I'm already on the road to recovery, and at the look of things, the cancerous cells are shrinking and disappearing. I'm not going to complain or try to give you some medical explanation. I just believe prayer still works. Whew, my secret is out and I feel much better."

The room fell silent, and every eye sat glued on Esther. Realizing their astonishment, she gave the more subtle version of her intent.

"My beautiful children, let me say this. I was hoping your father would've been here to hear this, but I've been waiting and it's time to address all these issues. He and I are one, so if I know, then he knows. This is the very reason why I asked all of you to come here. I'm tired of the bickering, the secrets, the lies, the division, and I expect everything to be out in the open. The time is over for holding past hurts and secretive skeletons. The devil has no power in this house, and he definitely won't run amuck in my family. Now time and life are short, and I'm not leaving this earth until everything is out in the open. I refuse to find myself in a hospital so you all can argue after I'm gone. I'm not submitting to hospitalization or death, but I'm saying the time for harboring anger and hate is over. I'm alive and kicking and I want it out now! Patricia, I'm starting with you."

Patricia clutched her chest and looked at her siblings, then stared at her mother. She couldn't fathom why her mother chose her to be the center of her discontent. For the first time, Patricia didn't want to be the center of attention, at least not when it came to her mother's stern approach. She threw her hands in the air and slammed her hands down on the granite countertop. Pointing at Gabrielle and convinced she was the least of her mother's concerns, she retorted, "Ma, why do you have to start with me? I'm not the problem, I'm not the confused lesbian causing issues."

Esther didn't flinch at Patricia's physical and verbal response. Rather, she made it abundantly clear of her position and her power. Clearing a space on the counter and exhaling, Esther gave Patricia a stern look with enough potency to warrant a free MRI. Establishing her posture, she rejoindered, "Patricia, I'm still your mother. You are not exempt and don't cut me off again. If you cut me off, you're going to find out whose personality is running through your veins. Don't let my age, these heels, and that cancer announcement deceive you. You might be grown, with your own child, but this is my house and I am your elder. I will not repeat myself. Blink if you understand! Don't speak!" Patricia blinked, acknowledging her mother's demand while Esther continued, "Thank you, now before I was rudely interrupted, I said I was starting with you and that's what I'm doing."

Jackson, Patricia, and Gabrielle looked at each other as though they were teenagers all over again. They all knew when their mother meant business. None of them heard her speak that way in years. Jackson wanted to laugh, but he disguised it with another choking episode. Only this time, his mother's loving attention and smile shifted to level red with Homeland Security a second away from calling. After being married to a marine, they knew her bark and bite had as much power and impact as a nuclear weapon, and none of them wanted it to detonate. Jackson immediately knew it was not the right time to laugh. Esther looked at Jackson over her glasses, and he instantly put his head back into his plate. Gabrielle didn't even bother because she wasn't up for the direct hit. Turning away and focusing on Patricia, Esther continued to explicate her position.

"Patricia, you stand there with a judgmental spirit and enough of the devil's pride to start a new branch of the military. What you need to understand is pride comes before destruction. I don't want you to self-destruct. Apparently, you don't have any real friends because if you did, they would've told you this by now. That's neither here nor there. You owe your sister an apology that would stretch from here to heaven's gates, so apologize to her for disrespecting her, for abusing her love, and for judging her. You have no clue what the truth is, but it's about time you learn."

Patricia found this to be an excuse for her to speak since her mother demanded an apology, but she sneered at her sister and retorted, "I don't owe her anything. It's not my fault she likes women! That's between her and God, so what do you want me to do?"

Patricia's cold-hearted attitude raised the emotional level of Gabrielle, bringing her to tears. Gabrielle's tears began to crash on her chest, and her soul sank like an exhausted, abandoned swimmer stranded in the darkness of the ocean. Esther, noticing Gabrielle's disposition, leaned in to Patricia and lowered her voice with the bass of a man.

"Don't push me. I said apologize to your sister."

Gabrielle, not wanting guised apologies, reprimanded her mother.

"Ma, you don't have to make her apologize, if she does, she'll only do it because you made her, it wouldn't be sincere anyway. I'm tired, I'm about to go."

Jackson chimed in with a preposterous look of confusion on his face.

"Wait a minute! I flew all the way here. What is this about? Gabrielle, you can't leave, you've only been here like an hour. This is ridiculous. What's going on with everyone? First, Ma gives the 'I have cancer, but let's move on' speech, then Tricia brought the pit bull out of Ma, and now Brielle is crying and trying to run out the door. What the heck is going on in here? Somebody say something!"

Patricia pulled up a chair and sat with her arms crossed with enough flames spewing from her aura to cause third-degree internal burns. Gabrielle chimed in to clear the air.

"Jackie, she's talking about why I chose to live a lesbian lifestyle."

Jackson didn't realize how long he'd been away from home. Flabbergasted at his sister's personal lifestyle, he said, "When did you become a lesbian? I always knew you liked men. We used to have our talks and the whole nine, now this." Looking at both of his sisters, he gaped his eyes and gave the marine look his father would give when he demanded an immediate response to a question. Anticipating an answer, he asked, "What? Talk to me! What is going on?"

Gabrielle exhaled and redirected her attention to Patricia. Somewhat frustrated at her brother's ignorance, she walked around the island, isolating herself from her siblings and her mother, yet generating a podium for her encore release. After giving Patricia's feelings no second thought, she fixed your eyes on Patricia and prepared to give Jackson what he asked for.

"Patricia, you're sitting there like you're better than all of us and you judge everyone like the world revolves around you. Well, I'm this way because of you. It's your fault! All these years I've hated you. I've been punished for being your sister, and you parade around like you're completely oblivious to what happened."

Jackson, starving for answers, hammered in for details while chewing his food.

"Brielle, just spit it out! You're being evasive. We'll never get to the root of the problem if you stay on the surface. What happened? I'm not trying to generate any additional heat in here because it's obvious both of you are hot, but we're family. Someone has to let it out. What's going on, Brielle?"

The tension in the kitchen was hotter than the fire needed to melt two tons of gold bullion. Gabrielle, exasperated, walked over and stood before Patricia with antagonism and rage that made Patricia jump back in her seat. Not even Jackson saw Gabrielle that angry. Raising her voice, Gabrielle made her brother and sister know the root of her anguish. Turning to look at both Patricia and Jackson, she elucidated, "I was gang-raped and left for dead by the same guys Patricia went to school with. I went to her school to visit, and instead, I was gang-raped and beaten. They tried to make it look like an accident, but it wasn't an accident. The entire time while Braxton and his friends raped me, they kept repeating Patricia's name. You know who they are, Patricia! Do you remember Braxton and his friends? They raped me because they thought I was you! That's where these scars came from. That's why I can't have children! That's why I don't go to church anymore! That's why I don't pray to God anymore! God allowed me to be raped and scarred for life for being Patricia's identical twin!"

Gabrielle redirected her attention and aggravation to Patricia, "I hate looking like you! I despise being born in the same womb as you! It's because of you and that nasty attitude. You pissed someone off, and now, I've suffered for your actions. There you have it! The cat's out the bag! Oh, and there's more. News flash, everyone, I'm not the only one in here with skeletons and darkness hovering over me. Tricia, you think you're so innocent. You think I don't know your little secret, Pattycake! Ma, I'm not the only one in here with a lesbian experience, isn't that right, Patricia!"

Esther grabbed her chest and looked at Patricia in unequivocal consternation. Jackson sat with his mouth hanging open as the food and saliva oozed from his mouth down the corners of his jaw. This jaw-dropping information was so far left field, not even the angel assigned to keep them from killing each other saw it coming.

Angered from being exposed and more infuriated that Gabrielle knew her secret, Patricia jumped to her feet prepared for battle despite her mother's top-level warning. If her mother thought the shouting was horrendous last time, she should've prepared the neighbors for this championship match. The shouting match began without hesitation, and Patricia came out raging.

"Why don't you shut up? You always have to try to make other people miserable because you're so miserable!"

"Well, Pattycake, if I'm misery, then you must be my company! You walk around here casting judgment on everyone! How about you take a good long look at yourself, Patricia! You swear you're so put together like your shit doesn't stink, please enlighten us on your little nickname and experience, oh, wait your nasty pornographic lesbian experience."

"Shut the hell up, Brielle! You're standing there lying on me to make yourself feel better!"

They bellowed in the presence of their mother, ready to use profanity like they were born on a naval ship. Jackson looked at both his sisters with his head turning as they took turns throwing verbal blows like it was a championship tennis match. The ball never slowed down, rather it sped up with more fire and power behind every hit. Gabrielle had the ball in her court, and just when Patricia thought she couldn't take the hit, she pummeled the ball back over the net.

"Lying! Lying! Did you say that I'm lying? Well, how about I clear my name of being a liar, how about that?"

Patricia didn't want her sister to talk, so she attempted to raise her voice to drown out Gabrielle by yelling, "Shut up, Gabrielle!" to no avail. Gabrielle was no longer intimidated by her sister's demand. Poised like a lion grazing the Serengeti Plains, she was ready to pounce on her sister after watching her gallivant around for years. Her confidence swelled within like the air of a blimp as she took a bold stance against her mirror image. Her fist slammed against the granite countertop with enough force creating a cannonball sound. Esther jumped in her own skin and Jackson sat floored at the impact of Gabrielle's temper. This was the first time they'd witnessed Gabrielle in a position of dominance, and she gave no thought to capitulation. Pointing at Patricia, she demanded all attention, and no one dared utter a sound.

"No, you shut up! Don't you raise your voice to me! I'm tired of you bossing me around. I'm going to say this, and I highly recommend you listen! Say something I don't like, and see if I won't punch you in the throat and make your teeth click! For years, I've been your shadow, your understudy, your irritating little pest that you attempted to lose. You cast judgment on me as though we weren't raised by the same parents, in the same house, nursed on the same breast, and grew in the same womb. How dare you look at me and condemn me to hell when you're Satan's secretary? It's time for you to face the reality you tried to run from! It's time for you to step into the confessional booth of life, but since you refuse to admit you're flawed and you continually walk with the air of deceit, please allow me to say it for you. Here it is! Jackson, Ma, your precious Patricia, the judgmental queen of evil, was in a lesbian relationship with Bobbi when she was in college. Remember how she made everyone think Bobbi was a man, well, let me tell you firsthand, Bobbi, spelled with an *I* not a *Y* is a woman! Pow! Bang! Boom! The cat's out the bag, now chase it down and try to catch it if you can."

Gabrielle paced the floor as if she were a high-powered defense attorney walking in a courtroom before a confused jury awaiting the convicting truth. Confident her case was airtight and not wanting to delay any further, she explicated her case, "Oh, wait, that's right, I'm not done with my case because I'm a liar and I have to clear my name! How do you know this, you ask? I'm glad you're asking me to prove it. Well, let's see, after I was brutally raped and beaten for being Pattycake's twin, Bobbi came to my rescue and called the police, but when she started talking to me, she kept calling me Pattycake. She was crying all over me, telling me how she was sorry that she wasn't there for me and how much she loved me. She said she saw me talking to Braxton at the party. She heard me telling everyone about the rumors of him around campus. She kept calling me Pattycake–repeatedly! Then she started crying all over me, again, kissing me and telling me how it never should've happened. That we should've never argued after having sex that day. I should've stayed with her instead of arguing with her about going to the party. Why are you standing there pretending this isn't real, Patricia? I would rest my case, but there's still more."

Jackson and Esther was the jury, and this jury was convinced without reasonable doubt. There was more to Patricia than any of them cared to know, but this unveiling left them speechless and intrigued. Patricia looked around and sneered at her exposure by way of her twin. She was prepared to respond, but the look on Gabrielle's face coupled with her subsequent comment humbled Patricia like a child wanting a hug.

"Don't you dare cut me off! Now, you're sitting there looking like you want to cry because you're stunned that I know your little secret. Well, you could imagine how shocked I was when Bobbi said it to me. I was weak, but I was wide awake for all of it. I heard every word she said. I even looked twice to make sure I was really talking to a woman! Bobbi was with me in the hospital and gave them all of *your* information, so when the nurse came in and we were in the room, the nurse called me Patricia and I told the nurse, in front of Bobbi, "My name isn't Patricia, it's Gabrielle. Patricia is my twin sister!" You should've seen the look on Bobbi's face! Apparently, no one knew there were two of you. Do you want to know how Bobbi got your cell phone number? It's because I gave it to her! I was the one who gave her your information. Bobbi didn't get it from your job. We still keep in touch. She was there to help me after what happened to me, not you. I was with *your* lesbian lover because she thought you were the one raped. She cried her heart out for you, but it wasn't you, Pattycake, it was me! Well, damn, Patricia! I've never heard you this quiet in twenty-five years! Jackson, have you ever heard her quiet like this?"

Patricia was speechless, and she was not alone. Since Gabrielle had the floor, she decided to go for the win. Gabrielle looked at her sister and spoke to her, "Look at you, Judas Iscariot. Don't worry, I'm should be I'll make you bless me if it's the last thing I do. If Jesus could handle Judas, so can I."

Thinking this would hurt Patricia, it did the opposite. Patricia looked at her sister and retorted, "I'll be your Judas Iscariot if it means bringing you to the cross for God's own glory. I'll be your betrayer, so you can be the raised lamb. Hell, you're already wearing the scars, there's just one more step. Go for it!"

Floored by the harshness of their comments, Esther addressed Gabrielle's comments with undoubting authority, "Gabrielle, my baby, even if you sweep that house out clean, be sure that you let the Holy Spirit back in to replace that evil spirit that you've evicted. You must let God in your heart so he can fill that unoccupied space, or the devil himself will return greater and with more evil spirits than before. This is nothing to toy with. The devil is real, but he has no place in here and in any of my children! Not on my watch! God is real! The Bible is truth! Matthew 12 is what I'm talking about, children. Don't you let that devil come in your house! I refuse to let him in this house! God is the greatest power, He shall not be defeated! I'm talking to both of you! Patricia, look at me, that goes for you too. You must let God enter in and replace that void. Oh, God, I hope you two are listening and receiving what I'm telling you!" Both Gabrielle and Patricia were more concentrated on their anger, though their mother's words touched their hearing. Esther refused to dwell in pleading with her daughters, but in dread of the power behind their words, she paced the room and pleaded the blood of Jesus. She began to pray harder and louder as she called on the name of the Lord. Taking some oil she'd prayed over, she began to sprinkle the oil around the room. Though she prayed and was in the personal presence of God's angels, her children's spirits were still warring. Someone had to ensure the Holy Spirit would come in. Esther dismissed their disdain and continued to call on the power of God.

The spirits and hearts that filled the room plummeted to the floor with no one moving to assist in their elevation. Patricia sat gazing into the pain of her sister's heartfelt words. For the first time, she'd realized just how removed she'd been from her sister's life and the overwhelming pain her sister must have felt. She'd finally realized just how self-centered she'd been all those years. Images and different situations flashed through her mind like a 100-mm camera's clicks between shots. Without hesitation, she tunneled back to the night of the party. She knew exactly who Gabrielle was talking about and who Braxton was. She'd forgotten all about the events of that evening. It had been nine years ago, and college days were far gone. However, there she was, right back in the overcrowded fraternity house with voices muffled speaking indistinctly in the background. Bodies pressing against one another, and there he stood. Surrounded by his friends as an entourage of evil spirits cheering on their main imp, Braxton hovered. She finally saw the anger and rage in his eyes that she ignored that night because her focus wasn't on his personal affect, it was on her elevation to demean anyone who crossed her wrong.

Tears leaped from Patricia's ducts uncontrollably, and she attempted to cup her eyes, but they found release and spilled over her hands. She began to sweat profusely as her entire body shook with fear, anguish, and helplessness. Imagining her sister lying there with the weight of those men pressing against her and holding her down was inconceivable. Imagining her muffled cries forever being erased in the air with no one willing to help her was debilitating. Envisioning Gabrielle's battered and bloody body lying there in a cesspool of masculine body fluids, she wept and wailed aloud in her mother's house. For the first time, she finally saw herself. It was her lying there, taking the brunt of her own negative actions. It was her clenching her muscles as the hands swung and met her flesh. It was Patricia who heard the ringing in her ears as she heard them tell her to shut up. She finally saw her own body lying there as the knife glided across her delicate throat with her blood running to the earth and her body falling faintly to the ground with nothing but the moonlit sky peering and casting a shade around her body. The eye of God watching over her, keeping her from death was there when no one else was. The light that pierced through the darkness and held her limp body, touching her weakened pulse giving it strength, calling to the angelic host to touch the lives of people and have them draw near to tend to this vessel. It was no longer Gabrielle lying there. She finally saw the life she'd lived there under the night sky with the air brushing her skin. She saw beyond what her very eyes could see. She saw death recede into the recesses of the night with the angels singing and praying unto God for another chance. She saw the hand of life touching her soul, reviving her again.

Coming back from the vision of Gabrielle's ordeal because of her own neglect, she looked Gabrielle over. Extending her arm to reach out and touch the bruised body that took on the abuse of men for her sake, she wept. Through her cloudy water-filled eyes, she was able to finally see clearly. She had finally noticed the deep scars on Gabrielle's body. Scars reflective of the brutal lashes that marked the body of Christ. She too was a lamb that took the brunt of sin for the life of another. The longer she peered through the eyes of her twin, she saw the innocent lamb grazing the field and being raised up from the earth into the arms of the Shepherd. Patricia arose and walked over to her sister and fell at her feet weeping. Throbbing in spirit from the pain of crying, she screamed out to God for forgiveness. As her voice rose, willed with the quivering of her words as she beckoned Jesus to forgive her for her sins, she pleaded with God to help her and her sister's pain. Patricia finally encountered a surreal instance of humility. She had a personal humbling experience where her prayer and attitude was not focused on personal gain or the profit of her own life. Rather, she humbled herself unto the God of her mother and grandmother, the God her father chased, the God her sister turned away from, and the God her brother ran from, knowing this same God had the power to accept her flawed and all.

Patricia called for her sister to forgive her and love God, pulling on her body and clasping her hands. Patricia continually apologized. Weeping, Gabrielle fell to the floor and wrapped her arms around her only sister and gazed into the eyes of her own soul, into the mirror image of her face, beyond the years of anguish, past the years of bitterness, beyond the veil of the devil's guise to harbor hatred toward her sister and God. Gabrielle broke through the ceiling of her own pit and cried out to God for his forgiveness and pleaded for her return to his bosom as her sister cleaved to her. It was as though she was the prodigal son returning home after coming to himself. She'd finally come to the vast knowledge that her resentment and actions were rooted in darkness, but because of the light of Christ permeating her heart, she was able to see her way home. Whispering in her sister's ear of her forgiveness and locking their bodies together, the two embraced as they did as children with love generating the rhythm of one heart.

Jackson dropped to his knees, calling on the name of the Lord. He submitted to the power of prayer and acknowledged God's perfect will. He declared healing over his own heart from the pain of Alexandria's death, from the heartache of hearing his mother's declaration of cancer, from the suffering of his sister's pain, and from the years of running in fear of his calling. Praying to God, he refused to run any longer. He denied his own plans and pleaded for the good plans and perfect will of God. Elevating from his private altar, he walked over, raised both Gabrielle and Patricia from their altar on the floor, and embraced his weeping sisters while praying over them. For a brief moment, he saw the face of the cabdriver and laughed within. This was the life-changing moment that would bring this called man of God through the threshold of his destiny. There was no great audience and approval of pastors and ministers prepared to lay claim on the birthing process God established, this was the personal moment where purpose, timing, and God's will concatenated. Jackson entered the holiest of holies and denounced any thought of looking back.

Encapsulated in the moment, he reached for his mother to come into the circle of prayer. Raising his voice with power and authority, he prayed louder for the presence of God to heal their hearts from the brokenness they'd encountered, but more so to deliver them from the bondage of malice, envy, and bitterness.

⁘

Silas returned from taking Payton to the party and walked in the house. Stepping into the kitchen turned sanctuary and bearing witness to the residual effects of God's presence, this disciplined man turned submissive in a matter of seconds. The years of serving God's people and working diligently in the kingdom while praying for his broken family would prove God's promises would manifest in due season. Silas remembered the day he heard God speak to him, and he remembered the day he told his family about the calling on his life. Silas assumed that he'd be postured before a great congregation, but after fifteen years of serving and helping others in the church, he never truly preached before a mass congregation. The years of teaching classes and submissive servitude were preparation for this iconic moment where spiritual wealth, God's timing, and fulfillment would align. Though trained in God's house, he quickly resolved that they years of praying, fasting, believing, and standing firm on the promise of God would occur in his life. In a moment of awe, he realized that his family was his church. They were his congregation and his true ministry. No longer would he pray for his son to accept his calling. No longer would he worry about his daughter returning to God or her sister experiencing humility. He would never doubt the prayers of his wife and her fortitude in standing girded with truth of the very promises of God. The years he invested in witnessing the power of God in the lives of others was upon him in his own home. It took Silas years to realize the essence of God's divine plan, and he welcomed it with an open heart.

Hearing his only son pray aloud to God, the sound of his only daughters wailing in the arms of their prayer warrior brother, and seeing his wife's tear-filled eyes brought this brawny military-defense trained preacher to tears. Trying to mask the emotions that swelled within, he wept as his silent prayers to God were manifested before his very eyes. Praying silently within his spirit, he opened his heart and submitted his flesh to the power and presence of God. This was not the extravagant edifice with chandeliers and clamoring parishioners pressing their way in to be entertained while listening to the preacher. This was the heart of his house and now his sanctuary. It was the one room where they would gather and watch Esther prepare meals, laugh with one another, share stories, and come together and have family Bible discussions with nothing but love swimming in the air. Prayers would be rendered to God for meals, but this time, prayer was coupled with worship, and this heart, this sanctuary, would beat to the power of God's own drum.

To see his family return to this sacred place of unity was a blessing far beyond the worldly success and natural wealth his children attained. This was a lasting and spiritual wealth that beckoned God's holy armament to stand at attention. He could see in the spirit the hand of God hovering over his wayward daughter who returned to Christ. The glory cloud enveloped his judgmental daughter's perception and taught her humility. The heir and seed from his loin who once battled with fear proclaimed authority over his family and his God-ordained calling while his wife's healing was truly established through her soul and her children. This was the wealth he'd asked God for. This was the wealth that many ignore. This was the triumphant moment that helped him to see the profound impact of God's timing and calling him into the ministry when he did. His lesson learned was the timing of God and the perfect plan of God would always come when the heart is ready to receive.

As Jackson ended his prayer for his family, his father, the priest of the house, walked over to the sink and washed. He anointed his head with oil, consecrated himself and his son, and prayed over his family. No one understood those many years ago when Silas shifted from not being eager to serve God to serving God with his life. The years of misunderstanding and assumptions would go down like the Berlin Wall. Though a decade and a half passed, God's manifestation was evident in this moment. Esther's prayers were finally confirmed. There was no doubt that God's calling of her husband and son was intended for a great purpose.

Taking the oil, he anointed them all and prayed for them. For the first time, both father and son were submerged in the oil and presence of God in acquiescence to God's divine order. The linked kinship would be likened to Elijah and Elisha, for the double portion would truly fall upon Jackson.

The Sanctuary

He that has an ear, let him hear.

*Matthew 11:15 (*NIV*)*

The city of Atlanta was peaceful, picturesque, and serene. Buildings embraced their concrete foundations as trees to their roots. Though the pavement endured rigorous abuse from the bustling activity of people and vehicles journeying to various citywide events, calm would eventually console the city for the evening. After a busy Saturday with events for every age group occurring at some venue within the perimeter to have a city engulfed under the umbrella of calm was worth cleaving. Saturday came to an end and would never be experienced again, for it would forever remain a day in the past. With the grace of God at the helm admonishing sovereignty over dominion, God pressed forward, showing mercy upon his land with the dawning of a new day.

The sun arose slowly above the city, warming and strengthening everything it touched. Shadows danced in the rays of the sun as though performing before God himself. The brisk winds chased the gentle cool air as if taking a dominant stance, yet the two conjoined creating a melodious rhythm of gentleness. The coupling of opposite temperatures exemplified a seasonal transition to come. However, on this particular day, the trees embraced their current season and swayed delicately in the gentle breeze that whirled about, kissing its colorful leaves as they gracefully parted from their rooted companion. Falling slowly with poise, the colored leaves frolicked in the cool, crisp fall air. There was a shift in the atmosphere, and nature embraced its transitional process. This natural transmogrification would foreshadow the spiritual affect in the lives of God's people. Residences across the city were consumed with people preparing for their personal worship experience at their respective places of adulation.

Jackson and Patricia both returned to Atlanta after their revelatory experience in their parents' home. On opposite sides of the city, the two would reunite at the one place that would cleanse their hearts, rejuvenate their lulled thirst, and restore their faith—Salvation Church. Patricia walked about her home with an eagerness to receive a word from God through her earthly spiritual leader. Though she prepared for her worship experience in the same manner on numerous occasions, this Sunday would entail a minor shift in the normal routine. On this Sunday, Patricia would be accompanied by a guest that would bring tears to her eyes, yet the sight of her guest coupled joy with anxiety. Doing a final look over in the mirror by the garage door, Patricia took a deep sigh of relief. The exhale of anxiety was replaced with the inhaling of confidence that overshadowed anxiousness. A hue of peace blanketed her spirit. Patricia smiled gently as a solemn tear escaped her tear ducts; only this time, she willingly permitted its liberation without any gesture of capture. Looking down with a sincere loving smile, she rubbed her hand across the face of Payton, extended her hand to feel the warmth of her little hand, and escorted Payton to the car. For the first time in what felt like an eternity, the two would journey together as a family; only this time, there would be no later division. Payton, overjoyed at her mother's touch, smiled and walked to the car. Entering the vehicle, they looked at each other and smiled, silently knowing this would embark the beginning of their new journey together, as mother and daughter.

As they prepared for their commute, Jackson too prepared himself for his worship experience. This time, Jackson would take additional time, making a detour to Buckhead to pick up his parents from their resort-style hotel. Though Jackson welcomed them to stay with him in his loft, his father opted for a weekend of hotel and spa treatments and amenities, and his mother followed suit. However, for a more personal effect, they would later stay with Jackson for the remainder of the week. Driving to pick up his parents, he thought about completely surprising Amber with their presence, but was temporarily sidetracked as he thought to call to his parents to ensure they were ready to be picked up. The morning was bustling with people preparing to encounter God and the transition of life in the midst of other believers.

    Amber, among those preparing, sang softly as she clothed herself. After rubbing herself down as if ironing out the wrinkles, she looked herself over in her mirror and headed for the door. After several weeks of listening to the encouragement of Jackson, she decided to join the Praise Team, so God and the church would hear the gift entrusted in her care. Jackson loved hearing her sing, and rather than hearing her only on a stage in a darkened club, he positively encouraged her to bring her gifts to light. This was also the therapeutic longing of Jackson's to hear Amber. He enjoyed listening to her sing, hum, or do anything that entailed music. To him, her voice was as calming as being in the presence of Jesus. Amber already considered joining the Praise Team, but reserved the thought as she became involved in other ministries. Having the support of a good friend and confidant only ignited the desire that was looming within. Before Amber pulled out of her driveway, her phone rang. Recognizing the ringtone, she answered with a smile on her face, "Good morning, Sunshine Puff." Jackson smiled and chuckled at her personalized nickname for him and responded with enthusiasm, "Hey, Beautiful, I know you're getting ready for church this morning, just wanted to let you know I have a surprise for you after church. Don't panic or worry, it'll be nice." Amber was elated that Jackson planned something special. As their relationship developed, she'd grown acclimated to him taking charge and doing the simplest of things to the greatest of things. The spontaneity of his personality always proved trustworthy, and she learned how to welcome the gestures of his love. However, she was still curious and inquired, "Okay, you know I love surprises, but what do you have up your sleeve this time?" Jackson assured Amber she'd like the surprise, but thought within himself if he should give her an inkling. They discussed his trip to New Jersey and his family matters, so he opted to give her some hint, "Well, this is something we've talked about, but let's just say, we're going to dinner with a few other people you've never met." Amber's mind raced, but she was mentally and emotionally prepared for anything. After moving beyond her past and embracing the blessing in her newfound present while journeying into her future, she remained optimistic, "Not a problem, I'm always ready to meet new people and enjoy new experiences with you. I'll see you in a little while. Be safe." Jackson welcomed her trust in him, "Okay, Hun, be safe too. See you in a bit." By the time Amber and Jackson hung up, her phone rang again, only this time she was greeted by her joyous friend Taylor. The two talked briefly as they both journeyed to Salvation Church. Meanwhile, across town, the church was filling up quickly.

Security directed the traffic that entered the parking lots. Parishioners flooded the streets with their feet creating a rhythmic melody as they journeyed toward the edifice. Families walked away from parked vehicles with Bibles and children in tow. If there was ever an announcement made that bringing your Bible to church would get you one hundred dollars, each member would have entered ready to receive. This was truly a Bible-based church where learning the Word of God was paramount. Before you could put both feet in the door, someone was there to welcome you with open arms.

The hospitality ministry embraced and greeted each person that entered the edifice. Once parishioners entered, they gathered in small groups embracing one another and welcoming fellow members and visitors to Salvation Church. Parents moved quickly to send their children, both adolescents and teens, to their respective ministries. Children and toddlers entered the Little Lambs Children's Department where the décor and atmosphere was formulated to appeal to the attention of children five and under. Everything was geared for their level of understanding and they loved it. They too were able to worship God and have a service that included singing, drama, puppets, coloring, and above all, learning God's word in tiny tot format. Parents signed their children in and received a vibrating pager that would alert them when it was time to pick up their children. While parents assessed their smaller children, Bernie was there for the teens.

Bernie walked through the halls conversing with teens as they prepared to enter the chapel for worship. Bernie waved at Amber as she and Taylor walked together. The two parted ways, and Amber continued to head for the sanctuary. Taylor greeted Bernie as she entered the chapel to help with the youth.

The youth ministry at Salvation Church was the highlight of the week for the youth. The teens and adolescents had their own worship service every Sunday, separate and apart from the adults, where the youth of the church ran the entire worship service. The adult presence was there to supervise and provide spiritual guidance, which was assessed by Bernie and other ministerial staff. All musicians, singers, praise dancers, sign language interpreters, ushers, and everything in between was handled by the youth. It was their worship service, and they praised God with all their might. The youth services filled up the chapel faster every Sunday. It grew just as fast, if not faster than the adult services in the sanctuary. Amid the crowd of people, Bernie noticed one teen that rested deeply in her heart. Eve walked through the crowd and walked directly up to Bernie and gave her a hug. Bernie was glad to see Eve continually return to their worship services. She quickly learned that Eve had a gift to sing that would make the angels in heaven cry and rejoice at the same time. After her initial introduction at the youth retreat, Eve quickly became involved in the church throughout the summer months and continued to melodiously sing with the teen praise team. She developed spiritual brothers and sisters that helped her along her journey.

In every direction, people were walking with their independent destinations in mind. Both young and old were gathered in Salvation Church to enter into worship, and a worship experience was an understatement for what they would encounter. The praise team sang harmoniously resounding as one voice humbly submitting to the presence of God. Without hesitation, Pastor Woods, First Lady Woods, the ministerial staff, and the congregation alike began singing and worshipping God. This was not the congregation that required a drill sergeant to stand before them and expel directives on when to shout, when to praise, or when to stand. This congregation was the stark opposite. They were set ablaze with the power of the Holy Spirit. Any and every attempt to extinguish the worship only ignited the praise-blaze to volcanic pressures. When the people entered into worship, it was sincere and unscripted. They came prepared to come before God, and that is what they did. People could be found shouting, dancing, or at the altar lying prostrate before God. Some would kneel before God wherever they found themselves, some would merely raise their hands with bowed heads and humbled hearts, while others would look toward heaven as if it were personal and let their tears communicate with God as though there were no other people in the sanctuary. However, you deemed your intimate worship unto God, no one looked upon their neighbor with judgment or scorn. The pastor and congregation alike made it abundantly clear that they were in complete submission to God and not man.

Among those in worship was Jackson, standing with his parents. Jackson smiled as he looked across the sanctuary and saw Jordan. Jackson almost didn't want to make eye contact with Jordan because there was bound to be some form of comedic episode. However, Jordan kept his eyes affixed on Jackson until the two managed to attain eye contact. They gave one another the silent grin of salutation. Jordan couldn't resist the temptation to joke around and made it clear he was excited about the dancing and shouting. With subtlety and a mischievous grin, Jordan rubbed his hands together, shrugged his shoulders, and pointed to a beautiful woman immersed in a shout. Jordan smiled at Jackson, like a kid eyeballing a new toy behind glass. As Jackson glanced over at the woman, he instantly reflected on Jordan's story about his personal relationship with God. Jackson motioned for Jordan to pray. Jordan observed Jackson's gesture and looked forward and focused as he looked at Pastor Woods. Jackson knew his comedic friend would be a hard nut to crack. Having him in service was one step, but God would certainly have to take two. After an hour of straight worship with singing and dancing, Pastor Woods arose before his congregants, and they slowly began to sit. Some remained enthralled in worship while others prepared to feast off the Word of God. With the worship transitioning over to sermon, Jordan's behavior caught Patricia's attention.

A few pews over sitting three rows up were Patricia and Payton. Observing the silent conversation from across the sanctuary, Patricia glanced behind her to see what or who had Jordan's attention. After combing through the parishioners, she noticed her parents first then Jackson. Tears filled her eyes because she was unaware that they were in town. Jackson glanced in her direction and smiled as he noticed her emotional state. She smiled at her family and pointed to Payton of their presence. Patricia thought to send Payton to sit with them, but letting go now would lead her back to square one. Patricia opted to keep Payton with her since this would be their first worship experience together in quite some time. Payton squeezed Patricia's hand as if silently affirming that she was happy in her mother's presence. Eventually, the time would come to release her to the Little Lambs, but for now, they remained together.

In the rear of the sanctuary, after years of devout denial of ever returning to God and God's house after her brutal attack, Gabrielle hesitantly entered the worship service. Years of walking, running, and intentionally dismissing God and the church collapsed in her parent's kitchen; however, the remodeling, restoration, and return to Christ would occur at Salvation Church. Even though she had been out of the worship scene for quite some time, she knew enough and learned enough from her parents that there were two things that would always get God's attention, kneeling in prayer with a heart of faith and shouting unto God in absolute humility. Nestled in her seat and hidden amongst those standing, leaping, dancing, singing, and rejoicing, she transitioned her posture and knelt quietly. She exhaled gently with her head bowed. Without uttering a word, tears plummeted from her eyes. Though physically clothed, she was spiritually exposed and naked before God with her heart pulsating at the foot of God's throne. She prayed silently and introduced herself to God as though they were meeting for the first time. Quivering lips and shaken to her core, she prayed as though she resembled the posture of Hannah in the temple in Shiloh. This time, there would be no priest to question her position. This intimate meeting was personal with guarding angels hovering near. Though her lips stopped moving, she remained with her heart open and ready to receive whatever God had to say.

Gabrielle was the last person her family expected to return to church, particularly since she proclaimed she never would. No one knew Gabrielle was in the rear the entire time because she was on her knees praying to God. Because various forms of worship were common at Salvation Church, she went unnoticed. Although she desired to be with her family, she feared that she'd still be rejected. Gabrielle left room for doubt, and Satan suggested that her family wasn't sincere in her parents' house.

Unsure if the deliverance in her parents' kitchen was genuine, she opted to crawl rather than run to her family. She warred over communicating with her mother, who was more receptive and understanding than the rest of her family. The entire time she journeyed to the church, she kept hearing that their sincerity wasn't real. Although when she knelt before God and entered into the Holiest of Holies, Satan himself could not enter. It was in that moment that she'd attained her true deliverance. In the solace of her heart, with no one there to comfort her cries of repentance and forgiveness, Gabrielle knelt before God and arose spiritually restored and prepared to surpass the thoughts of being rejected. Somewhat new and truly considered a babe after she'd operated in her carnality for so long, her first lesson to learn would be that she'd have to bring her flesh under subjection to the spirit of Christ. Though her mind and all that was familiar still entertained debate of contacting her mother, the Holy Spirit interceded with great authority and wouldn't give her peace for entertaining the negative thought. The Holy Spirit comforted her in the spirit where the physical touch was absent in the flesh. It was as if the angelic host continually pressed on her spirit, dissipating the carnal barrier she'd established so she wouldn't deviate off course. While in prayer, she heard no sound except the beating of her heart. Though she knew she had a voice, it was as though it too had been silenced. In a brief moment of intimacy with God, she heard a voice speak so clearly, "I am with you. I will never leave you nor forsake you. You have brought glory to God the Father. Go in peace, for you shall be received." She quivered and wept harder. She cupped her hands over her mouth, attempting to muffle her cries. Shaken to her core, her only response was repeated through her tears, "Thank you, God. Forgive me." There was no sound. Then in the midst of the stillness, God spoke again, "No longer shall you grieve. You have been forgiven." For the first time in years, she'd had a personal encounter with God where she quieted herself to hear God with her whole heart. After not being in an atmosphere of worship in years, though raised in the church, Gabrielle was ready the past pain, and the tearful release was her baptismal pool. She was unequivocally submissive to God and released the hurt and pain she'd festered in her heart. Her quiet, intimate worship with God was thrust into the reality of her present state. The volume that was once nonexistent arose, and the worship and praise pierced Gabrielle's heart like a two-edged sword. She was finally able to release and experience deliverance. After receiving confirmation from God, she called and texted her mother from her seat as she wiped her tear-filled eyes.

∽o∾

Esther didn't recognize Patricia or Payton in the service. After maintaining strict concentration in the service, she was snatched from worship and diverted when she heard her phone. In an attempt to quiet her phone, she immediately sat down. Partially embarrassed that she'd neglected to silence her phone, upon observing the missed call and subsequent text message alert and its sender, she dismissed any acceptance of embarrassment. Esther was lured into the text message and the sender faster than being led to Christ. Although she never gave attention to her phone, particularly during service, she appeared to be deeply distracted by her phone, and it was easily evident. Without delay, she responded to her text and awaited a response. She appeared on edge as if anticipating something catastrophic. Seated between her standing husband and son, she massaged the phone she placed in her Bible on her lap. On any given Sunday, Esther would never even consider looking at her phone during service, let alone holding it; however, this Sunday was different. Immediately, Silas leaned down and asked, "Why are you playing with your phone? You never have your phone out during service. Is everything okay?" Esther gently smiled at Silas, reached for his hand, and rubbed it. In a faint whisper intended for his ears only, she said, "It's about Gabrielle." Assured that his wife would assess the situation her way, he resolved to do what he knew produced results: he prayed to God. In response to his wife, he leaned in closer to her and wrapped his arm around her shoulder and merely said, "I believe God will do exceedingly and abundantly above all we could ask or think." Esther smiled and received the confident message from her husband. Meanwhile her phone, now on vibrate, began massaging her lap. Esther entertained the sender's message, and before long, she was sending text messages and eventually her husband nudged her to focus on the service. Esther looked at her husband over her glasses in a maternal glance of aggression, and he disregarded her focus on the phone and continued to listen attentively to the sermon. Looking back at her phone, she'd finally received the response she'd awaited.

Gabrielle sent her mother a message informing her to turn around to her left. Esther turned and practically leaped out her seat when she saw Gabrielle seated in the rear near the door. Gabrielle sat nursed on the next to last row before the door as if she was planning her amazing escape. Esther grabbed her face with one hand, catching the tears of joy that streamed down, while beating Silas repeatedly on the leg with the other hand. Jackson looked in his mother's face and immediately inquired, "Ma, are you okay? What's going on?" Esther quelled her tears and spoke to both Silas and Jackson, "Gabrielle is here. My baby is here." Silas spotted Gabrielle among the worshipers in seconds and nodded his head with a smile brighter than the sun. Jackson searched and noticed Gabrielle sitting alone in the sanctuary. Without delay, he excused himself as he arose from his seat to go tend to his sister. Jackson's movement caught the attention of Amber. She watched him walk to the rear of the church and embrace an unfamiliar woman. Jackson walked with such a rushed pace it was as though he arrived to Gabrielle with two giant steps. With the swiftness of an eagle and the power of an eagle's talons, he reached out and grabbed Gabrielle by her arms. Jackson held her so tight and so long that she cracked under the strengthened pressure of his grip. With their spirits unified, the presence of God was powerful and evident within their embrace. It was as if God himself enveloped her in his mighty hands. The quiet of the sanctuary made Gabrielle's muffled cries appear more amplified. Esther, hearing her daughter's cry and witnessing her son's gesture of supreme love, dropped her belongings and hurried to meet with her children. Silas made no delay in gathering their belongings and walked to be with his family.

Since they were in the rear, initially, there was minimal attention brought to them. However, with Esther and Silas's abrupt movement from the front to the rear, the amplified cry in the air, and witnessing her parents and siblings huddled crying in a circle, Patricia took notice. Patricia looked over to see her parents and searched the sanctuary to see them cleaving to one another. Without any warning, she dropped her head and cried out loud. She didn't have time to move; it was as if she'd been paralyzed and completely unable to free herself. Payton, with her delicate little hands, reached out to wipe her mother's tears. This simple, silent gesture only heightened Patricia's sensitivity as she broke free from her paralysis while holding on to Payton for dear life. The man sitting next to Patricia held her and Payton as if they were a family unit. His touch alone caused Patricia to further cry out, screaming for forgiveness. She belted out apologies between breaths as she rocked harder, holding on to Payton in the arms of a stranger. The strong, hypercritical woman, never once witnessed by others for such a public display, humbly sat without a care or concern for any man's opinion. The time was over for putting on airs. This moment caused for humility and sincerity of heart. With ruined makeup and bathing in her tears and sweat from such an emotional release, Patricia made her public appeal to God.

Pastor Woods observed the behavior and paused in his message. Sensing a shift in the atmosphere, Pastor Woods looked twice at the woman Jackson was embracing, and then, he looked at the closer pews. Partially unsure if he was seeing clearly, he spoke to the congregation, "Normally, I would never interrupt my sermon, but when you are in submission to God, you must recognize when the power and presence of God is at work. I believe God is speaking to the hearts of his people. Right now, where you are, take a moment to hear the voice of God speak to your heart. Don't ask God for a thing, just thank him for being faithful. Thank him for protecting you from the dangers you didn't know were lurking in darkness. If you experienced some danger, thank God for his infinite wisdom to lead you back to him. Praise God and thank him for his grace and his mercy! After all, you don't like a morsel of the pain you've been through! If you wear a scar from your past, thank God that he healed your wounds! Thank God that you're still warm and not ice-cold in a grave! Thank God for the angels that came to your rescue when you didn't think you would survive! Thank God for making you evidence for the world to see that you are a survivor! Thank God for shielding you! Thank God for loving you! Thank God for leading you! Thank God for forgiving you so you can forgive others! Now that you've thank God, be still and hear what God has to say. Open your hearts and receive him wherever you are."

Pastor Woods paused as he paced the pulpit as if following behind God, catching every word that fell from heaven. As he paced the pulpit, he began to thank God. The more he walked, the more his reflections increased. He was in awe of God's faithfulness and blessings. As a result, the louder he became. The parishioners began praying aloud unto God with triumphant voices of thanksgiving. The house filled with a resounding sound of thanks.

Pastor Woods walked over to Yolanda and whispered in her ear, "God is telling me he's placed a word in you." Without giving his wife any specific directive, he embraced his wife and their physical connection ignited their spiritual connection with such intensity that it was immediately evident they were on one accord. With a brief prayer between him and his wife, Pastor Woods followed God's lead. Pastor Woods handed the portable microphone over to his wife, and she ministered with power, anointing, and authority.

She immediately ministered about sexuality, restoration, and forgiveness. Women throughout the sanctuary without age barriers flooded the altar without instruction. They stood in groups, embracing one another and crying out to God. They embraced one another in prayer and others knelt in prayer. As the women were engaged in intense worship, Yolanda handed her husband the microphone, walked among the women in worship, and began personally praying for them and laying hands upon them. As the women engaged in worship, Pastor Woods addressed the men as heads and leaders of their families and households. Addressing these important details encompassed everyone in the sanctuary.

Pastor Woods then addressed the congregation as a family unit reflecting the whole body of Christ, "Although my sermon was underway, I know when the power and presence of God is at work and I must always take a backseat to God because he is the head over this body. I am convinced that God wants everyone in here to be released and delivered. The best way to go about that is often the hardest road to take. You must put pride, past hurt, anger, resentment, and fear aside and with sincerity of heart, forgive those in your life who wronged you. Sometimes, you can be the very offender, but you've mentally convinced yourself that you were the victim of the offense. However, the Bible is clear in Proverbs when it says, *'Whoever would foster love covers over an offense, but whoever repeats the matter separates close friends.'* Then it says, *'A person's wisdom yields patience, it is to one's glory to overlook an offense.'* We would be remiss if we didn't recognize that forgiveness and reconciliation are intertwined. Forgive and reconcile your differences this day. Don't let the sun go down another day on your anger so that the blessings of God may be released over your life. In order to be forgiven, you must first forgive as God has forgiven you."

Jackson and his family stood and wiped each other's tears as they looked at one another with sheer joy. They each asked the other for forgiveness as they took turns hugging one another. Others around them mocked this modeled behavior. This was the message that the entire congregation needed, and God used this impromptu moment to feed his sheep. Without prolonging the service and attempting to overshadow that power of God, Pastor Woods identified that God's will had already been fulfilled. In a prayer addressed to every person with a heart and ear, he rendered the benediction over his congregants, "*Now unto him who is able to keep you from falling and present you faultless before the presence with exceeding joy. To the only wise God our Savior, be majesty, dominion, and power, both now and forever. Go in peace trusting the Lord knows all things and has gone before you preparing the way. Amen.*"

Upon giving the benediction, some worshippers remained throughout the sanctuary engulfed in their private worship from the service. While others made a valiant effort to adhere to the duty of forgiveness and reconciliation. Pastor Woods's emphasis on the power of being overcome by the word of testimony and how one testimony of your previous experience would be the catalyst to deliver someone else from their affliction resonated on the lips of lingering parishioners. Though formerly dismissed from the service, some remained as they continued to embrace and fellowship. Simultaneously, the youth ministry dismissed from the chapel, and the youth slowly made their way to their various destinations and reconvened with the families. Among those repositioning themselves in the sanctuary were Amber and Jordan.

Amber was unsure if she should walk over to Jackson or wait for him to recognize her talking amongst other parishioners. Before she could give it another thought, Jordan walked over smiling and hugged Amber tightly. As they parted, he looked over her shoulder and noticed Jackson's family standing in the rear. Observing his new facial expression, she turned to see the delight of his attention. Jordan wanted to take Amber over, but paused to think. Before he could delve deep into thought, Amber redirected his focus to reflect upon the service, "Jo, God is the greatest power. I'm so glad to sit under such leadership and anointing. I'm so ready to live, I can honestly say, I've released today."

Jordan smiled, cleared his throat, and responded with his usual comical remarks as if receiving an award, "First, giving honor to God who is the head of my life. I would like to thank the pastor of this fine edifice for taking a backseat to God so we, the children of God, could get some heavenly manna." Before Jordan could continue, Amber laughed aloud, which immediately caught the attention of everyone in their immediate vicinity. Amber, embarrassed but enjoying Jordan's personality, popped him for playing in church and pointed to people still in prayer. She also noticed some of the deacons observing their lighthearted conversation in the midst of people who were still deeply intimate with God. Slouching within herself and pulling for Jordan, her comical partner in Christ, to go out with her to the vestibule, Amber mouthed her apologies to the deacons. The dynamic duo headed toward Jackson and his family while heading toward the atrium. Amber was somewhat relieved that Jordan would be her excuse. For some reason, she was nervous about overstepping, and she'd learned enough lessons about elevating assumptions that she'd opted to let the situation play itself out before leaping off mountaintops.

∽o∾

Meanwhile, as Jordan and Amber proceeded toward Jackson, Patricia was a few pews away and distracted by the gentleman who assisted her in her emotional outbreak. Patricia thanked the kind stranger for letting her wail in his arms. He welcomed her conversation and continued to create small talk. Unfortunately for him, his miniscule window for dialogue would end abruptly at the hand of Payton.

Payton began moving and twisting while trying to get Patricia's attention. Patricia mouthed for her to calm down and stop fidgeting, but she continued and increased in more obvious behavior that she needed Patricia's undivided attention. Between the man's conversation and Payton hopping, doing the bathroom dance, Patricia's attention was extremely short. For a brief moment, Patricia hadn't realized the situation because she'd been removed for quite some time in her parental responsibilities. However, her maternal light illuminated and she realized that it was no longer all about her. There was someone who took precedence and it became increasingly obvious. Payton, no longer able to contain herself, commented aloud, "Mommy, I really have to go. Gammy says I'm not supposed to hold it, and if I do, I have to say something." After a final brief exchange and a rushed apology, Patricia and Payton speedily walked across a pew and down the aisle to the nearest exit in search of a restroom. In her haste to get Payton to the bathroom, Patricia completely missed the opportunity to approach her family. Payton made it evident that she was the priority at that moment, and Patricia, in her new role, fulfilled her responsibility as a mother.

∽○∽

In the interim, Jackson immediately noticed Jordan and Amber smiled from ear-to-ear. Seeing them was certainly the necessary remedy required to lift his spirits and transition the emotional mood to laughter. Jordan and Amber were the two people who could transition and lighten a mood: Jordan, with his lifesaving personality, and Amber, with her radiating optimism. The two never let Jackson down when he needed a pick-me-up. Jackson whispered in Gabrielle's ear and asked if she was all right. She smiled and squeezed her brother, giving him silent confirmation that she was ready to smile after crying. Jackson still warned her about Jordan being a joker, but she was well aware of his colorful personality and welcomed anything Jordan entertained.

Jordan had to be the first one to make it known that he saw Jackson, but also wanted to address his mother before turning comical, "Is that the lovely, vivacious, my other mother, First Lady Esther Wilmington? Let me just say, from your more handsome son that didn't come from your womb, that I love you and I'm so glad to see you. Let me get a good hug before the colonel tries to separate us and keep you to himself." Jordan pushed past Jackson and reached out for Esther.

Esther laughed like a teenager through her tears and wrapped her arms around Jordan as if he were one of her children. Silas laughed, "Only you, Jo. You're the only man on earth that could hug my wife like that in front of me. Come here, son." Jordan and Silas laughed together as they embraced as if biologically connected without reservation.

"Now, Dad, you know a brother is jealous. I don't even need to tell you, but I'll say it anyway, you are a blessed and favored man because you know she's gorgeous. But before you think I moving in on Mom, please let me introduce you to my sister, both in Christ and friendship, Amber. Oh, wait, Jack, you introduce Amber. My bad, Jack."

Jordan stepped back and waved for Jackson to introduce Amber. Esther smiled and exchanged salutations with Amber by shaking her hand. Silas immediately looked at Jackson and smiled bigger than the rings of Saturn. Gabrielle, without hesitation, nudged Jackson so hard that he grunted and jerked as a result of her abrupt contact. Jackson grabbed his side and laughed as he pulled Gabrielle with him while extending his hand to Amber to formally introduce the woman he was prepared to make his wife.

"Mom, Dad, Brielle, I would like to introduce you all to the woman who has filled my heart and reminded me what love is all about. This is my heart, Amber Dawson." Esther's disposition changed instantaneously as she laughed and smiled deeply while disregarding the moisture on her face from her emotional reunion with Gabrielle. She was elated to finally meet the young woman who successfully managed to bring her son out from relationship hibernation. Even though she exchanged a simple handshake when Jordan introduced her, she reached out her arms with love evident in her touch and squeezed Amber tightly. Silas followed up Esther's excitement with a warm fatherly welcome. Jackson smiled, prepared to continue, but an usher approached and asking kindly if they could continue fellowshipping in the annex. The group gladly followed the usher's direction and left the sanctuary. Regrouping with the free and clear ability to laugh aloud and communicate, Jackson exhaled and continued to address Amber. Reaching out for Gabrielle, he reminded her of their previous conversation.

"Amber, I'm sure you were wondering who this beautiful woman was I held on to during the service. I told you I had a surprise and there were some people I wanted you to meet. As you can see with your own eyes, this is my sister Gabrielle, Patricia's identical twin. Of course, you already know Patricia, but this is someone not too many people have ever had the opportunity to meet, especially face-to-face." Amber was amazed, more so to see Patricia's mirror image standing within arms' distance of one another. Not wanting to be crass, Amber reached out for Gabrielle. Gabrielle welcomed the exchange and Jackson continued to lead his family, "Listen, guys, I've already made reservations for lunch. Why don't we head out into our cars and caravan over there to feast. You know how I am about time, so I don't want to be late. It's a new restaurant, Patricia was the one who told me about it, so I know it's going to be phenomenal. Plus, I'm hungry, so we need to head over. I must say this and I don't want anyone to get all emotional again, but I am ecstatic to have all of you in the same place and everyone is in great spirits. This is truly a blessed day. I don't know about you, but I needed that release today. God is truly a restorer, and I just want us to celebrate together as a family. You're my family and I love you all. Only thing is we're missing two."

They all looked about to see if Patricia and Payton were around. Curious of their whereabouts, he inquired, "Has anyone see Tricia? I know I saw her with Payton." Everyone looked around, but no one saw them. Jordan interjected, "Jack, I'm going to pass on lunch this time because I already made plans with Taylor, but I will call you later and see what everyone is doing and I'll come through then. If I see Patricia, I'll let her know the plan." Jordan walked around his extended family and said his good-byes as he walked over toward the chapel. Watching Jordan leave yet still searching for his sister, Jackson continued, "Okay, that's odd. I don't know where she disappeared to. All right, here's what we'll do, I'll call Tricia and let her know where to meet us, this way we'll all be heading in the same direction. Everything will work out and we can sit back, eat, and relax. Is everyone good with that?" His family nodded in agreement and they all headed toward the doors.

Gabrielle almost revved up the tears as they exited, but turned her head away in an attempt to refrain from being exposed again. Fanning to keep her tears at bay, she expressed her heartfelt sentiment. As the words came out of her mouth, she laughed heartily and exhaled deeply, "All I can say is I love you all. I can't wait to tell Patricia when I see her. I sincerely do love my sister. So let's hurry up and find her or call her so she can meet us and we can all be together."

Though Patricia and Payton were detained on the other side of the church, they too would be included so their family would be complete. All of their hearts were spilling over in delight as they journeyed out of Salvation Church and into the sun as a reflection of a new beginning.

The Truth Shall Set You Free

Is any one of you in trouble? He should pray. Is anyone happy? Let him sing songs of praise. Is any one of you sick? He should call the elders of the church to pray over him and anoint him with oil in the name of the Lord. And the prayer offered in faith will make the sick person well; the Lord will raise him up. If he has sinned, he will be forgiven. Therefore confess your sins to each other and pray for each other so that you may be healed. The prayer of a righteous man is powerful and effective.

James 5: 13–16 (NIV)

Taylor arrived at the church's office to begin her day of duties. As the operations manager, she put her parents' Ivy League educational investment to extreme use. Running a church with a growing membership of eight thousand plus members required structure. If anyone was apt for the job, Taylor Woods fit the mold. Walking into the office while singing her favorite gospel song, she was startled when she walked past the empty offices and Elias came around the corner. Exerting a startled yell, she jumped back and grabbed her stomach. Elias was always attentive to Taylor, so he reached out and comforted her frightened nature. Pulling her in, he gave her a hug and inquired of her protective stance for her stomach.

"Now, Tay, you know I come in early, but you on the other hand are a little earlier than usual. I'm impressed, but what's with the covering of your stomach? Usually, people drop what's in their hands. Frightened women cover their chest or grab their face, but you went straight for the stomach."

Elias stood there, awaiting an answer to quiet any rustling thoughts attempting to gather momentum in his mind. Taylor knew she wouldn't be able to easily break free from this conversation and attempted to divert his attention. The only thing she could think of was blame the time of day.

"Elias, you are going in on me already ready. It's too early in the morning for you to lecture me."

Elias looked at Taylor's physique and noticed that she looked more different than normal. Taylor was always very well put together, but her hair was frazzled and the small bottle of mouthwash protruding from her designer handbag was another sign. Elias helped Taylor to the sofa in the lounge and wrapped his arm around the back of the couch, pulling Taylor into his arm. Welcoming a comforting presence, she leaned in. Elias sat quietly for a moment, thinking of how to initiate his inquisition, but he shifted gears when he realized he was talking to his Tay.

"Taylor, no one else is here, and this is me you're talking to. I've been paying attention to you since I've met you, so you know you can't get away with telling me just anything. Talk to me and tell me what's with the covering of your stomach and the mouthwash in your bag. Yeah, I am a man of the cloth, the spirit showed me that mouthwash. Yeah, right. Talk to me."

Taylor looked down at her slumped handbag and noticed she was exposed like a crooked cop caught on tape. Knowing she would have to fess up eventually, Taylor looked down at her stomach, then looked Elias clean in the eyes and told him what he wanted to know.

"Elias, I'm pregnant and I'm having morning sickness, which is an oxymoron because it lasts all day. I'm not sure who the genius was that called it morning sickness, but I can guarantee you, it wasn't a woman. As you may be able to tell, I'm a little far along and the weight from the secret is more of a burden than the weight of my belly. These oversized clothes aren't really working either. I keep making excuses, but it's starting to get obvious. People see, but no one will ask."

Although it was obvious to Elias, he remained stunned that the woman he loved dearly had life growing within her womb.

Excited and partially jealous, he inquired, "Taylor Woods, my love, you're having a baby? When did you start having sex? Never mind, don't answer that. It was seriously a rhetorical question. My love is having a baby. When did you meet this joker? Who is this dude? Where is this dude? Why haven't I met this dude? I'm going to have to repent after I meet this dude!"

The two laughed as Taylor envisioned him choking Jordan. She could tell Elias was joking, but there was a hint of apparent irritation that he was not in the loop of Taylor's extracurricular activities. Trying to reassure him and calm his rising blood pressure, she smiled, saying, "Will you calm down? You're silly! He's great man. We have fun, and he's been around, you just didn't notice. See and I thought you paid attention to everything I do. Humph, apparently not. You know him, you probably know him better than I do. We've been dating for several months, but this pregnancy wasn't planned, that's for sure. Wait a minute, did you say, '*my love*?' Hannah is your love. After that night in Florida, oh, you do remember helping me to the bed, don't you? Wait, did you ask me when did I start having sex? Eli, do we need to go back to Florida?"

The two sank back in the couch and stared up at the ceiling. Unbeknownst to them, they weren't the only ones in the office. Pastor Woods was in his study with the surveillance system on, listening the entire time. Not wanting to rush and jump the gun, he wanted to let the natural order of things play out so he would compare it to the version told to him. Turning his head to observe the other monitor, he noticed Hannah walking down the hallway as well.

Hannah was troubled in her spirit and kept trying to figure out a way to talk to Elias. Every opportunity that arose for her to confess her barrenness and troubled past to him, she either froze or they were interrupted. Since she woke up in another cold sweat from another nightmare experience, she chose to rise above her fears and tell the man she loved most, next to God, that she had a secret. Her mind raced about his dream and vision of them having a family, but she fought herself not to cry. Walking and encouraging herself, she approached the door only to notice Taylor and Elias sitting on the couch in a comforting position with their backs turned to the door. Hannah lost the battle over her tears, but stood there silently, attentive to their conversation. Meanwhile, Elias reflected on that night in Florida and an immense smile leaped across his face. Trying to retain his focus through his joy, he shook his head in response.

"Taylor-Tay, don't go there right now. I'm trying to stay focused. I'm in a state of shock. Don't get me wrong I'm happy, but I'm just in a little shock right now. I was there and so were you, but I wasn't there…the night…you…man, Taylor, Florida. Whew, do I remember Florida! Taylor, you know I'm in love with my Little Miss Rudy. Now my LMR is having a baby, so what are we going to do?"

Hannah stood there, with the devil trying to sit on her shoulder and lead her down the path of evil thoughts. Was Elias having an affair with Taylor? Hannah thought of all the times people would comment about their close relationship, but she always dismissed the gossip because she had faith in her relationship and Elias's faithfulness. Thinking in depth, she pondered over Florida. What did he mean by Florida? How could they have had an affair without her realizing it sooner? Did he say baby? Was she having his child? The one thing she came prepared to confess is the one thing she overheard Elias speaking of with a woman she was aware he loved. Her heart began to sink, but the stillness in her spirit arose boldly. Shaking off the negative thoughts, she rebuked the notion and focused to hear what followed. Taylor began to respond to Elias's query.

"Elias, I have to admit I've loved you for years since the day we met in my father's office and you spilled that purple soda on your shirt, I knew you were special. You've been nothing but a great friend and confidant to me. I cherish our friendship and that's why I'm so comfortable around you."

"You know I always want you to be comfortable around me so you can talk to me. That's what I'm here for."

"You know when I knew I loved you the most, when you didn't do anything to me in the room that night. I knew I loved you and that you were unique. Remember, how we stayed up all night talking, laughing, and cracking jokes until the sky turned to morning. You were the only man that ever held me and had an opportunity to go beyond our friendship, but you respected me enough to keep our love and friendship solid. That's why I love you, Elias. Now I'm having a baby. Funny how life changes, isn't it? Okay, so here's the plight, someone has to tell my father, so you ready to let him know?"

Hannah wanted to escape her skeletal system and kiss all over Elias for his faithfulness. Though she still wanted to discuss Florida further, she considered the past irrelevant. Meanwhile, Pastor Woods sat quietly listening, with his mind flashing to all the times Elias was in his home and left with his daughter. He was proud of the wise decisions made by both Elias and Taylor, but he wrestled with the concept of his only daughter being pregnant out of wedlock.

Though many modern-day relationships deny the protocol of marriage before children, he always assumed his daughter would respect the values instilled in her since birth. He was never a traditionalist, but he practiced specific requirements and expected his daughter, of all people, to understand and respect his perspective. However, wanting to maintain strict order, he couldn't help but see his daughter and her smile. For a brief moment, he thought about Yolanda's reaction to having a little body running through the house. Instantaneously, he didn't consider the opinions of his parishioners or peers. He was elated that a new addition would be in his family. There were several thoughts bouncing around as this articulate, polished, and analytical thinker tried to make sense of the entire situation. Growing frustrated with his own thoughts, he sought the best decision maker he knew. He prayed silently as he sought God for wisdom and an open heart to receive his daughter. In the meantime, Elias addressed Taylor as they continued their conversation unaware of their private audience.

"Taylor, you know I love you, but you have to trust the love of your father enough to tell him yourself. I can hold you. I can be here for you when you want to scream and cry, but this one has to be done by you. Don't delay in telling him either. The longer you delay, the more painful it will be. He loves you, and I'm more than sure he'll understand. I know I love you and I understand, so you have nothing to worry about."

"I sure do hope so because I'm already feeling like I'm going to throw up. I don't need any extra stress. This nausea won't disappear. I feel like I'm having twins."

"You know it's funny you say that. I've been having dreams about having twins. I told Hannah all about it. Wouldn't it be weird if it were you in the dreams I've been having? Now God's sense of humor would really make me laugh on that. The only thing is that I know God told me about Hannah. I don't know what's up with her. Since I told her about my dreams, she always cuts me off and she's been acting weird. Has she talked with you or any of the other ladies? I know how women confide in one another."

"Well, Eli, just like you told me I have to confront my dad, sounds like you need to talk to the love of your life. You've loved her since I can remember. Ask her to spill her guts. Oh, wait… I'm about to spill mine first."

Taylor leaped off the couch at top speed, heading for the nearest trash can. The bathroom was too far away, and she couldn't contain the fluids any longer. Her morning sickness had completely dominated their conversation. Elias remained on the couch, holding his mouth while making faces because of the sound.

"Tay, do you need help? You make me want to throw up just listening to you. I hope Hannah doesn't go through this. I'm going to take her to lunch. I want us to talk."

Taylor couldn't get her head out of the garbage can. Instead, she just fanned to Elias and proceeded to regurgitate. Before Elias could get his phone out of his pocket, Hannah announced her presence. Taylor peeked above the garbage, but was thrust back into the pail.

"Good morning, Eli." Elias spun around on the sofa and smiled when he saw Hannah. Beaming with joy, he said, "I was just talking to Taylor about you. As you can see and hear, she's a little preoccupied at the moment. Come have a seat. Taylor, you sure you don't need anything? Let me get you something."

Taylor wiped her mouth and held her stomach as she motioned for her pocketbook. Feeling rather disgusted, she smiled at Hannah and walked toward the bathroom when she was halted in her tracks by her father standing in the doorway. Taylor stood there frozen like a deer in headlights when she saw her father's face. Knowing she'd just been throwing up rather loudly, she wasn't sure how much he'd heard. The feeling of faintness crawled through her nervous system like an invisible marine in the marsh. Pastor Woods, noticing the fatigue coming across Taylor's face, wrapped his arm around her and walked her into his office closing the door behind them.

He whispered in her ear, "I already know. You don't have to say a word. It's funny, for a quick minute, you looked just like your mother when she had morning sickness. Taylor, I love you and that's all that matters."

A father's delight and love for his daughter was captured in that office. That moment would have to pass because there was another sound that took precedence. Taylor bolted for the bathroom in the study as she went headfirst in the toilet. Her impromptu reaction was a mirror image of Yolanda during her pregnancy. He walked over to the bathroom and laughed, "Yup, you are certainly your mother's child. She was literally the same way. Conversations were always cut off when her stomach got to turning. She could smell bacon up to three miles away, it seemed. Back then, she always kept a toothbrush and toothpaste with her. Funny, how the life cycle is, huh? Now I'm in here and my baby girl has her head in the toilet. Here, let me hold your hair. Your mother never wanted her hair messed up, so if I was around, I'd always hold her hair. Now, sweetheart, I don't want you to get upset, but as your father, I will say this, I'm sending you to the spa. I want you to get the best pampering treatment they have for expectant mothers. That's Daddy's version of let's keep it right." Taylor couldn't help but to laugh and cry. She laughed as an outward sign of relief to his understanding and lack of harsh judgment; however, she cried as a result of her hormonal imbalance taking over. Her nose turned red faster than Rudolph's, and before she could comment on his loving expression, she went face in again. Pastor Woods merely leaned over and held Taylor's hair. "Don't worry, I'm here. I'll drive you to the spa myself." He rubbed her back and held her hair as they talked and laughed privately.

In the lounge, Elias smiled and looked Hannah in the eyes and said, "Let's go in my office. We need to talk." Not hesitating, he got up from the couch and motioned for Hannah to walk in front of him. Hannah was more focused on talking than location that she began to speak before they entered his office.

"Eli, I have to get this out or else it'll hurt more. Please just let me talk because you know how you can get in a conversation." Walking into the office, they sat together on the sofa. Hannah rang her hands as she spoke, "Eli, I know you said God has given you a vision of us having a family. To be honest, I thought for a moment, Taylor was having your baby, but I heard the entire conversation, so I'm glad you all have a genuine friendship. I'm also glad she's having a baby. Part of me wants to cry out, but I have to get this out. I'll understand if you want to leave, but there's something I haven't been honest with you about."

Elias's pulse raced like the engine of a Porsche. Not sure of Hannah's next comment, he braced himself for the impact. Hannah sat nervously as she told Elias of her tormented past.

Tears plunged to her lap as she held her head in shame, awaiting some form of feedback from Elias. Exhaling as he attempted to regain his breath, he rubbed his head. His thoughts flooded back to all the dreams he'd been having for months about having a family. He remembered all the times he'd heard God speak to him. Now thoughts of inquisition bombarded his spirit as he barraged heaven for answers. Hannah's tears grew as she sat in silence, watching Elias's reaction. Not knowing if she should touch him or continue talking, she silently consoled herself, growing more afraid with thoughts of him leaving her. Elias began to cry, not out of anger, but out of the pain Hannah must have felt. His heart melted as he envisioned her ordeal, and his weakness had been exposed. Breaking the silence, Hannah tried to talk to Elias.

"I know you may hate me for telling you this now. I was so afraid and ashamed. Plus, I know you're actively involved in ministry and I didn't want you to feel compromised. I know serving God is your life and I didn't want you to know anything about me that would bring disgrace to you, God, or your ministry. I always thought if I ignored it, it would disappear. It never has. I dream about it constantly. It's eating me alive on the inside. I don't want to take pills anymore. I've been on antidepressants for years, but they aren't working. Nothing is working. I have to be honest with you. I have so many flaws. I've been silently and secretly trying to handle things on my own, but there's no way I can keep living a lie."

Pausing briefly, she reached for her purse and retrieved a letter. Prepared to hand it to Elias for him to read, she opted to speak from her heart.

"I received this certified mail and I was so angry. I've taken several tests and the doctor says I can never have children. But there's a reason for that. I never told anyone! The *only* people who know are me, my mother, and my doctor. I never saw the doctor after it happened. I had an abortion when I was a teenager. My cervix was severely scarred after I'd been brutally raped and left for dead. As a result of the rape I became pregnant, but I was so embarrassed about what happened and I was going to college that I begged my mother for an abortion. I feel like I've been punished all these years for my decision, so my nightmares never go away. All I can think about is if I'd never walked down that street, if I would've never been out with my friends, my life would've been so different. This isn't something that's just water under the bridge, but it's my dark truth. My selfishness for wanting to keep you in my life is because you're a man of morale and great character, so when you dated me without wanting intimacy, I couldn't let you go. I'd finally met and found love after so many failed relationships. They wanted intimacy, but the thought of it made me feel like I was being raped all over again. Then you came along, and I started to believe and trust in love again–real love. When you were willing to wait until marriage I feared I'd never have that opportunity again, so I kept my secret to myself. I know this is extremely harsh news, but I can't continue with this lie. I love you so much, but I'm so sorry that I've done this to myself and to us. I *never* wanted to hurt you. I hope you can believe me. Honestly, I'm still being selfish because I want you to stay, but I'll understand if you want to go. Knowing Taylor is having a child and knowing how close you two are, I'm not sure if you'll ever want to stay with a woman who can't have any children. I'm *so sorry* if I've hurt you. Please talk to me. Say something."

Elias turned his head. Sniffling, he looked at Hannah with the tears in his eyes. Emotionally flummoxed, he continued to rub his head. His silent prayers to heaven were heard when the Holy Spirit reminded him to trust and believe in what he heard and the vision that was given to him. Not wanting to speak, he smiled and grabbed his wife and held her as they wept together. Hannah cried in fear, but Elias wept in faith. As the priest of their house, he encouraged his new wife.

"Hannah, it is not my place to judge you. There is no condemnation for those who are in Christ. Please don't allow the devil to deceive you any further. What you experienced is more than many can handle and what far too many have to bear alone. I'm so sorry for what happened to you. I don't believe under any circumstances that a person should be violated. I'm glad that you trust me enough as your husband to handle the obstacles that have come your way. However, I do not believe that it will negatively affect our marriage. People want the forever after, but refuse to deal with the valley lows between the mountain highs. For better or for worse, to me is translated, *Do not count it strange the fiery trial you must face, but be of good cheer, for you have already overcome.* You and I are one, and there is no sin or dark past that will cause me to leave you. I did not marry you because of children; I married you because *I love you*. Love keeps no record of wrongs. Now that we've discussed it, let's move forward together and grow from it in faith, not fear.

"Hannah, aside from your name having an overwhelming biblical depth, you have only confirmed to me the power of God. I will never leave you, and if we have to wait on God, I want you to know that God has spoken to me about *you* being my wife. He also spoke to me about *you* being the mother of *my* children. He has not spoken of any other woman to me but *you*. So as your husband, I'm here to tell you that God has promised us a family and I'm convinced he's going to bestow that immense blessing upon us. Hannah, I can have the faith to believe, but you have to believe with me. We are one, so we must journey into this as the one we are. I'll wipe your tears for you, but know I'll always be here to wipe your tears and make you smile. I love you."

Hannah was overwhelmed with joy that she continued to cry out of nervousness. Her heart warmed, and the weight she'd been carrying for years had been lifted and destroyed. It was as if the curse over her life had been broken. Through her teary eyes, her vision became clear. She saw in the spirit as the walls of depression, the nightmares, the artwork of her rapist, the doctor's reports, and everything that spoke against God disseminate.

Elias reached for two Bibles, took the letter from Hannah, placed it within the pages, and grabbed Hannah's hands as he prayed with his wife. After praying, he handed Hannah one Bible and kept the other for himself. Instructing her to turn to 1 Samuel 1, he began reading it aloud with Hannah. Tears filled Hannah's eyes and crashed to the pages of the Word of God as she received God's promise in her heart. Elias raised his voice as he read verses 19 and 20, "Early the next morning they arose and worshiped before the Lord and then went back to their home at Ramah. Elkanah lay with Hannah his wife, and the Lord remembered her. So in the course of time, Hannah conceived and gave birth to a son. She named him Samuel saying, 'Because I asked the Lord for him.' Hannah, ask the Lord and I'm telling you, like my name is Elias, God will bless us with a family."

Shaking uncontrollably, Hannah continued to weep and cry out to the Lord, making her request known. Elias tightened his grip on Hannah's hands as he neared the end of the text. Gazing into his wife's eyes, he lifted her head and began wiping her tears. Smiling and lifting his head toward heaven, he arose holding his wife's hand and held her in his arms. Whispering in his wife's ear, he comforted her, "Honey, I love you and you are my one and only wife. Let us go and be doers of the word." Hannah paused from her worship experience and yelled in laughter, "Eli! What are you talking about? Oh my goodness!"

Laughing within, she welcomed her lover, her husband, her priest, and her source—God. Elias began laughing, but with his faith in full gear with no remoteness of fading, he reminded Hannah of the value of God's promises, "All I'm saying is God is faithful, and in order for him to water the seed, it must first be planted. It's in the word, Hannah, let's go. The harvest is ripe, but the laborers are few. They better be few. I better be the only laborer in this field. I'm feeling a fresh anointing. The spirit is speaking and it's saying, 'Go home!'" Hannah and Elias laughed as they left the office and headed home.

Confessions of the Soul

By a new and living way opened for us through the curtain, that is, his body, and since we have a great priest over the house of God, let us draw near to God with a sincere heart in full assurance of faith, having our hearts sprinkled to cleanse us from a guilty conscience and having our bodies washed with pure water. Let us hold unswervingly to the hope we profess, for he who promised is faithful.

Hebrews 10:20–23 (NIV)

They overcame him by the blood of the Lamb and by the word of their testimony; they did not love their lives so much as to shrink from death.

Revelation 12:11 (NIV)

After months of conflicting schedules, business trips, personal life adjustments, and evolving relationships, the ladies were unable to convene for their lunch and spa dates. Finally having a day where they were all available, the ladies gathered together at Echelon Restaurant and greeted each other. Two by three, Amber, Hannah, Taylor, Bernie, and Patricia all laughed as they entered the newest five-star dining restaurant called *Atmosphere with Ambiance* with excitement for the opportunity to reconvene. Embracing one another as if returning to their collegiate alma mater for homecoming, they clapped hands, posed for pictures, and complimented one another like they hadn't seen each other in years. Patricia, always being the lead, broke away from the group to inform the concierge of their reservation with her A-typical personality and demanded superlative service. The other ladies continued to converse amongst themselves as Patricia returned with the hostess who guided them to their table.

Amber, Hannah, Taylor, Bernie, and Patricia all sat at the table, laughing and sharing stories from events at church and in their personal lives. They laughed and cried in tears from the verbal comedic demonstrations to enhance the stories of their lives. With all the laughter and personal life experiences, there was a missing link that sat like an elephant at the table. They each knew there were events in their lives that held each woman captive in her own solitary confinement, but laughter would play the perfect Oscar-winning role to evade their truths. Although laughter was good food for the heart, their spirits demanded release from their personal cells. Even though they were all laughing, it was subtly evident there was a need to escape the facade being portrayed and get to the root of some underlying issues. It was necessary to see beyond the veil and see beyond the person they each saw before them. Patricia, still overwhelmed by her recent encounter and revelatory experience from her mother's house and family deliverance at church, looked off and began daydreaming. As the always vibrant life of the party, it was evident there was a problem with her, and it didn't take much probing for Patricia to crack like a cold egg in boiling water. Patricia, refusing to care for the opinions of her peers, began to confess her personal demons to her friends.

"You know what, I'm tired! You all think I go to church because I'm perfect. If I could come clean right here, right now I would like to have you know I go and I praise God for not letting me act on some of my thoughts. I go because every chance I get to at least think about doing something right, I need to say, 'Thank you.' Now that's not the real reason why I go. I go because I need a hit every now and again. You know that hit when the word pierces your soul, but you know you need that cut, that brokenness, so you can be healed by God's hands. Doesn't it say something like the word is alive and powerful sharper than any two-edged sword, dividing soul and spirit, joints and marrow, exposing out innermost thoughts and desires. Bernie, that's Hebrews 4:12, right? I don't know, preaching is Bernie's department, but I go to church so I can get a cut and a hit. Lately, Pastor Woods has been used by God to pierce me because I am messed up. I'm not perfect y'all! I'd rather speak what I am—judgmental. I've been living a lie so long that the devil has been taking notes and attending my seminars for those in denial. I think he tried to call me and ask me for some tips, but he got my voice mail. I'm tired of lying, and I'm even more tired of being fake in church and in front of God."

Exasperating a sigh of relief, Patricia continued, "Whew, I needed that. I know you look at me, and from the outside, I look like I have it all together, I'm so sorry to inform you that you've been hoodwinked, bamboozled, and misled. You have no clue the countless nights I've cried from the shame of my past. I moved here, hundreds of miles away from home, to start a new life. It would make more sense that way. Journey to a new place where no one knows you and start fresh. Well, they say you can run, but you can't hide. Either confront Goliath and kill him or remain a slave. The Bible certainly did have it right, kill your fear or become its slave. Well, I didn't kill it, and I've been shackled by it ever since. When I was in college, I was young and curious, so I had a lesbian interaction. Okay, I'm still faking. I was in a relationship with a woman. When I graduated, I never looked back, and to prove my womanhood, I moved here, landed a great job for a fine executive, and worked him and my career. Then, boom, I got pregnant and Payton was born. I know, I know! The beautiful little girl I led you all to believe was my niece is really my daughter. I am the mother of a ridiculously gorgeous, smart vessel of light named Payton. Who knew Patricia had a child too? Yes, I am a mother! Kaboom, bet you didn't see that one coming!"

No one dared to utter a word. Though some of the ladies' minds were racing and their assumptions had all been quelled in these bold statements. They each knew they too were accountable for their own personal skeletons. With each ear fully attentive, they listened with their hearts as their friend revealed her truths with authority. Patricia was equally concerned with pouring her soul as she was with getting the waiter to pour her another glass of wine. After refilling her glass and taking a sip, she rubbed her hands on the goblet and continued, "I know this threw you for a loop. I can tell because you are sitting there with your mouths open. Close your mouths, it only gets better. After I had Payton, I shipped my child off to my mother in Manalapan, New Jersey, came back here, and focused on being successful so I wouldn't need to give myself over to a man any longer. That's right, I give advice, but I was a slave to a man for what I wanted and what he was willing to give when he saw fit, that is until I attained it on my own. You can *perceive* it as sleeping your way to the top. I *believed* it to be a plan of execution to work my vision. I needed him so I could learn what he knew for myself. I just went about the learning process the wrong way. He used me for sex, and I used him for his mind. Call it what you want. No bad blood in my eyes. I honestly learned a lot from a business perspective because he's an extremely intelligent, wise businessman and investor, but as long as our child remained out of sight, she was out of mind—at least for me. Financially, he's been there. Unfortunately, he was never physically there, and it's honestly my fault. He's argued with me about spending time with her, and he went as far as contacting my parents and traveling to and from New Jersey to see her. My mother welcomed the idea, and of course, my father didn't see anything wrong with his approach. I was so caught up into myself that I couldn't see what he was trying to do and what I was hindering him from having, a fulfilling relationship with his daughter. I felt he'd expose me, so I demeaned him and created havoc and chaos intentionally, so I could keep him to myself and further my vision. I was a reflection of absolute ignorance and selfishness at its deplorable finest. I was so ignorant I went off on him time and time again. I was being foolish. I don't know what I was thinking. I wanted to hide my truth so much that I kept my own child from her father. The crazy part about that is I grew up with my father in my life. Let me just throw this current disclaimer in about Payton and her dad. After much prayer and my overwhelming need to get the silverback gorilla off my back, I pleaded with him for forgiveness of my ridiculous behavior over the years. Now he and Payton are working on building a true father-daughter relationship. In essence, she's so happy, I'm at peace knowing she'll have a true loving relationship with the man who loved her despite my ignorance, and he's thankful to have her in his life. Well, at least one aspect of my life's rainforest has been cleared up. I'm telling y'all this is some demented stuff I've been dealing with. Here's another confession, I have major control issues. I needed to have control. Business and success, I can control, and it's proven and evident for the world to see. However, matters of the heart, family, and love—I fail miserably. In my ignorance and deep concentration to learn, build for myself, and establish my own career, I dismissed the value of tending to my daughter's needs. My visits to her weren't merely enough. All those business trips were visitation trips to see her with the occasional business in the process. It became so easy to ignore my truth and lie that I eventually lived it until my lies became my truth. I just kept burying my past. No one asked questions and no one from my past surfaced, so I was home free. Yeah, right! Ugh, I'm so tired of trying to maintain control of a runaway train. Apparently, God must have gotten tired of my foolishness too. The phone call that day when we were getting our massages was my past. Gabrielle gave my past lover my number because they know one another. I'll tell you about her in a minute. She came by my mother's house, and in an instant, everything I'd worked for would've been ruined. Don't brace yourself yet, I didn't even get to the family saga. Oh no, it doesn't end there! I found out that my identical twin sister, Gabrielle, bet you didn't even know I was a twin, was friends with my past."

Each of the women sat at the table in absolute awe of the information Patricia, their well-put-together friend, shared. Their silence and shock was evident, and they completely ignored everything going on in the restaurant including their meals being brought to the table. The center of everyone's attention was captive in the mouth of Patricia's and no one pleaded for an escape. Patricia continued as she completely acknowledged their attentive behavior, "See how we keep secrets! The cat's out of the bag on that one! Oh well, but I told you I have some issues, and if it could only stop there, I'd be fine, but I'm not fine and I'm exhausted from carrying this yoke, so, Jesus, listen up. I'm telling you in front of them that I'm giving my burdens, my past, my pain, my secrets, my problems, and my future to you. This burden, this yoke is so heavy that a deep body tissue massage won't fix. Trust me, I've spent enough money on them, and it's merely a temporary fix." After releasing a sigh to both gather her composure and continue in her thought process, she readdressed her friends.

"Now where was I? Oh, Gabrielle, my twin sister. Now, Amber, I know you know Brielle, but I'm not sure if the rest of you know her. By now, I'm sure someone has either mentioned or never mentioned anything assuming that it wasn't true. Either way, the truth is I have an identical twin sister. Life between us hasn't always been a bed of flowers. We started out extremely close, and then the college years parted us faster than the Red Sea." Taking a deep sigh in an attempt to hold back her tears, Patricia continued, "Ladies, I found out she was gang-raped, beaten, and left for dead because the people that assaulted her thought she was me. She was supposed to die, but God saved her. The scariest part is that it was intended for me. Do you know what it feels like to know that someone hates you enough to plot and execute a devious plan to kill you or attempt to kill you? The saddest part is they didn't want her, they wanted to *kill* me. As a result, my only living sister suffered and was mutilated. She's been living with and physically wearing scars as daily evidence of being my twin sister. It was all my fault! All she wanted was to surprise me by coming to my school so we could hang out. They didn't even know I was a twin because Gabrielle and I went to two different colleges. I'm just letting it all out the box, the bag, the house, the closet, and anything else you can think of. I'm coming out! Right now! They wanted to rape me. Not only did they rape her, but they also beat her and left her for dead. I keep repeating it because I can't think beyond someone wanting you dead. Man, she was left for dead because of me."

Patricia grew emotional at the thought and couldn't hold back her tears. At this point, she no longer cared for her makeup and what people in the restaurant would think about her crying in public at a table surrounded by women. She was releasing, and her tears were a sign of the burdens she bore. Exhaling and inhaling deeply, she continued through her cracked voice, "I can't even tell you what happened to them. All I know is Braxton, the ringleader, is behind bars for ten years because Bobbi persuaded my sister privately to pursue it before the statute of limitations was up. The other two each got seven to ten for rape and manslaughter. In actuality, Bobbi became an attorney as a result of Gabrielle's rape and assault. The blessing was that she personally handled the case pro bono and won. It was the case that sparked her career, and she's been successful ever since. So there you have it. Your perfectly put-together friend is washed-up and full of dirt. I was faking it every week in church like I had it all together and I was a farce. After that Sunday, when Pastor and First Lady Woods spoke about deliverance and forgiveness, I've been progressively striving to be a better person. I made amends with my sister and family, but I needed for you all to know so everything can be in decency and in order between us as well. You're my family away from my family. I hope we can advance our friendship both spiritually and emotionally where we can help one another in all areas of our lives. I'm definitely under intense heavenly construction. Well, one's thing is for sure, if God can love this hot mess, then there's still hope yet."

Hannah, overwhelmed with emotion, chimed in and laughed through her tears, knowing she too had a past that she needed deliverance from. She exhaled a sigh of relief that the opportunity finally arose for her to share her life's story.

"Well, since we're confessing and the Bible says that we're overcome by the word of our testimony, here's my dark past. I was raped by a serial rapist when I was a teenager. He was killed on impact in an accident after he raped me. Can you believe that, God punished him moments after he raped me? I don't know how God did it, but he did. The only problem is, I was still punishing him and myself. That's just part 1. Here's part two, now Elias, the one man I'm in love with, had no clue what happened. I didn't want him to know because I feared he would leave me because of infertility—as a result of the rape. The one thing he wanted and told me about was the one thing the doctors told me I couldn't give him—a child. The doctors said I'd be barren for life because of the man that violated me. There you have it! I'm in love and married to a minister in the church with a dark past that no one knew about except Pastor Woods and his wife. How did they know? They were the ones who took me to the hospital when they found me in the street the night I was raped. I sit in church screaming on the inside and harboring anger in my soul for being robbed of life before I ever had the opportunity to live. I've been living a lie. Dancing, shouting, and singing in church all while suffering in turmoil, not experiencing change. Every time I've been close to getting better, I'll have a nightmare. I'm exhausted of running and living in fear."

Smiling through her tears, Hannah proudly addressed her friends. All forms of embarrassment are a thing of the past. It was as if the devil himself walked away, waving the white flag of surrender as she spoke boldly and was giving praise to God. The difference with this praise was her confidence and faith in God was so powerful he had no place to hide.

Holding her head up and speaking clearly she continued, "I know without a doubt that God is real, God is a healer, and God is powerful and all knowing. I didn't realize how much I feared letting God take control of my life until I was tired of the devil's fear tactics. Don't get me wrong, the devil didn't take control; I gave him control by living and operating with a mind rooted in fear, intimidation, and ignoring the power and authority ordained by God in me. I also realized that Elias is a great man and I was about to ruin a wonderful relationship with a phenomenal man because of a horrendous experience with a man that never knew me, but raped me. Elias is the first man I've truly loved and the man God placed on this earth just for me, and I'm so thankful that he chose me to be his wife. We've prayed and cried together, and ladies, I'm here to tell you not to let the devil hold you hostage any longer. I'm no longer bound because God has all power in his hands. My rapist destroyed my life, and a doctor snatched a life from my body. The doctors told me I couldn't have children, but I'm sitting here today telling you that the doctors said no, but Jesus said yes! I'm twelve weeks pregnant, by my husband, with twins. God gave me beauty for my ashes and a double portion blessing for my trouble! He gave my husband a vision, and we came together as one and the evidence of God's vision is manifested within me, literally!"

Hannah rubbed her womb, smiling with a joy so profound that nothing could penetrate her spirit. Wiping tears and smiling, she carried on, "After years of torturing myself, God stepped in and I'm emancipated. I believe it was a result of confessing my skeletons and completely resolving the issues. I had to overcome one of my life's most difficult lessons—forgiveness and trusting God. How do you forgive someone you don't know? How do you forgive someone who robbed you of innocence? How do you forgive yourself? I wanted my husband to be open, honest, and completely trust me, but I hadn't done the same to him. I wanted him to forgive me, but I hadn't forgiven someone else. The way I treated my husband was essentially the way I'd been treated. The only difference was that I told him I loved him. I believe God wanted me to learn forgiveness, because I'd eventually have to seek it. I also believe he wanted me to learn to trust Him despite what my reality depicted. I'm convinced forgiveness and trusting God are the absolute hardest things to do, but are the most essential components within a true relationship with God. Ladies, all I can say is trust God, forgive, and believe! Don't allow deception to coerce you into a state of disbelief. At some point, we have to remind Satan he's under subjection to God. After all, he couldn't touch Job without God's permission. That means he can't touch or dominate us either. So that's my story and I'm sticking to it."

One by one, the ladies all shed tears and hugged Hannah for she had truly been a living example of God's promise made real. The ladies never realized their friendships held so many secrets. Taylor wiped away her tears as she began to confess her own sins. Being the daughter of a notable pastor wasn't the easiest thing to do, but living a lie was something she knew all too well. Taylor took a sip of water and poured her heart out.

"I know I'm not the easiest person to get along with, but I'm glad to know I fit right in. You have no clue what it's like to be the daughter of a pastor and not just a pastor of a small church, but a preacher's kid of a father that's all over television. People judge me before they know me. If I blink, someone's telling my parents, or my parents are telling me not to go here, say this, or do this, and let's not forget; I'm not to embarrass them. Now with the Internet and blogs, it's almost like being the president's kid. You can't do anything. Well, here's one for you that shouldn't be hard to see. I'm pregnant and just about due, and I'm not married yet at least. We've talked about marriage and we are getting married!" Taylor flashed her hand with all four carats of diamonds gleaming in the light. The ladies all shouted in glee for their friend's engagement, and Patricia couldn't help but give the thumbs up at the diamonds.

Patricia, almost prying the ring off Taylor's finger to appraise it, smiled. Turning toward Amber, she whispered, "I have to tell brother to take that ring he bought back. He needs my help I can see that already. It was good, but this is stunning. Oh no, I'll make sure brother takes good care of you. We must maintain the standard. Don't you worry! I'll go shopping with him to ensure you'll be set right! Hello! He can afford it! I might get him to get me something while we're at it. See, there I go again. Okay, Pat, get it together." Amber laughed, but sat pondering if Patricia was being facetious or if Jackson had purchased her a ring. Ready to leap out of the chair, she whispered to her spirit to calm down. She couldn't help but see herself as Mrs. Jackson Wilmington but didn't want to jump the gun. Not wanting to assume anything, she took Patricia's comments for face value and believed in her heart that God's timing would reveal all she needed to know. Amber redirected her attention back to Taylor as she continued.

Smiling jubilantly and accepting the compliments of her peers, Taylor commented, "I've been planning this weeding for months, but it's scheduled after the baby, so I can get my body back! You're looking at the future Mrs. Taylor Brensen. Even though I should be joyous about getting married, there was still the internal family saga. I was taught not to speak against my family externally, but I'm talking to my girls. Now that may not be much to you, but when my parents found out, I thought it would be like World War III and IV. I was actually surprised at their reactions. My mother was so excited, she started planning for the baby before I could get the words out of my mouth. Initially, my dad was hurt, but he continued to express his love for me so he turned out okay. Y'all, my father is so sweet and precious, he even held my hair while I puked up my guts when I had morning sickness. I was absolutely shocked, but he said I reminded him of my mother when he saw me. I was so thankful that he understood.

The weird thing about it all is that my parents understood, but it was the other parishioners who had a problem. It's not like I'm a teenager, I'm an adult woman with an Ivy League education. I don't know, but the larger I grew and the more questions people raised, it became a problem. Now, until I'm married, I'm privately considered a hindrance to the morale of his ministry—at least according to the congregants. My father loves and adores me and made sure to let me know. He's forgiving and trusting, but it's the people in the church that have the most judgment. Some have gone to him personally expressing their disbelief in my personal life. One lady went as far as telling my dad to have me come before the congregation and apologize and completely remove myself from all aspects of ministry. The woman wanted me ousted from the church like I'm the modern day plague! I'm not a child. I'm grown, but I've been subject to a microscope of perfection and I've failed miserably. However, my child will be here soon, and my success and liberation shall be evident to all. I'm tired of wearing the mask of my parents. I'm sorry that I've embarrassed them, but I can't live for them, I have to live for me. I don't think they understand, but eventually, they will. Now, when I do get married, since the chicken came before the egg, you are all expected to be in my wedding party. At least, I'll already have a flower girl."

The women all smiled as they welcomed Taylor's invitation to be part of her wedding. Taylor kept her child's sex a secret, but since exposing secrets was the theme of the day, there was no need in hiding. The women rejoiced for Taylor while Bernie's thoughts peered through the forest of her valley.

Bernie sat there partially intimidated by her past, but knew she too needed a release. She knew that the spirit of deliverance was present, so hiding behind her past would only create greater tension within. Praying silently for the healing power and deliverance of her fellow friends, Bernadette shared her story.

"I know you all see me with the youth at the church, and I would think that my relationship with God isn't just evident, but

I want you to know it's real. I understand like you, ladies, what pain is. There's a purpose for it, and there was a breaking to get me to this point. I'm sorry I can't relate to your heartache of being raped or dealing with the skeletons of not being able to have a child or maintaining the mirage for the sake of your parents or having a child and being a lesbian. However, I would hope that after I share my past with you, ladies, there would still be the same, if not higher, level of anointing within each of our lives and a greater respect for our spiritual maturation."

No one was ever privy to the personal life of Bernadette. They always saw her in church as active with the youth. The persona displayed within the sanctuary was one of dominance, strength, and authority. It went without question that her relationship with God was pure and intimate. This was evident within her character and her active participation within ministry. The anointing on her life was evident, but the process to achieve such greatness was bought at a hefty price.

Pausing to take a deep breath, she looked around the restaurant and, in an instant, thought she saw someone from her past. In a momentary daze, she wondered if she was hallucinating or if she actually saw someone she'd known years before. Shaking her head to refresh her thoughts, she prayed silently. Bernie's internal battle to share her previous life required a calculated resolve for her to attain victory. On one side, her spiritual self resolved for God to be glorified through her life as Jesus utilized the apostle Paul. However, her carnal self opted to consider the opinions of others, which could prove detrimental as with the demise of King Saul. She'd successfully lived her new life clear of judgment and disgrace. To share her personal story amongst women whom she'd deemed sisters would inevitably place an overcast in their hearts regarding her character and the transmogrification process God ordained. Surrendering within her spirit, not to carnal acceptance, but for God's glory, she looked into the eyes of her peers and shared her very private testimony with the anticipation of overcoming her past and fulfilling her destiny.

"You beautiful women are all astounding with great triumphant lives as a derivative of tribulations within your lives. Had God not caused you to engage in the essential preordained plans he had for you, there would be no witness within your lives. You, me included, stand as witnesses before the world to exemplify fortitude and grace. As much as I would like to solely encourage you in how to be examples, I'd be remiss if I didn't reveal my truth."

The ladies sat partially intrigued because they thought they knew everything there was to know about Bernie. Whenever Bernie conferred with anyone, she was a representative of heaven. They'd partially deemed her to be the most notable role model for how they should serve and live a life of Christ. Flummoxed by Bernie's newfound approach to share her life, the remained attuned to every word that fell from her lips.

Bernie continued, "I grew up in the church and witnessed some horrible things. I know I never talk about my family and it's with good reason." Pausing in her statement, she turned toward Taylor to address her personally while addressing all her peers, "I definitely wasn't a preacher's kid, but I understand the expectation of behavior you have to maintain, Taylor, so I can partially relate. However, my situation is nothing remotely close to yours. My uncle was the pastor of the church where I grew up and my mother was on every committee and in everything you can muster up at the church, so we practically lived there. It's no surprise that I saw people come and go. It's also no surprise that in watching people and listening to my mother, I heard and saw things. My uncle was always a little bit different. He married a beautiful trophy wife to cover up and prove to my family that he was a man, hence making him not different," she said with sarcasm, "stay with me."

Laughing to herself, she proceeded to build her case. "He never really wanted to preach, and being honest, I can't judge if he called himself or if God called him, but I do know that he saw church as a means to counsel people, preferably men. Most of the men left the church or remained for a certain amount of time, then eventually left. For years, no one ever said anything. Some people wondered and even spread rumors, but because no one ever confirmed the rumors, life at the church went business as usual. Unfortunately, my uncle grew extremely comfortable, and his encounters with men in the church grew more frequent. I'm not sure what intrigued him to venture into younger men, but he fancied this particular young man. He counseled and met with the young man for some personal issues he had in his life. I'm not sure what was going on in the young man's life, but I know his counseling sessions with my uncle went south faster than a crashing plane. Unlike the other men, he approached this young man more aggressively and against his will. The young man he molested told his father and his father came on the one day he knew he would be there, Sunday. Before he shot him, he shouted and yelled at my uncle for making his son a queer. You know, *queer* was the term they used back when people weren't politically correct. Then, he killed him in front of the entire congregation. Ladies, my uncle was shot in the chest on a Sunday morning. I was young and knew what was going on, but didn't understand all the details. I knew enough to know that it could've been avoided. All I know is it turned me away from church and God, partially because I thought if I came to church and someone didn't like me, they'd kill me, and the other part was because of all the things that went unspoken of in church. I was confused, frustrated, in shock from witnessing a murder—in church—angry, and bitter. Instead of anyone answering any questions or talking about it, they dismissed me as being too young to understand. For me, that wasn't a good enough answer. I blamed God because he allowed it to happen. I blamed my mother for not communicating with me. I blamed the man who killed my uncle—in church. I blamed the young man for saying something that led to my uncle's death. I blamed my uncle for being perverted and being the example of what a man of God represented or the stark opposite. He was the only example I had before me that I was also a relative. I was even angry with all the people who knew or thought something but never said a word. I just blamed everyone. So I did what I thought in my mind, at the time, was the right thing to do—I turned away from God and the church.

"Now don't get me wrong, all churches weren't and aren't like the church I was raised in. I'm just telling you my personal experience with people using the church for their own selfish, deceitful means. God has a way of punishing people for such deplorable acts. People who play church and demean the house of God as just another building demonstrating no reverence will be held accountable at some point. Now that's just my opinion, but I believe it to be true and my experiences are driving this opinionated truth.

"Therefore, getting back to me and leaving my opinion alone, I grew older and began dating a gentleman that altered the course of my life as I know it. Initially, I was unaware that he was an atheist. After time, I learned that he was a devout atheist, and before I could blink, I partnered literally with the devil. I let the devil in my life, my heart, and my bed all because of suppressed anger for what occurred in my past. Harboring hatred, bitterness, and allowing malice to take root in your heart is dangerous territory. Well, the roots grew, and I transitioned my once overly dedicated life to Christ and transferred that same energy to absolute denial of God the Father, Jesus Christ the Son, and the Holy Spirit. Ladies, I was what some would consider the publicist for the atheist next door. I turned away and denied God faster than the cock crowed three times before Peter denied Jesus. I promoted all things against God to whoever was ready to listen. Since I grew up in church and I knew the Bible like my name and I could argue with the best of them. I did this for about seven years, and then, I was hit with some startling news. I found out I was having my first child.

"When I was pregnant, I began having horrible dreams that I'd never experienced in my life. My dreams were always dark and dismal. I was always running or being chased by some form of darkness or scary-looking person. I would fight creatures and animals in my dreams. I was more stressed out when it was time to go to be than I was when assessing a new case. My pride would consume me, but out of frustration or desperation, I'd talk to my partner, and he'd convince me that I just needed to relax. I didn't even realize how much I was in the dark. I will say there was a good side to having a mother who stalked God. While I was in my personal hell, my mother was constantly calling me and praying for me. I'm almost embarrassed to say that I would sneak to talk to my own mother. It was like I was hiding God and anyone connected to him in every facet of my life. My mother, on the other hand, didn't care or fear anyone or anything. She would leave messages when she was doing nothing but praying. She would even have her friends from church pray over the phone. You know I went to an old-school church where those old mothers knew God! They would call you out! So when I tell you they kept calling and rebuking Satan and praying, *trust me*! To be honest, I actually listened to their messages. I am a living witness that the effectual fervent prayers of the righteous avail much. My mother and her friends prayed the hell out of me literally! After hearing all that prayer, there was no way I could stay in hell. Come to think of it, I'll have to invite them to a luncheon. I'm telling you, they will pray and cast out any evil spirit that thinks about being present. I've seen it, I've lived it, I know it, and I believe God placed those women in my mother's company to keep her strong in God and to pray me out when I didn't have the sense to pray for myself. Between my horrendous dreams and the harsh reality I was living, there were some things going on with me that transitioned me back on the path I was always ordained to journey. God has a way of arresting your attention and I learned the hard way. All that time I dedicated to denying God and the name of Jesus came to a screeching halt on the highway. Being honest, the only time I prayed or called on Jesus' name in years was when I was screaming in pain after being in a car accident. I completely dismissed denial when that semi-tractor trailer plowed into me. I should've died in that car. There was no way on earth I was supposed to survive after that accident, but God spared my life. I didn't understand then, but I'm thankful for it now.

"Not too long after, I was in the accident that should've rendered me dead, I was in a coma for eight months, and the entire time, my baby, who surprisingly survived, kept growing, but I was literally in hell. I saw evil for what it was and the stress on my body because of what was going on with me internally caused my child to be stillborn. I had a caesarian section while in a coma and never saw my child. When I awoke from hell, honestly and literally, it was only after God himself told me that I would be given another chance at life. The life I had with the devil was snatched away to spare my life. It sounds horrible, but I was having a child with a man that I should've never intertwined with from the beginning. I can relate to Saul on the road to Damascus on a level that many people can't. I don't tell people this because they look at me crazy and want to judge me. They don't realize that God can and will change your life and your heart. I've been cut and broken literally. My child was cut from my body without my knowledge, and I had seven bones broken in that accident. I'm sitting here today to tell you the wrong roots were dug up, and the Potter put me back together again. When Jesus delivered me from hell, I swore on my life that I would commit my life to him in any way he wanted me to serve. I'm convinced God spoke to me, so I've been used to touch the lives of his people. Since then, I've been working in ministry fervently like never before. I worked just as hard when only two people showed up as I do now when hundreds show up. This is years in the making, and I can't take credit for anything. God gave me grace, and I don't take that lightly. At one point, I wouldn't have told a soul. You see how long it took me to tell you, ladies, but now I believe the recent events in life and at the church are God's warning for his people to speak up. No more hiding in the shadows ashamed and afraid. It's time to be set apart and be the standard that God requires of his people. At this phase in my restored and rejuvenated life, I'll tell anyone who has an ear.

"Now, I pray with my mother and those women from her church. I intercede for people all the time because I know it was the prayers of those intercessors that saved my life. I believe God heard me in that car. I also believe he used that accident to jump-start my life back to his original plan. I'm also convinced he heard my mother. To make sure he hears me now, I call him all day long. Every chance I get, I'm in God's face, seeking him, and thanking him. You know what? I'm not ashamed one bit, rather, I'm thankful. I know God cleared my schedule up for me to come here today because this was what my soul and spirit needed.

"You ladies have to share your testimonies with others. All of our experiences are not for us to harbor within ourselves for fear of man's judgment. God allowed us all to survive our storms, trials, tribulations, and tests to bring glory to God, not bow our heads in shame for what some human being may think. This is ministry. This is what true ministry is, and Jesus didn't stay in the synagogues to teach. He was out among the people. He was hearing their stories and touching their lives and their bodies. Some didn't get their healing and deliverance until they opened their mouths. I'm here to tell you from being on assignment and working for the devil, he wants you quiet. Your silence gives him power. The longer you remain silent, the stronger he grows. You know why you've been 'functional devil advocates'? It's because you refuse to empower yourselves and know that the God in you and the spirit in you has more power than the devil could ever have. Satan knows you only have to believe the slightest bit, and he'll be destroyed. You feed and mature him in your mind, through your fears, and in your lives when you remain silent, embarrassed, and timid of the God-ordained power in you. Starve the devil and feed your spirit. In order to do this, you have to confess with your mouth, believe in your heart, and believe that Jesus is Lord. The keys to salvation are clear. Open your mouth and make a declaration. Once you start talking about something and start bouncing your thoughts off others with the same thoughts, your belief in what you're saying grows. This is what the devil fears most. All I'm saying is send the devil running in fear of you operating in your authority with God's grace at the helm!"

Bernie had the ladies floored at her personal testimony. Aside from their attention being hostage to her words, the support of her statements captivated their hearts. Patricia couldn't keep silent any longer. Belting out a comment and cutting Bernie off, she leaned in and stared deeply into Bernie's face. Before she could take the emotional route, Patricia opted for the theatrical performance of her life.

"Dag, Bernie, let me find out you're supposed to be preaching! You're about to make me tear this restaurant up. I'll start the running ministry in here and bring it to the church." Patricia belted out to the waiter in the corner of the restaurant, "Waiter, can I get a plate for my sister over here so we can pass that plate and take up an offering! She needs tuition money for seminary." Patricia laughed heartily as her girlfriends joined in the laughter. Patricia couldn't help but keep her theatrics going. "Girl, I'll make it rain in here for real. I'll pay for your first semester, touching my spirit like that. Bernie, girl, you have me looking through my phone trying to call heaven. Every time I call, the angels keep saying he's already there with you. Wait, let me ask Jesus because y'all know he's sitting in that seat." Turning to the empty chair, Patricia addressed Jesus as though he was wrapped in flesh and occupying the seat. She inquired, "Um, Jesus, why are we just having this lunch? I could've been living better a long time ago. What's up with that?"

The ladies all burst out in laughter as Patricia jokingly tried to lighten the mood in their newfound sanctuary. All of them had jubilant tears filling their eyes and soaking their skin and blouses as they obtained true deliverance, not in a church because they each silently realized they were reflections of the true church. The restaurant became the sanctuary, and they were able to enter into the presence of God. They learned how to see beyond the spiritual veils people hide behind in sanctuaries across the nation and around the world. They all learned how self can be the greatest obstacle, while self-preservation and pride are the fuel feeding the devil. The scales from their spiritual eyes fell as they could see clearly beyond what was before them. Life was no longer the oppressor, and the devil's guise had been exposed. The power and presence of God permitted them to have personal relationship with 1 Peter 1:6–9. Bernie continued to explicate her new position in spiritual maturation.

"Ladies, as your friend, I've learned and I'm learning that our obstacles and challenges have not been afforded to us, so we delicately place them in a safety deposit box confound to the heavily guarded depository. God entrusted each of us to survive our seasonal tribulation so he can be glorified. We are not challenged to be reserved. We are challenged to continually flow and deposit into others. Almost as if we are equated to being rivers, so we flow into the greatest of waters, the ocean. The beautiful thing about a river is that it empties out into an ocean. I implore you to consider the reason you're a river and why it empties into the ocean. The river can't flow into a lake because it's confined nor shall it release into a pond because it contains an even smaller restriction. Rather, the river empties into the ocean because it is limitless. When the rivers are running and flowing through you, it's because God's power is always graceful and moving."

Patricia sat astounded by her friend's words and couldn't help but comment on her remarks.

"Look here, Pauline, Paulette, I'll just call you Paul because you're telling it like it is. You really did journey on the road to Damascus, didn't you?"

Bernie laughed and reflected of her journey, but instead of retorting with a long response to feed Patricia, she smiled and welcomed God's peace and proclaimed, "I now know how to see beyond what my eyes can see. I can't see God, but I can see his presence everywhere." The women sat around the table, amused by their own survival. They clapped hands and worshipped God for his grace and magnificent power still alive and at work in their lives.

With a quiet, peaceful smile cascading across her face, Amber sat in a meditative state. Knowing that her past wasn't as immense as her peers, she too had a life unbeknownst to her counterparts. Amber looked around and paused within herself, pondering if she should share her life's story. She knew she had underlying issues within her life, but she recalled her dream and the reflections of her past that created a nightmare in her mind. In her intellectual mind, she rationalized each woman as they each gleaned the fields of their lives as if killing the weeds of her personal garden. They'd identified the root cause of their pain and were overcome as a result. Was it pertinent to speak against the future she'd already prophesied over by rehashing things of old? Shaking her head, Amber continued in the vacillating thought. There was really no need in resurrecting the dead of her past, particularly since she was living a phenomenal present with an expectancy of a future destined for greatness. She thought of her newfound love with Jackson and how elated she'd been since finally meeting a man versus entertaining temporary fixes. Fortunately, Amber vested that she'd attained her joy and peace, but she still had a memory, and it desperately sought to return to what was familiar—pain. Though not fainting to her past nightmare, she also considered, while in her season of isolation, how she transitioned her mind-set to attain positivity while confronting the root cause of her pain. It was in that time that she recognized the source for her relational qualms with men, her father. Smiling upon her reflective thought, she recalled her conversation with her dad and the emotional roller coaster that jolted within when she traveled to get past the hurdles of confronting her root. However, after her visit with him and the undeniable power of forgiveness that dug up all matter of bad soil, she deemed it unnecessary to harvest that which was resolved. Rather, she smiled and merely stated aloud among her peers, "Ladies, my past is behind me and I am adamant on pressing toward the prize that is destined ahead of me. If God holds no remembrance of former things, neither should I. Rather, I will bask in knowing that old things have passed away, and I embrace my life as all things will become new." Lifting her glass to toast her own victory, she was received by each woman as if they too were waiting to toast to their future.

Looking around the table, it would have never been evident that each woman had her own skeletal idiosyncrasy that propelled each to the sanctuary weekly. Their individual walks with Christ and the baggage they carried had finally been cast upon their Savior, eliminating them from anguish and emotional trepidation. No longer bound, they each rejoiced and celebrated their emancipation from their past and spiritually humbled themselves before the Lord in adoration of his presence. The restaurant transitioned from a place of fine cuisine to feasting on the presence of Christ who is/was their true bread of life.

With the afternoon sun beaming through the picturesque window, cascading a heavenly hue upon the beautiful warmed skin of each woman, the door opened, shading the essence of the person in the sun. Walking closer into the restaurant, her attributes became obvious to the onlookers within. Among those who recognized the face was Bernadette. Tapping Amber, she pointed to the young woman. With a welcoming smile racing across Bernie's face, she openly acknowledged the young woman's presence, quieting the group and arousing their attention. Captivated by Bernie's sudden focus, the women all smiled as the young woman neared the table. Taylor smiled, but became emotional instantly. Her hormonal imbalance had taken effect. Bernie arose as she hugged the young woman and barraged her with a slew of questions.

"Hello, honey. I haven't seen you in a while. What are you doing here? I know you're still coming to the church, but I see you, then I don't see you. Where have you been? Wait before you tell me because I honestly don't think you ever told me your name. I'd like to introduce you to some of my best friends. You've already met Hannah at the retreat and I'm sure she looks familiar. This is Taylor, you already know her from the church, Amber, you also know her from the church. and Patricia, you may not know her, but she comes around. Please tell everyone your name so you can be properly introduced."

The young woman greeted all the women at the table. then addressed Bernie, "Well, you know I never did tell you my name at the retreat, but don't worry about my old name. which was Fearful, I have a new name, my real name."

Bernie looked perplexed at the young woman's comeback, but continued to listen. Patricia sat on the edge of her seat. endowed in curiosity as she fought herself to remain bridled. Unfortunately, Patricia lost the battle and retorted.

"Okay. Ms. No Name, well. on behalf of my peers. it's nice to meet you. Man. these young girls today are fierce."

Noticing her verbal feedback from Patricia, she continued to clarify.

"I never really told people my name because in school they'd tease me about it. I didn't realize until recently that my mother did something right when she named me. I also didn't know that I'd have to have so many hardships in order for my name to make sense, but in the end, God knows all things. My old name was death and disease, which means absolutely nothing because since I came to that retreat I experienced a personal revelation, manifestation, and growth in my relationship with God. I've been changed. My name was hurt and pain. Miss, I don't know you, but when people saw me, what they really saw was a façade. I walked around as a functional Christian atheist. If you don't know what that means, let me help you understand. I was going to church sporadically, but I harbored anger and hurt in my heart because of what happened to me, so I didn't really believe. I didn't believe because I couldn't see beyond my pain. I couldn't see beyond my trials and emotional ridicule. Now all of that has changed. Miss, people know me as Eve. I'm not really sure why I was embarrassed by my real name. Looking at some of the things I've encountered in my life, I believe my name says more about me that I could ever explain. I'm growing to learn how to be comfortable in my own skin. I'm tired hiding behind veils, and I refuse to hide any longer. If you would like to know my name, it is Evidence. You can call me by my real name, Evidence."

Patricia leaned back into her chair and crossed her arms. Unbeknownst to the young woman's story, Patricia welcomed her to a seat.

"Okay, Evidence, well please have a seat. I don't know you, but today since we're giving out new names and since I pledged the best sorority, how about I give us a line name. I think I like Destined for Divine Deliverance. Apparently, you've come at the right time because we're all sharing our stories of deliverance, so you fit right in. Okay, now since you have a unique name that sounds like a line name, you can call me Overcomer. How about you, ladies? Bernie, we already know you're Paul, Pauline, or Paulette, something along those lines. Anyone else have a new name?"

Bernie chimed in response to her sarcastic friend's inquisition.

"Patricia, excuse me, Overcomer, I have a better name for you. It might be a little hard for you to digest, but God is able to touch even you. Why don't you become Humblina for a moment and let this young woman speak. You'll never be the same."

Throwing up her hands in submission, Patricia whispered her apologies to Evidence and fanned for her to continue.

"Thank you, Ms. Bernie. Well, I'm Evidence, both on my birth certificate and in reality, because when you see me you no longer see the face of AIDS. I'm evidence because when you gaze into my eyes, you no longer see despair and desolation. I no longer wear the crown of shame and the coat of disease. I may not look like much to you. I may not have a beauty queen or pageant princess flare. I may not be a daddy's little princess or a mother's mirror image. I'm not a footstool to a man or a punching bag to an abuser. I am evidence that God still exists. I am evidence that God is faithful. I am evidence that God is a healer. I am evidence that God still saves. Some people only thank God or call on God for material things and a bunch of junk that a natural disaster can destroy in one fell swoop. What is a house going to do for me when death is banging at the door? What is a car or millions of dollars going to satisfy when my tomorrow isn't promised? Monetary gain has no ability to profit from my life. I have been thrust in a position to love God and trust God, despite people leaving me, abusing me, and regardless of my material gain. Like you said, Ms. Bernie, I'm convinced God postured me to endure my season of trial to show me that God was all I ever needed. I didn't realize God was all I needed until God was all I had. I don't have a mother or father to lean on and friends are more seldom like meteors crashing to the earth. Out of all those who left me, God was there and remained faithful to me. I'm living proof that I've been tried and survived. Cases in courts across this nation are overturned when new evidence arrives in the courthouse. I'm evidence that the devil slammed the door on my case and prepared to walk away victorious, but God's heavenly host burst on the scene with new evidence to present to God. Once my angels came with the new evidence, I was freed and the devil was defeated. I'm not ashamed to tell anyone that I lived at the feet of the devil with his arsenal of disease plaguing my body. I'm not ashamed to tell anyone I was abandoned by my mother, sexually abused, beaten, and raped by my uncle and his drunken friends. I'm not ashamed to tell anyone that I had a baby when I was twelve, even though it died, not because I was being grown, but because my drunken uncle couldn't distinguish a child from a grown woman, then invited his friends to join in. I'm not ashamed that I had to run the streets. However, I am overjoyed that God sent an angel in the form of my neighbor to rescue me. I'm not ashamed that I had to die before I could experience life. I'm not ashamed at all because when the devil stood in court and proclaimed that I had been tried and found guilty, I sat there and cried out to Jesus and he stood up and said, 'That's all I was waiting for.' When everyone else left me for dead, Jesus stood up for me and told the devil to go to hell. So there you have it. I'm not ashamed to tell you, Ms. Patricia, or anyone else, that it doesn't matter what my name was or who people perceived me to be. What matters is that my name is Evidence! Eve is my nickname, but my real name is as unique as my life–Evidence! When you see me, recognize that it's not me you see. Open those pretty eyes of yours and see beyond what your eyes can see! I stand before you as proof beyond a shadow of a doubt that God is alive. He is not dead. He is in the miracle business and Jesus' blood still heals. For that reason, I am his chosen child, tried, travailing, and triumphant. Since you asked, please don't ever forget, I am Evidence. Anymore questions?"

The restaurant and every living soul in the place fell tranquil and soundless as the earth before it was formed. Awaiting the breath of life to release the stillness upon the patient souls, tears fell, creating the sea, while hearts began to beat and take shape creating new land. God's presence was evident and lives were forever changed that day in a restaurant, in God's presence, basking in God's glory. The women experienced deliverance at the hand of God in the atmosphere that allowed them each to elevate to a place in God they could only attain once they were able to see beyond what their eyes could see.

I pray this book and poem allow you to always recognize discernment and s*ee beyond what your eyes can see*. Living within you is a great and mighty king, a son, and a savior. God bless.

The King Within

Beautiful skin massaged by God's own hands
Formed in his likeness and image with preordained greatness
Embedded within your soul's journey;
Unable to relinquish hope of the unknown, yet inevitably
You persevere along the lit path
Guided by that which lives within.

Your eyes, bright as starlight
Illuminating in darkness
Beckoning those who dare to glance
They pause,
Mesmerized by the indisputable power that resonates within you
A King.